Twilight of One:
The Plague of Decompose

Nina R. Schluntz

Llumina Press

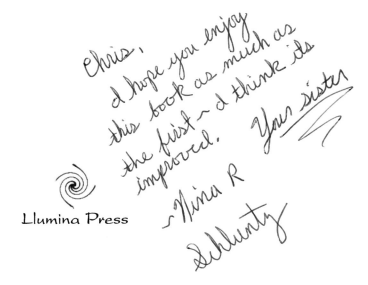

© 2007 Nina R. Schluntz

All rights reserved. No part of this publication may be reproduced or transmitted in any form or by any means electronic or mechanical, including photocopy, recording, or any information storage and retrieval system, without permission in writing from both the copyright owner and the publisher.

Requests for permission to make copies of any part of this work should be mailed to Permissions Department, Llumina Press, PO Box 772246, Coral Springs, FL 33077-2246

ISBN: 978-1-59526-718-4

Printed in the United States of America by Llumina Press

Library of Congress Control Number: 2006911162

Part 1

The Plague

Dee slumped against the bathroom door and wiped some of the blood from his face. He blinked his eyes, trying to clear his vision. Why had he chosen someone so old? Her eyes were bad—not unhealthy, but the vision was horrible. He couldn't see a thing. And he wasn't about to start wearing glasses. Dee leaned his head against the cool metal door behind him. He could smell the rank odor of blood from the woman lying on the floor. He rubbed his eyes again and wished he knew what he was doing. He had just murdered a woman in a church bathroom, stolen her eyes and wedged them into his own empty eye sockets. Now he could see, but would his powers work?

Knock-knock. Someone was rapping gently against the bathroom door. Dee nearly screamed in fright. He jumped away from the door and quickly scanned the room, trying to assess the situation. He was in a one-stall bathroom with a sink and toilet. Blood was everywhere; he had been rather sloppy since he'd been unable to see what he was doing. If he opened the door, the person was bound to see what he had done. He focused on the mirror as his vision cleared. Apparently, the Decompose plague in his blood liked its host to be healthy.

He needed a stone to pass through the mirror, didn't he? That was how everyone else had to do it. But maybe, just maybe... Dee reached out with his hand and pressed his fingers against the glass. He only touched the reflection of his fingertips. No luck; he needed a stone to pass through the mirror. He concentrated, and his new green eyes began to glow bright red. He reached out with his mind and entered the mind of the person on the other side of the door. A human mind—a mortal. The man was defenseless against Dee's telepathic powers. Dee focused his energy, and the man passed out. Then Dee quietly opened the bathroom door. He saw the man on the ground and knelt down, not sure what to do next. He grimaced slightly at a twinge of pain. Dee was always in pain. It wasn't so bad in his human form, but he was always hurting. He reached out and grabbed the man's wrist. Dee closed his eyes, and for a brief moment, felt no pain. For once, Dee was healthy. The constant battle inside him eased as he passed the Decompose plague into the man before him. But the relief didn't last long, and the constant, numbing pain returned. Dee opened his eyes to see the man reduced to a skeleton, clothed in the man's wardrobe. Dee backed away, startled by what he had done.

"Oh my God," a woman said in a hushed tone. Dee backed away from the dead man and looked down the narrow hall. A middle-aged woman was covering her face in surprise. Dee's eyes glowed red, but he couldn't enter her mind quick enough. She let out a shrill scream, which was cut short as Dee raised his hand. The air quivered between them, and the woman fell to the floor. Dee closed the palm of his hand as he realized the Decompose plague could be made airborne.

The scream had surely alarmed someone. Dee had to do something, quickly. He opened his palm again and hoped his destructive power could be used for more than just killing people.

Dee stepped outside the church, slipping out the back exit. He was on the top of a cement staircase. The stairs seemed to twist and sway beneath him; he grabbed the railing with one hand and clutched his head with the other. He wasn't sure what had just happened, but on some level he had enjoyed it—the feeling of being alive, the pain-free moments, and the feeling of infinite power. Now the pain crept back on him, as his body resumed its never-ending war of healing itself while another part of him feverishly worked to kill him.

"You know I can't let you leave, mate."

Dee recognized the voice and opened his eyes to see Scully standing in the parking lot at the bottom of the stairs. He took a moment to admire the strange grace of the skeleton, whose velvet cape swirled elegantly in the breeze as he posed with his samurai sword ready.

"I have no fight with you, Scully. Just leave me be, and I'll do the same for you," Dee told the ghoulish figure as he descended the stairs. Dee had become accustomed to the pain, and he walked toward the skeleton with confidence.

"Darlene's fight is my fight. You know that," Scully growled. He raised his sword, ready to take action if Dee came too close.

"Darlene." Dee paused for a moment, as if the name puzzled him. She was his niece. Darlene's mother had been a cat, leaving her some unique features. "She claims to be the most powerful witch alive, doesn't she?"

"I don't think she would like the use of the term 'witch,' but you are correct," Scully agreed. Dee heard sirens in the distance. His eyes glowed briefly, and the sirens came to an abrupt stop. The silence hung in the air, increasing the tension between them. "What are you doing, Dee? What did you do?"

"Well, I certainly did something, didn't I? You should be more concerned about your immediate circumstances Scully. Like why Darlene, with all her power, never returned you to your human state."

"Did you kill those people Dee? How many people have you already killed? I saw what you did to the church. You've only been…"

"Why, Scully? Why didn't she heal you? She's more powerful than the dragons, isn't she? They cast this curse on you, and she could have removed it. Why didn't she, Scully?" Dee shouted.

"I don't know!" Scully shouted back, shaken. He had been cursed by the dragons for having an affair with one of their maidens and was now doomed to walk the earth without flesh.

"Because she didn't want you to be normal, Scully! She's a freak, and she knew that as long as you were a freak too, you would stay with her. But if she made you look normal again, you would leave her. I mean why would you stay with a cat freak like her?"

"You're insane, Dee. How can you talk about this while you destroy the world? Just stop it," Scully begged. Dee's eyes stopped glowing and returned to their normal violet hue. There was no difference between his original eyes and the eyes he had stolen.

"You'd give anything to have your old body back, wouldn't you? To have flesh again? To be able to feel the bodily pleasures the dragons deprived you of?"

"They deprived you, too, mate. They kept you locked up, just like they did me. But that's no reason to lash out at the world," Scully countered. Dee had been held prisoner by the dragons to protect the world from the plague that resided in him.

"I'll give you back your life, Scully. All I ask in return is that you give me mine," Dee said softly.

"Making a deal with you is like making a deal with the devil," Scully whispered.

"Only with me, you can keep your soul," Dee said with a grin.

Before Scully could agree to anything, Dee grabbed his wrist. He half expected Scully to cut his arm off with the sword, but instead the skeleton dropped his sword in surprise. Muscles, tissues, organs, and ligaments that had long since been taken away, swiftly returned. Dee let go of him and bit his lip in an effort to hide his pain. Healing someone temporarily allowed the Decompose plague to get ahead in his body.

Scully took a few steps and stared in wonderment at his hands, then quickly reached up and felt his face. His brown eyes widened as he realized he was clothed in nothing more than a cape and hood. He quickly untied the cape and wrapped it around his waist. Dee took a moment to catch his own breath. He shrugged off Scully's appearance. Although Scully stood over six feet and had an Australian accent, he was of Asian descent.

Scully said nothing, and Dee did likewise. Instead Dee walked down the street, away from the collapsed church, while Scully went into the alley. Dee wasn't sure if Scully was still an enemy, but he felt confident that Scully wouldn't be hunting him. Darlene, however, was more than likely still alive back in that rubble.

Darlene woke up, feeling pain all over her body. She opened her eyes to darkness. She moved her hands and worked them free, then twisted until her arms were free, too. She reached up and pushed whatever was on top of her, off to the side. She sat up and brushed more debris from her black-furred body. Aside from the soft fur and cat-like eyes, Darlene looked like a normal woman. It took her a while to free her legs, and when she tried to stand, she felt a twinge of pain in her right ankle. She limped a few steps and paused, as she realized she didn't know where she should be going. She recalled seeing Dee standing in the center of the church, as the walls crumbled down all around him. Then the wall next to her had fallen on top of her. In a way she had been thankful, the screams of the dying had been too much for her to bear. She looked around the rubble, trying to spot some sign of life.

"Hello? Is anyone there? Help me, please," a woman's voice cried out. Darlene looked around but couldn't see anyone. She tried to make her way to the front of the building, where the voice seemed to be coming from. She tripped on something and fell to the ground, flat on her face, and her sprained ankle sent a burst of pain up her leg. As she spit blood from her mouth, she saw a hand protruding from the rubble. A prosthetic hand.

"Jaff? Daddy?" Darlene croaked, surprised at the rough sound of her own voice. She began clawing at the fallen plaster and boards. But she was too late. Jaff McPowin was dead. She stared down at his stone-cold face, covered in white dust from the plaster. A tear stung her cheek and caused her pain as the salty liquid touched a cut. She quickly wiped it away, cringing at the pain her touch caused.

She forced herself to her feet and refused to look down as she made her way out of the building. She reached the cement steps at the front entrance and looked down so she wouldn't fall. She instantly forgot her own pain and clasped her hand over her mouth. Dee had destroyed more than just the church, far more. As far as Darlene could see, the houses and buildings had been leveled. Nothing but piles of rubble remained. A few people were out in the streets, wandering aimlessly. Dee hadn't killed them all? How was that possible? A woman came running down the street, screaming as if death itself were on her tail. Behind her, a man was in pursuit. People paused and watched, but did nothing to help her.

How could people turn on each other so quickly? It had only been a few hours. Darlene began to head down the stairs, ready to trounce the man, when she saw another man sprint from the nearby bushes and tackle the woman. Both men fell upon the woman, and stayed on top of her. Darlene couldn't tell what they were doing. Dusk had hit, and the streets were barely lit. By the time Darlene reached them, the woman had stopped screaming; she was dead.

"Get off her!" Darlene screamed, still not understanding why they were hovering over her. One man looked up and growled, his mouth full of flesh and blood.

Darlene backed away. They were eating her. Why? Both men seemed fine, perfectly healthy, and surely they weren't starving to death so soon. She backed away and the men forgot about her and went back to their meal. She cautiously walked away and went around the block, wanting to put the ugly scene behind her.

Darlene decided to find a mirror so she could ask the dragons for help; she was in no condition to battle Dee alone. A mirror was the only way to travel to Dragon Island. She heard footsteps behind her and a damp hand grabbed her shoulder. Darlene screamed and kicked her would-be attacker in the chest. She visualized a man's hand, covered in blood, grabbing her shoulder. Instead, she turned to see a woman in a bathing suit fall to the ground.

"I—I was in the pool. I had just dived in, and when—when I came back up, everyone was gone, dead, or something. What—what happened?" The woman looked like she was in shock, but at least she wasn't trying to eat people.

"I'm sorry; I can't help you," Darlene told her softly.

"I'm hungry—so hungry. Why am I so hungry?" the woman murmured. Darlene backed away and decided it would be best to avoid people from now on.

"I came to you for help," Darlene growled, sounding much like her feline ancestors.

"And we did help you. The White Dragon tended to your wounds, and we offered you sanctuary. I doubt Dee will come here," the Black Dragon told her. He resembled a Chinese dragon, looking more like a snake than the four-legged, winged lizard he truly was. He stroked his long whiskers as he watched her with his beady black eyes.

Darlene rubbed her shoulders, trying to warm herself, but after traveling through town after town that had been destroyed by Dee, she just couldn't seem to rub the chill from her bones.

"If I hadn't found that mirror, I would still be out there. Do you know what is happening?" Darlene asked. The Black Dragon sighed and laid down on the floor. His dark scales glimmered with moisture.

"Dee is spreading a plague."

"He's decomposing the world," Darlene snapped. "Buildings, homes, everything falls to rubble as he passes. People die left and right, and those lucky enough to survive feel like they are starving to death. Some of them are resorting to cannibalism. You can help them. Together, we can stop him."

"The Red Dragon will never agree, Darlene. What happens in the world is no concern of ours," the Black Dragon told her simply. There were Five Royal Dragons, each with his own unique power and distinct features. All were roughly the same size—equal to a two-story building.

"I know you hate humans; don't think I've forgotten the civil war. But you can't let him destroy the world." Once, the dragons had been divided. The White and Black Dragons had wanted to destroy the humans, but the other three dragons had objected.

"We can't interfere, Darlene. Can you imagine what will happen if we just show up and start fighting Dee? What will the humans think of us? What will they think we are?"

"I don't know, but imagine what they think now!"

"I imagine they are thinking about how hungry they are, or whether their city will be the next to be infected," said the Black Dragon. Darlene searched his expression, hoping to see a hint that would tell her he was joking, but she saw nothing.

"I want to talk to the Red Dragon myself," Darlene told him gruffly.

❖❖❖

"You what? You actually think we would help these humans? Decompose is their problem. Let them use their nuclear weapons to stop him," the Red Dragon scoffed. Darlene looked around the cavern at the Five Royal Dragons and one dragon maiden. She didn't see a sympathetic eye in the lot.

"Fine—then give me the power to stop him. Your power, combined with my own, could stop him," Darlene suggested.

"So you want to use the dragon powers again? The Black Dragon already did that once, without my consent. Those gifts cannot be borrowed, Darlene. It is a lifetime agreement. There is no such thing as a temporary dragon maiden." The Red Dragon was the beefiest of the dragons, with large, bat-like wings, long legs, and several fin-like fans decorating his head and running the length of his back.

"Not even to save humanity? You'll never have new maidens if Dee kills them all!"

"We've been observing the plague," Veron said. Darlene hadn't even noticed him. He was a small, wingless green dragon, only the size of a turkey. "When Decompose infects a population, roughly ninety-three percent of the population is killed. Of that surviving seven percent, only two percent are reduced to cannibalistic acts. The rest seem to be regrouping and are likely to live full, normal lives."

"Five percent. So out of the entire world, only five percent are going to survive? How many of them will be killed by the cannibals? And who's to say Dee won't go back and finish them off?" Darlene snapped.

"We have yet to see Dee do anything of that sort."

"The world's only so big—" Darlene growled as she grabbed her forehead in frustration. "It's only been two weeks—tell me, how much of the world has he destroyed? How many continents?"

"Perhaps you misunderstood; the figures I gave you encompass the world. Every continent has been affected," Veron told her.

"What? How is that possible?"

"The plague is airborne," the Red Dragon told her simply. "We don't even know where Dee is. He can infect any part of the world, at any time, from any location."

Darlene sank to the floor, pulling her legs up to her chest. She hadn't realized things were that bad. The dragons didn't seem to understand that eventually everyone would be dead, and by the looks of it, "eventually" wasn't very far away.

"Fine, you win," Darlene said.

"I don't think this is a matter of winning or losing," the Red Dragon pointed out.

"No, you've always wanted me to be your dragon maiden. You give me the powers of all Five Royal Dragons, and I'm yours for life."

"You would give up your freedom to save these pathetic humans? You aren't even a full human yourself," the Red Dragon said in awe.

"Do we have a deal or not?" Darlene asked.

Dee woke with his face covered in dirt. He pushed himself off the ground, wondering why he had fallen asleep in a pile of dirt. He sat back on his knees and wiped the dirt from his face. He opened his eyes and squinted against the sun. Was he in a desert? He had that groggy, dizzy feeling again. That meant the plague had re-infected him. He had overextended himself this time. Although the bliss of being pain-free was great, it was an enormous drain to funnel the plague out of him and infect others, causing him to pass out in odd locations, like the middle of a desert. The dizziness passed, and Dee felt the numbing pain of the infection—similar to the pain you feel when starving. Not that Dee knew what that felt like—he hadn't eaten a bite of food since he was a toddler.

Dee shaded his eyes with his hands and looked around. He didn't think this place had been a desert before. It was time to start walking, at least until he was out of the desert. He needed to find living creatures, so he could begin spreading the plague again.

Darlene finished strapping her belt around her waist. The belt had one stone from each dragon on it, and a Royal Dragon Gem rested on the top of her red staff. The dragons used gems to pass their powers to others. She was dressed in glittering white cloth. The skirt went down to her ankles, and a slit on the left side went up to her mid-thigh. She wore a matching tank top that showed her furry midriff. On each wrist she wore gold bracelets, and around her neck she wore a black necklace. It was all too flashy for her taste, but it was what the dragons wanted, and she now had to obey them.

Darlene led her horse, Boots, through the mirror; he was incredibly resistant. The palomino pulled back on the reins as Darlene led him through. She knew how he felt; she wished she didn't have to go, either. Veron passed her a compass, telling her that Dee should be directly south of where he was sending her.

Darlene heard the crunch of glass under her silver boots and the horse's hooves. She looked around the darkened room. They were in the living room of a once-beautiful home. The house had once been quite classy, judging by the remains of the curtains and furniture, most of which were broken and torn. She saw splatters of blood here and there and wondered if the house's occupants had been injured during the plague or if they had turned on each other afterwards. She paused and gently put her hand on the horse's forehead, bringing him to a stop. She heard something. It sounded like a dog eating. The slobbering, wet sound sickened Darlene. She moved forward slowly, pulling the hesitant horse with her. They reached the front entrance, and that was when Darlene spotted the source of the noise. A woman was crouched on the ground, partly behind the couch, hovering over a body. The woman was covered in blood, and a chunk of flesh dangled from her mouth. She didn't even look up.

Darlene wished she could do something, but she had to stay focused. She continued on and stepped outside. One of the floorboards on the porch gave way under the horse's weight, and it took a few minutes for Darlene to get the two of them off the porch.

She climbed on the horse's back and tried to block out the screams she heard throughout the city. Cries for help, cries of death, cries of doom. She fought back her tears and closed her eyes. She glanced down at the compass and made sure they were heading south, then gave the reins a sharp snap, and Boots took off. She tried not to pay attention to the people wandering the streets. Most were cannibals. Those who had resisted the urges were likely holed up in their houses, or so Darlene hoped. Why didn't the cannibals attack each other? Could they sense who was infected? Was the flesh of the non-infected better? Boots had trouble running on the broken-down streets, the cement was decayed and numerous times, Boots tripped and almost fell. But she didn't want to waste any time getting out of this city. A woman suddenly ran from her house at them, carrying a bundle. Darlene wondered if it was a child. The woman's screams confirmed Darlene's suspicion.

"Por favor, llevaos a la creatura! Por el amor de Dios! No lo dejeis que muera aqui; por favor ayudeme!"* the woman cried. Darlene made the mistake of looking at her and saw tears of despair rolling down her cheeks. Darlene started to slow Boots as she considered taking the child. Then she saw six of the dazed cannibals making their way towards the woman. They were moving slow, waiting to see if Darlene would stop so they could attack her, too.

Darlene closed her eyes and kicked Boots in the sides, encouraging him to hurry on. He didn't seem to object, even if he didn't have good footing.

It wasn't long before the decayed ground turned into brownish dirt. It reminded her of a desert, but this was Argentina; it was supposed to be well-forested country. As they continued, Darlene realized how easy it would be to get lost; everything looked the same—just more and more sand. No land markers of any kind. She was grateful for the compass, although she wasn't sure what good it was going to do her when it came time to pinpoint Dee's exact location.

Luck seemed to be on her side; a large dust storm was headed their way. There was no wind, which meant it had to be Dee, or some form of Dee. She brought Boots to a halt in the path of the oncoming storm. She hoped her plan worked. The cloud of dust was moving remarkably fast. If it passed them, Darlene wasn't sure they would be able to catch up with it.

*"Please, take my child with you! Please! Don't leave him here to die; please help me!"

She raised her hands and closed her eyes before softly mumbling an incantation to create a reddish force field. She opened her eyes and watched the dust storm charge forward until it rammed into her force field. The cloud paused for a moment, then rammed again. Darlene fell to her knees as she struggled to keep up the field. The force field collapsed as the dust settled, and Darlene saw the beast. It was Dee, in the form of the hideous Decompose monster. Apparently he made better time traveling in that form. The monster's head was a skull, a distorted skull, similar to a gorilla's. His ribs were exposed, and various organs were visible. Other bones protruded from the beast's skin, as if the monster had extra bones and there wasn't enough room in his body to keep them under the skin.

She looked up at him, wondering why he wasn't taking advantage of her weakness. The force field was gone. There was nothing to stop him. The beast opened its jaws and took a deep breath. Darlene raised her hands, knowing what was coming next.

A giant plume of red fire issued forth from inside the beast. Darlene managed to get a force field up in time to keep from being burnt alive. Then a giant paw swept down on top of her. Darlene let the force field fall as she rolled out of the beast's grasp. He swatted at her, as if she was nothing more than a tiny insect.

"I've learned some new tricks since we last met, Dee!" Darlene yelled, hoping to slow him down or trick him into morphing into his human form. But the beast paid her no heed. She barely managed to keep out of his grasp.

Darlene rolled onto her back and used the power of the Gold Dragon to turn the nearby sand into gold. Then she flung the bits at him. He paused, raising a paw to block the tiny projectiles. She formed several of the golden dust particles together and formed a dagger, which she then propelled at him. It went right through his paw. He gave an inhuman scream and bashed his paw into the ground, shattering the metal. She changed tactics, and used the Black Dragon's power to turn invisible, which was useless, as she left clouds of dust behind her as she ran. Becoming visible again she faced Dee and sent a spray of ice towards him, courtesy of the Silver Dragon, hoping to confine him behind a wall of ice. He just opened his jaws and sent a burst of fire at her, melting the ice before it could reach him.

Then he did something Darlene had never thought she would see. He stood on his hind legs, and an orange-colored cloud formed around him. She quickly formed a force field around herself. She looked at Boots, but he was too far away for her to protect. The cloud grew darker, then popped, just like a balloon, and the contents oozed out. Darlene watched the flesh rot right off Boots, decomposing him to dust. The cloud suddenly dispersed, as if it had a mind of its own. As the infection spread, Dee started to change. The hideous monster before her began to heal. His exposed ribcage covered itself in flesh and grew a layer of black fur. His skinless skull became covered in muscle and tissue and elongated. He fell to his four paws as his splintered toes solidified into hooves. The beast shrunk to the size of a horse, perhaps slightly larger than a Clydesdale. His rounded teeth became square, like those of an herbivore. A single horn protruded from the base of his skull and a shaggy mane of black hair sprouted along his elongated neck. He gave his new black tail a shake.

Darlene's jaw dropped. He had morphed into a black unicorn. The true form of a Meta-morph. She had always been told that her Uncle Dee was a quarter Meta-morph, his mother had been the daughter of a Meta-morph. It was also rumored that Dee's grandfather and father had been the same person, her own grandfather. But Darlene wasn't sure how much of the family's history was true. Was that what he had been trying to morph into all these years, but had instead changed into that hideous monster? The unicorn pranced merrily for a moment. Darlene would have thought the creature beautiful, but the glowing red eyes ruined the effect. The unicorn reared and kicked his front hooves in the air, then gave a whinny. As soon as his front hooves hit the ground, he took off running. A cloud of dust followed in his wake as Dee galloped into the distance, continuing north to the Caribbean.

Darlene waited until she could no longer see any hint of orange particles in the air, then she dropped her force field. She grimaced as she took her first breath of air, but thankfully, she felt no pain. Then she realized how long of a walk she had before her. She had no idea how far she would have to travel to find a mirror.

Just as dusk began, she saw a dragon in the distance, flying towards her. She wondered if the heat was starting to get to her, if she was seeing mirages. But in a few minutes, the Red Dragon landed next to her.

Twilight of One: The Plague of Decompose

"This dust looks familiar," the dragon scoffed. Darlene glared at him, not caring if the dirt looked like the dirt in his territory back on the island. "What happened? Veron told us he infected another area and recommended we search for you."

"All five of you came looking for me?" Darlene asked, surprised.

"Well, I came; let's just leave it at that," the dragon told her. "Let's get you back to the island, so you can—"

"No. No, I'm not leaving until I finish this. I have to kill him."

"You tried that, and you failed," the Red Dragon said simply.

"But I learned from the experience. I know how to beat him now. I've been wandering out here in the middle of nowhere for hours. I've had time to create a plan. Now I just need to find him."

"You've been out here for nearly sixteen hours. You need rest," the dragon said.

"I can't rest until he is stopped. I can't let him kill anyone else. Please, I pledged my life to serving you. All I ask is one more chance to beat him."

"You want me to fly you to him, don't you?"

"It's the only way I can catch up to him," Darlene said in desperation.

"I still don't understand why you care so much about these humans, but a deal is a deal. I won't help you fight him, but I'll help you find him," the Red Dragon said reluctantly.

They were nearing the northernmost point of Bolivia when they finally spotted a cloud of dust that could only be created by Decompose.

"That's him," Darlene told the Red Dragon as she tightened her grip on his claws. He carried her in his hand as he glided across the countryside. "Get us ahead of him. I know how to stop him."

The Red Dragon brought them to the ground, gently dropping Darlene on the green grass. Decompose hadn't infected this area yet, although Darlene was sure the cannibals from Brazil had already ripped the area apart.

Darlene turned and faced the oncoming beast. She took a deep breath and prepared to create the force field.

"I don't think I'll stick around for this," the Red Dragon decided. He kicked off with his hind feet and lifted himself up into the air. Darlene had hoped he would change his mind, but evidently, he wasn't going to. She turned back to Decompose and found him closer then she had thought. Decompose, back in his monster form, leaped into the air and clawed at the Red Dragon. He reminded Darlene of a house cat tackling a sparrow, if the cat and sparrow were the same size. The Red Dragon issued a gargling sound as Decompose thrashed at him with his front paws. Darlene assembled her red staff and placed the Royal Dragon Gem on the top. She secured it and charged toward Decompose. She couldn't beat him as long as he was awake, but if she could use the gem to put him asleep, she would have a chance. The Royal Dragons had used their combined powers to create a gem that would put Dee into a coma; it had been used when he was first imprisoned on their island.

When she was within two feet of Dee, he suddenly backed away, leaving the tattered dragon to bleed to death. She thrust the staff at him, aiming for his skull. He raised his right paw to block it, but it was useless. The effect of the gem swept over him, and Dee fell to the ground. He morphed back into human form in a last attempt to move far enough away from the gem to be free of its effects. But Darlene grabbed the staff and rushed at Dee, placing the gem on his chest before he could regain consciousness.

She quickly disassembled the staff. It broke down into three pieces, one of which held a sharp dagger. She thrust the dagger into his skull, killing him. She pulled the dagger out, only to watch in amazement as the wound healed. Puzzled, she stabbed him in the chest, directly in his heart, only to watch him heal once she removed the dagger. Frustrated, she thrust the dagger back into his skull and left it there. She checked his neck for a pulse and found none. But if he was dead, how was he healing himself?

Then to her utter surprise, his eyes opened. Darlene gasped, but before she could respond, Dee shoved her off, and the gem tumbled to the ground as he stood. He was still dead. The dagger protruded from his skull. How was this possible? Darlene was unable to move; she just sat on the ground in amazement. Dee reached up and pulled the dagger out of his skull. He tossed it to the ground next to her, as if mocking her attempt to kill him. The wound again healed, but as soon as Dee's pulse returned, he let out a groan and fell to his knees, losing consciousness again.

"That's… why…we…never…killed…him," the Red Dragon whispered, speaking as loudly as he could manage. "Once…he dies…he becomes…unstoppable—invincible."

"Then we won't kill him," Darlene decided. "We'll just imprison him again. Better this time."

She looked up and saw the White Dragon approaching. The other dragons must have known the Red Dragon had been injured. She was amazed at how quick they could be when they wanted.

All five of the Royal Dragons were present as Darlene finished the last touches on Dee's new prison. Rather than put it on Dragon Island, Darlene had put the prison in one of the areas Dee had already destroyed, forcing him to live in his own mess. They found a valley in southern Peru that fit their needs perfectly. The area was surrounded by mountains, and thanks to the Gold Dragon, entrances to the valley had been sealed off. A row of Royal Dragon Gems dotted the tops of all the mountains, creating a helix above the skyline, making it impossible for Dee to escape over the mountains. The only way out of the valley was through a crevice in the side of the mountains. A dozen Royal Dragon Gems dotted the opening, so even if half of them were removed, the force field would remain.

"It's finished," Darlene said as she placed the last gem in the wall.

"I want an additional barrier put up, one that will keep anything that enters the valley from leaving it," the Silver Dragon commanded. He was covered in glimmering silver scales too shiny to look directly at in the sunlight. He looked like the meanest of the dragons, and often was.

"But why?" Darlene asked, not understanding.

"I don't want people wandering in there and making friends with that creature. I want people to hate this place, to dread it. Part of Dee's punishment should be isolation. Force him to live in the world he was creating. A world with nothing alive but him," The Silver Dragon growled as he tapped his long fangs against his equally long talons.

"Sounds just. Make it so, Darlene. Force him to live in isolation," the Red Dragon agreed.

"Do you want me to make it so no one can enter it, either?" Darlene asked dryly.

"No," the Silver Dragon quipped. "If no one can enter it, people will become curious. But if they can enter it and not leave, and if they know Dee will kill them as soon as they enter it, it will deter them from coming here."

"Agreed," the other dragons mumbled. Darlene sighed and looked into the valley at the sleeping Dee. She had left a stone on his chest, and she planned to leave it there until her work was finished. But in the end, she wanted him to be awake when she left him to his punishment. She wanted to be the one to tell him he was trapped here forever.

Part II

Valley of Death

Rick showed no fear as his tormentors dragged him along the ground. He knew he would be able to escape; he always escaped. Especially when he was dealing with humans. They were such a weak species. He had stopped listening to their crude jokes and boasts of pride, waiting for the perfect moment to break the rope that tied his hands behind his back. He twisted his feet, trying to decide if he could also break the rope around his ankles. The dragging stopped and Rick tensed, wondering if this was his opportunity.

"Here we are, boys," one of the men said. He claimed to be the one in charge, the self-proclaimed sheriff of the village in which Rick had been caught. Like the humans had any sort of authority. Rick knew the man wasn't a sheriff; only the dragons held such positions. Maybe he was the slave of the dragon who was the sheriff, but it didn't matter to Rick. The man had been so upset to find Rick stealing chickens from his henhouse that the humans hadn't wasted time informing the dragons. They had taken the law into their own hands. Once Rick got free, he planned to find a discreet way to inform the dragons of this little band of renegades.

"Show him," the man said in his gruff voice. Someone reached down and pulled the blindfold off Rick's head and twisted his neck so he would look where they wanted. Rick had to close his eyes. Sometime during the dragging, the sun had come up. He didn't like the sun; his home planet never got bright like this one did. Being stuck on this scorching planet was torture enough without humans adding to it.

"That's where you're going, Zalite. Does it look familiar?" the gruff man asked. His comrades grunted in satisfaction. Rick opened his eyes just a sliver, but tears blurred his vision; it was too damn sunny out for him to see anything.

"You know Zalites are practically blind in the daylight. Just tell him," one of the other men said. Another arrogant human that thought he knew about Zalites. Nice, Rick thought. Rick could see just fine in the sunlight; it just took a few minutes for his eyes to adjust.

"It's the Valley of Death, Zalite," the gruff man said softly. "You're going to meet the only other creature on this planet that's killed more people than you. Although with you, it might be a close call."

The others all laughed at his joke as Rick tried to figure out what they were talking about. He wasn't up to speed on what the humans believed. He had a feeling that the Valley of Death was a religious reference, where they believed the devil dwelled. What was the name the humans had given their devil?

"That's right, Zalite, you're going to meet Decompose," the man told him, trying to scare him. Rick relaxed—stupid humans and their religious tales.

"Decompose isn't a real being. It's just a plague that destroyed majority of your world thirty-six years ago, and the Valley of Death is—" Rick paused as he remembered what the Valley of Death was—a place still infected with the plague. If they threw him in there, he would become infected.

They must have noticed the change in his demeanor, because they began grabbing and pushing him. He needed to make his escape now. Rick fought back with all his might, which was quite a bit mightier than the humans could fathom. He hadn't counted how many of them there were, and he couldn't count them now with his eyes unadjusted to the scorching sun. Just as he broke the binds holding his wrists, he was pushed to his right. He hit the ground hard and spit dirt from his mouth. No one was touching him anymore. He didn't even realize it at first. His eyes adjusted to the bright sun, and Rick opened his eyes to find a dozen men watching him from only a few feet away.

Rick was on his feet in a heartbeat, ripping the rope from around his ankles as he got up. He only made it a few feet before he touched something that sent a jolt of pain through his body. The air in front of him rippled red. An invisible force field divided him from the townsfolk. He backed away, assessing the barrier. He guessed it to be about fifteen feet high and ten feet wide. What the barrier didn't cover was blocked by layers of golden stone. His gaze went higher and higher,

Twilight of One: The Plague of Decompose

and eventually the wall ended, but it was an impossible angle to climb, as if the valley was surrounded by a dam.

"Sorry, Zalite. A spell was put on this valley to keep the *infection* from escaping. Once something goes in the valley, it never comes out," the gruff man told him, and he and his band laughed at Rick's predicament.

Rick had to admit that made sense, and it was just like the dragons to use magic in such a way. He wondered what he would die from first—the plague or starvation. Maybe neither, if Dennis would hurry up and find him. Surely there was a way to get out, if someone on the outside of this valley was helping.

Rick heard a twig snap behind him and turned away from the men. He wasn't sure why he was even bothering to pay attention to them anymore, *they* weren't going to help him. A snarling gray wolf was approaching him. A living animal. The stories were wrong, or maybe the plague had dissipated on its own. If a wolf could survive here, so could he. The wolf shook its head, and Rick noticed a clump of skin hanging from its neck. Then he noticed the blood-stained fur. The animal reeked of death. Zalites, unlike humans, had retained their animal instincts, and Rick knew this animal was dead even before he saw the decomposing flesh writhing with maggots on the wolf's neck. Still the beast continued towards him, his eyes glowing red. The wolf wasn't the only creature moving in the valley. All around him, dead animals rose from the ground. Some barely had any flesh left on their bones. Rick wondered how he could fight an army of the dead.

The wolf lunged towards him, and Rick raised an arm. The wolf was surprisingly light, and Rick's blow smashed it against a nearby tree. The wolf's body fell to pieces, much as one would expect a week-dead carcass to do. Then the body began pulling itself back together. His temporary distraction cost him as a lioness tackled him, pinning him to the ground. She must not have been dead for as long, for she had some weight to her body, but the smell was still wicked. On Zalita, Zalites kept pets that were larger than the lioness, and more aggressive, too. Rick had wrestled with his pet all his childhood; wrestling the lioness just brought back memories. He reached up and snapped the lion's neck. He heard the bones break. But it had no effect on the feline, and she just opened her mouth to swallow his face. Rick closed his eyes, fearing the cat intended to gouge his eyes out. Rick felt a muggy paw on his forehead as another dead creature tried to pry his eyes open. Rick screamed. Rick never screamed. When he was six and broke his leg, he hadn't screamed. But as his eyes were forced open under the scorching sun by a band of dead animals, he screamed.

He opened his eyes and found himself meeting the gaze of a fat, disgusting rat. A jittery raccoon was holding his eyelids open, the lioness still pinning him to the ground. Rick looked into the red eyes; they had a mesmerizing nature. Rick felt the hot breath of the rat against his cheek and realized the rat wasn't dead. The rat was alive, and pretty healthy, judging by its bulging tummy. But it still had red eyes, just like the dead animals. What did this plague do? What was it going to do to him?

The rat shivered and made a whiny, guttural sound as it stared at him intensely. Rick had had enough. He jerked his head forward, ramming it into the lioness' head, nearly smashing the rat in the process. The rat jumped to safety as the raccoon flew out of Rick's line of sight. With the two smaller pests gone, Rick freed an arm and forced the lion off of him. He was on his feet in seconds.

In those few moments that Rick had been distracted, the dead corpses had fallen to the ground, as if all the life had suddenly been sucked out of them. All except the rat, who skillfully skipped over the unmoving corpses, heading to the thicker brush.

"Not so fast, you little frkrak," Rick cursed as he chased the rodent. He had only taken a few steps when something struck the back of his skull, sending sparks of pain through his head. As he lost consciousness, he wondered if this was the beginning of the plague's symptoms.

When Rick came to, his arms were bound behind his back. This time, his captors hadn't been wise enough to bind his ankles as well. He was slumped against a tree, and his head still pounded. He opened his eyes slowly and saw his captor. Rick tried not to let his captor know that he was awake; he wanted to keep the element of surprise. His captor was a male, with blonde hair. He seemed normal enough, but looked crazed. Rick wondered if he was dead; he couldn't tell.

"You're not human," the man said.

Rick didn't respond, pretending sleep.

"I know you're awake, I'm telepathic. I can't read your thoughts, but I can see enough to know you're awake."

Twilight of One: The Plague of Decompose

"You sound like you've never seen an alien before," Rick said slowly in his deep voice. English wasn't the easiest language to learn, not compared to the Zalite language. But Rick was smart and had managed to pick it up after being trapped on the planet for fourteen years with Dennis, the only other Zalite.

The man seemed shocked at Rick's comment. He took a step back. "What are you?"

"I don't think that's any of your business," Rick told him. He twisted his wrists and wrestled his hands free. He got to his feet, but a familiar red force field formed around him. He paused, unsure if it would be as painful as the one blocking the exit to the valley.

"I think it is," the man said, his eyes glowing red, just like those of the dead corpses. Rick took a deep breath. Maybe he should have started going to the Dragon Temples.

"You're faster than any human I've ever seen. Your eyes are iridescent—if I didn't know better, I would say you could see in the dark. You don't speak with any accent I've ever heard before, and I can't control your mind. So a part of me believes you, but you need to give me reasons to let you survive," the man said calmly.

"You're a sorcerer," Rick murmured.

"I don't do magic tricks," the man responded. "There's a reason I'm trapped here. Is there a reason you're here?"

"I don't think that's any of your business," Rick responded.

"You're going to die here, whether I kill you or not. So there's no reason to not cooperate. I can help us both get out of here, but not if you don't give me a reason to help you."

"If you can survive in here, so can I. Maybe I'll grab the next fool tossed in here and recruit him to help me," Rick countered.

"Survive? You think I survived? I was already dead when they left me here!" the man shouted. "Well, in a manner of speaking. You could say I'm dead, or you could say I'm immortal. It's one of those conundrums, like saying a glass is half-full or half-empty. But you're alive; there's no question about that, so the real question is whether or not you want to stay that way."

"Why don't we start this friendship off on the right foot by getting rid of this little force field," Rick suggested.

"After you tell me what you are."

"Drop the force field, and I'll tell you, but only if you'll tell me who you are," Rick countered. Rick had a feeling this man had been trapped here for a long time.

"I'll drop the force field after you agree to help me, not before."

"I'm not negotiating anything until you drop this force field."

"Dead men don't sleep," the man said simply, and he sat down with his back against a nearby tree. "I have all the time in the world."

Rick stood for a moment, surprised that the man had given up so easily. Rick hadn't managed to gain anything, but he hadn't given up any information, either. He wasn't sure how long he stood there before he sat on the ground as well. Two could play this game. The man hadn't so much as moved a muscle.

"You know, the longer we wait, the weaker you're going to become, and the harder an escape is going to be," the man told him.

"I'm a tough species," Rick responded. Day faded into night. But as the sun began to come up again, Rick started to doubt his ability to outlast the man. And as the sun set on the second day, he became concerned that the man hadn't so much as moved in nearly two days. He had never seen a human do that. Warlock or not, the man should have gotten up to drink something.

"My name's Rick, I'm a Zalite, from the planet Zalita. My co-polite and I crashed here fourteen years ago during the pursuit of Sapoquates, an alien species from Sapoquatis. They were coming here to research the plague that destroyed much of this planet thirty-six years ago. The dragons forced us to land, destroying our ship and technology. The people on my planet don't know I'm here. After the Sapoquates were attacked and stranded here as well, all hope of rescue was lost. Sapoquates aren't much into rescuing downed ships and most likely put a warning beacon in orbit to prevent further losses. So we are all trapped here. Now if you could get rid of this force field so I can get something to eat and drink," Rick said.

"You never said why the humans left you here, and you haven't agreed to help me escape."

"The humans just don't like me, and if it's a fair deal, I'll help you escape—so long as I get out, too."

"Deal," the man agreed. The force field was removed, and the man's eyes changed to what Rick assumed was their original color, although he had never met a human or alien with eyes such a shade of purple.

"Are you going to tell me who you are?" Rick asked.

"Name's Dee, but most of the people on this planet know me as Decompose."

"Heh, that I doubt; everyone refers to that plague as 'decompose.'"

"I am that plague," Dee told him.

Rick started to laugh again, but the man was serious. Dee *had* been trapped here for a long time; he must have lost his mind. Or perhaps he had been insane from the start. Maybe that was why he had been banished here in the first place.

"The passageway is the only way out," Dee explained. "Whenever someone touches it, it creates a surge in power; however, if one of us touches the field first—"

"Then the other touches it, the surge won't be as strong for the second person," Rick finished.

"Yes, and the second person should be able to endure the pressure," Dee agreed. "And on the other side, the force field can be disabled by removing ten of the twelve stones arranged on the wall."

"Freeing the person still in the prison," Rick concluded.

"Yes."

"Well, I guess the question is, who gets out first? That's quite a leap of faith—to trust the other person to actually free you," Rick said as he ran a hand over his hairless scalp.

"You can go first," Dee told him. "I trust you."

"Really?" Rick asked.

"Why shouldn't I?" Dee asked him. They looked at each other for a moment, then Rick looked at the sun as it began to rise.

"All right then," Rick agreed. "Let's do this."

"I might pass out for a few minutes after you get through the barrier, but I'll be okay."

"Right, the whole dead guy thing, right?" Rick asked.

"Can't kill someone who's already dead," Dee agreed with a grin. He stepped forward and placed his fingers a few inches away from the force field. Rick looked through the red-glazed wall and into the waist-high golden grass. All he could see beyond the valley doorway were hills and hills of tall grass. He wondered how far the townsfolk had dragged him.

"Ready?" Dee asked.

"Yeah," Rick agreed, as he crouched into a runner's starting position. He was going to have to be fast; if he stayed in the crossfire of the force field for too long, the pain would cause him to pass out, and he wasn't sure which side of the force field he would pass out on or how safe it would be to be unconscious on the other side of the force field. He couldn't see what kind of creatures lurked in the golden grass.

"Here goes," Dee said as he thrust his hand against the field. Instantly, the red pulses of energy increased in the area he was touching and faded to a pinkish color elsewhere. Rick charged forward, gritting his teeth in preparation for the pain. To his surprise, the burst of electrical energy only lasted a few moments, then he found himself on his hands and knees on the other side of the force field. He looked back into the valley and saw Dee lying face down on the ground. He debated whether he should free the man. Neither had confessed why they had been banished to the valley, although Rick doubted the man's crimes could be any worse than his own.

He looked up at the golden cement surrounding the doorway, and sure enough, he saw ruby stones embedded in the rock. He looked farther down the wall and saw other red stones. Exactly as Dee had told him, there were twelve—evenly spaced around the doorway.

"Walk away," a deep voice said. Rick turned away from the doorway and looked at the speaker, who stood surprisingly near him, his face shadowed by a brown hood. Rick hadn't heard the man approach. He broke out in goose bumps as he saw the weapon the man wielded. He held a bow and arrow, the arrow already nocked and aimed at Rick's chest. Judging by the black fur covering the man's hands, he was probably just as quick as Rick—at least quick enough to fire the arrow before Rick could get out of the way.

"Doesn't that look like what I'm doing?" Rick asked.

"I heard the deal you made. If you try to free that beast, I will kill you," the man said without a hint of humor.

"Well, Mister Valley of Death Guardian, where were you three days ago, when I was thrown in there against my will?" Rick asked. "That guy helped me get out; *you* could have prevented me from going in."

"That's not my job. I'm just here to keep him in there. So you can walk away and pretend none of this happened. Or I kill you."

"You Earthlings don't make getting out of the Valley of Death easy, do you?" Rick asked as he saw a familiar figure rise from the grass behind the guardian. Dennis had arrived. It was about time, Rick thought. Dennis was slightly taller and a lot skinner than Rick.

"Walk away," the guardian repeated. Dennis was only a few feet away now; he joined his hands together to form a single fist, then slammed the man between his shoulder blades. Rick saw a brief glimpse of shock in the man's eyes, or at least imagined it—he still couldn't see the man's face. He watched the man crumple to the ground, disappearing in the tall grass.

"What took you so long?" Rick asked. Dennis looked at him, uncertain how to respond. Then he noticed the unconscious man behind the force field.

"Should we help him? That's what you were arguing about with this guy, right?" Dennis asked, annoying Rick. Dennis wasn't someone Rick would have chosen to befriend, but there hadn't been much of a choice in the matter—he was the only other Zalite on the planet. At least Dennis's brain came in handy once in a while; he was a smart Zalite.

Rick looked back at Dee, who was still unconscious, and shrugged his shoulders.

"Naw, leave him. He's not worth the effort—just a crazy loon. Probably better off in there, anyway," Rick decided. He never looked back at the valley as they left or noticed the pair of glaring red eyes that watched him leave. Rick wasn't the only one who could pretend to be asleep.

Rick hadn't been the first person thrown unwilling into the valley with Dee. But he had been the first who had agreed to help. Usually the person killed themselves the first chance they got, before Dee had a chance to talk to them. The Zalite's betrayal made Dee bitter. He avoided the passageway to the valley for nearly a year, not caring if someone was thrown in. They would die, or kill themselves.

One day, he had wandered closer to the passageway than usual, and he heard the faint voice of a woman. Curious, having nothing better to do, Dee made his way to the entrance, keeping out of sight. At the passageway, a sheep paced back and forth on Dee's side of the force field. On the other side, a woman was trying to figure out how to get her sheep back.

Animals often wandered into the valley. Dee usually didn't pay attention to them. They didn't live for very long once they entered—only rats seemed able to survive, and that was only because they fed on the carcasses of the animals that died. But never before had Dee seen someone trying to help an animal get out. Most people thought the animal was instantly infected if it entered the valley. Removing it could mean genocide. Or so the humans thought.

Dee watched the woman fret over the sheep, and the sheep fret over the stressed woman. Finally, the woman sank to her knees, crying, and the sheep laid down and bleated for help. It was a sad sight. Dee wondered where the stupid archer was; this was just the kind of situation he usually took care of. Finally Dee succumbed and walked toward the passageway.

The sheep sensed him and instantly got to its feet, looking terrified, obviously sensing he was unnatural. Dee looked the sheep in its eyes and calmed it down. The woman noticed the silence and looked up, obviously expecting to see the sheep dead. When she saw Dee, she started screaming and mumbling words Dee didn't understand.

"I'm sorry, but do you speak English?" Dee asked.

The woman looked at him with fear in her eyes.

"You want your sheep back? Right?"

Again, the woman said nothing.

"I can help you. I can free your sheep. All you have to do is remove a few of the stones around this doorway, and your sheep will be free."

The woman dried her tears and stood. She had a very slender figure—she was gorgeous. Or maybe she just looked gorgeous because he hadn't seen a living woman in so long.

"Yes, my sheep. I need my sheep. My father will be furious if I return without it," the woman said without an accent. Perhaps she had just been mumbling her words, and not speaking a different language, as Dee had thought.

"That's fine; he'll never know about this. All you have to do is remove the stones around this doorway, and the sheep will be all yours," Dee told her, almost unable to believe how easy it was.

"Yes, yes; I can do that," the woman said excitedly. She reached over and grabbed at something Dee couldn't see on the wall. He assumed it was one of the stones. Then Dee heard the swoosh of an arrow and saw the woman fall to the ground. The archer stepped out of his hiding place in the golden grass and walked up to the woman. He grabbed her dress and proceeded to drag her away.

"She just wanted her sheep. You could have let her have that. Or you could have told her to go away. You didn't have to kill her," Dee growled. But the man didn't talk to him. He never talked to him.

The sheep protested, as if it knew its owner had died. The archer looked at the animal, annoyed. He let go of the woman and drew an arrow. He shot one at the sheep. Dee wasn't about to let the sheep die. Its owner had given her life for it.

Dee raised his hand, intending to catch the arrow midair. Instead, the arrow went into the palm of his hand. The archer readied another arrow, and Dee threw up a force field around the passageway, keeping things from entering the valley. The man shot a few arrows, but when they bounced away uselessly, he stopped and resumed dragging the woman.

Dee watched him go then took the sheep away from the doorway, to where there was water and vegetation. He would make sure this sheep lived a full life, and someday, a free one.

It had been nearly three years, and Dee had managed to keep the sheep not only alive, but healthy. Almost as healthy as the rats. Dee paid little attention to the passageway, but when he heard activity near it, he would sneak a peek. Today was one of those days. It sounded like another mob, probably here to toss someone into the valley as punishment.

Dee tied the sheep to a tree so she wouldn't wander off and get close enough to the passageway for the archer to shoot her. Dee had been forced to pull an arrow or two from the sheep's hide on more than one occasion.

Dee reached the passageway in time to see a group of ten men toss a burlap bag into the valley. That was odd; usually the victims weren't in a bag. Maybe it wasn't a human. But why would they toss an animal in a bag into the valley, either?

There definitely was something alive in the bag, though; Dee could see it kicking and squirming, even from his distance. The men began tossed rocks and stones at the bag, cheering themselves on. That was unacceptable. Dee couldn't stop them from tossing people into his valley, but he could stop them from torturing the victims once they were in. He took a deep breath and morphed into the form of Decompose. He had used this method to frighten citizens before. He issued a roar and watched the townsfolk freeze like statues. Decompose took a few giant leaps and landed in front of the passageway, close enough to the people to see the whites of their eyes. He opened his jaws and breathed fire. It hit the barrier, but it still sent the men running and screaming. Long after the men had left, Decompose continued to blow fire, hoping it would force the archer to distance himself, as well. Decompose shivered as the pain of being in this form increased. He shrunk back into his human form and looked down at the still-twitching burlap bag. Dee created his own force field around the doorway, just in case the archer decided to kill his new company.

"What is going on out there? Is there fire? I feel fire—smell it, too. Did you set me on fire? Who is out there? Anyone? Am I alone? Hello? Hello?" the whiny voice asked, over and over. There wasn't much of an accent in the voice, but it didn't sound normal. It almost sounded reptilian, if there was such a thing. Another alien? Perhaps the kind Rick had mentioned.

"Hello," Dee told the bag. It fell silent for a moment.

"Ah, yes, there is someone. Good, good. Can you be a good old rasptiyn, and let me out of here?" the hissing voice asked. Dee stared at the bag, not sure if he wanted to see what this thing looked like.

"You're in a burlap bag. Just pull it open," Dee said, deciding the voice belonged to a male.

"Do you not think I would have done that if I could?" the voice asked, without a hint of sarcasm.

Dee sighed and reached down. He grabbed the bag with both hands and gave it a pull, tearing it in two. He took a step back, wanting to keep his distance.

A greenish arm reached out, the fingers elongated and webbed, with no fingernails. The skin looked slightly damp, like a frog's. The creature sat up, and Dee had to bite his lip to keep from showing his shock. Rick had been an alien, but aside from his freakishly bald head and iridescent eyes, he had looked human. There was no mistaking this creature for human.

The alien's body was muddy green; he almost looked like a frog in human form. His skin was so thin, Dee could see purplish veins under it. The creature did look muscular though, with strong legs and arms which probably made him a very good swimmer and jumper. He crouched on the ground, much as a frog would.

The face was the most amazing. He had large eyes, like an insect. He didn't seem to have a nose; instead, Dee noticed three gill-like slits on his throat. The alien's lips were narrow, barely noticeable when his mouth was closed. He was hairless—a slimy green mass of flesh. He wore a tattered brown cloth around his waist that looked like it could be unfolded to cover his upper body as well.

The creature looked at Dee and stood with eerie agility, like a lizard or snake. It was taller than Dee expected, making him seem even more snake-like. Tall, slender, and muscular—how had he been trapped inside a burlap bag?

"Greetings," the creature said as he extended a hand. Dee didn't take the offer, and stared into the creature's black eyes. He saw nothing—he couldn't read this guy's mind any better than he had Rick's.

"Where might we be? Is there water near here? I am so very thirsty," the creature said as he dropped his hand.

"You're in the Valley of Death," Dee told him casually. The creature seemed startled and gave a little jump.

"Surely you jest? If this is the Valley of Death, that would make you—"

"Decompose?" Dee replied. The creature backed a few feet away from him.

"The plague," he gasped as his little gills flexed in panic. Dee had to try hard not to laugh.

"Don't worry; there is water," Dee told him.

"So, all I must do is jump through the force field while you are touching it, then remove the gems from the wall, and we shall both be free?" the alien asked. Dee nodded. The alien had been in the valley for barely a day, and already Dee felt he had made a friend for life. The alien went by the name of Aquatis, and he was indeed one of the Sapoquates Rick had mentioned.

"That's all there is to it," Dee affirmed as they neared the doorway. They paused a few inches from the force field. Dee had brought the sheep with them, tying it to his wrist. He couldn't think of anything better to do. "There is one more thing."

"Yes?"

"On the other side of the force field, an archer guards the gateway. He'll try to convince you to leave me here. Otherwise, he will kill you."

"Ah, I see; you might have mentioned him earlier," Aquatis remarked.

"Is that a problem?" Dee asked.

"We shall see, won't we?" Aquatis told him. "Let's do it."

Dee nodded and reached out with his hand. He placed the palm of his hand against the force field and was instantly overwhelmed with the surge of power. He managed to keep his hand on the force field until he counted to ten, exactly how long he had told Aquatis he would have to get through. Dee let go as he lost consciousness. The last thing he heard was the soft bleating of his sheep.

Aquatis felt a numbing pain as he leaped through the force field. He landed on the ground on the other side of the passageway, crouching like a frog.

"I suggest you leave," a voice growled at him. Aquatis looked up to see a hooded man standing before him holding a bow and arrow. Aquatis looked into the valley and saw Dee unconscious on the ground, the sheep tugging at its rope.

"You must be the archer," Aquatis said.

"And you must be the outcast Sapoquate," the man countered. "Like I said, I suggest you leave, now."

"I will not leave without my friend."

"He's not your friend. You know that. He's the reason your ship crashed here. You know as well as I do that he deserves to rot in that valley."

"He deserves a second chance."

"I'm starting to see why the other Sapoquates kicked you out of their community," the archer said. "But I really don't care. You either walk away, or I'm going to kill you."

"I'll leave. I agree that risking my life for such a pathetic creature is not worth it. However, I trust you no more than I do him. So I would like a vouch of faith."

"That was a pretty quick change of heart."

"Maybe for your human mind."

"What's a 'vouch of faith'? I assume you mean a gesture of faith."

"Yes, my apologies. I wish to shake your hand."

"Not happening."

"You let your guard down long enough to shake my hand, or you'll have to shoot me," Aquatis said stubbornly.

"You think I really care which way this goes down?"

"You're guarding this gateway for the good of humanity, aren't you? Such a man wouldn't kill someone if he didn't have to," Aquatis reasoned. The archer just looked at him from behind the shadow of his hood, his yellow cat-like eyes glaring.

"If you ever come back around here again, I'll kill you. No questions asked," the man said.

"I don't plan on ever coming back," Aquatis agreed. The man lowered his bow, carefully keeping an arrow still nocked in it, and extended his other hand to Aquatis. Aquatis took his hand, and before the man could realize what he was doing, Aquatis was off his feet. He twisted in such a way that only a fellow amphibian without a stiff skeletal system could have copied him. His left foot kicked the archer in his right side, while his other foot hit the ground and kicked up. The archer went flying through the passageway, into the Valley of Death. Before the archer had finished passing through the force field, Aquatis was on the top of the archway, using his sticky palms and feet to keep his grip. An arrow flew through the passageway. If he had been just a few seconds slower, that arrow would have went straight through his soft skull.

Dee woke in time to see the archer fly through the passageway. That had not been part of the plan. The man launched an arrow before he hit the ground, a good fifty yards from the passageway. Dee quickly got to his feet and pushed the sheep behind a nearby tree, hiding it from the archer. Dee untied the rope and left one end of it next to the force field, the other end tied around the sheep's neck. Dee had to stall and hopefully give Aquatis time to remove the stones. He ducked into the nearby brush, concealing himself.

It seemed frogs had been created quicker and more agile than cats. McCaw got to his feet and let loose a blood-chilling roar. Of all the times to break his oath to not use his magical powers, this seemed ideal. He got to his feet and shot another arrow at the force field. But the power had already been restored, and his arrow bounced off. Not that it mattered. The frog-like alien was nowhere to be seen. That meant he had either left—or he was removing the stones.

"No," McCaw whispered under his breath. He ran towards the force field, realizing that he wouldn't be able to do anything once he reached it.

"Why?" a voice asked. "Why did you always kill them?"

McCaw froze and raised his bow and arrow. He had almost forgotten about the decompose monster. He searched the plains and brush, looking for it. He had tormented this creature for a long time. He didn't want to know what it wanted to do to him.

"All she wanted was her sheep," the monster said as he jumped out from behind a nearby bush. McCaw was quicker than a human and easily stepped out of the way. The decompose man-creature let out a sharp cry of pain as McCaw shot an arrow into his thigh.

McCaw prepared another arrow, aiming to shoot through his skull. The creature got to his feet as if he wasn't injured at all, catching McCaw off-guard. He kicked at McCaw's knees, tripping him for a moment, and the arrow lodged itself in the man's ankle. When McCaw got back to his feet, he saw the man running away, as if nothing was wrong, although he had arrows protruding from both legs. McCaw watched him for a moment, then he raised his bow and shot another arrow, then another, and another. He would not let this creature leave the valley alive.

Dee felt a stabbing pain in his ankle every time he put pressure on it and a stream of blood running down his other leg. Why had he left the doorway? What had he been thinking? Now he had to run all the way back and race the archer the whole way. But the archer wasn't racing him, he was just shooting arrows at him. And he was a damn good shot. Bam—in the shoulder; bam—in the right knee; bam—in the back, right between some ribs. Dee was sure it had struck a vital organ because things started getting a little fuzzy after that, and he had trouble breathing. Bam—another in the back, higher this time; it hit the lungs. Bam—in the back again; this time, it definitely hit an organ because Dee went numb. His heart stopped. Bastard shot an arrow in my heart, Dee thought ironically. He knew more arrows were hitting him, but he couldn't feel them anymore. He was almost to the force field when his right knee gave out. He tumbled to his chest and rolled over. He looked down at his knee to see a half-dozen arrows. Dee was lucky his calf hadn't fallen off. He sat up to pull a few arrows out, and an arrow slammed into his left eye. The force knocked Dee back, and he tumbled to the grass and clutched at the arrow, not enjoying his limited vision. He looked up and saw Aquatis tugging at one of the gems. It took a moment for this to compute. His mouth moved slowly as he tried to form words. He looked to his right, where the sheep waited for him. The rope. His mind focused on that. He ignored the arrow in his eye and grabbed at the rope.

"A—Aquat—tis," Dee shouted, having trouble remembering his name. "Stop, stop. Put the gems back. Put the gems back now!"

Dee lifted his head and saw the archer running towards them. He gave the rope a sharp tug, coaxing the sheep through the passageway. He hoped the archer couldn't shoot while he was running. Besides, he had already done all the damage he needed. He had immobilized Dee; now he just needed to reach him. The sheep hurried past Dee and dashed into the brush. The rope slipped through Dee's fingers. He stared at his fingers a moment; he hadn't even felt the rope.

"Dee, I can't put this stone in until you get out of the way. It'll put the field back up," Aquatis shouted, pulling Dee back to reality. Dee rolled onto his stomach and heard a loud crunch and pop. He wondered if it was just the arrows breaking in half, or if it was his bones. He didn't bother trying to stand up; he grabbed at the ground in front of him and dragged himself along, but that was too slow, and Dee decided to just roll through. He gave himself a quick push and rolled at an angle to the left. He came to a stop on his side and looked back at the force field. The archer was close.

"Now! Do it now!" Dee shouted. Aquatis put one of the stones back, and then scurried over to another hole and put another stone in. The archer slammed into the invisible force field. Aquatis put another three stones in before the archer had recovered enough to try again. This time, the archer fell to the ground, unconscious. Aquatis finished putting the stones back and leaped to the ground next to Dee.

"Are you okay?" Aquatis asked. Dee looked at the alien with his good eye and smiled.

"Yeah, just give me a minute to get these things out," Dee told him. He sat up and grabbed at the arrow in his skull. He gave a sharp tug and pulled the arrow out, backwards through his flesh. He held the arrow in front of him and saw his eyeball on the arrowhead. Dee stared at it until his vision fully returned. He blinked both eyes; he was able to heal better than he used to. He began grabbing at the arrows in his knee.

"Wait! Dear Exnith, wait. If you break the arrow in half, you won't have to pull the arrowhead through. It won't cause as much damage that way," Aquatis told him. The lizard-like creature reached over and snapped one of the arrows, then easily pulled it out.

"Amazing," Dee murmured. He followed Aquatis's example and began snapping the shafts in half before pulling the arrow out. When he was finished, he got to his feet. "We should start moving. I don't know how much time we'll have before the dragons realize I've escaped."

Aquatis stared at him for a moment. "But you still have at least two dozen arrows in you," he said.

"I'll pull them out as we walk," Dee said as he pulled two arrows from his ankle and another from his calf, freeing one leg of protrusions.

"The tales of you are disturbingly accurate," Aquatis told him as he began walking down a path in the waist-high golden grass. "There's a village not far from here; we can stop there and get you new clothes."

It wasn't until Dee pulled the last arrow out—the one in his heart—that he realized the sheep wasn't with them. He dropped the arrow to the ground and felt a sharp pain in his chest as his heart started pumping again. He bent over and placed his hands on his knees, trying to catch his breath. The pain subsided, and Dee took his first breath in over twenty minutes. His lungs ached, but after a few minutes, he began walking again and caught up to Aquatis.

Part III

A World Ruled by Dragons

It didn't take Dee long to begin disliking the golden grass. It was too tall; at times it towered over him and slapped him in the face. He pushed it out of the way and tried to follow Aquatis. He still wasn't sure what had happened to the sheep; he hoped it was okay.

"There should be a well up ahead. I am in desperate need of water," Aquatis told him. Dee looked up, only to be slapped by another strand of sharp grass.

"Tell me something, Aquatis. Why did the dragons strand you here?" Dee asked as he brushed the grass out of his way.

"They feared we would liberate the humans," Aquatis said simply.

"Liberate the humans? From whom?"

"Why, from the dragons of course. Who else?"

"What do you mean? The dragons enslaved mankind?" Dee asked as he stepped into a clearing. Before them stood a well built from golden bricks, with a golden roof, rope—even a golden bucket.

"Well, they didn't, at first. I think the Five Royal Dragons were content to leave humanity to fight amongst themselves. But after the Queen was born, she had different ideas."

"Queen? Fight for themselves? Aquatis, I've been trapped in that valley for the past forty years. Would you mind filling me in?" Dee asked.

Aquatis lowered the bucket into the well, watching with eager fascination as it sank into the murky darkness.

"After the Decompose plague plundered the land, some of the survivors became sick. People became cannibals. Mother and child turned against each other. It was horrible. Their skin turned gray, and no one was ever able to examine them and find out why. But it was believed that the sickness gave their flesh a rotten taste, so they wouldn't eat each other—only those who were not infected. Cows, deer—anything with meat on it. But animals were a rare commodity after the plague, and they weren't about to take up fishing. Aquatic life was the only thing unaffected. Well, it turned into a war. Cannibals against humans. Greenland and Iceland were overrun with people trying to seek shelter. But those two countries closed their borders and refused to allow entrance," Aquatis said. He paused as he heard a splash. "Doesn't sound too far down, does it?"

"The water? No, not at all. What happened next? How did they deal with the cannibals?" Dee asked as Aquatis jumped on the rim of the well and peered down.

"Well, for about ten years, they didn't do very well at all. The humans tried to reach deserted islands, but most were lost at sea. Others created forts in which to hide. But they couldn't hide forever. The cannibals were slow, stupid, and functioned only on instinct, but they had a hypnotic power. All a human had to do was look at them, and they were paralyzed. The cannibals could eat them at their leisure. The losses were horrendous," Aquatis said. Then, to Dee's surprise, he jumped into the well. Dee hurried forward and peered down, hearing the splash as Aquatis hit the surface of the water.

"Aquatis? Are you alright?" Dee asked.

"Yes, I'm fine. Just enjoying a nice swim," Aquatis called back, his voice echoing.

"So what changed? After those ten years?"

"The dragons took pity on us," a woman said. Dee turned and saw a woman in a simple yellow dress holding a wooden shepherd's cane. "I believe your sheep has wandered into my flock."

"Then—then you may keep him," Dee mumbled. He hadn't seen a woman in so long, her beauty made him struggle for words.

"I thought everyone knew of the history of our land. How is it you do not?" the woman asked.

"I—I have been in isolation for quite some time," Dee told her, unable to look away.

"The dragons are the greatest blessing anyone could have asked for. They built for us walls to surround our villages, providing us with safe havens. They taught us the way our dragon gods wished us to live, and they chased the cannibals from the land, forcing them to hide in abandoned cities, and come out only in darkness, when the dragons cannot see them," the woman continued.

"They sound—" Dee began, then he paused. Had she called them "dragon gods"? "I find it hard to believe they would be so charitable."

"It is unwise to speak unkindly of our dragons," the woman warned, but her tone remained friendly.

"What did they ask for in trade?" Dee demanded.

"They asked for nothing, only that we worship them and give them the respect they rightly deserve."

"And provide a virgin sacrifice whenever they need one. And do their every wish and whim. They enslaved mankind," Aquatis said as he crawled out of the well.

"They saved us."

"And it only cost you your freedom. They took away the people's technology, cast them back into the dark ages," Aquatis clarified.

"Disgusting cretin. How dare you speak like that and immerse your filthy body in our well water?" She distorted her face in disgust and raised her shepherd's cane against him. Dee stepped between them and pulled her staff away from her. She screamed in frustration and charged, attempting to push Dee into the well. Dee swung his arm at her, striking her across the face. She fell to the ground, unmoving.

"Dee, what did you do?" Aquatis exclaimed as he climbed down from the well. He went to the aid of the woman then looked up and shook his head. "You killed her."

"She deserved it," Dee said with a dismissive shrug.

"Dee, you cannot go around killing people like this."

"Why are you objecting? She called you names; she wanted to kill you."

"That doesn't matter. You didn't need to kill her. She wasn't a threat to you."

"No one's a threat to me. That's beside the point," Dee told him. "Was she telling the truth? Did the dragons use my plague to enslave mankind?"

"Truth is, Dee, if the dragons hadn't intervened, mankind would be nothing but a bunch of slobbering cannibals. My species didn't arrive for another ten years after the dragons took over. We wanted to help the humans reclaim their technology, maybe even move to a healthier planet, but mostly, we were here to study the plague. The dragons didn't want us meddling. So they stranded us here. The humans don't welcome us because the dragons hate us so much. No one will openly kill us because the dragons don't condone murder. But no one greets us warmly, either."

"That's not right," Dee growled.

"Well, I agree. We Sapoquates should be treated with some respect."

"I did not destroy the world so the dragons could take it over. I hate them," Dee continued, ignoring Aquatis.

"I think it's a little late to be worrying about things like that."

"What do you mean? There're only five dragons—simple enough to kill," Dee told him.

"Five? Dee, there are thousands of dragons. Once the Queen was hatched, the dragons began multiplying. They are like bees."

"Then maybe we should kill the Queen. The dragons have always been easier to deal with when they have no leadership. They never would have defeated me if they hadn't formed that alliance with each other," Dee said.

"We'll sort all this out later. It's getting dark; we should probably go to the nearest village for the night," Aquatis told him.

"We?"

"Well, yes; I mean, you haven't been outside that valley in nearly a half-century. You need a guide."

"And you need a bodyguard," Dee finished.

"Is there something wrong with a mutual relationship?" Aquatis asked softly.

"Betray me, lizard, and I won't hesitate to kill you," Dee warned.

"I would imagine not," Aquatis agreed.

It didn't take long before the golden grass had turned to reddish sand. Dee was grateful to be rid of it. Dee looked ahead and saw a red fort in the distance.

"All Five Royal Dragons have forts?" Dee asked.

"Of course. The Red Dragon Fort is the closest to your valley; we'll stay here," Aquatis said.

"Are you sure it's wise to stay at one so close? It won't be long before they notice I'm missing."

"Actually, it probably will, if you and I keep a low profile. The dragons don't check up on your prison. Unless that archer figures out how to escape, it could be quite some time before they discover you are missing," Aquatis countered.

"I see," Dee said softly as they approached the fort's gate. He could see red dragons, about the size of horses, walking along the top of the wall. Keeping watch, no doubt. It sent a chill up Dee's spine. He had never seen them so organized. It was as if they were all working with one mind. It made Dee wonder how literally he should interpret Aquatis' comparison of them to bees.

A red dragon spotted them and leaped off the wall. He landed on the ground in front of them, then popped his neck and sat back on his haunches. Dee watched as the fish-like fins fluttered gently in the breeze. Dee remembered killing red dragons back on the island—they were the easiest to kill of the four kinds of dragons he had fought. He had never fought a Gold Dragon. Red dragons had hides like iguanas— no special hard scales like the silver dragons. Their spikes were small and dull, unlike those on the white and silver dragons. Their teeth, though sharp, were little, unlike the grossly large teeth found in the white and silver. They didn't move with special agility, like the black dragons. Their special power was fire, a very easy power to overcome.

"Long ways from the swamp, aren't you, Sapoquate?" the red dragon asked.

"Yes, my lord. I require a safe haven for the night," Aquatis told him with a slight bow. Dee felt sick watching his friend be congenial to the dragon.

"Well, you know the rules. Sapoquates are allowed in only at night and must leave at first dawn," the dragon told him with a ruffle of his fins. The dragon eyed Dee. "Is he with you?"

"Yes, we met in the field and traveled together. He, too, seeks shelter," Aquatis told him.

"Odd. I have been working this post for quite some time, and I've never met you. What happened to your clothes?" the little beast asked. He walked up to Dee, grabbed at his pant leg, and stuck a clawed hand through one of the holes the arrows had made. Dee felt the dragon's warm scales against his knee. He bit his lip and tried not to smack the dragon away.

"A minor accident," Aquatis told him.

"I did not ask you, frog boy. I asked the human," the dragon said stiffly. He looked up at Dee, but Dee didn't respond. The dragon sat up straighter, reaching the same height as Dee. His red eyes burned into Dee's violet ones.

"Since when do dragons care what happens to a human's clothes?" Dee asked, trying his best to not sound odious. The dragon's fins stiffened and Dee knew the dragon had taken offense at his remark. "I had some issues with rats in my home. And most recently, I had a run in with a briar patch."

The dragon pulled his hands back and took a step away. "You need a better home and better manners. Perhaps you would do well to pray for prosperity and luck in the temple during your visit," the dragon said rudely. He looked up at the tower and locked eyes with another dragon at the top. They both nodded, and the gate began to lower.

It took three dragons at different locations to lower the gate. But the dragon visiting with Dee had only looked at one of them. Were the dragons communicating telepathically? Dee didn't dare use his powers here; one of them was sure to notice his glowing eyes.

"Hey, hold up. You look familiar. What's your name, human?" the dragon asked. A moment ago, the dragon said he'd never seen Dee before. Had one of the other dragons recognized him?

"Aquatis," Aquatis told the guard calmly. The guard raised his paw, and the gate stopped moving. Dee could see inside the village and knew that if he made a run for it, he could make it inside. He could probably mix himself in the crowd and lose the dragons.

"You must be mistaken," Dee told the guard as he quickened his pace.

"I am never mistaken," the dragon snapped. "I have only seen those eyes on one other person."

"You're much too young to have ever met me before," Dee said coldly. The guard squinted his eyes and flicked his fingers. The gate finished lowering.

Dee noticed the guards watched him closely.

Aquatis leaned in close and whispered harshly in Dee's ear. "You almost got us killed back there! Why did you say that? Do you know how suspicious they are of us now?"

"I think they're telepathic. I don't understand how that is possible."

"Telepathic? Are you saying what you did back there was some sort of test to find out?"

"No, they proved it without my help. Be happy I didn't kill anyone," Dee said with a grin.

"I guess," Aquatis agreed. Dee worked his way through the crowd just as a woman cried out in alarm.

"My baby, my baby! Someone please help me!" the woman screamed. The crowd moved out of the way, and Dee spotted a woman fretting over a child, who was on the ground, having spasms.

"I'm going to go get something to eat. Do you want anything?" Aquatis asked, ignoring the scene the child was creating.

"No, I don't eat. Go ahead. I'll wait here. It'd probably be best if I don't go inside with you dressed like this."

"Right, I'll get you some clothes while I'm in there," Aquatis said as he walked off. Dee looked back at the woman whose child was still twitching on the ground.

"You need to get this child to a white dragon," a man told her.

"But we do not have the money to reach a White Dragon Village, nor enough to pay for his aid," the woman explained.

"They charge you?" Dee exclaimed. "I thought they were gods. Why would they charge you for that?"

"It is an honor to be healed by a white dragon, not a right," the woman explained calmly.

Disgusted, Dee knelt next to the woman and reached out with his right hand. He placed it on the child, and the child stopped convulsing. Dee's eyes glowed red as he searched for the problem behind the spasms. He found it and cured the child. Dee pulled his hand away and blinked as his eyes returned to their normal color. The onlookers stared at him.

"He has the eyes of the devil. He is a demon," a man whispered.

"He has been sent from hell to kill our children."

"Summon the dragons!"

"Kill the child!"

"Yes, quickly; he has been infected with the demon's disease!" another man shouted. The woman pushed herself away from her child and didn't shed a tear as the men began to beat him.

"Wait!" Dee shouted. "I didn't infect him with anything. I cured him."

The people ignored him, and Dee heard a loud pop as the boy's neck was broken. Dee pushed them away and looked at the dead child. A few red dragons began to fly over to see what the commotion was about.

"You won't infect us, demon," a man proclaimed and spit at Dee. Dee raised his hand and stopped the spit in mid-air.

"You want to see me infect someone?" Dee snapped as his eyes began to glow red again. The crowd began to move away, forming a circle around him.

"Break it up, break it up." Four small dragons dropped to the ground between Dee and the people. Smaller than the gate dragons, they were only the size of ponies. "You should all be at the ceremony, anyway. We want maximum attendance."

"Oh, yes, the new maiden offering," someone in the crowd exclaimed. Most of the people sent a last glare at Dee and left him alone with his now-empty threat. He let the spit drop to the ground, and his eyes returned to normal. Aquatis appeared next to him, munching on a vegetable of some sort.

"I found a man who will sell you clothes for a reasonable price," Aquatis said. Apparently, he hadn't noticed the bedlam.

"Why didn't you tell me I'm hated as a demon?" Dee asked.

"I didn't think it would come up. Besides you're not a demon, you are *the* demon. Satan, the devil—ruler of the dead."

"But if someone has glowing red eyes, they are considered what?"

"A demon. Why do you ask?" Aquatis asked.

"You didn't think I needed to know that?" Dee asked.

"Who would be foolish enough to do something like that in public? Come on, let's get you some clothes," Aquatis suggested. Embarrassed, Dee changed the topic.

"Tell me about this maiden offering everyone is going to see."

Dee and Aquatis walked back onto the street in their new clothes. Dee used his telepathic power to convince the merchant to sell them the clothes for free. Even Aquatis's rags had been replaced. To help conceal their identities, they wore robes with hoods. Dee thought they looked a little like monks. The crowds had thinned, and Dee looked around, wondering where the people had all gone.

"We should find a place to sleep for the night," Aquatis said.

"First I want to check out the maiden offering ceremony," Dee told him.

"But there will be dragons there, and you don't seem to get along with them very well," Aquatis pointed out.

"I don't care; I'm going. It's up to you if you want to come or not," Dee said roughly. They pulled their hoods up and followed the remaining pedestrians towards the congregation at the center of the city.

The city seemed to be built around the temple—a huge red building that reminded Dee of a castle from a storybook he used to look at as a kid. In front of the temple was an open, circular area. He guessed it to be about half a city block long. In the center of the circle was a foot-thick red pole. At the top of the pole was a carved dragon head. The circle was made from little red bricks, the only part of the village that was paved. Everything else was dirt.

"We shouldn't be here," Aquatis whispered into his ear.

"These dragons took over because of what I did; I think I have every right to see what they've done with that power," Dee countered. The crowd kept off the red bricks, but a large number of people crowded the rim of the circle. A few people stepped back and created an opening to Dee's right. Dee gently pushed a few people out of the way so he could get a better look. Two men held a young woman by her shoulders. She was younger than Dee expected—only twelve, if that. They had her clothed in a long red dress, and they had tried to make her look pretty, but she was crying. Her brown hair was tangled, and there were smudges of dirt on her dress. Apparently it had not been easy to get her this far. Now that she saw the stake ahead of her, she began to scream.

"Why are they doing this?" Dee asked. "Surely there are women who would willingly do this."

"It is an honor to be chosen as a dragon maiden. She will be immortal," a red-haired woman standing next to Dee said.

"Dragon maiden? That girl is only a child! Why couldn't they find an adult—someone that wants to do this? She's screaming, obviously she doesn't want to be a dragon maiden," Dee remarked rudely.

"It's not easy to find a virgin. Sometimes the children must be chosen," another person said from behind Dee.

"It's no wonder I killed so many of you," Dee muttered. Dee ignored the harsh whispers from Aquatis telling him to stop. Dee pushed his way to the front of the crowd and stepped onto the red bricks. A dark shadow fell over him, and the girl fell silent as the men finished tying her to the stake. Dee looked up and saw a red dragon, slightly smaller than the Royal Red Dragon, land gently on the roof of a building next to the circle. Small bits of debris rolled down the side of the wall under the weight of the great beast. He folded his wings to his body, his red hide shining gently in the setting sun. He paused a moment to take an elegant pose, as if preparing for a photo shoot. The two men that tied the woman fell to their knees and bowed, burying their faces against the warm bricks. A ripple effect began as everyone in the circle went to ground. Dee glanced at Aquatis and saw him motion to follow along. Then Aquatis dropped to the ground, as well. Dee started to lower himself, but was too slow. He was already the only person still standing. He looked back at the dragon and locked eyes with the beast.

"What kind of insolence is this?" the dragon roared. Dee felt a chill—the beast spoke with the same mannerisms as the gate guard.

"My Lord, he is a newcomer and does not know our customs," one of the men who had tied the woman told the dragon. He jumped to his feet and pushed Dee to the ground, kicking him behind the knees. Dee dropped to the ground and allowed the man to push him down.

"Ensure that this does not happen again. The Queen does not like such mistakes," the dragon said. "Arise, my people."

The people in the crowd stood, but kept silent in respect. The man pulled Dee up with him and shot him a dirty look. With a sharp push, he shoved Dee off the bricks and back into the crowd, where he was grabbed roughly. Dee looked at the ground and his eyes glowed red as he sent an electric shock through his body, giving everyone near him a painful but harmless jolt. They stopped touching him, and Dee looked up to see the dragon leap elegantly from his perch and land on the red bricks in front of the woman.

"This is the woman you provide me with to become my new maiden? She is but a child," the dragon objected.

"My Lord, you asked for a virgin sacrifice. Such a task is not easy. Men will rape their own daughters to prevent them from becoming dragon maidens," the man who had forced Dee to bow explained.

"Perhaps you should teach people that sacrifice is a good thing!" the dragon roared. "I refuse to accept a child! Find me a beautiful woman!" the dragon roared in fury. Dee saw him take a deep breath. That usually meant one thing. Fire. Dee's eyes glowed red as he prepared.

"I want a maiden as gorgeous and elegant as the other dragons'! This is a lousy sacrifice!" the dragon whined. He blew the fire at the stake, intending to light the woman on fire. Dee raised his hand and created a blue force field around the woman. Dee blinked in surprise, he had never created a blue one before. He wondered what had he done differently. The girl's hair stood on end, as if she had a bad case of static electricity. He had created an electric field around her; he must have still had electricity in him from shocking the people around him.

The hot fire hit the blue force field, and the arena erupted in electricity and fire. Sparks flew into the crowd and lit people's clothing on fire. The once peaceful crowd began screaming and racing for cover. The dragon stopped blowing fire as sparks stung his eyes. He wiped at them, trying to clear his vision. It was Dee's chance. He dropped the force field and ran forward, skipping around smoldering bits. The smell was rank. He reached the girl and found her unconscious, hanging limply in her ropes. Her skin was dark and smudged with dirt or ash. Her hair was singed and frizzed. Dee looked at the dragon. It was busy wiping the ash from its eyes, and Aquatis was nowhere to be seen.

Dee wasted no time. He quickly ripped the ropes that held her and accidentally dropped her on the ground. Dee fell to the ground with her; the sun had finished setting and it was now dark. The only light came from the smoldering fire. She had stopped breathing, so he placed his hand on her face and healed her lungs. He pulled his hand back, but she was still unconscious. He heard a roar from the dragon—he had almost forgotten about it. He grabbed the child, tossed her over his shoulder, and ran into the darkened streets.

Dee finally stopped running when the flames from the fire dissipated; he feared tripping on something in the darkness. He laid the girl down and looked at her. She was still asleep. Dee touched her face again. It was so soft. He sent a sharp jolt of pain through her body. She jerked and opened her eyes; they were wide with terror. He couldn't imagine what it had been like for her inside that bubble of electric energy. She looked at him, opened her mouth wide, and her chest moved as she gasped. If she had been a dragon, he would have thought she was going to blow fire at him. Her ear-piercing scream echoed through the streets. Dee covered her mouth with his hand and looked into her eyes. He entered her mind easily and forced her to calm. He pulled his hand back, but kept looking in her eyes, searching her memory. He was filled with a surge of power as he realized he could do with this girl whatever he wanted. He could change her memory to make her think he was her father, or make her fall madly in love with him. She could become his slave, doing his every wish and whim. He could make her believe she was a mighty warrior, sworn to protect him. But then he would be no better than the dragons, who made these people worship them. He had caused the humans enough grief; it was time he started making things better for them. Dee could destroy humanity—could he heal it? He pulled his mind from hers and looked at her, trying to make himself appear unthreatening.

"It's okay. The dragon didn't want you. You're free to go home," Dee told her softly.

"He—he wanted to burn me. Why? Why am I not dead? Who are you?" the girl asked in bewilderment. Her fear changed to adoration. "You saved me."

"Listen," Dee began. He didn't want the little girl getting attached to him. He had things to do, and he didn't have time to take care of some kid.

She jumped forward and threw her arms around him. Dee cringed. He had never been hugged before, not since he was a small child. He pushed her roughly away, not used to someone being nice to him, and not sure how to react. In an odd way, he liked it. And he wasn't sure that was a good thing.

"Go home, kid," Dee told her, trying not to sound too mean. "Go home and live your life. Have sex with someone so you don't wind up in this situation again."

Dee looked away from her, deciding that the situation was taken care of. He needed to find Aquatis and lay low for the night. The girl jumped on him again and pressed her face against his. He felt her wet lips on his. It was like kissing a frog, an action Dee would have thought repulsive, yet he felt something he'd never felt before. He kissed her back and goose bumps broke out on his skin as she wrapped her arms around him. He heard a dull thud behind him and felt something smack him on the back of the head. He pulled away from the girl, but she clung to him.

"What are you doing?" Aquatis snapped at him.

"She—she kissed me," Dee told him dumbly. Aquatis grabbed the girl and pulled her off.

"Go home. Get. You don't want to tango with the devil, do you?" Aquatis asked.

The girl looked at him, puzzled.

"Dee, make your eyes glow."

"No, I don't want to scare her, she's been through enough."

"Dee, just do it so she'll go away!" Aquatis shouted.

"You don't—" Dee began, but he felt a sharp pain in his throat and all that came out of his mouth was a gurgling sound. He reached up and felt blood, then a sharp wooden stick protruding from his neck. He moved his fingers along it and found a smooth arrowhead. Dee tried to say "archer," but no sound came. A warm coppery taste filled his mouth. He spat and saw a splotch of blood. Aquatis hadn't figured out what had happened; he was glaring at the girl, still trying to get her to leave. The pain was searing. Dee was afraid he was going to lose consciousness. He stood quickly and shoved Aquatis out of the way, pushing him next to the building.

"What are you doing?" Aquatis asked, annoyed. "There is no need to push me."

In the darkened alley, he hadn't noticed the blood or arrow, not that Dee's hood and robe helped. The fort's wall was only a building's length away. If they jumped the wall, it would take time for the archer to follow. Dee frowned. No, it wouldn't take the archer that long; he looked like he was a half-breed cat, like Darlene, and he remembered how agile Darlene was. Dee reached up and broke the arrowhead off. The jerk drove a rush of blood from his wound, and Dee began to shiver.

"Ccgart, the archer? He found us already? How did he get out of the valley so quickly?" Aquatis asked, perplexed. He reached out to grab Dee and pull him to safety, but Dee pushed him away.

Dee glanced back and saw the girl running across the street. He hoped the archer would let her go. He felt another arrow impale his back, but it didn't feel like it had hit any organs. Dee gave a sharp tug and pulled the arrow from his throat. He felt dizzy, and the world seemed to spin. Then the pain was gone. He touched his neck; it was still wet from blood, but there was no gaping wound.

"You have to get out of here," Dee said.

"The guards must have suspected something and sent someone to check on the valley. I should have guessed. I can't believe we let our guard down like this."

"Aquatis, you have to go," Dee said sternly.

"What? Dee, I can't leave you."

"Jump over that wall and get out of here. If he attacks us at the same time, I won't be able to help you," Dee said as he felt another arrow strike his left shoulder.

"Dee, I can help you!"

"I can't fight him and worry about you at the same time. Now go!" Dee shouted.

"Okay, but promise you'll find me. I'll go to the swamp where my people live. Do you think you can find it?" Aquatis asked.

"Yes, just go, now!" Dee shouted, then felt another arrow strike his neck. Painful, but it didn't cause much damage. He watched Aquatis turn, and with two short jumps, leap over the fort wall. Dee took a deep breath, and was pleased when he found it painful—that meant he was still alive. He heard footsteps approaching. Dee rolled onto his back and pretended to be more injured than he actually was. He waited until the man's shadow was over him, then opened his eyes and looked up. The man's eyes reminded Dee a lot of Darlene's. They glowed like a cat's and had a single black sliver in a pool of gold. Dee thought the eyes very beautiful, then he shook the thought from his mind and got down to business. He had to give Aquatis time to get away.

"Sorry pal, I'm not dead this time." Dee raised his hand in unison with the archer's bow, and the arrow shot into the palm of his hand. But Dee didn't care, he hadn't been trying to block the arrow, anyway. He sent a blue current of energy at the archer, only he wasn't trying to protect him as he had the girl. The archer started to convulse, and Dee saw ripples of blue energy cascading around his body. Then Dee's pain was gone, having bled to death. Dee knew he couldn't beat the man in hand-to-hand combat, so he ran for the wall. If he could jump the wall or climb it, it would probably give him enough of a lead to remove some of the arrows and prepare for another attack. Dee ran until he was about five feet away from the wall and jumped. He slammed into the cold brick and heard a crunch as his nose broke. Dee stumbled backwards, glad he had been unable to feel the pain of the impact.

Dee looked back at the archer and saw him slowly getting back to his feet. He had dropped his bow and arrow, so it would take a few minutes for him to prepare for another shot. Dee started ripping arrows out, not bothering to break the arrowheads off first. First the arrow in his neck, then his shoulder, then the one farther down his back. He could barely reach it, so he pulled it out through the front. He felt pain as the arrow scraped his insides. He dropped the arrow and turned, seeing an arrow strike the dirt in front of him. The archer's aim was off; he was probably still a bit shaky from the jolt Dee had given him. Dee ran toward one of the buildings near the wall, jumped again, using the wall for leverage, and landed higher. He used telekinesis to give himself an extra boost and flung himself over the wall. He hadn't planned it out well, though, and fell belly up on the soft dirt on the other side of the wall. He heard a crunch and realized he had fractured something vital. His back, perhaps? He couldn't move. He closed his eyes and counted slowly backwards from ten, hoping his body would heal itself before the archer climbed the wall.

Dee opened his eyes and looked at the wall; he was about five feet away from it. He felt pain in his back; he was alive again and slowly healing. He waited. Still no sign of the archer. Dee sat up cautiously. He listened, and heard in the distance the sounds of chaos from the fire he had started back at the circle. He looked away from the wall and saw that thick woods bordered the area. He would have to travel through them to get away. He would have to wander around until he found more people and ask them to help him find the swamp, or at least give him directions. Dee wondered if the archer had jumped the fence somewhere else and was doubling back for him. Dee stood and searched his body for stray arrows then moved into the woods. It did him no good just standing by the wall. Aquatis had run off and didn't appear to be coming back.

Dee walked into the woods, looking back at the wall every few steps. The woods were silent. He heard no birds or small animals. Maybe that was normal. He didn't know what things were like, now that his plague had changed everything. Between the darkness and the thick woods, it wasn't long before he could no longer see the wall. He kept going, hoping to stumble across a village or cottage. Anything. He found it eerie that his footsteps were the only sound. He was so preoccupied with the lack of sound that he jumped and screamed when he felt someone firmly grasp his shoulder. He pulled away in fright and slammed into a tree trunk.

He looked at his attacker and saw a woman standing there, her arm still outstretched from reaching out to him. He tried to calm himself and took a few deep breaths.

"Sorry, I didn't hear you," Dee said. She didn't respond. She looked odd in the moonlight. Her skin seemed pale, almost gray. He decided it was a trick of the lighting, but her ragged clothes and knotted hair were not so easily dismissed. She looked like she hadn't bathed in months, if ever. Dee noticed a rotten stench; he couldn't believe he hadn't noticed it sooner. She smelled like a rotting carcass. Dee raised his hand to his nose and breathed through his mouth.

"Are you okay?" Dee asked. She was still holding her hand out to him. She opened her mouth a few times, as if she was trying to say something, but no sound came out. Then she stuck her tongue out and licked her lips. Dee took a step away from her, suddenly uncomfortable. She looked at him like he was a juicy steak on the grill. Was this one of the cannibals? An effect of the plague? Dee took another step away. She followed, making a moaning sound. He met her gaze. When he looked into her eyes, he felt oddly comforted. She wouldn't hurt him; she was just a harmless old bag lady. He couldn't take his eyes from hers as she came closer and grabbed his arm. Her hand felt cold and clammy at first, then the feeling faded. She didn't look as dirty as he had originally thought. In fact, she was kind of cute, almost pretty, and her hair was well-groomed.

She led him through the woods. Dee wasn't sure where she was taking him, but he was too tired to ask. The sun began to rise as they reached a village not surrounded by a wall. It was a regular little town, the kind you would see in a western. Dee remembered watching westerns as a boy. His arm itched. He began to scratch it. The woman next to him seemed upset by this.

"Don't scratch. It will make it worse," the woman said. She sounded like someone's grandma. Not a comforting tone at all.

"Why does it itch?" Dee asked, but even as he asked, he found himself not caring. He felt the itching on his legs, and almost a tickling sensation on his abdomen.

"You must have rubbed against some poison oak in the woods," she said. Dee nodded. That made sense.

He felt sleepy, but he didn't understand why. He didn't normally sleep at all.

"You look tired; you should come with me. You can sleep in my home," the woman said. There was no one else in the village. It was deserted.

Twilight of One: The Plague of Decompose

"Where is everyone?" Dee asked.

"Sleeping. As should you. It is very early in the morning," the woman said.

"Yes, that's right." Dee remembered watching the sun rise. Though as she told him this, he noticed the sun wasn't in the east. It was already coming down in the west. Where had the time gone? It was puzzling. The tickling feeling was all over his body now, but not in his right leg anymore. He didn't feel his leg at all. He reached down and tried to touch it, but the woman grabbed his arm.

"Come, let me give you a tour of our town. I think you will enjoy it," she said with a warm smile. She was dressed in clean clothes; hadn't she been wearing rags earlier?

Dee didn't know why, but every time he looked at the sun, it seemed to have moved significantly. He saw the sun rise and set, but it never got dark. The woman was still showing him the town, but he had a strange feeling that they had been on the same street the whole time. He had never seen any of the other townspeople. Somehow he didn't think they were still sleeping, but every time he tried to think about it, he lost interest.

The woman was showing him a building, telling him historical facts about it. He was vaguely aware that she had told him this before. But he still listened intently because he didn't really remember what she had said. He felt a pain in his chest. He reached up and grabbed at his chest. He felt like he was having a heart attack or stroke. The woman looked at him oddly.

"Oh dear," the woman said to him. "I really have enjoyed this."

"Enjoyed what?" Dee asked as the pain disappeared, almost as if he had just died. The woman was gone, and Dee found himself staring up at the sky—it was blue, without a cloud in sight. No sun, either, he thought. He was laying on the ground, flat on his back. He heard smacking; it sounded like a bunch of dogs were eating sloppily. Dee tried to raise his head so he could look, but his neck was stiff, as if he hadn't moved it in days. He forced his head up; he wanted to know what that sound was.

He saw eight people on their knees next to him, eating something; they were the ones making all the noise. They had their hands up to their faces, ripping at clumps of meat. He wondered what they were eating. They were covered in blood. The woman he had met in the woods was to his right, next to his head. She was gnawing on something. Another was next to her, then one farther down, with five others on his left. One reached, and Dee heard a loud pop—like a bone breaking—and saw the man hold up his find. It almost looked like a human rib bone. Perplexed, Dee lifted his head higher.

What he saw horrified him. He was cut open, gutted like a fish. The eight people were eating him. Dee felt sick, then saw his stomach and realized it would be impossible for him to throw up. His body was hurrying to heal itself, but the damage kept coming. The person on the far left reached down and grabbed at his guts, pulling out a long strand of intestines. That did it. Dee screamed and screamed; he couldn't think of anything else to do. The people paused, unsure how to react; they had never had this happen. The pause gave his body a chance to heal. Dee suddenly felt scorching pain; he looked down and saw his heart take a beat. Then he was standing next to the woman. He stood there, gasping, not sure what had just happened.

"Are you okay? You passed out for a moment. But you seem okay now," the woman said. He eyed her warily and backed away, but already he was forgetting why he didn't trust her. The illusion didn't last long this time, and Dee felt the pain again. It was unbearable; he screamed and found himself staring up at the sky again. He felt someone hit him roughly across the face.

Had one of them actually hit him? The pain went away again, and Dee realized he was dead. He was starting to catch on: when he was alive, they had a way of entering his mind and creating illusions. He was momentarily amazed that they could do that to a powerful telepath like him. He turned his head to the left, and saw a crowd playing tug-of-war with his leg. He lifted his head and looked down, but his body had already grown it back.

"I'm the meal that keeps on giving," he said out loud, mildly amused at his predicament. Then he saw the woman playing with his intestines again and that really unnerved him. He looked to his right, where the woman who had been messing with his head was. She had been the one to hit him, too—he was sure of it. He reached up with his arm; it moved slower than normal, but he thought it pretty good for someone who had been eaten alive for days.

He smacked the woman on the head, so hard that she tumbled backwards. He swung his arm and screamed again. Somehow, he managed to sit up. One was still holding onto his intestines. Dee reached out, grabbed her head, and snapped her neck. He pushed her limp body away and pulled his intestines away from her. The other six people started trying to push him back down, three of them staring into his eyes.

"I'm afraid that doesn't work on dead people," Dee told them and head-butted the nearest one.

He wasn't sure how, but he managed to get to his feet. They were perplexed at his behavior and stared at him, amazed. Dee grinned. He doubted they had corpses get up and walk off on a regular basis. He took a few steps forward, then a few more. He was having trouble walking. He looked down, wondering what the problem was, and found he was tripping on his own intestines. He stood there for a moment, not sure what to do. Then one of the cannibals dropped and started gnawing on them.

Dee cried out and kicked at the man. He reached down, gathered up his intestines, and tried to stuff them into his gaping wound as he walked. The people kept their distance, but followed him. Dee couldn't outfight them in his condition. They weren't afraid of him and would overpower him with sheer numbers. Even if he somehow managed to fight them off until his body was healed, he would simply become victim to their mind control again. And if he somehow managed to avoid that, the pain he would feel once he became alive would probably be enough to knock him unconscious, anyway, leaving him helpless.

He looked around and found himself walking down the street he had seen in the illusion. Only this time, there were people everywhere. But they weren't attacking him. They just kept staring at him. He realized dimly that they were trying to use their powers on him and didn't understand why it wasn't working.

He needed a plan before he came back to life. He looked at one of the houses nearby. *What the hell,* he thought. Dee went up the three stairs and across the wooden porch, holding his intestines in his hands. He didn't have to worry about coming back to life anytime soon; he was leaving one hell of a bloody trail. He hugged his organs against his chest, opened the front door, and walked inside. It was musty and took Dee a moment to adjust to the darkness. There were only three people inside, crowded around each other, gnawing on an arm. Dee looked away, he didn't want to know if it was his.

He was in a kitchen—a very dusty kitchen. There were three doors, the one he had just entered, one that was closed, and another that led farther into the house. Dee wasted no more time. He moved to the closed door and realized he was limping. He was starting to feel pain; he was coming back to life. *Shit.*

Dee pushed it open, holding himself with one hand again. It was a closet. It wasn't a very large closet, but it was a place for him to lock himself up so he could heal and figure out how to get out of this mess. He reached with both hands and moved the clothes around, making sure the closet was empty. His organs were hanging out of his chest, but they seemed bloodier and less droopy. Satisfied, he stepped inside and turned around. He saw the people who had been following him walk into the kitchen. A moment of panic overtook him, and he slammed the door shut.

He leaned against the back wall, with the dusty clothes parted on either side of him. He heard the doorknob turn. He couldn't see because it was so dark. He lunged forward and grabbed at the knob, refusing to let it open. He held it with one hand and fumbled for something with which to wedge the door shut. He was going to pass out soon, so his body could heal. He pulled something over and felt it—a croquet set. He felt at least four mallets. He grabbed one and turned it lengthwise, bumping it against the back wall. Dee found that he could wedge it between the door and the back wall. He grabbed another and did the same, then wedged two against the floor and door.

Satisfied, he leaned back against the right side of the closet. He reached and felt his intestines—they still weren't inside his body. He started to shiver, going into shock. Dee started to see spots and then felt a fiery pain in his stomach. He bit his lip to keep from screaming, then he slumped against the back wall, knocking one of the mallets from its place.

When Dee woke up, he felt wet, and he could still hear the smacking sound of someone eating. In the darkness of the closet he pictured someone, perhaps a child, gnawing on his calf. Dee screamed as he realized that it was possible a child had hidden in the closet with him. It was even more possible that they had entered his mind again and he hadn't entered a closet at all, but was instead stretched out on the dusty kitchen floor.

Twilight of One: The Plague of Decompose

Dee screamed and kicked in panic. He heard thuds and felt objects hit his legs. He thrashed harder as he decided that someone was definitely in the closet with him. He wasn't sure how long he kicked and screamed before he finally settled down. He started coughing from the dust. He was buried in a mountain of clothes that had fallen off their hangers. Dee pushed the clothes off him and heard the door creak. He had kicked the mallets out of place. He grabbed the doorknob just before the door opened. He pushed and heard it click back in place. Breathing deeply, he listened to the thuds and pounding of people on the other side and wondered how long he had been trapped.

After the pushing lessened, Dee used one hand to search for the mallets, and wedged the door shut again. He leaned back against the pile of clothes. He tried not to panic—that had almost gotten him killed. He was alone in the closet. He had to believe that. If they were in his head, they would not let him be this scared, or remember so vividly what had happened. He felt his abdomen. It was healed. He was normal. He sighed heavily and slumped back. He didn't want to leave the closet. As soon as he walked outside, they would be in his head again. If he killed himself, it would only make him invincible to their mind control. They could still overwhelm him by sheer numbers. He doubted they would stand by and watch him again. This time, they would probably tie him up so he couldn't get away, and he didn't like the idea of spending an eternity being eaten alive. He fumbled in the darkness and preoccupied himself with finding new clothes to wear. His were all torn up.

Unsure what he was wearing, and coughing mildly at the dust, he tried to figure out what to do. Their powers worked like his. They needed to look him in the eye to get into his head. If there was a way to get past them without looking at them, he would be okay. It was impossible to walk around with his eyes closed; he'd open them by accident eventually. He slammed his fist into the pile of clothes and pulled up a scarf. An idea hit him. What if he tied the scarf around his face? Covered his eyes with it, so they couldn't make eye contact. They would try to rip it off of him, obviously. But just because he couldn't use his mental powers on them, that didn't mean he couldn't use other powers. He could create a force field around himself. It might work. He wrapped the scarf around his face, covering his eyes so no one would be able to look in them, or vice versa. He took a few deep breaths and calmed himself. Then he removed the mallets, and before he could change his mind, charged out the door. He heard several people fall and he quickly put up a force field.

He didn't feel anyone grabbing at him, although he heard them moaning and moving around. He felt his way along the kitchen counter and out the door. He fell off the porch, but he never let his guard down. He got back to his feet and started walking. This could take a while. He could wander in circles for days. The cannibals could eventually trick him, and he would have to do this all over again. He started walking aimlessly, occasionally running into a porch or tree. He thought about running and trying to lose them, but he had no idea how fast they were, and he could fall and injure himself. No, walking was best. He pictured himself walking in circles around the same street on which he had been trapped in the illusion. He was so distracted with trying to figure out how to deal with the situation that he didn't notice when he stepped forward and felt nothing under his foot.

He couldn't feel the ground anymore. Air rushed up at him—he was falling. What the hell had happened? Had he walked blindly off a cliff? The thought hit him as ironic, but before he could laugh, pain surged through his body and darkness ensued. He opened his eyes and found that he wasn't in pain, which meant the fall had killed him.

"I won't die in a closet, but I will die falling off a cliff," Dee muttered to himself. If he was dead, he should take advantage of the moment and see if he was rid of the cannibals. He heard a dog barking. The barking came closer and soon sounded like it was right next to him. It took a few moments before his arms would respond.

"Hank, you stop that racket, hear me?" a man called. He had the slightest hint of a southern accent. Dee remembered watching southerners in movies. Dee's hands finally moved, and he tried to tear the scarf off. He heard the man whisper something under his breath.

Dee winced as the bright light shone into his eyes. How long had it been since he looked at the sun? How long had he hid in that closet? He blinked his eyes and let them adjust, then looked and saw the dog. It was black and white—some kind of coon dog or sheepdog mix. Dee didn't know for sure. He had been a pretty big dog fan as a kid. Then he noticed the man standing next to the dog. Dee slowly brought himself to a sitting position. He heard the bones in his back pop back into place. He wondered if the man heard it, too.

Twilight of One: The Plague of Decompose

The man was very dark skinned—a black man, Dee thought. He was wearing a straw hat and flannel shirt, and looked at Dee, amazed.

"Hi," Dee said. He couldn't think of anything else to say. He wasn't sure if the man had seen him fall. Maybe the dog had just led him over.

"Are you okay? That was quite a tumble you took," the man said.

"Yes, yes, I'm sure it was. Did you see me fall?" Dee asked.

"My dog heard it," the man said. "Are you injured?"

"No, no, I'll be fine; just give me a minute," Dee bent his knees and heard them pop loudly. Slowly, he made his way to his feet. "Name's Dee," Dee said, trying to sound nice. The man looked at Dee's offered hand and hesitantly shook it. "Is this your—uh—"

"Farm?" The man finished.

"Yes, farm. A farm," Dee agreed. He saw a red barn and farmhouse in the distance, surrounded by rows of crops. Dee was reminded of his picture books of various animals—the name of the animal written in big, bold letters. Dee had never gotten past CAT and PIG. Spelling the bigger names like HORSE was a mystery to him. He looked at the growling black and white dog and spelled D-O-G in his head.

"It's my potato farm," the man told him. "My name's Dominique, and this here is Hank, my farm dog."

"And what a fine dog he is," Dee said gently. The man seemed nice enough; at least he wasn't trying to eat him. "Do you know of a swamp where the Sapoquates live?"

"Why, yes, it's a day and a half's travel by horse. It'll take you three days on foot. Why are you heading there?"

"I have a friend I need to meet up with. Would you be willing to take me there?" Dee asked.

"I'm sorry, my crops are almost ready for harvest. I can't leave," the farmer said sincerely.

"I see. What if I make a bargain with you?" Dee asked.

"Like what? I could sell you one of my horses."

"No, no, I need you to go with me. I don't know my way around. I just spent who knows how long trapped up there with those cannibals."

"That was you I heard screaming? Amazing. And you got away uninjured?"

"Let's just say I'm okay now."

"Fair enough. But I still can't go with you. If you hung around until I finished my first harvest, I could take you to the nearest village with me."

"Which is? What color?"

"Red," Dominique said, puzzled.

"I can't go there. Is there another one?"

"A white one is a few miles out of your way, if you're going to the swamp."

"White—that should be okay. What if I made your crops bigger and gave you a better harvest? Would that be payment enough for you to take me to the swamp?" Dee asked.

"You're just going to wave a wand and make my potatoes grow?" the farmer asked sarcastically.

Dee bent, pulled a potato from the ground, and held it up for the man to see. It was the size of a tennis ball. His eyes glowed red as he enlarged the potato to the size of a basketball. Then he placed it on the ground.

"Cut it open if you want; you'll find it's a good crop," Dee said, satisfied. He looked at the man to see him staring in shock. He seemed paler.

"Demon—you have demon eyes. You are possessed," the man accused as he backed away. The dog began barking again, sensing fear.

"No, please, you have to listen to me. I know the dragons have told you that I'm a monster; they say I'm the devil. But you have to trust me. They mislead you. They are not gods; I can kill them, just like you can, if you try," Dee said, trying to look non-threatening.

"You lie! Demon!" Dominique shouted; his dog barked louder.

"Why would I want directions if I were an all-powerful demon? Why of all things on this hellish planet would I want directions to a swamp? Tell me that. And if it fits with your twisted dragon religion, then I'll cast a plague on your farm, and you'll live in a swamp for the rest of your life!" Dee shouted. He had just fallen off a cliff after spending the past few days locked in a closet and being eaten alive. He wasn't in the mood to argue religion.

The man stared at him in shock. Even the dog stopped barking.

"I have a friend in the swamp that needs me. Would a demon care about a friend? Would he even *have* a friend? Would he run away from cannibals? I am not a demon; I am just lost and frustrated and hoping that a kind stranger will help me." Dee dropped to his knees, covered his face, and realized he was almost ready to beg the man for help.

"I don't know what you are," the man said, "but you look like you are in a bit of trouble. I know the dragons wouldn't take kindly to me helping someone like you. I have a bed-ridden wife that can't take care of herself, never mind my five-year-old daughter."

"Daughter?" Dee asked, spreading his fingers so he could see the man.

"That's right. Why?" Dominique asked suspiciously.

"She's in danger of becoming a dragon maiden, right? I can help you with that."

"What?"

"I mean—" Dee took a deep breath. "I didn't mean that. I—I don't know what I'm trying to say. I can heal your wife, though, and I'm against the dragons taking women against their will. I'm going to start a war against them, but I need to find my friend first."

"I already lost one daughter. I believed myself to be a religious man, but when they took my little girl—" The man wiped a tear from his eye. "Demon or not, I'll help you if you promise to help me get my daughter back."

"I don't know if can promise that. But I can promise you everything I mentioned, and I'll do my best to help your daughter," Dee said.

"All right, let's get away from this cliff before those damn cannibals try to come down here. We'll get you to my farmhouse and clean you up. You're covered in blood and starting to attract flies."

Dee got a better look at the farmhouse as they neared. He was certain Dominique was the real deal—he had been dead when he first met him, so he couldn't be hypnotized. And the dog's barking had proved the dog was real. None of the cannibals kept pets. Dee was confident that what he was seeing was real. But there was something about the farm—about it being so close to the cannibals' village, yet not overrun. Something didn't add up, and it made Dee uneasy. Maybe he was paranoid, but there was something about the run-down look of the house and barn, about the way the place looked—something about the way the farmer seemed so carefree.

They reached the house, and the farmer opened the door. The dog obediently laid down on the porch. Dee glanced around. Something was wrong, he could feel it. Dominique held the door open for him. Dee didn't even want to step on the porch. Maybe it was because in the last house he'd entered, he'd been forced to hide in a closet. Maybe it was because he hadn't been in a real house since childhood. Either way, Dee didn't want to go in there.

"If it's all the same, I'd rather wait out here," Dee said quietly.

"Don't be silly. Come inside and get cleaned up. We have running water, and one of my farmhands is about your size. He always keeps a spare set of clothes here for when he gets messy. You can change into them."

Dee took a step forward, then another, and slowly made his way up the stairs. He walked into the house and glanced around, half-expecting to see cannibals idly chewing on corpses. He found instead a normal little farmhouse. Nice furniture—nothing too fancy—but functional. Dominique led him down the hall and showed him the bathroom. A few minutes later, he returned with a handful of clean clothes.

Then Dee was standing in the bathroom alone, unsure of what to do. He hadn't taken a bath in what seemed like forever. He walked up to the bathtub and stared at it. After a few minutes, he turned one of the knobs. Water rushed out and went down the drain. A plug—he needed a plug. He found one connected to the tub by a chain. He put it over the drain and the tub began to fill. He turned the other knob, and the steam rising in the room lessened.

After he took his clothes off and sank into the rising water, Dee felt the uneasiness rising again. He turned the water off and grabbed a bar of soap; at least, he figured it was soap. It was a large yellow bar. He had never used a bar of soap before. His parents had always used that no-tears stuff that came in nice-smelling bottles. Dee wrinkled his nose, then scrubbed the blood off of his skin—he'd started to notice how badly he smelled. Was it him? He paused for a moment and sniffed. Something in the house reeked. He hadn't noticed before. He washed his hair with the soap, not caring if he was supposed to.

Dee dried off and dressed in farmer overalls and a plaid shirt. He yanked the plug and watched the filthy water rush down the drain, then he turned and opened the door. He was barefoot; he couldn't remember when he lost his shoes. The smell was worse in the hall. Dee didn't leave the bathroom; instead, he leaned out and determined that the odor was coming from one of the rooms down the hall.

"He's going to help us. Yes, I know you don't want me to leave, but I need to. It's for the best. I'll have Ernie stay. He can— Yes, but—" Dominique was saying. He seemed to be having a one-sided conversation. Dee wondered who he was talking to. Cautiously, he walked down the hall. Dominique was in the room emitting the foul odor.

Twilight of One: The Plague of Decompose

Dee looked in the room and saw Dominique kneeling next to the bed. He had his arm stretched out in front of the person lying on the bed. His bed-ridden wife, Dee realized. Dominique was still talking.

"I know you find Ernie strange, but he won't hurt you. No, I think you're exaggerating. He would never—I don't think—" Dee stared at them in bewilderment. She wasn't saying anything, but Dominique was talking to her as if she was responding to him, and there was something wrong about the way he held his arm, the way it was right in front of her face—almost as if— And then Dee heard it—a slight, very slight, slurping sound. For a moment Dee couldn't breathe or think. He saw a small girl's hand under the comforter on the bed, and there was a slight bulge under the comforter where the girl's body should be. But it wasn't moving, and as Dee stared at the hand he saw flies landing on it. That was what the smell was—the girl's body was decomposing. Dee felt sick and grabbed the doorframe for support, making a thudding sound. The woman lying in the bed sat up. Dee tried to look away, but it was too late; his eyes locked with hers. He was in the illusion now, and he didn't know what was real and what wasn't.

"What are you doing?" Dee asked. He wanted to run away, but couldn't.

"Dee, this is my wife, Debbie; I was just explaining that you're going to help us," Dominique said.

"And I was just telling my husband that the farm needs him—I need him. I don't think he can go with you right now," the woman said. Her voice was soothing, calming. Dee looked around the room. The girl sat in the bed next to her, a smile on her face as she played with her dolly. Dominique was holding hands with his wife. The smell was gone, and the room seemed brighter than it had before. The paint was fresher—not as chipped and worn.

"We won't be gone long," Dee told her. He moved forward. Dominique had been alive; he had been real. Dee had to help him. He wasn't sure what he was doing was really happening, but he had to try. He felt a pain in his head, and his thoughts fuzzed. She was fighting him. Dee looked at her for a moment. Maybe she really was sick; her powers didn't seem as strong as the others' had been. He could still discern what was real and what wasn't, although his thoughts were confused.

"She's right; I really should be here with her," Dominique said as he looked lovingly at her.

"Why are you sick?" Dee asked.

"She was helping me out in the fields a few weeks ago, and a rogue cannibal came up and attacked her. I managed to kill the thing, with Hank's help, of course, but she's been sick ever since."

"And stuck in this bed," she finished.

"Is it contagious?" Dee asked.

"What?" they asked in unison.

"The cannibalism."

"That's silly," the wife said.

"No, no it's not. It was originally a plague—it makes sense that it could be passed on to others."

"That's why I haven't taken her to a doctor. Some people say that same thing. It's crazy talk," Dominique said.

"Dominique tells me you think you can rescue our daughter," the wife said sweetly.

"Yes, yes, and improve the potatoes," Dee confirmed. "I need to work on the potatoes."

"That's right; it's part of the deal. He's going to help me have a huge harvest," Dominique confirmed.

"I'm going to go outside and get started on that."

"I guess that will give us a couple of days to work this out. Maybe I'll be feeling better by then and I can come with you," the wife suggested. Dee wasn't sure why, but he didn't like the idea.

Dominique got up and walked him out of the bedroom. Dumbly, Dee wondered why they were leaving the room. Then he remembered the potatoes. They stepped outside, and Dee saw the dog still lying there. The pain in his head lessened, and Dee remembered feeling that something was wrong. Panic began to rise as he decided that something *was* wrong. The house looked like it was covered in a fresh coat of paint. It was all so clean, so tidy, so perfect—and the sun, that damn sun. He remembered the sun. She was weak, weak—Dee mulled that thought over in his head. They might still be in the bedroom—but he had a feeling she wasn't that good. Not yet. There was still a chance some of this was real.

"I think I'll be able to talk her into it. I'm going to check on the horses; maybe we can head off first thing in the morning. That way, I can get Ernie and have him help me with the harvest. It's going to be a big one, right?" Dominique looked at him with a big grin on his face.

There was only one way to sort this out. Dee didn't like it, but he saw no other way.

"I need you to do something for me," Dee said.

"Of course. Oh, you're probably hungry, aren't you? I'll see if I can rummage something up in the kitchen; that's usually Debbie's department, but—"

"No, no, I need you to give me something sharp—like a pick, or a stick, something." Dee searched the ground.

"Like this?" Dominique grabbed a stick from the ground. It had been part of the white picket fence that went around the yard. Dee looked at the fence—it was there, without a single missing plank. And yet, Dominique had found that stick just lying there.

"Yes, that will work," Dee decided. He touched the tip; it seemed sharp enough. He backed against the house and braced himself. "I need you to ram it into my chest—right here." Dee touched himself above his heart.

Dominique stared at him. "I don't understand. You want me to kill you?" he asked, puzzled.

The dog stood up. It saw something Dee couldn't see.

"I know it doesn't make sense, but—" Dee's mind raced. Everything was so fuzzy; he couldn't think straight, but maybe if he felt like that, so did Dominique. "I'm wearing new armor. I need to test it. I want you to ram that stick into my chest with all your might, so I can see how well it holds up."

"Really?" Dominique grinned as he realized he wasn't going to actually hurt Dee. He got into a runner's stance and wiggled his body eagerly. "You ready?"

"Yes; just do it," Dee was glad the farmer hadn't asked any questions. He braced himself against the wall and looked to his right. He heard a scuffling of shoes, and Dominique ran at him. Then he felt a sharp pain as the stick plunged into his flesh. Dee's jaw dropped as pain surged through him. Had Dominique missed? Was he still alive, just impaled with a picket fence? He felt Dominique give the stick a twist, and Dee screamed, then the pain stopped. It just stopped, and the colors Dee was seeing faded away. He felt Dominique trying to pull the stick out and heard Hank barking.

"I don't think it worked. Did it puncture you?" Dominique asked. Dee realized he was slumping against the house; he had almost collapsed. He pushed Dominique away and stood straighter. He saw people walking slowly through the fields. Were they connected to each other? Had the woman told them he was here? Had they set this up? Had they left the farmer alive, just so Dee would run into him and fall into this trap? He hoped they weren't that smart and that this was all a coincidence.

The woman was too sick to use her telepathic powers properly, and too sick to hunt for food. She had lived off her husband and eaten anyone he brought to her. The cannibals coming to the house now were probably just following him. He had been the perfect meal. Well worth climbing down a mountain for.

He looked at Dominique and saw his arm wrapped up in a sheet—a makeshift bandage. He wondered how long she had been feeding on him. How long it would be before he became infected, too? He heard a shrill scream and turned to the house, just in time to see the farmer's wife jump from the porch and land on top of him. Dee felt the stick twist as they rolled around on the ground. Hank, the wonderful dog, came up and bit her in the neck. Again and again, he bit her, until she went limp. Dee hefted the woman off him as the dog continued to growl. He looked at Dominique, expecting him to be surprised. He figured he would be back to reality, but instead, he just stood there. If anything, he seemed in more of a daze—almost as if— Hank barked shrilly and backed away. Dee turned his head and saw a man standing there, his eyes locked on Dominique.

Dee wondered where he should go. The thought of running back into the house wasn't pleasant. Hank was barking so much Dee couldn't think. He heard a horse cry out, then another. The barn. The barn was likely secure. Dominique wouldn't want stray animals going in it.

The cannibal stared at Dee, wondering why he was moving. Dee grabbed Dominique—it was like trying to move a mannequin. Then Dominique started to struggle, fighting Dee all the way. Hank ran alongside them, barking. Dominique punched him in the face, but Dee barely noticed. He reached the barn and tossed Dominique inside. Hank was already in, and Dee pulled the doors together and jammed them closed. Hank just growled softly now. Dee looked around the barn: it was pretty dark, but light slipped in through the boards. He saw two horses, both restless. Dominique got to his feet, moved to the doors, and started to unlock them. Dee shoved him roughly to the ground.

Twilight of One: The Plague of Decompose

"I have to get to my wife. Can't you hear her screaming?" Dominique asked. Dee listened to the silence. He needed Dominique's help. He didn't know the first thing about horses, but he thought they could outrun the cannibals. And they were big, very big—and beefy. They were both chestnut with blonde manes. Dee looked at the dog.

"Do you see anyone, Hank?" Dee asked, feeling stupid to be talking to a dog. The dog sneezed, and Dee took that as a no.

He leaned against some bales of hay and pulled the stick from his chest. Dominique got to his feet slowly; he seemed pretty weak. The pain hit Dee and he dropped to his knees, vaguely aware that the dog was whining. Dee closed his eyes and counted slowly to ten. He thought dryly that he ought to learn what came after ten, because sometimes it took longer than that for the pain to stop. He heard a squeak as the lock was undone on the doors. Dee jumped to his feet and pushed Dominique out of the way, just in time. He put everything back in place and took a deep breath. He looked at Dominique, thinking his skin looked ashen. He had better try this quick, or Dominique was going to eat him.

Dee knelt on the ground and put his hand under his chin. Dominique looked up, but he didn't see Dee. His saw something else entirely. Dee looked into his eyes—it didn't matter if he looked back. He entered his mind; it was a mess. He saw the man outside, and he saw through his eyes. Then the connection was broken, and Dominique went limp in his hands. Dee's eyes glowed red as he healed the man.

"You can't fall asleep on me, Dominique—not now," Dee growled. From the corner of his eye, he saw Hank stand, looking alarmed. Dee heard it, too. The cannibals were outside—lots of them. He could hear them scratching their fingernails against the wooden panels.

Dominique looked at him—actually looked at him. Some of the color was back in his face. He seemed confused. Then his eyes widened. His mouth moved, but he couldn't form words. Dee considered going into his mind and deleting some of his memories so he wouldn't have to live with the memory of walking into his sick wife's bedroom to find her eating their five-year-old daughter. He had a feeling Dominique remembered things that happened after that, too. Dee had been right; Dominique had been bringing supper home to his wife for weeks now. Dee couldn't figure out how much of it had been real, and how much was fake, but he was pretty sure there used to be seven workers at this farm, and they weren't around anymore.

"Jolene—I have to get her. Something is wrong with Debbie—it's not safe. I have to—" Dominique started. Dee grabbed him by the shoulders.

"Do you remember me?" Dee asked. The man nodded his head, after a moment.

"Good, that's good. We have to leave here now. I need you to hook those horses up to that wagon back there, and I need you to do it now," Dee said gently.

"Jolene—did you see her? Did you?"

"We can't help her. Please, just get the horses ready,"

"I haven't feed or watered them in days," he said, his voice full of guilt.

"I'll take care of that. I can make them better," Dee said, speaking softly. He was afraid Dominique was going into shock. Dee started to get up so he could see the condition the horses were in, but Dominique grabbed his arm.

"The dragons were wrong about you. You aren't a demon. You're an angel," he said matter-of-factly. Dee felt a wave of guilt.

"No, they're right. I created those things. Only a demon would do that," Dee said, not sure if he should have told him. Dominique nodded.

"We all make mistakes," he said as he got up and went to the wagon. "We should hurry. If too many of them get down here, it won't matter if we have horses or not. We won't be able to move an inch."

The horses were harnessed to the wagon. It was a flatbed, with no top, and a bench in the front to sit on. It was perfect for hauling produce, but not much good for anything else. Dee pushed everything that had been on the cart onto the ground, feeling splinters of wood stab his bare feet as he worked. He sat on the bench next to Dominique. The farmer wasn't talking much and looked a little dazed, but he had gotten the horses hooked up. He was still useful. Hank jumped into the back of the wagon, as if he knew they would be leaving.

"Belgian draft," Dominique murmured softly. Dee looked at him, puzzled. "That's what they are—the horses. Best money can buy. Great workers. I've always taken such pride in them. And she made me offer to sell one of them to you. She made me neglect them for days."

"She wasn't your wife anymore. She was sick," Dee said.

"How are we doing this? They affect you, too, don't they? Just Hank that's immune."

"I've been thinking about that. I don't think they can affect animals. I think the horses will run away from them. You and I are going to blindfold ourselves and trust the horses to get us out of here," Dee said as he began tearing at a burlap bag.

Dominique looked at him dumbly. "You've got to be kidding. The horses could go the wrong way; they could lead us to the cannibal's village."

"Horses have instincts. When I infected the world, I didn't kill nearly as many animals as I did humans. The animals knew what to do, how to avoid the plague," Dee said as he tied the blindfold around his face. "The horses know where to go to get away from the cannibals. They will probably go where you usually take them, out of habit. With luck, they will take us right to the white village."

"I guess it's worth a shot. But these are tame horses; they aren't going to trample anyone. And horses don't break down fences, so they won't break down these doors, if that's what you were planning," Dominique said. Dee pulled the blindfold down and looked at him.

"Maybe you should have kept oxen instead of horses," Dee said, trying to make a joke. Dominique didn't laugh. "It's okay," Dee continued. "You just shake the reins, and I'll make sure our path is clear. We demons have special ways of moving things out of our way. Now, put this on, and make sure you can't see."

"This is suicide," Dominique said as he tied the bag around his face.

"Well, it was last time. Hopefully, it won't be this time," Dee said. He put his blindfold back on. "Get ready."

"Blindfold on, reins in hands," Dominique said flatly. He didn't seem to have any energy left for emotion. Dee had the feeling that the only thing keeping him going was the fact he had something to think about. He'd had to harness the horses and move everything out of the wagon. Now he had to get out of the barn. What would he do when he had nothing to do but think about the past few weeks?

"On my mark," Dee said. He reached out with his mind and created a force field around the wagon and horses. They whinnied softly, surprised. Dee had created a telepathic link with the horses, so he entered their minds and comforted them, telling them what they needed to do. Then he electrified the force field carefully, making sure all the energy was projected outwards. He shot a jolt of energy at the sliding doors, and they burst open. The horses didn't hesitate. Dee almost fell from his seat as they dashed forward, literally becoming a rolling ball of electric energy.

Dee grabbed Dominique's shoulder, reassured by his presence. The man jumped, then leaned towards Dee, almost as a small child would.

"It's okay; we'll be out of here in no time!" Dee shouted; it was hard to hear himself over the hissing of electric energy and the thunder of the horse's hooves. It was a bumpy ride, though. Dee grabbed the seat with his other hand and wondered if Dominique was right. Not all animals had good instincts. Especially tame animals, like these horses. Dee couldn't even begin to name all the species he had caused to go extinct. Baboons, monkeys, gorillas—just to name a few; in fact, he was pretty sure all the primates had gone extinct. They hadn't been smart at all, and somehow he remembered his adoptive father, Mortimer, telling him they were the smartest mammals alive. Not anymore, Dee thought. He was airborne for a moment as they hit a bump. He heard Hank whine, but Dee thought he sounded okay. Vaguely, Dee wondered what the sun looked like.

Dee wasn't sure how long the horses ran; it seemed like an eternity. He was beginning to think he had spent his entire life on the wagon, being jerked around on the bumpy trail. The sound of the horses' labored breathing seemed as familiar as his own, and he had to keep reminding himself that he probably hadn't been on the wagon all that long. Eventually, the bumps became a little less rocky. The sound of the horses calmed as well. They had slowed down.

Dee gave Dominique a gentle shake, wondering if the man had fallen asleep. He jumped and leaned away from Dee. There was no doubt in Dee's mind—the horses were walking. The only question was—why?

"They're probably thirsty," Dominique said. He had to shout to be heard over the crackle of electricity and the clip-clop of the horses.

"They wouldn't have slowed unless they felt safer," Dee reasoned.

"Unless they have a false sense of security from your force field," Dominique argued. Dee was surprised; he hadn't told Dominique about the force field.

"Either way, one of us will have to look and see if the cannibals are still here," Dee answered.

"I don't see how that will do us any good. As soon as we look, they'll enter our minds and make us think it's safe," Dominique said.

"Correct, but they can't do it right away. You'll have a few seconds before they have control of you."

"I notice you didn't use the word 'we,'" Dominique pointed out.

"I think you should look," Dee said.

"Why? You're more powerful; you'll have a better chance of resisting them, then I will."

"If they get in my head, this force field will come down. We won't have a chance. Besides, who would you rather they have control of? A normal human, or a demon?" Dee asked.

"Thought you said you weren't a demon."

"It's as good a way to describe me as any."

"Okay, so I tell you what I see, and we hope I can say it before they get in my head."

"No, we hope they aren't out there at all. You ready?" Dee asked.

"Yeah, here goes," Dominique said. Dee heard the tension in his voice. Dominique took a deep breath, then held it. Silence.

"Dominique, did you not understand what I said? If you pause like that, I can't trust you—" Dee began. He felt the seat below him move; Dominique had gotten up. He felt the wagon come to a halt, heard Hank's claws against the wood in the back of the wagon, and Dominique's ragged breath.

"I knew this was a bad idea," Dominique mumbled. "I need you to drop the force field."

"Dominique, I can't do that—not until I know it's safe," Dee said as he tried to think what to do.

"That damn force field is making a lot of noise, and it really stands out; we don't want to attract attention, so turn it *off*!" Dominique snapped.

"I don't understand what you are so worked up about."

"Then take that blindfold off!" Dominique shouted.

Dee worried that they had made a mistake. The cannibals were probably all around them, just waiting for him to drop the force field. Hundreds of them, just waiting.

"Would you hurry up?"

Dee didn't see what choice he had. Drop the force field and let them attack him without seeing the attack, or take the blindfold off and be sucked into their reality. He decided to drop the force field first. That way, he would at least hear the screams of the horses. He might just have a chance. Might. He relaxed, and the force field went away. He sat there, rigid, waiting. But the horses remained calm; so did Hank. He felt nothing but the wagon's gentle rocking, caused by Dominique jumping around. Dee wondered how long he should wait. Then he heard the gentle gurgle of a river and the splash of fish. Dee took a deep breath; he had to look. He slowly untied the blindfold, keeping his eyes closed for a moment. He felt the gentle bounce of the wagon as Dominique jumped off and heard him making squishy sounds in the mud. Dee opened his eyes.

It was cloudy, almost like it might rain. They were surrounded by trees, but it was easy to navigate the wagon through them. A gentle mist rose from the ground; he peered over the edge of the cart and studied the dark mud, speckled with bunches of green grass.

"Where are we?" Dee asked. The forest didn't look like the one Dee had been in before.

"Black Dragon Territory. Not a good place to be," Dominique said, not bothering to look at him. He was checking the horses. "They need water before we can get out of here."

"Is this a swamp?" Dee asked.

"Yes, and not a friendly one. There are snakes, crocodiles—all sorts of dangerous animals—around here. And we can't pull the cart through this mud. That's why the horses slowed down—they were having trouble."

"Is this the same swamp the Sapoquates are in?" Dee asked.

"Yes, but there are easier ways to reach them than this," Dominique said. "We'll find water and then backtrack. We'll go around the long way, through White Dragon Territory, then slip into the Black Dragon Swamp nearest the Sapoquate camp."

"But it would be quicker to go straight from here to there," Dee said.

"And more dangerous. I'm not risking myself or my animals. You are welcome to go that way if you want," Dominique said as he unharnessed one of the horses. "If you want to speed things up, help me take the horses to the river to get some water."

Dee climbed down from the wagon and felt the mud squish under his bare feet. He really needed shoes, although the mud was soothing against the slivers embedded in his soles. He took the horse's reins. He hadn't realized just how large the animal was. Dee was slightly intimidated; he couldn't even see over its back. The horse lowered its head and looked at Dee with big, dark brown eyes. Dee could almost see his reflection in them. The horse moved to sniff Dee's shoulder, but Dee stepped away and slipped in the mud. He fell on his back, but managed to keep hold of the reins. As he laid in the mud with the horse's head hidden by the mist, he realized that if this horse wanted to get away from him, there was no way he could stop him. Unless he morphed into Decompose.

"Dee, you okay? I have the other horse ready," Dominique called. Dee heard something sniffing the ground, and a wet nose sniffed his neck. Dee almost screamed, then realized it was Hank. It was the first time a dog had licked him. Its tongue was smooth—soft. Dee patted Hank on the head and found the dog's fur silky.

"Hank? Where are you, boy?" The dog obediently trotted off to join his master, leaving Dee alone in the mud. Dee really didn't want to get up. It was kind of peaceful. The chestnut horse pulled gently on the reins, and Dee saw a giant gray hoof land in the mud next to his head. The horse had blonde socks. He thought they might be white, if the horse was cleaner. The hair around the hoof was longer, too, as if he were wearing pompoms.

"Dee, did you hear me? Are you okay?" Dominique asked again. Dee started to sit up, then saw something move in the mist. Or did he? The mist was moving, as if there was a breeze, but Dee felt no wind, and the mist only moved in that one spot—as if an animal moved through it, invisible to the naked eye.

"I'm fine," Dee said softly. "Dominique, you're a religious man, right?"

"Yes, I go to the temple twice a month, just like the Royal Dragons want."

"Then I'm assuming you attended some sort of Bible study as a child that taught you about the dragons—what their various powers are?" Dee asked.

"Of course. Why?"

"Are the rumors true that black dragons can make themselves invisible?" Dee asked.

"It isn't a rumor."

"Then it's not true," Dee asked, relieved; it was just an isolated breeze.

"No, it's fact. I saw a black dragon materialize in front of me when I was ten. It was amazing," Dominique corrected.

Dee searched the mist, looking for dragons. He started to notice the odd swirls everywhere. Dizzy, trying not to panic, he sat up and pulled himself to his feet. He looked at Dominique, who was petting his horse's forehead. Dee's horse was still looking at him, as if to ask what they should do next.

"Why do you ask?" Dominique asked.

"The dragons don't like me very much," Dee said flatly.

"That would make sense—you being a demon and all," Dominique said with a chuckle.

"A demon? Decompose, have you been demoted? Or have you been lying to this poor old man?" a male voice asked. Dee didn't like how close it sounded. He turned to find himself face to face with a black dragon.

The little creature had stood on his hind legs, holding a tree trunk for balance. He was smaller than the Royal Dragons. By holding onto the tree, he towered a foot above Dee, but he still wasn't taller than the horse. His black scales had little droplets of condensation on them, and the long black whiskers that extended from the tip of his snout had water dropping from their tips.

Other dragons appeared. Some hung on trunks; others were almost completely hidden in the mist. Dee counted over ten dragons—probably twice that many. Dee was glad the horses weren't spooked by the dragons. They had probably known they were there the whole time.

"So nice to see you again," Dee said dryly.

"My, my—you are smarter than I gave you credit for. Figured out who I am already, did you?"

"Somewhat, yes."

"I am the Queen; I control all the dragons, Dee. I will hunt you to the ends of the earth, if I must. You need to go back to the valley. I can't leave you running around. You might decide to destroy the world again."

"If I hadn't destroyed it, you wouldn't be in control now," Dee said.

"Yes, that was nice of you. But the Royal Dragons told me of your powers. You destroyed us once. I don't think history will repeat itself."

"They didn't have a queen back then."

"That's right. We dragons are unbeatable when united. Why don't you surrender? Save us all the trouble," the black dragon requested.

"Why don't you tell my niece she'd better start hunting me again? She's the only one who can catch me," Dee said with a grin.

"You don't know that, Decompose. I've never had an opportunity to try."

"I don't see you here, and I know these dragons can't catch me." The last comment did it. The dragon on the trunk lunged at him. Dee fell back, aiming to land next to the wagon so he could roll under it. But something went wrong, and he landed on something. He twisted and saw another dragon under him. It twisted and rolled him up like a python. The horse, whose reins Dee had dropped, whinnied and reared. The front hooves crashed down on the dragon's face. Dee heard a crack and the dragon went limp, falling in loose coils to his feet as Dee stood. Other dragons moved to take his place. The Queen was right—the dragons did fight better now.

"What do I do? What do I do?" Dominique asked, over and over. The dragons ignored him.

"Tell me the way to the camp, then we go our separate ways," Dee shouted.

"You don't know the way; you'll get lost," Dominique said. He was near panic.

"I can't take you with me; I'm sorry," Dee said gently. Dominique jerked his head to the left. Dee took that as a sign for the direction he needed to go. The dragons were nearly on top of him. He climbed onto the wagon, jumped into the air, then morphed into Decompose. With his new mass, he easily leaped over the wagon and crashed into the trees left of Dominique. He didn't look at the farmer as he passed; he didn't want to see the terror on his face. That was the last idle thought Dee had—between the numbing pain of this form and the constant battering of the dragons, he didn't have time to think of anything else.

He moved like a steam shovel, plowing the trees and foliage in his path. Dragons tore at his back, arms, and legs. Dee tried to touch their minds, to control them, but he couldn't. The Queen's power was as strong as his own. He was going to have to kill them. What was the quickest way to kill a dragon that loved dark swamps? Dee didn't have to ask twice. He stepped into water only a few feet deep and sent a jolt of electricity through his body. The dragons screamed in anguish. Dee trembled as the current raced through him then he started to run again. Faster and faster, with no dragons slowing him down, he ran on—until he lost his footing and slipped down a muddy hillside. He realized he had an opportunity to lose the dragons and morphed back into human form. He came to a stop at the bottom of the hill, covered in mud. He rolled over and looked up. There was so much foliage it was impossible to tell where he had fallen. He was safe; he had lost them. Then he remembered they could be invisible. He needed to get out of Black Dragon Territory. There was no fog or mist around here, no way to see them coming. He heard the shrill cry of a dragon. He had never heard them scream like that. He looked up and saw a dragon fly by. The Queen must have decided against invisibility. He didn't know how smart this queen was. Maybe she was letting him see one dragon to lure him into a false sense of security. He looked around; things weren't as wet and humid here. He had to be at the edge of Black Dragon Territory. Had he gone the wrong way? He got to his feet and began walking towards drier land. If he left the Black Dragon Territory, he would have to worry about cannibals. If he went to a village, he would have to worry about dragons. And if he stayed here, he had to worry about invisible dragons. He didn't like this dragon world, not one bit. Something needed to change. He paused as he realized something.

He was Decompose. He had created this world—at least part of it. The Queen could protect the dragons from his powers, but she had no control over the cannibals or she would have killed them already. Dee made them, and he could finish them off. Why hadn't he thought of it before? He felt silly for fearing them. They were basically a human version of him—humans infected, but not to the point where they died. All he had to do was infect them a little more, and they would die. The trick, of course, was to infect only the cannibals, and not every living creature. He would only be able to cleanse a small radius at a time. But the cannibals didn't seem to travel quickly. If he got rid of the ones in his immediate area, it was unlikely they would continue to be a problem. He wasn't sure how large a radius he would be able to create, but since he wasn't killing everyone, and since he hadn't made one in a while, it would probably be bigger than those he made before.

The only problem was that he would eventually pass out and be left vulnerable. It was a risk he had to take. He knelt in the grassy mud, behind a bush. It would be tricky, trying to kill only one kind of being. He closed his eyes and concentrated.

Hank cowered behind one of the wagon wheels. Duchess, Dominique's horse, tugged on her reins but stayed at his side. Dee's chestnut horse, Roy, had brutally attacked one of the dragons and was still stomping the beast's carcass. Dominique feared the dragons would turn on the horse, but they ignored him, just as they ignored Dominique. The dragons had acted with a single mind. They wanted Dee, and only Dee.

Dominique hadn't moved, though; he didn't want to attract attention, and when Dee had morphed, Dominique had been unable to move, frozen in terror. It was the beast that cast the plague and was painted in murals on temple walls. It guarded the gates of hell and was the monster in the stories told to children at night to make them behave. Dominique was a religious man, but he hadn't really believed the monster was real. It was comforting to doubt that such an evil existed. That the plague had been a natural phenomenon, not cast by a living creature.

Now he was forced to believe, and worse yet—he had helped it. It had helped *him*. It had done something the dragons had never done. Granted, it may have only saved him because it needed help. But its last words—*I can't take you with me, I'm sorry*—those were unselfish words. The beast had left him because it hadn't wanted the dragons to hurt him.

He had done the only thing he could think of—he told it which way to go. The progress of the beast had been quite noisy. The creature had gotten lost almost immediately. Dominique was pretty sure it had headed back towards White Dragon Territory.

Now Dominique was faced with a dilemma. What to do? Go on with his life, continue worshipping the dragons, and hating Decompose? Or help his friend, a man who had saved his life? The dragons had never done anything to help him. And even now, alone in the swamp, he realized the dragons should have offered to help him, to give him directions out of the swamp. Hell, they should have at least asked if he was okay. Dominique didn't generally lose his temper, but he suddenly felt immense hatred for the black dragons. Gods or not, they should have cared about him—at least a little. They claimed to care about him when he went to the temples. They claimed to have protected humans from cannibals and the Decompose plague. Decompose had kicked their butts, and Dominique had watched it happen. His own horse had kicked their butts. He pondered this. His horse had killed one of them. His horse had killed a black dragon. A god. His horse had killed a god. Was that possible? It made sense that Decompose had been able to kill them. An immortal should be able to kill an immortal. But his horse was just a horse.

Dominique walked to the other side of the wagon, pulling Duchess with him. Hank crawled out from under the wagon. Dominique stared in amazement as his horse stomped the carcass. It was barely recognizable. Dominique grabbed Roy's reins and pulled the horse away. Reluctantly, the horse backed up, still breathing hard.

The dragon was dead, bleeding real blood. He watched it for a few minutes, wondering if it would come back to life. He had seen Dee die, too. He had seen him bleed. In fact, Dominique had seen him die twice, but both times, Dee had healed himself. He had come back to life, as an immortal should, but this dragon, who was supposed to be a god, just laid there. Dead.

Dee was the real deal; Dominique had no doubt of that. But these dragons were frauds. They had special powers, but they were just like regular animals. They could die…

The farmer looked around nervously as he realized the discovery he had made. The dragons probably didn't want him to know it. They would probably come back for him, to silence him. The dragons had kept their mortality secret for decades, but Dominique doubted he was the first person to see one die, which meant they did something to people who learned the truth.

He had a feeling that the next time he crossed paths with a dragon, they would not ignore him. Their behavior made sense now. They hadn't stopped to see if he was okay or continue the façade because they already planned to kill him. He just wasn't a priority. They could come back and get him. He was just a normal human. What could he do?

"I can become the devil's right-hand man—that's what I can do," Dominique proclaimed. He had to find Dee. He needed his protection and his help, just as Dee had needed his help. He tied Roy to the wagon and stood on the bench to climb to Duchess's back. Then he pulled the reins over her head and gathered Roy's reins.

Twilight of One: The Plague of Decompose

"Come on, Hank; we have to find Dee before those dragons find us," Dominique said as he gave Duchess a gentle kick in the ribs. They hurried through the swamp, following Hank's nose. Dominique stopped only to let the animals drink. Hank lost the trail crossing the shallow river, but he quickly found it again, and they continued their search.

"Dead, all of them dead," the man bragged proudly.

Scully couldn't help but overhear.

"They were working their hypno jazz on me, then all of a sudden my head cleared, and I saw about fifty of them all around me. They gagged and gasped, then fell to the ground, dead."

"Sounds like Smith blood was too much for them," another man quipped, then he laughed with a few of his friends.

"Got that right, but look at this—they had been gnawing on my arm, right? But look—not a mark—like a white dragon healed me. But there weren't any dragons around," the man continued as he rolled up his sleeve.

Scully took another sip of beer and looked away. He was in a smoke-filled tavern in one of the white dragon villages. They were the most pleasant. At least, the women were the most pleasant. He smiled as a large-breasted waitress passed his table. He sat by himself, as he always did, unless he was in the company of the other sex. Tonight he was on the prowl for a new companion, but he had been distracted by the talk of the cannibals' mysterious deaths. This man was the fifth to boast of his miraculous escape.

There was no dismissing the heightened security of the villages. The dragons had been edgy for weeks. Something was going on, something that even the dragons were worried about—and he had never seen the dragons concerned about anything. He'd heard about the dragon maiden escape three weeks ago, and how one of the red dragons had been left blind from the incident. The red dragon had made a public appearance to prove he was fine. A white dragon had probably healed him. It may have even been a different dragon. They all looked the same to him.

He picked up his mug and drained the last of the beer, then left a few coins on the table to pay his tab, including a generous tip for his waitress. He walked out of the tavern, taking the long way around, catching bits of conversation along the way.

"Nothing but bones and bits of clothing left."

"Had six of them out in my barn. They had been feeding on my livestock for months, and I hadn't even known!"

"Damn wife was one of them—she'd eaten the kids! Hadn't killed me though, but look—all the wounds gone—amazing!"

"All over the trail—the wheels on my carriage kept getting caught in their bones."

"Animals are coming back, did you hear them?"

"You think the dragons did it?"

"Naw, they would have done it sooner; must have been something else."

"But what?"

"Had eaten my damn horse, and tied me to a tree, saving me for later."

"How many?"

"Counted seven skulls. Kept one for a souvenir."

"Ha, I want one!"

"Kids are finally sleeping easy."

"'Thank the Queen,' is all I can say."

Scully pushed the door open and walked outside. He actually did hear the call of animals. It was dark outside. Usually, the animals were quiet after sunset. Something had happened. He walked to where he had tied his horse. He gave her a gentle pat on her speckled head. She was Halayi, a beautiful chestnut appaloosa filly with white snowflakes on her face, sides and back, plus white stockings that turned dark brown at her knees. She had a white mane and tail to match the stockings, and tan hooves that were almost the same shade as her chestnut body. Her nose had a white snip on it, too, making it pinkish on top. She was fifteen hands at her shoulder, a mere thirteen inches shy of Scully's height of six-one. He easily looked over her and saw a rather large woman make her way down the dusty street. Scully thought she was disgusting, but no one would ever tell her. No one insulted Lorna; no one dared.

She waddled past him with a determined look on her pudgy face. Scully couldn't help but grin. If she had been about a hundred pounds lighter, he would have taken pleasure in trying to court her. He imagined Lorna was a handful in bed. He meant that as much literally as metaphorically. She was five-six. In a way, she was attractive, but for someone as tall and lean as Scully, she just wasn't compatible. Scully was afraid she might roll over and crush him.

"Lorna, did you hear?" Scully shouted. She paused to find him in the darkened streets then she smiled.

"You mean the cannibals?" she said with a grin.

"Yeah, do you know what caused it?" he asked.

"Scully, I didn't do it, if that's what you're asking," she said with a shake of her head.

"I didn't do it, either," Scully confirmed.

She took a deep breath, as if she needed the extra oxygen to manage the walk over to him. Then she put her pudgy hands on Halayi's back and gently stroked the horse as she spoke.

"I don't think Ethan is capable of doing it," she said softly.

"I know he can't. Although he's the kind of person that would try."

"Well, I'm his cousin, so I would know. And I'm telling you he doesn't have any friends that could do this, either."

"What about his new girlfriend—do you think she might?"

"Impossible, I've met the girl. She's a little saint, but as mortal as anyone," Lorna said matter-of-factly.

"If it's not any of us, then who?" Scully asked.

"Maybe the dragons did it."

"They just suddenly decided to turn over a new leaf and kill the cannibals. You know as well as I do, they would never do that. If it wasn't for those cannibals, they wouldn't be able to keep humans in check."

"Then who?" she asked, staring at him with her brown eyes.

"The dragons went on a witch hunt after they took over, killing anyone with magical talents that refused to join them. They couldn't find some, like you and I, and they made a special exception for Ethan because he helped them once. But no one is capable of killing all those cannibals in one sweep."

"Except the man that created them," Lorna pointed out. They both fell silent at that.

"There is no such man," Scully said flatly. "And you'd best remember that."

"I'm no fool, Scully. My Aunt Rachel told me about what my brother was doing. I've talked to Ethan, too. So don't treat me like one of these mindless humans. I know what happened," she snapped.

"There's no way he could have escaped. No possibility," Scully said, trying to stand his ground.

"I think he has. That little monster is free again, and this time it's going to be an all-out war with humans stuck in the middle and us forced to choose sides. Tell me, Scully, whose side will you choose?"

"That decision was made for me years ago," Scully said softly. "And you have no idea what that monster is."

"He's an abomination my brother created and left for others to clean up."

"Clean up? Lorna, you can't clean him up, he—" Scully began, but stopped himself.

"What? You think it's wrong for me to take responsibility for the mistakes my brother Jaff made?"

"Yes, I do. That's what Darlene tried to do, and she ended up giving her life to these dragons. There's more to the story than you know, Lorna. That abomination is your brother," Scully said in a hushed whisper. He pulled on Halayi's reins and climbed on her back.

"That's ridiculous. The only son my father had was Jaff, and he's dead."

"He's also your nephew," Scully added.

"The only nephew I have is McCaw, and he's been missing for nearly sixty years."

"McCaw, huh. I'd forgotten about him. But he wouldn't do this, even if he is still alive. Your father had a child with your sister, Rai."

"That would explain why the poor girl killed herself," Lorna said with a sigh.

"Her baby survived—he's Decompose," Scully said. "I thought it was time you knew."

"My family leaves too many details out. Good day to you, Scully. But you never answered my question. Whose side will you be on?"

"Hopefully the same as you," Scully said as he gave his horse a kick in the ribs. He hoped Lorna would be on Decompose's side because he didn't want to see the two of them in battle.

"She wants me to what?" Darlene exclaimed as she sat up on her sunny red rock. She had been njoying a nice cat nap in the afternoon sun, when the Silver Dragon woke her.

"Some of my dragons are going with them, too; she wants you to go as well."

"I thought the Queen said she could handle Decompose on her own. She didn't want my help," Darlene complained.

"There was an incident earlier today. Thirty-four black dragons were killed," the Silver Dragon said glumly. "We want to make sure that doesn't happen to my dragons."

"No offense, but your dragons are better skilled than the black dragons. I'm sure they'll be fine."

"They ambushed him, Darlene, and they couldn't even slow him down," he said in a hushed whisper. He didn't want to frighten the other dragons. He had been alive the last time Dee fought the dragons. He remembered how badly they had done against him, and he feared a repeat of events. She looked away. His glimmering silver scales reflected too much sunlight; it hurt her eyes.

"Dee only needs to see a trick once to learn it," Darlene said softly.

"He may not be able to cloak himself like black dragons do."

"But he'll be able to see them now. No, you can't surprise Dee twice—not with the same trick," Darlene agreed. "Do you know where he is?"

"No, but that is being taken care of. The Queen hired expert trackers. She just wants you and my dragons to go with them. After the trackers find him, you can take over."

"Fine, but I'm taking Sheena with me; she'll be useful. If nothing else, she can distract Dee and give me an edge. Who are these trackers? Are they fighters?" Darlene asked.

"The Queen wasn't sure I should tell you." The Silver Dragon hesitated.

"Why? Who are they?" Darlene insisted.

"The Zalites," he said softly. Darlene glared at him.

"You're not serious."

"The Queen promised to get them off the planet if they helped us recapture Decompose. They're good trackers, Darlene; they'll find him."

"But you can't trust them."

"That's why you're going."

"I can't believe this."

"There's one other thing you should know."

"And what's that?" She slid off the rock and held her hand up to block the sunlight reflecting off his scales.

"Dee did something a few days ago. Something that we couldn't conceal. People are starting to suspect something is happening."

"And that would be?"

"Dee killed all the cannibals."

"What?" Darlene dropped her hand, looking at the dragon despite the pain it caused in her forehead.

"Four days ago, all the cannibals died. All at once. It was just like what happened forty years ago. Only this time, only the cannibals were targeted."

"But what do you mean *all* of them? Dee can only affect a limited radius. He never created a sphere bigger than Australia. The cannibals are scattered all through the world. How did he kill them all in one casting?"

"Only three continents have people on them. The others are uninhabited, so destroying an entire species in one shot doesn't mean quite what it used to."

"It's still a big area! How did he do that?" Darlene shrieked, turning away and closing her eyes.

"Our best guess is that he can affect a bigger area if he's only targeting a specific thing. Before, he was destroying everything."

"Does the Queen know what this means?" Darlene asked. If Dee wanted, he could kill someone without having to be near them. He had become the most powerful being on the planet, and she had let him become that—let him mature in that stupid valley for forty years. She gave him the opportunity to perfect his powers, and now he was more deadly than ever.

"That's why the Queen wants him dealt with now," the Silver Dragon said. She now understood why the Silver Dragon sounded so frightened. She was fighting to remain calm herself. *And the Queen wants me out there fighting him—just great,* she thought, *just great.*

Lorna pounded on the door. He still wasn't answering. She had traveled for three freaking days and now her stupid cousin wouldn't answer the door. *Don't you piss me off, kid,* she thought with a scowl. *Wouldn't want me to mess up that pretty face of yours, would you?* Finally she saw a light turn on inside and heard footsteps coming to the door. The door opened and a sleepy-eyed Ethan stood before her in his pajamas. Only Ethan would wear pajamas with little horses on them. Most men outgrew that kind of thing.

"I thought you'd never answer the door," she grumbled.

"And I thought you'd never stop pounding on it. Do you hear the dogs barking? You probably woke half the neighborhood."

"Don't you back-sass me, boy. I'll wake you up in the middle of the night if I want to."

"It's two in the morning! For the Queen's sake, Lorna, I just got married two weeks ago. I'd think you could show a little—"

"Shush. For someone so sleepy, you sure are talkative. Now, move aside; let me in." She used her massive weight to push him out of the way.

"Lorna, please. What do you want?" Ethan complained, running a hand through his blonde hair; she couldn't recall having ever seen him with hair so messy.

She was in the kitchen now, and Lorna glanced around quickly. Such a small kitchen—how could he live like this?

"Ethan? Who is it?" a very feminine voice called from farther back in the house, in one of the rooms that was still dark. Lorna couldn't see her at first, then she stepped into the hallway and rubbed her puffy eyes in the sudden light.

"This doesn't concern you, darling, go back to sleep," Lorna said with a dismissive wave of her hand. The woman obediently sank to the floor and fell asleep.

"Lorna! For the Queen's sake! Was that necessary? She might have bumped her head! I—" Ethan began as he tried to get past her to reach his fallen wife.

"She's fine, and stop using the Queen's name in vain. I thought you liked her."

"You misunderstand, dear cousin. I said I liked her more than you. And if I have to have some woman dominating me, I would rather it be the Queen Dragon than my—"

"Shush, shush, child—always with such a tongue on you. I'm here about the second son my father had," Lorna said. Ethan woke up a bit and looked at her with wide blue eyes.

"What are you talking about?" Ethan asked, trying to look confused. But Lorna saw through his façade.

"Don't even think of playing dumb with me, Ethan. I know your parents took care of Rai when she was pregnant. Now tell me what you know of the child she had," Lorna demanded.

"You came all this way, woke me up in the middle of the night, and put my wife in a coma, just so you could ask about a baby your sister had sixty years ago?" Ethan said, trying to smother other emotions with anger. Lorna slapped him with a pudgy hand and his pale cheeks reddened at her touch.

"If I recall properly, Rai was one of the twins my father had with a Meta-morph, but it's recently been brought to my attention that the child she had was also my father's son, not his grandson. Is this true? And don't act like you don't know what I'm talking about. I know you lived with your parents 'til the day they died."

"My parents took care of Rai before she had her baby, but we assumed the child died," Ethan grumbled, refusing to make eye contact.

"Ethan, you just got married; it would be a real shame if you suddenly found yourself unable to perform in the bedroom, wouldn't it?"

He looked up at that. He had remained a virgin until the day he got married. What she proposed to do to him was more than ironic. It was cruel.

"Now that you mention it, I do recall Mother saying something about how Jafar's incest was irrefutable, but it wasn't something we talked much about. I never knew if it was true."

"And when you worked with Jaff on the island? You never asked him?"

"There were rumors that Rai had killed the baby out of shame. She died because she refused to go to a hospital when she was in labor. She ran away from home, and we found her body days later. It was a sensitive issue, especially with her twin sister, Tai. I didn't think it would be polite to bring it up," Ethan said coldly, trying to point out that unlike her, he thought of such things.

"When you were on the island, what exactly were you helping Jaff do?" Lorna already knew the answer, but she wanted to make sure he understood.

"Creating a spell to kill the Meta-morphs."

"And you did this?"

"Yes."

"Did you take into consideration that there was a quarter Meta-morph in the world somewhere? Did you take into account how the spell would affect him?" Lorna asked, waiting for it to sink into Ethan's sleepy head.

"Of course not. We thought the baby was dead. And Tai had kept in touch with my parents so we were able to get her an antidote." He wasn't getting it.

"How would this spell have affected that baby?" Lorna asked.

"It would have killed him, then brought him back to life. Just like the spells we cast were supposed to do. Only it didn't work on the island because the dragons started killing them before we had a chance to cast the second spell," Ethan told her irritably. They had cast two spells? Suddenly she understood; it made sense now.

"That's what it did to a full-blooded Meta-morph, but that baby wasn't."

"Maybe it only killed part of him then healed that same part, I don't know. It doesn't really matter. I already told you he's dead."

"Ethan, what if that first spell you cast moved into the human blood when the second spell was cast? Isn't it possible that the second spell, meant to heal him, would be stuck always trying to find that first spell to counteract it, but never succeeding? Leaving that person stuck in limbo? Never quite dead, but never really alive?" Lorna asked.

"Yeah, but that would mutate the person and give him—" It finally hit him.

"Special abilities? Like the power to infect the entire world with a deadly plague? Or kill all the cannibals in a single day?" Lorna asked.

"Sure," Ethan said, paler than usual.

"Powers—just like Decompose," Lorna finished.

"Sure," Ethan agreed. He looked like he was going to pass out. "The Meta-morphs had telepathic powers, too. That would explain why the cannibals have that power."

"Well, congratulations, Ethan. You created the devil. And he's your cousin."

"It's time for you to right your wrongs, Ethan. I'm offering you a chance at redemption. You created that monster, and since Jaff's dead, you're the only person who knows how to get rid of it," Lorna said as he packed his bags. The sun was starting to come up, and his wife was already outside, getting their horses ready.

"You want to hunt him down and kill him?" Ethan gasped. He looked at her, horrified. It had taken her four hours to calm him down, he'd been nearly hysterical after he had realized what he had done.

"Kill him? Ethan, he's family! You're going to cure him. We're going to find him before the dragons do. Then we'll head up to Jaff's old lab on Dragon Island, and with my help, we'll cure him."

"What if he doesn't want to be cured?" Ethan asked.

"We'll worry about that when the time comes. But I'm betting those spells have him in a world of hurt, and he'd give just about anything to be normal again," Lorna decided.

"Is it just the three of us going?" Ethan asked.

"If you mean you, me and that stick of a wife you have, then no. We're going to meet up with an old friend of mine. We'll drop your wife off with a few of his girlfriends and go after Decompose."

"How are we going to find him?" Ethan asked.

"My friend? He already knows we're coming."

"No—Decompose. It's going to be hard to find him before the dragons do."

"Well, Ethan, that's what you're for. Decompose is a quarter Meta-morph. Cook up one of your finder spells that you use to catch lost chickens or cows and orient it to find Meta-morphs."

"I can't believe I'm doing this," Ethan muttered under his breath. Lorna let the comment go; he'd had a long night.

Dee's head hurt. He felt worse than ever. Maybe he should have just killed the people the cannibals had been eating. It had taken too much effort to heal them. But he knew how they felt, and he felt sorry for them. The pain was unbearable. He figured he'd probably been dead for a few days, and now he was coming back. He was sore and stiff; he couldn't move—it hurt too much. He tried to open his eyes but they wouldn't work quite right. He felt something hot, wet, and soft against his cheek.

He heard a whine, and the hot thing went away. Then he felt something else on his face—something cold this time—a damp cloth. Then his mouth was pried open, and the cloth was pressed against his tongue. A few drops of water trickled down his throat then the cloth was back on his forehead, gently patting him. Dee tried to open his eyes again.

"There he is. I was starting to think you were never going to wake up," a familiar voice said. "Don't think I've forgotten about those potatoes you promised me."

Dee's eyes opened, and the pain in his body dwindled to a dull ache. Dominique was leaning over him with a white cloth in his hand.

Hank was next to him; they were moving. Forgetting about his pain, he sat up and looked around. They were on the wagon, passing through a field of green grass a few feet tall. Dee saw open skies all around them. It made him nervous.

"I don't like it, either, being out here in the open like this. But don't worry. In a few hours, we'll be in the forest and we'll leave the wagon behind. By nightfall, we should be in the Sapoquate village," Dominique said with a smile.

"You didn't have to do this," Dee told him, and his voice cracked. "Did it work? The cannibals?"

"I had a feeling you did that. Yes, it worked. You created quite an uproar. It's all people are talking about in the villages."

It was mid-afternoon when they reached the river. Dee stopped walking and brought the horse to a halt. Dominique looked at him, puzzled. Dee had felt safer in the forest; he didn't like large bodies of water.

"Don't worry, the river is shallow. Only waist deep. We can walk through, and Hank can swim, so don't worry about it," Dominique said.

"I don't like water. Can't we just walk around it?"

"Dee, it's a river. A river isn't something you can walk around. It's not like a lake or pond," Dominique said. Dee just stared at him. "You don't know how to swim?"

"No, I can't swim," Dee said simply. He didn't know why he couldn't. But for some reason, when submerged in water, he just sank, then drowned, as if his body weighed too much to stay on the surface of the water. He couldn't use his powers underwater, either. That scared him more than anything. *I could get stuck in the mud, drown, and never get out*, Dee thought. And drowning was, to Dee, one of the worst ways to die.

"All right, I'll go first; just walk where I walk, and you'll know it's safe. Sound good?" Dominique asked.

"I don't suppose I have much of a choice," Dee decided. He watched Dominique step into the water. The horse went with him. The water went up to Dominique's waist and didn't even touch the horse's belly. He was tempted to climb on top of the horse. But his fear of riding horses was even greater than his fear of water. Hank jumped in the water and swam across. Dee waited until he saw the dog walk out of the water and shake himself off.

"Just keep hold of the horse, and you'll be fine. Roy will make sure you make it across okay," Dominique said comfortingly.

Dee took a deep breath and stepped into the mud at the edge of the shore. The horse went ahead of him and stepped into the river, pulling Dee with him. He slid for a moment in the mud and almost fell. In a panic, Dee pulled on the reins with one hand and grabbed the horse's mane with his other. Roy stopped and waited for him to regain his footing. Dee just stood there, not wanting to move. The water lapped at his ankles.

"Come on, Dee—just think—in a few hours, you'll be seeing that friend of yours," Dominique said. He was right; Dee knew it. He had to cross this river. He took another step, then another, slowly moving into deeper water. It was cold, and soon his pants were soaked and sticking to his skin. He kept a firm grip on the horse with both hands, his right on the mane and his left holding the reins. He could do this, he repeated to himself over and over. He was halfway across the river, and it was up to his waist, tugging at his shirt. Then his left foot came down, but there was nothing under it. Dee fell sideways as his right knee gave out. He tightened his grip on the horse, but Roy wasn't about to be pulled down with him. The horse reared, and for a moment, Dee thought the horse might be able to pull him out of the hole he had stepped in. Dee let go; he wasn't sure why. His fingers lost their grip, and Dee tumbled backwards.

The roaring water was loud in his ears. It overwhelmed him. He opened his eyes and saw the surface of the water disappear. He tried to grab at something, anything, to stop his fall. But there was an abyss in the middle of the river, and Dee was falling, falling. He hit the bottom and laid there, staring up at the surface of the water. He saw the sunlight trying to reach him. The water was so loud, he couldn't hear anything. He tried to breathe and felt the water rush into his lungs. He was drowning. He was dying. Stuck at the bottom of an abyss in a damn river. The pain eventually went away, and the water didn't seem as loud.

Dee sat up and managed to get to his feet, holding onto the sides of the hole for support. That's what it was—a hole. It wasn't an abyss—an abyss didn't have a bottom, right? It was a hole. Dee dug his fingers into the mud and tried to climb. He slid back down, but didn't give up. He dug his toes into the mud, too. That did the trick. He reached up, hand over hand, foot over foot, and climbed out of the hole, just like a mountain climber. He almost dreaded reaching the surface. Coming back to life after drowning was even more painful than drowning.

It seemed like he had spent his entire afterlife climbing out of the hole. He finally reached the top and saw the horse's footprints in the mud. The horse had continued without him. Dee paused for a moment, resting his arms on the edge of the hole. He debated standing up and taking that first painful gulp of air then decided against it. The last thing he wanted was come back to life then slip and drown again. He crawled out of the hole and went across the rest of the river bed on his hands and knees. He reached with his left hand and felt a clump of dry grass. He pulled himself up and lifted his head out of the water.

He took a deep breath and instantly started coughing. Water and stomach bile poured out of his mouth and onto the shore. Dee shivered in pain as his lungs burned. He dragged himself out of the water a little farther, then rolled onto his back. He heard footsteps behind him, but he couldn't speak; he was still coughing. He squinted in the bright sunlight and opened his eyes to see a wooden stake crash down into his right eye. The pain only lasted a moment, then Dee stopped shivering and looked with his remaining eye at his attacker, a person Dee remembered all too well.

"I told you this would be easy. Help me tie him up; I don't want to take any chances with this guy," Rick said as he turned and spoke to someone Dee couldn't see. Dee slowly got to his feet; he only had a few moments to react before Rick did. Dee did the only thing he could think of. He head-butted him.

He heard the crunch as the stake shattered Rick's skull and Dee pulled back. He had to take a few steps before he was free. Rick fell to his knees in agony, covering his face with his hands. Ironically, Dee had gouged out his left eye. Dee was surprised; he had thought that move would kill Rick. Zalites were apparently made of stronger stuff than humans.

"Oh my Rectqil, Rick, Rick are you okay?" a tall lanky man asked. He took a few steps towards Rick, then hesitated when he saw Dee still standing there. The man had the same iridescent eyes Rick had, but Rick was more muscular and slightly shorter. And unlike Rick, who was bald, save for stubbles of hair—proving that he shaved his head regularly—this guy had a few inches of brown hair on his head that stood straight up, making him seem even taller.

"What did you do to my potato farmer?" Dee asked as he wiped some of the blood from his face.

"He's fine, he's right here," the man told him, gesturing to his right. Dee saw Dominique sitting on the ground with his wrists and ankles tied. Dee knelt next to him and ripped the ropes off. The tall man didn't know what to do.

"He's going to die; please, you can help him, can't you?" the man asked.

"Are you okay?" Dee asked Dominique.

"Yeah, I'll be okay. But I think they're working for the dragons," he said. Dee nodded.

"Dominique, I need you to do me a favor. I need to get this stake out of my head, so I'll be able to fight the dragons when they get here. Do you think you can stomach that?" Dee asked. Dominique nodded. He placed his hands on the stake and pulled. Dee tried to help, but it was no use. The stake didn't budge.

"I think your skull is starting to knit together, and it's knitting the stake into the bone," Dominique said grimly.

Dee didn't want to spend the rest of his life with a stick stuck in his head. He looked at the spiked haired guy who was looking mournfully at his unconscious friend. "Are you as strong as he is?" Dee asked, pointing to Rick.

"If you're asking if I can pull that out of your head, yes, I can. But you should be asking me if I *will*, since you killed—"

"He killed me first," Dee snapped, then forced himself to calm down. He took a deep breath of air and realized dumbly he hadn't been breathing. Of course he hadn't, he was dead. "I'll heal him, but I can't do that unless I'm alive. If you pull this stick out of my head, I'll save your friend. Do we have a deal?"

"Deal," the man said, and lunged at him. The man reached and grabbed a branch above Dee. Swinging on the branch, he kicked the stake with his left foot, then dropped to the ground and grabbed the end of the stick hanging out of the back of his head. With one swift pull, he tore the stick from Dee's skull. Dee fell to the ground, wondering why the guy hadn't warned him. Wouldn't it have been easier to take it out the same way it had gone in? Dee opened his eyes and couldn't see out of his right; it was still all bloody. His head throbbed. He looked up, and a few feet away, he saw Rick lying there, unmoving. His chest wasn't moving; he wasn't breathing. If Rick died, Dee couldn't bring him back. He could only heal someone when they were still alive. But Dee wasn't completely healed himself. If he waited, Rick would be dead. Still on the ground, on his stomach, Dee grabbed Rick's forearm with his left hand. I can do this, Dee thought to himself. It'll only last for a little while. Dee forced himself to heal Rick, letting the blood continue to gush from his own head wound.

Dee saw spots of light behind his eyelids and he felt dizzy. This is it, he thought, I'm going to pass out. Then Rick was done, he pulled his arm away, and his own breathing finally steadied. Dee rolled to his side and breathed through his mouth, trying to forget the pain. A cloud block out the sun, and they were all cast in shadow. Dee looked up and saw a dragon above them, and numerous other dragons appeared as the seconds ticked by.

"I'm sorry," the tall man was saying. "I didn't expect it to play out like this."

"Dennis, what are you talking about? What the wesroff happened?"

"I made a deal with him; I helped him, and in return he saved your life. Technically that's twice he's saved your life," Dennis pointed out.

"So?"

"So this isn't right anymore," he said flatly. Dee ignored them and looked up the river bed. He didn't have enough time to recover; it was all over. Then he saw it—a gray wall in the distance. Dee squinted; it actually wasn't that far away. What were those things called? He remembered his father Mortimer driving him across one once. There had been a huge body of water on one side, and just a trickle of a stream on the other. His father said it kept the water from flooding the towns on the other side of the wall during heavy rains. A flood.

"What color dragons are they?" Dee asked, surprised at how weak he sounded.

"Silver, why?" Rick said.

"Silver is a heavy metal, and those dragons are covered in it. Their scales, claws, and spikes are all made out of it," Dee said softly. "Can Zalites swim?" Dee blinked his eyes and found that he didn't want to open them again. His right eye still burned from the dried blood in it.

"Of course, we can swim; our planet is covered in more water than yours is," Rick snapped. "I don't see what any of this has to do with our situation. Those dragons will be here in a matter of minutes."

"Silver dragons can't swim. They weigh too much," Dee said softly, his eyes still closed. He reached with his right hand towards the concrete wall, and using the last of his strength, he sent a bolt of energy at it. The last thing he heard before the icy waters rushed over him was Rick shouting something in his native tongue, then Dee succumbed to the darkness that beckoned to him.

Rick felt the water rush over him and then pull him down. His body hit trees and branches; he felt them tearing at his skin. Rick hadn't had time to take a proper gulp of air before the tide had hit him. His lungs were starting to burn, but a Zalite could hold its breath for almost ten minutes, so regardless of whether his lungs were full of air or not, he would survive—for a while, at least. He opened his eyes. Zalites had great underwater vision. He saw dirt, roots, twigs, and other debris being swept away in the current, which swirled and tried to pull him deeper, but Rick wouldn't let it. He wasn't about to die, he'd come too close already. He fought back, swimming with all his might. His feet were like lead blocks—then he remembered his shoes. He couldn't untie his boots, not in this current. He twisted and squirmed until finally he was able to rub his feet together and push the boots off.

His feet free, Rick found it much easier to swim. He had thought about swimming with the current, but that was where the dragons would end up, and he didn't want to be with them. He saw glimmers of silver below him—a fair number of the dragons had been pulled down; as Dee had predicted, they couldn't swim—not with all the metal on them.

He swam higher and higher, trying to reach the surface. He knew the tide would be worse, but he needed air; his lungs were killing him. If he could just take one good breath, he'd be okay. Then he would wait out the current under the water, where it wasn't as strong.

He was almost to the top when he saw a fluff of blonde hair, almost like a dead rodent. Then he saw the human body attached to it. It was Dee. Rick almost kept going, then remembered that Dee had saved his life not once, but twice. He had a feeling the count was up to three now. It was likely those dragons would have killed him after seeing how Dee had helped him.

Rick grabbed Dee under his arm, then tried to swim up again, but Dee weighed more than Rick had bargained for. For a minute, Rick made no progress; he considered letting go, getting some air, and coming back for Dee. Then he looked down and saw one of the dragons trying to swim up. Its eyes glowed unnaturally in the darkness. If Rick let go, he would sink, and the dragons would rip him apart. Rick swam harder, wanting to deprive the Queen of this victory. His body slammed into a tree trunk, and he dug his fingers into the bark. He felt his fingernails tear away. The bark cut into his fingertips, but he didn't let go. He braced his feet against the tree and slowly began climbing it. It seemed to take forever, but finally he felt cool air brush against his hand. He took another step up with his right leg and pushed. His head reached the surface of the water, and he gulped air.

Satisfied, he pulled Dee up and hung him over a branch. Free of his burden, Rick turned, still kicking his feet under the water. He held onto the tree trunk with one hand and looked around, hoping to see any sign that Dennis had made it out okay. He heard a groan and looked over to see Dee slip off the limb. Rick pinned Dee's body between himself and the branch. It was only a few inches above the water, and the tide still tugged at Rick. He braced one leg against the trunk then noticed the water level sinking. They were on a hill, he realized dumbly. If he moved farther up, he wouldn't be sucked under again, or so he assumed.

He heard a dragon roar and looked up. Some of the silver dragons had avoided the water. Rick decided it would be best to stay low, near the water, at least until the dragons decided to move farther down the river.

They reached the top of the hill just in time to see the dam break. Lorna knew it had been caused by Dee. She had seen the burst of violet energy come from the trees, and then everything was thrust into chaos. There was no way to tell where Dee was now, but Lorna, Scully, and Ethan were safe—the tide hadn't reached the top of the hill, and now the water was receding. They could cross the river, if they crossed in one of the shallow parts.

"You're sure he's still on the other side?" Scully asked, his filly prancing. Scully was having a hard time getting her to calm down. The explosion had really spooked her. Somehow, Scully managed to remain in his saddle and keep the horse from darting into the woods. Lorna's own horse, a pure black Friesian, was dealing with the stress better than the young appaloosa. He was older than Scully's horse, and he trusted Lorna. If she didn't think the water was going to sweep them away, neither did he.

"That was the last reading I got. I think he keeps, uh, dying or something. 'Cause his, uh, signature keeps going away. I don't really know," Ethan said doubtfully. He held a pearl-like orb the size of a tennis ball, and used it to figure out where Dee was. Every so often, he held his hand up, the sphere floated a few inches from his palm, and he magically knew which way to go. She had thought he was making it up until that energy burst. His horse, a bay quarter horse, didn't seem spooked by the rushing water, either. Lorna figured she could probably shoot the horse in the leg and it wouldn't move a muscle. It had to be really dim-witted, Lorna decided. 'Cause if it trusted Ethan to keep it safe, it couldn't be smart. If it came down to her depending on Ethan to save her life, she would cut her heart out and save herself the worry.

"Yes or no, Ethan? Do we cross the river or not?" Lorna asked.

"We cross the river, I suppose, he said. She looked away and rolled her eyes. I'm being led through a forest by an idiot and his magic pearl, she thought dryly.

"Then follow me, boys," she said and gave her horse a sharp kick in the ribs. She heard the others following, and they made their way down the sloped hill. The horse's hairy hooves splashed in the shallow water, avoiding the sharp chunks of concrete that jutted out of the waterbed. They were over halfway there when Ethan cried out. She couldn't hear him over the thunderous roar of the river.

"What?" she shouted.

"He's on the other side! The other side of the river—the side we were just on!" Ethan screamed.

Scully looked at her and shook his head in frustration. She knew how he felt. She wanted to give Ethan a hard smack across the face and knock some sense into the kid. Scully looked up and frowned.

"Look at the dragons!" he shouted. "They're flying in low this time!"

"Think they're coming after us?" she yelled back. Ethan didn't seem to be paying attention to their conversation.

"No. Look, they're taking big breaths; look at how their stomachs are expanding!" he yelled.

"So? I don't know jack shit about these dragons! I hate cold weather, so I don't go near their territories!" she shouted back.

"We should get out of the water, now!" he said, with a look of concern.

"Why?" she asked. Then she saw one of the dragons upstream; he opened his jaws and blew silvery fire onto the surface of the water. She watched in amazement as the water froze, mid-current.

They were waist-deep in the river water; the current had lessened, and Rick didn't think the tide was going to go any lower. Rick had braced Dee against a thick tree branch, and he had started coughing and waking up a little while ago. Rick looked up and saw the dragons swooping down closer to the water than he expected.

"Why are we still in the water?" Dee asked, his voice hoarse.

"Some of the dragons are still flying around. I wanted to keep us concealed. The water and trees are doing a good job. They haven't spotted us," Rick said.

"They're not all dead?" Dee croaked. He lifted his head, and it seemed like it took a tremendous effort.

"No, but we're safe. I don't know where Dennis and your friend are, but I'm sure they're fine. Dennis probably got your friend out of the water safely. He's nice like that," Rick pointed out.

"Are they silver?" Dee asked. His voice sounded better, but he still seemed exhausted.

"Yeah—same as the ones you drowned. I figure we'll be okay as long as we stay in the water," Rick said.

"No, we have to get out of the water now," Dee said, a hint of panic in his voice. Rick watched as he reached a weary arm up and grabbed at a branch. Dee started to climb the tree, but he couldn't move very quickly.

"Dee, I don't think we are in any danger," said Rick, still in the water.

"Rick, I don't have time to explain. Just trust me and get out of the water, *now*."

It took a great strain on Dee to climb the tree. He only went as high as he needed to get out of the water, then he hugged the trunk, his breathing ragged. Rick decided that if Dee was willing to climb a tree when he was barely conscious, maybe there was good reason to listen.

"I still don't think this is necessary," Rick said, but he reluctantly climbed an adjacent tree, only going as high as Dee.

Dennis barely had the energy to drag himself out of the water. He pulled the black farmer, who was dressed in flannel, along with him. He held the man by the back of his shirt. The farmer coughed water and gasped for breath. Dennis waited until the water was only a few inches deep, then he dropped the farmer into a puddle of water. Dennis rolled his shoulders and popped his neck. He'd nearly died in that flood. In all the chaos, he'd seen the potato farmer struggling to stay afloat. Dennis was amazed he'd managed to swim to the surface in the first place. So Dennis had helped him reach the shore.

"Thank you," the man said between gasps. Dennis looked at the river. He saw people crossing it near where the dam had been. He knew they couldn't see him, but thanks to his enhanced Zalite eyesight, he could see them. They were each riding a horse, heading to Dennis' side of the river. The last man in the line stopped and raised one of his hands. An object in his hand glimmered. Dennis squinted, but he still couldn't figure out what the object was.

"Name's Dominique. I guess I'll forgive you for that incident earlier," the man said with a chuckle that ended in a fit of coughs. Dennis looked away from the people; he doubted they had anything to do with him or Dee.

"Dennis," he told the man, then he offered him a hand to help him up. "My name is Dennis."

Lorna didn't hesitate when she realized what the dragons were doing. She didn't want to know what would happen if the freezing water reached her or her horse. She gave the horse a kick in the ribs, and he took off running. Her breath made clouds of fog, and she knew she wasn't going to reach the shore in time.

Scully shouted at Ethan to move, but the boy didn't notice. His puzzled expression changed to paralyzed fear when he looked upstream and saw the freezing water coming at them at an incredible rate. Scully acted quickly, his decades of samurai training not forgotten. He pulled his feet out of his stirrups and crouched on his horse's back. With luck, his horse would be able to reach the shore if she didn't have him as a burden. She was young and fast. Scully pulled his samurai sword from the horse's saddle and gave her a sharp slap on the hindquarters. She took off running, and Scully jumped and prayed.

He had to time this perfectly. If he landed too soon or too late, they would die. And Scully hadn't spent eighty-five years as a skeleton to die as a frozen Popsicle, just because some stupid kid locked up in the heat of the moment. Scully felt like he was flying as he went over Ethan's horse; as he feared, he had judged the distance between them wrong. He was up too high; he couldn't grab Ethan and pull him along, so he did the only thing he could think of. He used his sword.

His blade slid easily into Ethan's left shoulder. The leverage was all Scully needed. He pulled on the sword, sure that the pressure was on the flat of the blade. It would do him no good to cut Ethan's arm off. He swooped down and kicked the horse in its belly, then grabbed Ethan with his free arm. He pulled the kid up and off the saddle and away from the horse. For a moment, the two looked as if they were dancing in the air, then they crashed to the ground, Ethan hitting first, then Scully rolling over him, pulling his sword out as he went. His right shoulder hit the ground hard, and he felt cold nipping at him through his clothes. He was on ice. The river was frozen. The water had frozen while they were in the air.

Ethan writhed on the ground, exaggerating the wound. Scully knew it wasn't serious. He looked up and saw the quarter horse, frozen stiff, a layer of frost covering its body. Scully shivered, reminded of how easily that could have been them.

Lorna knew she wouldn't reach the shore in time, especially when she heard Ethan's gut-wrenching cry. She saw a branch up ahead, her only chance. She jerked on the horse's reins and forced him to jump over the branch. She knew he wouldn't be able to make the jump with her on him, so as they went up, she let go of the reins and grabbed the branch above her head with both hands. She kicked her feet back and pulled them out of the stirrups. The horse was airborne for barely ten seconds, but that was long enough. The Friesian's large hooves crashed down on a new surface—solid ice. Then he lost his footing and slid awkwardly, almost falling. He twisted to the right, and his left side slammed roughly into a tree. The horse came to a stop, breathing heavy, but still breathing. Lorna lowered herself slowly to the branch below her. It bent slightly under her weight. Her arms burned from the exertion, unused to supporting her massive body.

Rick heard the scream, but couldn't see where it had come from. It sounded like a man, but it wasn't Dennis. Maybe it was Dee's friend. He wasn't sure. He felt cold nip at his fingertips—the same ones still bleeding from his climb out of the water. He pulled one of his hands away from the tree trunk and felt bits of flesh come off his fingers. He looked at his hand in amazement. He had frostbite. Then he looked down and saw the frozen river below him. He looked at Dee in the tree across from him, only a few feet away. Dee was slumped over a branch, his eyes closed. The frost didn't seem to bother him. Silently, Rick counted in his head the number of times Dee had saved his life. By his count, Dee was up to four.

Dominique had already reached the shore, but Dennis was just stepping out when something grabbed the tail of his coat and jerked him backwards. His long, black coat dragged slightly behind him on the ground. He liked it—it covered his footprints when he walked. He caught himself before he fell and twisted to see what he had snagged it on.

It was still in the water, but the water wasn't water anymore—it was ice. Dennis looked at it for a moment, then tapped it with his foot. He had already put his boots back on, and the hard surface chipped the ice.

"Hey, uh, Domin—whatever. You know what caused this?" he asked. The farmer looked back as he finished wringing out his own shoes. His eyes grew large.

"The silver dragons did that. I can't believe they would freeze the whole river, but I don't know who else could," Dominique said.

"You make it sound like the dragons are the good guys," Dennis scoffed. He tugged at his coat and tore the piece stuck in the ice.

Lorna made her way slowly out of the tree and stepped onto the iced-over lake, keeping one hand on the tree to help her balance. She looked at the palm of her other hand and saw little cuts on it. Those are going to get infected, she thought glumly. She looked over the river and saw Scully and Ethan, partially hidden by the frozen horse. She heard

Ethan screaming. He sounded like he was dying. He sure as hell better not, she thought.

Lorna ignored the screams and went to her horse. Its front leg was bleeding, and it had a gash along its side. She took the saddle off to see the wound better. She needed to get the horse off the ice before it started to thaw. She saw Scully's on the shore, nodding its head, looking at them but refusing to walk on the slippery surface. A shadow fell over Lorna, and she looked up. The dragons were still circling.

"Scully!" she shouted, but she could barely hear herself over Ethan's screams. And if she couldn't hear herself, there was no way Scully could hear her.

"Ethan, you're fine, just calm down," Scully said. But Ethan was panicking. Scully was afraid he would pass out from lack of oxygen. Scully was trying to look at the wound, but Ethan was wriggling around too much.

"Ethan, you need to stop moving around so I can see your wound," Scully said calmly. The ice around him was turning pink from Ethan's blood. Ethan's skin was pasty and sweaty. He's going into shock, Scully thought. He grabbed the kid by the shoulders and pushed him down, then looked him in the eye.

"Stop moving, now," Scully said sternly. Ethan stopped, but he still screamed. "And if you don't stop yelling in my ear, I'll cut your tongue out."

It was a totally empty threat, but it worked. Scully looked at the wound. It was a clean cut, deeper than he had thought it would be, but superficial. As long as they stopped the bleeding and kept it clean, Ethan would be fine.

Scully grabbed Ethan's right hand and pressed it against the wound. He didn't have any bandage material, so they would have to make do with firm pressure until they could reach one of the horses.

"I need you to apply pressure right here, okay?" Scully said. Ethan nodded, in a quick snappy manner. "All right, we're going to stand up now. It's going to be slippery."

Scully put his arm around Ethan and helped him to his feet. He seemed wobbly, but okay.

"Ethan, where's the orb? The one you were using to find Dee?" Scully asked.

"On my horse; it's in a pouch," Ethan said softly; he sounded calmer. He looked at his horse to point out the pouch to which he referred, but when he saw the frozen remains of the animal his right hand fell, and blood spread onto his clothes. "My horse—that could have been me. I—I almost died. Sweet Queen, I almost died."

"But you didn't," Scully said, then reached over and pressed the kid's hand against the wound again. He turned away, raised his sword, and sliced at the ice until he freed the pouch Ethan had referenced. He brushed the last of the ice off, ignoring the dragons flying overhead. They weren't after them, and Scully figured if he ignored them, they would do likewise. He pulled a leather string out of his pocket and tied the pouch to it. Then he tied it around Ethan's neck.

"It'd be in your best interest to keep this pouch on you," Scully said. He held the pouch in front of his face for emphasis. "Your ability to find Dee is the only reason I have to keep you alive. I'm not going to risk my neck to save you again if I don't have a damn good reason, understand?"

It was an empty threat, but Scully needed the kid to get his priorities straight. It seemed to work, and Ethan nodded his head again. It took a few minutes to reach the shore, where Lorna was waiting. She had his horse, and her own.

"He okay?" Lorna asked.

"He's not a frozen popsicle, so I would say yes," Scully said. He stepped off of the ice and onto the hard dirt. The mud had frozen as well, but Scully didn't care. He turned Ethan around and pressed his back against a tree trunk. "I want you to sit down. Lorna, I need you to look in my bag—the one on my horse. There should be some dressing in there we can use for this wound."

It didn't take Scully long to dress the wound; it was already clotting. He wrapped clean cloths around Ethan's arm, and thought about going back out to the horse to see if he could salvage any more supplies. Lorna was cleaning her hands. Scully noticed blood on her horse, then saw that it had its right foot raised. A small trickle of blood was forming a puddle on the ground below it. She couldn't ride, and Ethan's horse was dead. Scully's was the only uninjured horse left. They couldn't continue—not like this. There was no point in going back for the supplies. They had to go to a village, get new horses, and find a white dragon to heal Ethan.

"Scully," Ethan said softly. Scully looked at him, he had his back against the tree and was sitting down, resting.

"Yes?"

"I think there's someone on this side of the river. It's not Dee, though; the orb said he was on the other side, and there's no way he crossed over so quickly. But there's someone over here with magical powers. It's messing up my orb spell."

Ethan had the orb in his right hand and was using it. Maybe my threat was more effective than I thought, Scully told himself.

"Someone else? Like who?" Scully asked.

"I don't know. Maybe a dragon maiden? I mean, there are a lot of dragons around. It would make sense."

Scully agreed.

"Can you pinpoint where they are?" Scully asked.

"That's the funny thing. They should be right over there." He gestured with his left hand, then winced and lowered it. "They're close enough we should be able to *see* them."

"Unless they're invisible," Scully whispered. The black dragons had that power, and could pass it on to their maidens. And since Darlene had that little alliance with them, she had mastered that trick as well. He prayed it wasn't her. He didn't want to confront her. Not after he had betrayed her.

"Invisibility cloak, eh?" Lorna said, placing her hands on her hips. "How old school. I learned how to do that when I was five."

Scully was about to ask if she knew how to reverse it so they could see who it was, when she clapped her hands together with a loud *smack*. It echoed in the silence of the frozen forest.

"Powers great, powers grand, make unto us an enemy seen. Let us behold who passes by; let us not be surprised," Lorna said, and snapped her fingers. A woman appeared out of thin air. She wasn't paying any attention to them; she was focused ahead, downstream. She was scantily clad in black, her long dark hair pulled back in a ponytail. Her staff had been broken into two pieces, one of which had a two-foot blade sticking out of it. She moved through the trees at a steady pace. Her hair and breasts jiggled with each step, and Scully silently thanked the black dragons for having such good taste in maidens. She was a lean woman, possibly of mixed Latino descent. The black halter top and mini skirt, meant to allow flexibility of movement in battle, were pleasing to the eye. Scully wondered why she would ever want to be invisible. He dropped his eyes to her knee-high boots and wondered how she could be so quiet while trotting through leaves and twigs. Darlene taught her well, Scully thought; time to find out how well.

"Go after her, Scully. I'll follow and get there as soon as I can," Lorna said.

"My pleasure, Lorna. And take your time," Scully added with a grin. Then he darted into the woods, as silent as his prey.

The screams on the river seemed to last forever. Rick had been tempted to find the source of the noise. But then it stopped, and only silence remained. Whoever it was had probably died. He climbed down from the tree and stepped agilely onto the ice. Dee was still clinging to the tree he had climbed, slumped over a branch with his eyes closed.

"Dee," Rick whispered. "There are too many dragons around. We need to move away from here."

Dee opened his eyes. The sudden movement startled Rick, but he tried not to show it. Dee leaned away from the branch, rolled his neck, then cupped his forehead in one hand while holding onto the branch with the other.

"You're in no condition to confront the dragons; we need to slip away and find somewhere safe for you to rest." And for me, Rick thought. His muscles were getting stiff. Dee nodded and began to climb down from the tree. He touched the ice tentatively with his feet, and Rick noticed for the first time that he was barefoot. Granted, Rick was, too, but he still had his socks on; it was something, at least. Rick took his trench coat off and ripped two strips of material from the bottom.

"Hold up," Rick said. Dee paused, one foot on the branch, one on the ice. Rick lifted up the foot that was on the ice and wrapped it with the cloth. Then he did the same with the other. "All right, that'll have to do for now."

Dee finished climbing down and the ice cracked under his feet. It had to be at least a foot thick, and yet it threatened to break under Dee's weight. How much did he weigh, Rick wondered. He decided not to test the strength of the ice, and led him to the shore. From the bank, Rick paused. He saw a horse frozen in the middle of the river, but it was too far away for him to tell if it still carried its rider.

"Where are we going?" Dee asked as they began walking away from the river.

"I want to put some distance between us and the dragons. Then I'll look around and see whether or not Dennis survived. In the meantime, maybe we can find you some shoes."

"That's fine for you, but I was heading to the swamp," Dee said.

"The swamp? Why go there? Nothing but black dragons and Sapoquates in the swamp."

"One of those Sapoquates is my friend," Dee said. "If you'll kindly point me in the correct direction, I'll be on my way."

"The swamp is on the other side of the river. You'll have to walk across it to get there. Judging by the way the ice cracked under you, I doubt you'll make it across. And if you do, the dragons are likely to see you."

"Well, that's no concern of yours, now is it? I don't recall us agreeing to stick together," Dee said dryly, but he sounded exhausted.

Rick stood in front of him, his face inches from Dee's. He bent down so he could look him in the eye. "Those dragons know I helped you. I'm as good as dead if they find me. And you're so weak right now you're as good as dead if they find you. So the only option for either of us is to work together."

"Like we did back in the valley," Dee commented.

"I would think that after what we've just been through, I'd have redeemed myself."

"Oh, yes, jabbing me in the skull made me forget all about your betrayal. I don't think of you as a friend, Rick. I never will. Just point me toward the swamp, and I won't kill you when I take my leave of you," Dee said steadily, getting some of his strength back.

"You'll be lost before you've taken five steps. You need me."

"I don't need help from someone who stabs me in the back."

"Then why are you asking me for it? I'll probably just point you in the wrong direction, anyway," Rick said, trying to keep his voice from rising.

"Maybe I already know the right direction, and I was just testing you," Dee snapped.

"Then let's just say I failed. Why don't you start walking?" Rick growled. Arguing with him was like arguing with a child. Half of it didn't make any sense; Rick was getting nowhere.

The woman was ignorant of Scully's pursuit. He was starting to wonder if it was a ploy, and he was going to find himself ambushed.

Then he spotted what she was after. In a clearing, right next to the frozen river, were two men. One was dark-skinned and dressed like a farmer. He was the shorter of the two, by at least half a foot. It was hard to tell exactly how tall the other man was; with the spiked, dark brown hair, it was a tough call. But he could tell he was taller than himself, by at least a few inches. He focused his attention on the man's clothing. Not many people walked around in black trench coats. But Zalites did. He couldn't tell for sure though—he couldn't see the man's eyes. Scully wondered what Dee was doing hanging around with Zalites.

The woman reached the clearing first and slowed her pace, giving Scully time to catch up. She approached the two men with her blade raised, ready to strike down the taller of the two. Scully burst into the clearing, visible to the two men. Scully saw the glimmer of the tall man's eyes and tried to hide his disgust. Zalites were not liked. Scully had heard too many stories of Zalites raping and stealing.

He dashed forward, knowing that if the dragons wanted these men dead, he wanted them alive. As he charged towards the woman, to the men it appeared he was attacking them. He reached around the woman and blocked her blade with his own. He saw the shock in her gorgeous brown eyes and dodged the tall man's fist. He pushed the woman back, and she went into a fighting stance. Scully did the same.

"Wait, I don't think he's after us," the dark man said, putting a restraining hand on the other man's arm, holding him back.

The woman charged and Scully blocked her blade with his. She bent in close, and Scully smelled her. She was wearing a very faint perfume; it smelled like roses. He resisted the urge to bend closer and take a whiff of her hair, anticipating her kick to his groin with a twist of his body and a gentle fling of his interlocked wrist. His move sent her backwards with a stumble. Before she could recover, he swung with his sword and harmlessly sliced one of her bra straps. Her cleavage sunk a few inches lower, teasing him. He grinned and prepared for her attack.

Infuriated, she gave him a nasty look and charged, roaring with anger. Scully again blocked her blow, this time skipping to his left as she passed. He flicked his blade and tripped her with its flat edge. She fell to the ground, her face smacking the frozen mud, but she didn't slow down; she rolled to her back, spitting out a tooth as she went. She rolled away from Scully and towards the other men. Scully saw the problem—she was working for the dragons, and she would willingly die to finish her task. Killing Scully so she could safely kill the men wasn't an option. It was a risk. Scully didn't like fighting people that crazy; they were unpredictable.

"Forgive me, sheila," Scully said softly, then flung his sword at her. He closed his eyes, not wanting to see the beautiful woman take her last breath. Then he heard the sound he knew all too well as the sword struck its mark and the gasps of the men as they saw their attacker materialize, followed by the roar of dragons overhead. The Queen could see everything the dragons saw and had the power to manipulate every move they made. She would not be pleased. The dragons weren't going to ignore him anymore. Now would be a really good time for Lorna to show up, Scully decided.

"Who are you?" the tall man asked.

"Mak Scully—I'm an old friend of Dee's. I'm assuming you are, too?"

"He was on my farm—saved me from some of the cannibals," the dark man said. "But he didn't mention you; he said he had a friend in the swamp with the Sapoquates. I assumed he was talking about a Sapoquate."

Remind me not to tell this guy any secrets, Scully thought.

"Yes, well, leave it to Dee to leave out details—like what species his friend is," Scully said with a smile. "Where is Dee?"

"We got separated in the flood, and I think you're lying," the tall man said.

"Whatever would make you think that?"

"'Cause you came here on horses, and no one living in a swamp would be riding a horse." Scully's smile faded. He had blown it.

"Did I hear you say your name was Mak Scully? I was under the impression you were a skeleton. A dead one at that," a voice called. Scully faced the dragon as it landed. Other dragons swarmed above them.

"My death has been greatly exaggerated," Scully told him.

"Why would you risk your neck for Decompose? That is an interesting puzzlement," the dragon mused.

Lorna reached the top of the hill just as the dragon landed. She dropped to her stomach in the grass so she wouldn't be seen. Dozens of dragons circled in the air. She didn't have time to reach them, and she wasn't sure how long Scully's charm would keep him alive. She'd hoped to make it out of here without getting on the Queen's wanted list, but it seemed that option was no longer available.

Lorna slowly stood and clapped her hands, feeling a sizzle of power. She didn't know why she always clapped her hands before casting a spell. Her father never had, and neither had her brother. But after clapping her hands, she felt the power increase, even if it was only in her mind. She didn't like twitching her fingers like a grandma knitting a sweater. Lorna preferred to vocalize her spells, but she always got results, so no one had ever criticized her—at least, not twice.

"Powers great, powers grand—send a wind to knock them off their silver knockers." She opened her palms to the dragons, and her hair blew into her face as a wind swept up. It roared in her ears for a few seconds, then she closed her palms and brushed the hair from her face.

That finished the dragons, at least for the time being. They were either knocked to the ground so roughly that the impact killed them, or were gouged by a tree on the way down. The dragons twitched helplessly, and Lorna smiled. She had wanted to do that for a long time.

"Come on, boys! Won't be long before she sends more! That woman is going to be royally—" Lorna began. A sharp pain burned her chest.

She looked down to see a long silver claw sticking a few inches out of her stomach. She tasted copper in her mouth and realized she was going to die. The idea had never occurred to her before.

"Lorna!" Scully screamed, and he ran towards her, but she knew he would never reach her in time. All the dragon had to do was snap her head off, and it would all be over. She felt oddly calmed by the idea.

Ethan heard Scully scream and knew something had gone horribly wrong. He ignored the pain in his shoulder and pulled the orb out again. He'd panicked before and almost gotten everyone killed. Now he was being treated like a child because of it—told to stay behind and wait because he was more likely to get in the way than he was to provide help. As Scully had so rudely put it, his sole purpose was to find Dee. And that was what he was going to do because it sure sounded like they needed him. He held the orb in front of him and was surprised to find that Dee wasn't far away—just on the other side of the river and up the hill. He took a deep breath and got to his feet; he would find Dee and bring him back to help. He had to do something. He couldn't just sit here.

He climbed up on Scully's horse and headed across the river.

"She saved us," Dominique said in almost a whisper, but Dennis still heard. Dennis went into action; the man with the sword was fast, but not fast enough. Zalites were faster than humans. He zipped by the man, and was on top of the dragon before it even registered that he'd moved.

Dennis jumped into the trees to level the playing field. Dennis dropped down above the dragon and landed on its long neck. The metal scales were cold; it didn't even feel like a living creature—more like a moving statue of silver. He hugged the beast's long neck with his legs, clutched it with his hands, and with a sharp jerk, snapped it. The beast went limp. He jumped off and landed on the ground before the dragon's body had a chance to smash the woman and he snapped the claw off at the paw, knowing that the woman's bleeding would increase if he pulled it out. He helped her lie on the ground, supporting her head so she wouldn't choke on her own blood.

"No, no, Lorna; no, you can't die on me," Scully said as he reached them. He put his sword away and fell to his knees next to her.

"Ethan," she whispered, her voice weak. "Protect Ethan and help him right his wrong."

"Don't talk, don't talk; it'll make it worse. Try not to move," Scully said.

"Who's Ethan?" Dennis asked.

"Her cousin. He was helping us find Dee. He's the only one who can track him," Scully said.

Dennis was about to point out that he had tracked Dee just fine when Dominique reached them.

"Is that him?" Dominique asked, gesturing to the river, where a man on a horse was crossing at a slight trot.

"Yes, that's him, on my horse," the man grumbled.

"Going after Dee?" Dominique asked.

"That or running home like a scared chicken."

"Dee can help her; I've seen him do this kind of thing—if we find him before it's too late," Dominique continued.

"Then what are you waiting for?" Dennis asked. "You're the only person Dee will listen to. I saw the way you got him to cross that river. Go after Ethan and help him bring Dee back."

"Right, right," Dominique agreed, suddenly nervous. He turned away and took off after the man on the horse.

"She won't last long; there's no way Dee will get here in time," Scully said mournfully. The woman had closed her eyes, but she was only asleep. Dennis could feel her pulse in her neck.

Rick watched Dee storm off. Of course, he was going in the wrong direction. The river was to the east, and Dee was walking northwest. Rick walked after him, keeping a distance of about six or seven feet.

"You're going the wrong way," Rick told him.

"I'm not listening to you anymore. Dominique found me once, and he'll find me again. Until then, I don't care which way I'm going," Dee replied, not bothering to turn around.

"Dominique is probably dead. Along with his dog and horses. You're on your own," Rick tried to explain.

"You have no idea how happy that makes me," a woman said. Dee had just stepped into a clearing, but Rick didn't have a good view of it; there were trees in the way. He saw Dee raise his hands, then he collapsed to the ground.

Rick burst into the clearing. A woman unlike anything Rick had ever seen was kneeling over Dee. She placed a red stone on his chest and smiled. She was covered in black fur, and she moved like an animal, more alert than any human Rick had met. She was dressed in sequined silver—a skirt that went to her ankles and a matching halter top. Her black fur was longer on her head, reminding Rick of the mane on a lion—all frizzy and tangled. She looked like a cat and moved with the same grace. But Rick needed Dee, more than he was willing to admit. He couldn't let this mutant steal him away.

Scully did his best to apply pressure to the wound, hoping it would slow her blood loss. Her skin was pasty. He didn't want to know how weak her pulse was. She's a big girl, he thought, she has lots of blood; she should be okay for a while.

"Hey, Scully," the Zalite spoke. Scully looked at him. He was holding her head up to keep her from drowning in her own blood. Scully hated that the Zalite was helping him and despised the fact that he'd been the one to save Lorna.

"What?" Scully asked, trying not to sound as annoyed as he felt.

"When you pulled your sword out of that woman, was she dead?"

"No, but I'm sure by now she is," Scully said, visibly annoyed.

"Well, I think she made a pretty rapid recovery."

"What?" Scully looked back over his shoulder. Down the hill, where he had been a few moments ago, should have been a woman slowly dying—bleeding to death from her wound. Instead, he saw nothing. There might have been a puddle of blood, but he couldn't see it from here.

"Where did she go?" the Zalite asked.

"She's invisible again. I don't understand how, she's a black dragon maiden. She shouldn't have the ability to—"

"To what?"

"Heal herself," Scully whispered. "That maiden must have been carrying a white gem. If we can get it from her, we can heal Lorna."

"But we can't see her. And she's going to try killing us," the Zalite pointed out. "Can you still see her? You could before."

"No, that was Lorna's magic; it's worn off."

"Well, you're a warlock aren't you? Cast another spell," the Zalite said. Scully didn't like being ordered around.

"I don't have enough power to counteract a dragon spell. Only Lorna does," Scully said.

"But you can do other spells, right?"

"Good job, Zalite," the woman said, looking up as he approached. Rick looked her over. She was short. Very short, compared to him—a full foot shorter. She barely stood five-two. She was muscular, though; Rick could tell, even with fur covering her body. If he were a normal human, with human strength, it would have been no contest. She would have dropped him in a heartbeat, regardless of his size. But Rick was a Zalite. The pet dog he'd wrestled with as a kid had been bigger and stronger than a human body builder. His only problem would be if she used magic.

"I'm afraid I'm going to have to rescind my services to the Queen," Rick said as he slipped his trench coat off. He was going to enjoy this.

"Is that so? How about if you just leave, and I'll pretend I couldn't find you?" she asked.

"How about not?" Rick asked. She wasn't expecting him to attack. She was used to people fearing her. But Rick didn't fear anyone, especially not a human. He walked up to her and slammed his fist into her face. She was thrown off her feet and flew at least three yards through the air, until her back collided into a tree trunk. She sank to the ground, blood dripping from her nose. Such an impact should have knocked her unconscious, if not killed her, yet she recovered in a few seconds. She climbed to her feet, slightly off balance, and wiped at the blood on her face. So she was tough; Rick still didn't care.

"What did you do to him?" Rick asked as he walked towards her again. She began making sharp little movements with her fingers. Rick wasn't sure what that did, but he didn't like it. He dashed forward, before she could finish what she was doing, and slammed his elbow into her neck. She fell sideways and caught herself on a tree before she hit the ground. She was recovering too quickly. It wasn't normal. Rick saw the gems attached to a belt around her waist. Didn't the maidens use those gems for magic?

She used the tree as leverage to mount her own attack. She kicked at him with her right leg, twisting her body in the air. Rick didn't budge. He grabbed her calf with one hand and gave her leg a sharp twist. He heard the crack of bones and knew he had fractured her knee in multiple places, and probably broken her tibia and fibula. She screamed a catlike sound that Rick had never heard a human make. He gave her leg a final jerk, pulling the knee out of its socket then he let go, dropping her to the ground with a thud. He bent and removed her belt. Then he remembered her finger movements.

He looked at her. She was lying on her stomach, shivering in pain, but still awake. Her leg was twisted at a disgusting angle, the foot aimed the wrong way. He had twisted her leg a full 180 degrees. He reached down and grabbed her right arm, laying it palm down on the ground. He stomped on her delicate hands, wishing he still had his boots. He could have caused more damage. But he grinned as he felt her finger bones shatter. She didn't scream; it was taking all of her strength not to pass out. He finished her right hand and repeated the procedure with her left. Then he crouched next to her and held up the belt.

"Now, why don't you tell me which of these little stones you were using to heal yourself, and maybe I'll give it to you—if you tell me what you did to Dee," Rick said. She looked at him, desperate. She was like a fox trapped in a snare, ready to gnaw her own foot off. She was in too much pain to talk, let alone explain what she had done to Dee, so he plucked one of the stones off the belt. It was black. He held it out for her to see.

"Was it this one?" he asked. She looked at him, but said nothing. He dropped it to the ground and crushed it under his feet.

"Hope not. How about this one?" He held up a red one, and again got no response. He crushed it, too. Then he pulled the white one off. That one got her attention. She raised her eyebrows and widened her eyes.

"Ah, so the white one, huh? Why don't you gather your thoughts and tell me how to wake Dee up?" Rick said. He held the gem inches away from her face, taunting her. "I didn't hurt your ability to talk, so get on with it."

"Of course I can do other spells—just not spells that directly counter a dragon's spell," Scully snapped. He searched the woods, hoping to see leaves move or twigs snap.

"Can you make it rain?" the Zalite asked. Scully looked at him, puzzled.

"Make it rain? Why would—" Scully began.

"Warlocks are always making fire, so I figure they can make rain, too. Can you?"

"Yes, I can make it rain, but I don't see—"

"If you make it rain, we'll be able to see her," the Zalite said calmly. Scully realized he was right. They wouldn't be able to see her good, but the rain would hit her and create an outline of her body. It was worth a shot, anyway.

Scully stood, reached into his small pouch, pulled out some grayish-purple sand, and flung it into the air. He waved his hand back and forth in it, spreading it around. He closed his eyes and envisioned rain—a gentle downpour. Then he felt the raindrops on his face and arms.

The rain had come out of nowhere, but it slowed Ethan. He had come to a stop and was muttering angrily to himself. Dominique caught up to him, breathing heavily, glad he was in fairly good shape.

"Ethan?" Dominique asked. The man jumped in fright, almost falling off the horse. "Your friends sent me; I think one of them said his name is Scully. They need your help. The woman—Lora, I think—she's been hurt. They need you to find Dee so he can help her."

"I—I can't," Ethan stammered.

"Yes, you can; that's where you were going, right? I'm Dee's friend; he won't hurt us when we reach him, I promise."

"No, I lost his signal. Something happened to him. He died or lost consciousness. I can't find him," Ethan said. Dominique saw tears running down his face, although it was hard to tell in the pouring rain. "I'm sure Dee is fine. Just lead us to where he was last," Dominique said.

"I can't; it doesn't work that way. She's going to die, isn't she? Lorna is going to die, and it's my fault." The man buried his face in his right hand, overcome with sobs. Dominique looked away; this guy wasn't going to be any help. I found Dee once on my own; I can find him again, Dominique thought. Hank—he'd had Hank to help him then. He wondered if Hank had survived the flood.

"Hank!" Dominique shouted, but his voice sounded small in the thunderous rain. "Hank! Here boy!"

"Go to hell," the black-furred woman said between gritted teeth. Rick frowned.

"Not used to begging for your life, are you?" Rick asked. He dropped the white gem in front of her face, then smashed it as he had the others. And for good measure he crushed the gold and silver gems, too. Then he turned away and went back to Dee, to figure it out on his own. He picked the ruby off his chest. It was bigger and differently shaped from the other red gem he had crushed.

"Wait," the woman called. Rick ignored her; it was pointless to bargain with him now. He had destroyed the only thing she could want from him. "Please, don't help him. You don't know what he's capable of,"

"Sure I do, kitty cat. He's what I came to the planet to get. He's the most powerful weapon in the universe. Don't tell me you actually bought all that talk about following the Sapoquates here. And you don't think the Sapoquates wanted to research this planet for science, do you? We were racing here, trying to find the weapon first. Whoever found it would become the dominant species in the universe. Looks like I won," Rick said with a grin. "And now I even know how to control him."

He twirled the gem in his fingers for emphasis and relished the look of failure on her face. He put the gem in his pocket and grabbed Dee, tossing him over his shoulder. He couldn't bring himself to finish her off, so he left her in the clearing to die. Some wild animal would probably finish her once dusk hit.

The rain fell in gentle sheets—a nice warm fall, not cold like the dam water had been. Scully searched the area, hoping to see the woman. Dennis tried his best to keep Lorna comfortable. He wiped some of the rain from his face and looked around. He had been proud he'd thought of the rain, but he had a feeling the swordsman didn't like him. Then he saw her. He had figured he'd see her before Scully. His eyesight was better.

"Scully, I see her," Dennis said.

"Where?"

"I'll take care of it," Dennis told him.

"What do you want me to do?" Scully asked.

"Just keep acting like you're looking for her; make her think she's safe," Dennis said. He waited, pretending not to notice her as she came around, approaching Scully from behind. He saw the rain run down the blade of her weapon as she raised it to strike Scully.

"We should just go back. We aren't doing anyone any good standing here in the rain," Ethan said. Dominique didn't like how easy this kid was giving up.

"Is that orb of yours working yet?" Dominique asked.

"No, he's still unconscious," Ethan sighed. Dominique had called for Hank a while, but with no luck. He leaned back against one of the trees. He understood Ethan's desire to give up; it was tempting.

"At least the silver dragons will leave. They don't like the rain," Dominique pointed out.

"I was getting a strong reading of another maiden a little bit ago, but her signal is fading, too. I wonder what happened," Ethan commented as he looked into his orb.

"What? You've been getting a reading, and you didn't tell me?"

"Well, it's not Dee."

"Are you still getting the reading?"

"Yes, but it's not Dee."

"So? Maybe she captured Dee. Lead us to her."

"Are you crazy? You want to take on a dragon maiden alone?"

"We need to find Dee."

"I'm not going after a maiden by myself. I'm going back to Scully and Lorna. Maybe we can help them without Dee." Ethan turned the horse around and started back across the river. Dominique had no choice but to follow.

❖ ❖ ❖

Dennis waited until the last possible second, then he lunged forward, over Lorna's body. He grabbed at the woman, pulling her away from Scully. He wrapped one arm around her, then grabbed the wrist that held her weapon. He squeezed her wrist until she dropped it; as it left her fingers it became visible. She squirmed and tried to break free of his grip, but it was like a mouse struggling to break free of a lion. He let go of her wrist and pulled her body against his. He covered her nose and mouth with his hand and her struggles increased. He held her for a few minutes, but she still struggled. Dennis was puzzled—she should have passed out from lack of oxygen.

"You need to get the gem off her; I can't hurt her if she still has it," Dennis told Scully. He had been watching them struggle, not sure what to do. Scully dropped to his knees and began feeling the woman's body. He patted her down like a security guard, searching the invisible woman for a stone. Dennis tightened his grip and resisted the urge to snap her neck. She began stomping his foot with her high heeled boots; thankfully, he could barely feel it through his boots.

Rick carried Dee away from the clearing and waited until he was sure they were far enough away from Darlene that she wouldn't be able to find them if, by some stroke of luck, a dragon found her before she died. He put Dee on the ground and looked at him. He was still asleep, almost in a coma. Rick took the gem out of his pocket. He placed it on the ground, then stomped on it, just as he had the others.

Rick slapped Dee across the face. Droplets of water splattered. The rain was annoying, and Rick reached up and wiped it from his brow. Finally, Dee murmured, and his eyes fluttered open. Then his eyes got huge, and he jumped to his feet, pushing Rick away.

"Darlene! Where? Where is she?" Dee asked, looking like a frightened rabbit.

"She's gone. I took care of her."

"Took care of her? How is that possible?"

Rick gestured to the crushed stone at their feet. "How else do you explain that?"

"You took on Darlene? For me?" Dee asked, not believing him.

"Yes, and she was a pansy once I took her stones away. Now, are you still going to march off on your own, or shall we stick together and find the others?"

"You beat Darlene," Dee said, as if the words sounded funny to him.

"Yes, I did. Are you coming?"

"I can't beat her. And you did," Dee said amazed.

"Well, you beat the dragons; I can't do that. I guess together, you and I are just unstoppable, huh?" Rick said.

"We're definitely something," Dee mumbled.

Scully pulled a gem off the woman's belt, and she became visible. In his hand, he held a black gem. He saw the white gem tucked away in the pouch around her waist. He yanked it off and hurried over to Lorna; she was still alive, but barely. He placed the gem on her stomach and realized dumbly that they needed to remove the claw before it could heal her.

"Dennis, I need your help."

"I'm kind of busy; this woman won't pass out."

"We need to roll her over and pull the claw out; I can't do that alone."

"Fine." Dennis slammed the woman's head against the nearest tree and watched as she fell to the ground, unconscious.

"Did you kill her?" Scully asked.

"If I wanted to kill her, I would have just snapped her neck," Dennis said dryly. He got on his knees across from Scully. "How did you want to do this?"

"Push her up on her side; I'll hold her up like that, and you pull the claw out from the back. As soon as it's out, roll her onto her back, and I'll put the gem on her," Scully said.

"You want me to roll her towards you?" Dennis asked.

"Yes."

"Okay, let's do this." Dennis grabbed at her armpit and pushed her onto her side. She was a heavy woman, and Scully was glad Dennis was so strong. Dennis grabbed the claw with his free hand and pulled hard. It came out easily, and a flood of blood came with it. He eased her onto her back, and Scully quickly put the white gem over her wound, which now gushed blood freely.

"You sure you know how to work that?" Dennis asked. Scully wondered the same thing. He wasn't sure if he needed an enchantment of some sort, or if he needed special training to operate the gems. It wasn't working; the stone was covered in blood and doing nothing.

❖ ❖ ❖

"You're telepathic, right?" Rick asked. Dee looked like he had his bearings about himself again.

"Yes, that's right."

"Think you can use those powers of yours to find Dennis?" Rick asked.

"I can try," Dee agreed. Rick watched as his eyes started to glow ruby red, then he winced in pain. "Someone's dying."

"What?" Rick exclaimed. "Who?"

"This way, I don't know who it is, but Dennis is with them. And Dominique is concerned about them." Dee took off at a run down the hill, towards the river.

"Dee, we can't cross the river, not with the dragons around!" Rick shouted as he ran alongside him.

"The dragons left!" Dee shouted back. "The rain drove them away."

"I still don't think you should go out there. That ice barely held you before. And now this warm rain has softened it up. You'll sink, Dee!" Rick shouted.

"You're right; we'll never make it in time," Dee agreed. His eyes glowed again, and Rick watched in horror as Dee morphed into something Rick had only seen in his nightmares. The giant beast leaped over the river in one huge jump. Rick just stood and watched in amazement. He really was Decompose. Rick hadn't quite believed it until now.

Scully heard the beast coming, and at first thought it was going to be a dragon. Lorna's pulse was quickly fading—the useless gem tossed aside. Dennis said maybe if they woke the maiden up she could operate it. Then the hideous monster was coming right at them. It had bounded across the lake in one leap, and now it was clawing its way up the mountain, knocking trees out of the way. In no time, it was standing on all fours, Dennis directly below its exposed ribcage. The memories came rushing back. He would never forget those days or his fight with Decompose. He couldn't move; he couldn't think. One of the giant's claws came down on top of Lorna, and the beast shrunk into Dee, the human that had given Scully back his flesh.

Scully heard Lorna gasp, and her eyes fluttered open.

Dee's own eyes glowed red. He looked at Scully and recognized him.

"Dee! Dee! Oh, thank the Queen you got here in time. Is she okay? She saved me from the dragons; she saved all of us," the dark-skinned man shouted as he raced up the hill. Ethan followed in his stead, holding his bad shoulder. He looked incredibly pale.

"Dee! You can't go tromping around like that! Someone will see you and—" another man shouted as he ran up the hill. He looked a lot like Dennis, only bald, and wore a matching black trench coat. He fell silent as he saw the group.

"Scully? Why are you here?" Dee asked, puzzled.

"Is this him?" Lorna asked. She tried to sit up and reluctantly, Dennis let her. She looked at Dee with wide-eyed excitement.

"Dee, we're here to help you. This is Lorna. She's your sister, and that's Ethan, your cousin. I told them about you and—" Scully tried to explain.

"Help me? What are you talking about? I—I don't have any family."

"Why, sure you do, I was Jaff's sister, we have the same father," Lorna said. Dee glared at her.

"Mortimer Talberg was my father. Jaff used me as his personal puppet for ten years. He's not my family," Dee said.

"He did what?" Ethan exclaimed. "I—I'm so sorry. I had no idea. But you have to believe us; I helped Jaff. I helped make the original plague, the one that killed all the Meta-morphs. It infected you because you're part Meta-morph. We didn't think you were alive—your mother—"

"You know nothing. You are here to help me? Why didn't you help me when the dragons put me in a coma, or when Jaff enslaved me, or when they imprisoned me? Where were you then?"

"I didn't know who you were!" Ethan shouted. Dee walked over to him, and Ethan shrunk away. "I thought I knew what Jaff was doing. I had no idea he'd gone back to the island. But I am here to correct it. I can fix you, cure you."

"Cure me? My father, Mortimer, said the same thing to me," Dee was standing only a few feet away from him now. Ethan cringed.

"Oh, God," Ethan closed his eyes, and Scully thought he could see him shiver. But Dee hesitated.

"What did you say?" Dee asked. Ethan opened one eye and looked at him.

"'Oh, God'?" he said again.

Dee took a step back. "No one believes in God anymore; the dragons are gods now."

Scully thought Ethan was going to pass out from fright.

"How old are you?" Dee asked.

"Didn't your mother ever tell you it's not polite to ask a warlock how old he is?" Ethan asked, trying to lighten the mood.

Dee did not smile. "My adoptive mother was killed by my adoptive father. I never met my biological mother," Dee said flatly.

"She died in childbirth," Lorna said. "She ran away from home and left you on the steps of an orphanage. When she went into labor she was very ill. I'm sorry no one ever told you."

Dee took a few steps away from Ethan. He didn't know what to do.

"Dee, we should get out of here; the dragons are going to come back as soon as it stops raining," the other Zalite said. Dennis had gotten up and was standing next to him. Dee looked at the falling rain and raised his hand. The rain stopped. Scully held his breath.

"I'm going to the swamp to find my friend Aquatis. Whoever wants to come is welcome. I don't care," Dee said with a dismissive wave of his hand. The dark-skinned man hurried over to him.

"Is he a Sapoquate?" Scully asked.

"Yes, he is. What difference does it make?"

"Dee, you can't trust the Sapoquates; you shouldn't even be trusting the Zalites," Scully said.

"And this is coming from you? I have no reason to trust you, either, Scully. You have no room to talk," Dee snapped.

Dee and Dominique walked off, heading towards the swamp. Scully helped Lorna stand and Ethan walked over. The two Zalites fell in step behind Dee and began following.

"Well, that's it, then. He doesn't want our help," Ethan said, satisfied.

"That is not it," Lorna said. "We are going with him, and we'll explain things better after he starts to trust us. Scully, go get the horses. Ethan, start walking. I don't want you falling behind."

"Wait a minute; I'm not going with them. They're going into the swamp. I did not sign up for that. Not only are there blood-thirsty black dragons in there, but those Sapoquates are going to murder us," Ethan whined. Scully looked away and made his way down the hill to get the horses.

"And we are going to be there to help Dee when he finds that out," Lorna explained. Scully was surprised at the amount of patience she was showing Dee and Ethan. He'd never seen her act so nicely. Her close call with death had done her some good.

Scully shifted the weight of the burlap bag he was carrying. Ethan's condition was deteriorating, so they'd been forced to put him on Scully's horse. Lorna's injured horse couldn't carry anything beyond the young dragon maiden, which forced Scully and Lorna to carry most of their supplies. Dennis had offered to help, and eventually Rick had helped as well.

The maiden was awake, her wrists tied to the saddle. They had placed an enchanted brown sack over her head, making her blind and deaf. Even if the Queen could see and hear through her, it wouldn't make a difference. Lorna led the horses through the muddy swamp. Scully walked alongside, keeping an eye on their surroundings.

Ethan had passed out again, and it looked like the blood-stain on his shirt had gotten bigger.

"I don't like this, Lorna," Scully said as he shifted his bag again.

"I know, Scully. No one is forcing you to come; if you want, you can turn back," Lorna said.

"You guys wouldn't survive ten minutes without me," Scully said with a grin. "I'm going to go talk to him. Maybe I can convince him to stop for the night. I don't want to meet the Sapoquates at all, but if we have to, I'd rather do it in the daytime."

"Agreed," Lorna said. Scully took that as permission. He passed the Zalites, who were mumbling to each other. They went quiet when he walked by.

"Dee, can I have a word with you?" Scully asked.

"As long as it doesn't require me to stop," Dee said without looking in his direction.

"Dee, Ethan is bleeding again. We need to stop so he can rest. And Lorna's horse is wounded as well; its limp has been getting worse. And I think I can speak for everyone when I say we are all tired."

"And I suppose you are hungry, as well?" Dee snapped.

"Dee, we have been walking for a long time. Food and rest sound pretty good," Dominique chipped in. Scully saw the bags under his eyes, and the tired look in them.

"It would be best if we meet the Sapoquates in the morning; we would seem like less of a threat," Scully explained.

Dee stopped walking and gave an exaggerated huff. He looked around at the forest as he contemplated what to do.

"I don't know how long Aquatis has been waiting for me. I don't want to waste time reaching him," Dee said, still not looking at Scully.

"One more night won't harm things. We can leave at sunrise, after a good night's rest," Scully said.

"Oh for Zit's sake, let's just stop for the night. I can't stand the whining," Rick complained as he dropped the bags he was carrying. "Dennis, let's see if we can catch something to eat."

Dennis didn't even wait to see if the others were stopping. He dropped his bags and followed Rick.

"And if we're going to have some sort of leader for this assemblage, my vote is for Scully," Rick said as he left. The mist quickly swallowed them.

"Don't get lost!" Scully shouted.

"Fine. Break camp," Dee grumbled.

"I think you mean set up camp. You break camp when you're getting ready to leave," Lorna said. Dee pretended he hadn't heard her.

Rick caught a wild rabbit, a big one. It smelled wonderful to Dominique. Lorna started a fire and Rick began cooking it over the flames. Lorna had also packed some canned goods, so they each enjoyed a tin of beef stew. She had packed more than enough food, something Dominique didn't find hard to believe. Judging by her size, he guessed she loved food. She and the Zalites were the first to finish their cans. Scully was busy putting a trail of light purple sand around the campsite. Most of his luggage was full of it. Dominique found that odd. He took another forkful of beef, surprised at how hungry he was. Ethan was slumped against a tree on the other side of the camp. The fire was in the middle, and the horses were tied to a tree to Dominique's right. The clearing in the trees wasn't quite a perfect circle—more of an oval.

Scully finished the circle and sat next to him. He picked up his can of stew and began eating it, glancing worriedly at the horses. Their baggage was next to the horses and their saddles had been removed. The woman they had taken prisoner was tied to a tree outside the oval, behind the tree Dee was leaning against.

"What's the circle for?" Dominique asked.

"It keeps anyone who means us harm from passing it. In other words, it will help me get a good night's sleep," Scully said as he took another bite of stew. Lorna went over to Ethan, trying to get him to eat.

"Anyone have a problem with me going down to the stream to get some water?" Dennis asked. He held up a pot. "I can fill some of the canteens, as well."

"Go ahead, but don't go alone," Scully said.

"I can't go; I need to make sure the rabbit doesn't catch fire," Rick said.

"I'll go," Dominique volunteered. He glanced at Dee, expecting him to object. But Dee just stared into the flames.

"How are you holding up?" Lorna asked Ethan as she watched Dennis and Dominique leave the protective circle. Dusk had hit hours ago, and the darkness was overwhelming. She had never liked camping, especially when their father took them. He always brought along some new girlfriend and practically ignored her and Jaff. Jaff had always been so quiet back then; Lorna didn't even know if he had enjoyed the camping. He had just sat by the campfire, staring at it, much like she saw Dee doing now.

"It burns," Ethan said softly. She held the can of soup to his lips and tried to get him to take a sip. He spat it out, repulsed. "I want water."

"You need to eat. This is chicken broth—good for you. Now drink," she ordered. Ethan glared at her.

"What's wrong with him?" Dee asked as he approached.

"He has a shoulder injury. We're having trouble stopping the bleeding," Lorna said. Dee crouched down, joining them.

"I don't want your help. I don't deserve it," Ethan said as he forced down a swallow of broth.

"Of all the people here, you deserve my help the most, don't you? Aren't you the one who made me the way I am?" Dee asked.

"And that is why I don't deserve your help."

"You made a god, Ethan. Don't you think you should at least enjoy my abilities?" Dee asked with a grin. "Or do you think of me as a devil, too?"

"You are a man infected with a disease I created," Ethan said flatly, his hand trembling.

"Whatever you think, I think you're slowing us down, and I need you to keep up tomorrow," Dee said.

"Your concern is heartwarming," Ethan told him dryly.

"Nonetheless." Dee reached placed his hand on Ethan's wound. Ethan screamed. Lorna couldn't tell if it was in pain, frustration, or fright. She didn't remember it hurting when Dee healed her. He was still screaming when Dee let go, but stopped as Dee got to his feet. Ethan already looked better—the color back in his cheeks. He pulled the bandages away from his chest to look at his wound. There wasn't even a scar.

"You might want to fix the black horse, too! It is slowing us down as well!" Ethan screamed.

"You could have thanked him," Lorna commented.

"He forced his healing on me. You don't thank a person for that. Rick, can I eat some of that rabbit?" Ethan asked, ignoring Lorna. Lorna decided it was time to get some rabbit herself.

"Do you hear that?" Dennis asked. Dominique shook his head. Of course he didn't hear it, Dennis thought, his hearing isn't as good. But Dennis could hear it—the gentle slap of footsteps in the mud. It turned into splashes as the footsteps reached the stream. Dennis braced for the attack.

"I hear it now," Dominique agreed, his voice strained.

Dennis tensed as the steps got closer. He thought about how far away the camp was. He wondered if Dominique could reach it if he tried to stall the beast. It would be better for one of them to survive than for both to die. He considered screaming. Someone up at the camp would hear and come to help. But it might give their position away. There was no guarantee that the beast knew where they were. He might still have the element of surprise. He wished it wasn't so dark and foggy; he couldn't see a thing.

Scully watched as Dee got up again and walked over to the horses. He was proving himself useful. He had healed Ethan, and now he was healing the horse. Granted, he was doing it for selfish reasons, but still—he was helping them. It was a start.

Rick finished cooking the rabbit and moved it away from the fire, saving some for Dennis to eat when he returned. Scully had been impressed at the Zalite's willingness to share. Dee and Scully were the only ones who hadn't eaten. Rick sat next to Scully, holding the rabbit's hind leg in his hand. He bit a chunk off and looked at Scully. His eyes looked strange in the reflected firelight.

"You don't like Zalites very much, do you?" Rick asked. Ethan was nearby, lying on the ground, getting some sleep. Dee was on the other side of the campsite, with the horses.

"Honestly? No, I don't," Scully said, confident that no one else could hear him.

"May I ask why?"

"Do you need to? I've heard the same stories everyone else has," Scully told him.

"I do need to ask. I want to hear you say it," Rick said, pausing as he chewed.

"Fine, I've heard about how Zalites go from village to village, raping women and stealing. You disgust me."

"Well, there's your problem. You view us as people," Rick pointed out. "We aren't people by any definition of the word. Sure, we may steal something to help us get by, but we would never rape a woman. And if we did, no one would consider it rape—more like horrific murder."

"I don't follow," Scully said.

"Here, touch my arm." Rick held it out for him to feel.

Scully ran his fingers along the arm, not understanding. Then he realized that although Rick's skin looked normal, it felt wrong—like he was petting a porcupine. The skin was silky and smooth when he petted the arm downwards, but if he went up, tiny needles pricked his skin.

"Our entire bodies are covered in barbed needles. Including—" Rick paused to clear his throat, "our reproductive parts. Female Zalites have tough, thick skin. They go into heat yearly, but mating is painful to them. When semen is released, it creates a burning sensation, which causes them to pull away. So males are covered in barbed spikes, like a burr. We attach ourselves to the females, making it impossible for them to remove us until we retract the spikes."

"The spikes don't cause more pain?" Scully asked, amazed.

"No, the female is built for it. From what I understand, a human female would die from such trauma. A Zalite breeds on instinct; we don't have the same desires and urges a man like you would."

"So you don't think about mating unless you sense a female Zalite in heat?"

"Right; from what I've heard, it's quite the opposite of the human male," Rick said with a grin, taking another bite from his rabbit leg.

Dennis felt like he had been waiting forever. His muscles ached from tension. The footsteps were close now; the animal was smaller than he originally thought, but that didn't mean it wasn't a dragon—he had seen dragons as small as chickens. Then, in the fog, he started to see the outline of an animal. He heard a soft growl. The animal was the size of a wolf, and at first that was what Dennis thought it was.

"Hank! Oh, my Queen, Hank!" Dominique dashed towards the canine. As the fog parted, Dennis got his first good look at Hank, who was the size of a wolf, but colored differently. He was long-haired with spots of black and white. "It's okay; it's just Hank, my Australian shepherd."

Dennis petted the dog and ruffled his droopy ears. Dennis watched them for a moment, then resumed filling the water containers.

"I can't believe he found us, let alone survived the flood. I wonder if my horses made it, too. Good old boy," Dominique told the dog joyfully.

Scully was laying in a bed that smelled of roses; the sheets were made of fine satin. He rolled over and took a deep breath of the scented material. Georgia's bed always smelled so good. So did she. Her hair was always done, her clothes always pressed and pretty. Her scent lingered even after she had long left the room. And his own clothes retained her scent as well. He rolled to his back and grinned as he saw her descend upon him. Her curly red hair hung down to her shoulders and teased him, hiding her breasts from view.

Then her lips touched his, her tongue peeked out, and she sloppily licked his cheek. It was hot and wet. She had never licked him like that before, but he found it strangely arousing. Wisps of hair tickled his cheeks. But the hair was rough, like whiskers. Not soft and silky like Georgia's hair. Scully, roused from his slumber, felt the cold, hard ground below him. But still he felt the licking tongue. At first, he thought it was the dog Dominique had brought back to camp last night. He raised his hand to push the beast away, but when he opened his eyes, he saw something else.

Nostrils flared, and the pink tongue flicked out again, enjoying Scully's salty skin. It was a horse, but it was so large; the head was at least twice the size of his appaloosa's. Scully pulled back, startling the horse with his sudden movement. It curled its lips, flashing large teeth. Scully saw a large gray hoof coming at him, and he screamed.

That wasn't so smart, either. The excited horse gave a scream of its own. In the morning sun, Scully saw it clearly. It was a light chestnut with a blonde mane and tail. The horse stood easily over eighteen hands—a monster of a horse. He had to be a draft of some kind, but Scully couldn't put his finger on the breed. His shrill scream had awoken the others in the camp, and Scully heard their mumbles as they woke. The horse reared and churned its front feet in the air. Scully had never feared a horse before. He loved horses. But he'd never been near one this huge. He preferred Arabians, quarter horses, Morgans, standardbreds, or thoroughbreds. He had never been around working horses. Even Lorna's Friesian was slighted by comparison, and Friesians were a heavy breed.

The ground shook as the giant horse came back down. He stomped, and Scully feared being trampled. He scrambled around the tree trunk, not daring to stand up, for fear of seeming aggressive. The earth shook again, and Scully saw another, equally large horse on the other side of the tree. It was of the same breed, although as this one reared, striking at him, Scully noticed it was female. Her front hooves chipped at the tree trunk and bits of bark rained down upon him.

Scully raised his hand to keep the bark from falling onto his face. He heard the others shouting to each other, but he couldn't understand what they were saying. He heard his own horse crying in fright, but not a peep from Lorna's horse. Then the dog started barking. And suddenly the dog was right next to him, barking fiercely at the female horse. The black and white shepherd darted between the mare's legs and forced her to back up. Scully expected to see her give him a swift kick. Instead, the dog was the dominant one. The male horse whinnied and nipped at Scully's shoulder, grabbing a mouthful of his shirt. The response was immediate—the dog dashed over and nipped the big horse's muzzle. The stallion promptly let go and took a few steps away.

Then the others arrived. Dominique reached the horses first, gently petting the male's muzzle, calming him. The female reared a last time, and the ground shook as she came down. Then the Zalites were next to her. Lorna came over with some rope, and soon crude bridles and reins were made for the horses. Ethan was next to another tree, his eyes wide with fright. He hadn't budged. Dee seemed slightly frightened himself. The horses were under control now, and Scully's breathing slowed to a normal pace.

"I can't believe they survived," Dominique was saying. Scully stood and looked at the dark man.

"These are your horses?" Scully asked.

"Yes, I use them on my farm," Dominique said. "I figured the flood had killed them. Amazing they found us."

"Yes, how very loyal," Scully said, still a little shook up.

"Are they saddle-broken?" Rick asked.

"If you mean can we ride them, yes, of course. Contrary to their recent behavior, they are quite mild-tempered," Dominique assured them.

"Good, then let's get going. The sun is already coming up, we can reach the Sapoquate camp in a few hours. If no one objects," Dee decided.

"I have some granola bars we can eat on the road. For breakfast, that is," Lorna said.

"All right, let's move out then. I'll have the maiden ride with me. The rest of you split up the uh, what kind of horses are those, anyway?" Scully asked.

"Belgian draft horses," Dominique said proudly.

"I'm not getting on one of those," Dee said stubbornly.

"We'll make better time if we ride," Rick said.

"Ethan, you ride up here with me. Just give some of these packs to the other horses so we don't put too much weight on him," Lorna told him. Ethan hurried over and helped her, relieved that he wouldn't have to ride one of the monster horses. They removed all but one of the saddle bags, and gave the others to the two large Belgians. Scully got his horse ready and went to the maiden. She didn't say a word as he forced her onto Halayi's back. He tied her ankles under the horse's belly so she wouldn't be able to jump off. By the time he got on himself, the others had packed everything up.

Dennis and Dominique were on the female draft. Rick was on the other, but Dee hadn't mounted yet. Odd. He was practically indestructible, but terrified of sitting on a horse. In the end, and after much persuasion, Dee finally climbed a tree so he could reach the Belgian's back. Then they were on their way. It didn't take long for Scully to get the feeling they were walking into trouble. The ground became muddy and they had to slow.

"Do you hear that?" Dennis asked. Scully was in the lead, the other three horses following in a line. So far, the maiden had behaved well. Scully slowed his horse, but didn't hear anything.

Hank heard it, though. The black and white dog was growling. He had been trotting alongside Dominique's horse, but now he tensed and fell behind. Lorna and Ethan were last in the procession. The dog starting trotting to keep up when he fell behind them.

"I hear it," answered Rick, directly behind Scully.

"I don't sense anything," Dee commented.

"Dee, don't use your powers unless someone tells you to. I don't want anyone to see your eyes glowing," Scully said, not bothering to look back. He searched the barren trees, trying to see what the Zalites were hearing. He didn't have to search long.

His horse sensed it first and gave a quiet whinny. The other horses answered. He brought Halayi to a stop, and the others did the same.

"In the trees," Dennis whispered. But he didn't need to point it out. Scully saw the shadows dancing in the trees. If he didn't know better, he would have thought they were monkeys.

"What do we do?" Rick asked. Scully had been pondering the same question. In the end, he knew there was really only one option.

"We came here to find them, didn't we?" Scully told them. "Dee, those are the Sapoquates,"

As if cued, one of the Sapoquates dropped to the ground in front of Scully's horse. Halayi gave a frightened whinny and tried to rear. Scully pulled her down. It was the closest Scully had ever been to a Sapoquate. He didn't like it. They were disgusting—like giant frogs in human form. The Sapoquate's large eyes stared at him, holding a stick with a sharpened stone at the tip. He put the tip against Scully's throat, but it was no real threat to Scully. He could draw his sword and slice the Sapoquate's throat before it could injure him. Although, with those springy legs, the alien could be faster than he looked. Some lizards were quite agile, and he had a feeling the Sapoquates took after them.

"Why are you here? The territory you have entered is forbidden to your kind," the Sapoquate said, his voice electronic and inhuman.

"I'm looking for Aquatis," Dee said from the horse behind Scully.

"Aquatis?" The Sapoquate pondered the name, but Scully saw that the man knew who they were talking about. He heard dull thuds as other Sapoquates dropped from the trees. There were now three Sapoquates surrounding each horse, one on either side, and one in the lead, taking the reins from the rider.

"Yes, Aquatis; I'm a friend of his. He helped me, and I've come to find him."

"Aquatis is a liar and cheat. What involvement have you with him?" the Sapoquate asked.

"My friend," Scully spoke up, cutting off Dee's response, "is here to repay his debt to Aquatis; it is a private matter. We will be willing to discuss it openly if Aquatis is present. We will say no more until you take us to him."

The Sapoquate eyed him for a moment. Scully found it disturbing—how their skin glistened in the sun.

"Very well, we will take you to him. But you must dismount and allow us to blindfold and tie you. We can't have outsiders learning the location of our camp. We will take you to Aquatis and afterwards lead you from the camp. Safely," he said.

Scully knew the others weren't going to want to consent, but he saw no other way to reach the village peacefully. He looked back at the other horses, but the Sapoquates had already taken hold of all the reins. His companions looked at him, awaiting his response. Scully wondered how he had become their leader. He didn't remember volunteering for the job.

"Weapons, as well?" Scully asked, although he was the only one with a weapon. In a way, he would be the only defenseless one—the others had powers the Sapoquates couldn't take away.

"Leave your weapons on the horses," the Sapoquate told him.

"Very well," Scully said solemnly. He dismounted and tied his sword to the saddle. He glanced back and saw the others doing the same, although some were having trouble getting off their large horses. He saw one of the Sapoquates grabbing the maiden off Halayi.

"Be careful, it's best not to remove that bag," Scully told them.

"We must remove the bag, so we can place a proper blindfold on her," the Sapoquate told him.

"Trust me, she is blind, and more. Please, she is our prisoner and it's best if—" The Sapoquate wasn't going to listen to him. Another Sapoquate restrained him, binding his hands. Rick was still free; the Sapoquates were tying Dee first.

"You can't take that bag off," Scully protested. Rick understood. He grabbed the maiden and in one quick motion, snapped her neck. Then he succumbed to the four Sapoquates that pulled him away and tied and blindfolded him. It was the last thing Scully saw before his own blindfold was strapped on.

Dee had the feeling they were walking in circles, probably to confuse them so they wouldn't be able to find the camp later. Finally the group came to a stop, and the blindfolds were removed. Being blindfolded reminded him of being blind. The memories were not comforting. Scully was in front of him, and they were tied together with one long rope. He looked behind him and saw Rick, then Dominique, and everyone else, all in a neat line behind him. All had their wrists tied and were tied to the person in front of them.

"Can you untie us now?" Scully asked.

"I will take you and the so-called friend of Aquatis to see him," said the leader. "But I will leave your wrists tied." Two Sapoquates stepped up and untied Dee and Scully. "Follow me."

Dee looked at the camp for the first time. The Sapoquate homes reminded him of those he had seen people in the Amazon make. Nothing fancy—just thatched huts of tree branches and trunks, arranged in a circular pattern, with several campfires in the center. They were led along the inner edge of the circle until they reached a hut with two guards in front of it.

"After you," the Sapoquate said. The guards stepped aside, allowing them to enter.

"How are you holding up, Ethan?" Lorna asked. She was the last in line and could tell Ethan was upset. No one was happy about this embarrassing capture. She hoped Scully knew what he was doing.

"We should have ditched him back when he said he didn't want our help," Ethan mumbled. Lorna's ankles hurt, and her feet were swollen. She wasn't used to being on her feet so much. It was taking a toll on her body.

"I see our horses," Dennis spoke up from in front of Ethan. "It looks like they haven't disturbed our things."

"This is all wrong," Rick said from the head of the group. "They should have killed us when they found us."

"Unless we are more useful to them alive than dead," Dennis remarked.

Lorna realized that these two knew a great deal about the Sapoquates. Weren't their worlds at war? None of the Sapoquates were near. They seemed to sense that no one was going to make a break for it. Dennis and Rick didn't seem to care if they overheard their conversation, either.

"Why would they want us?" Rick asked.

"Dee mentioned Aquatis. I think that made us gain value," Dennis said softly.

They fell silent for a moment. Lorna shuffled uncomfortably. She wanted to sit down.

"I think they were expecting us," Dennis continued. "I think this was a trap. Think about it. Aquatis freed Dee, then they conveniently were separated and Aquatis told him to come here."

"Why didn't they just kill all of us except Dee?" Ethan snapped.

"They know how powerful he is. Dee could have killed them all if they had attacked us," Dennis concluded.

"Then why not have Aquatis greet us? Dee trusts him more than us. If Aquatis had given the order to kill us, Dee wouldn't have given us a second thought," Ethan said.

"Something's wrong," Rick repeated. The group fell silent. Lorna rubbed her ankles together. She wished Dee and Scully would hurry up.

It took Scully's eyes a moment to adjust to the darkness inside the hut. The only light was what drifted through the open door and the cracks in the walls, which were abundant. Finally he saw a figure in the middle of the round hut tied to a long pole that extended down from the ceiling and went through the roof. He was on his knees, bleeding. At least, Scully assumed the dark fluid coming from various wounds and his mouth was blood.

Twilight of One: The Plague of Decompose

"Aquatis!" Dee exclaimed. He dropped to his knees and reached out to him.

Scully quickly realized he was going to attempt to heal him, which would expose him as Decompose, and Scully hadn't decided if it was a good thing to let the Sapoquates know or not. He pulled Dee back.

Dee looked up at him, questioning. "I have to help him."

"Let's find out what his crime is, first," Scully said, as if he were talking to an anxious child.

"His crime?" the Sapoquate that led them into the hut asked. "He was exiled from our encampment for attempting a coup. Then he returned, claiming that he had befriended the great beast known as Decompose. He thought it would earn our trust. Of course, none of us listened to his nonsense. He claimed to have gone into the Valley of Death and freed the beast, but that they were separated after being attacked by an archer."

"You beat and tortured him for claiming to have saved Decompose?" Dee asked, alarmed.

"We tried to get him to tell us the truth. He insisted Decompose would come to us. It was nonsense. We tied him here, waiting a few weeks to see if Decompose arrives. If not, we kill him."

"Why do you want Decompose?" Scully asked.

"It is the ultimate weapon. If our world was to gain his power, we would conquer the galaxy. There would be no wars; one planet would rule all," the Sapoquate told them with a glimmer in his eye. It made Scully shiver.

The Sapoquate tied to the pole looked up weakly. As his eyes seem to clear, he saw Dee. He smiled weakly and opened his mouth. Scully didn't wait to see what he would say. He did the only thing he could think of—he kicked him.

"Why, the arrogant creature, how dare he make up such lies!" Scully shouted as he kicked Aquatis in the gut, knocking the wind from him. Aquatis coughed and spit green slime onto the floor.

Dee yelped, startled. "What are you doing?" he asked, pushing Scully away from Aquatis.

"I'm furious," Scully shouted. "Sir, please leave me and my friend alone with this cretin. I assume you don't mind, since I'm sure; you have already done far worse to him."

The Sapoquate seemed to grin, although it was hard to tell. Dee just seemed confused.

"Of course. I'll be right outside," the Sapoquate told them with a nod. Scully waited until he left. The door to the hut was still open, and they could hear him if he spoke too loudly.

"Dee, you have to listen to me," Scully said, but Dee wasn't listening. He was going to his friend.

"That was a clever ruse," Dee said. "Pretending to hurt Aquatis. Now we can heal him and get out of here. Can we take them? The Sapoquates in the camp?"

"Dee, we're not taking him with us," Scully said softly.

Dee looked at him.

"He was using you, Dee. He's not your friend."

"How dare you say that?" Dee accused, getting to his feet.

"Weren't you listening to him?"

"He saved my life. I have to save his."

"It was all planned out. He was thrown into your valley, hoping to win your friendship so he could rejoin the camp. And he'll do it again the first chance he gets," Scully explained.

"He's my friend. He wouldn't do that. I trust him."

"You had every reason to trust him. But now you need to trust me. Please, Dee," Scully pleaded. Dee looked from Scully to Aquatis, not sure what to do. "I know you can't read his mind. You can't prove whether he betrayed you or not. But you can read my mind. You can prove to yourself that I'm not lying. I want to help you."

"But you don't know Aquatis. You don't know if he really betrayed me," Dee said softly.

"But I know how people think, Dee. I've been living in this world for a long time. You've been in isolation. I know people, Dee. This was a set up. He was just thinking about himself."

"You don't know how old I am. I'm older than I look," Dee said, stalling until he decided what to do.

"Dee, I'm three hundred and seventy-two. You're only sixty. I'd say I win that contest," Scully said with a smile.

Dee's eyes widened. "You're older than Jaff," he said. Scully wasn't sure if it was a question or a statement.

"I went to school with Jafar McPowin, Jaff's father and yours. I'm not like Jaff. Jaff was a foolish young man, always striving to be better than his father. I saw him grow up, and I saw the bitterness in his eyes. It was contagious. Jaff's children had the same problem—all that competition. You saw it between Lillian and Darlene, didn't you? You remember that?"

"Yes. But you spent some of your life in isolation, too," Dee reminded him.

"Almost a century—nothing, really. Gone in the blink of an eye," Scully winked for emphasis. "Will you trust me, Dee?"

Dee took one final look at Aquatis. His eyes seemed glued there.

"You can still read my mind if you want," Scully reminded him.

"No, I don't need to read your mind. You can't read mine, so it wouldn't be fair, would it?" Dee said.

"Okay, then. We leave this place, and Aquatis stays. Agreed?" Scully asked.

"Okay. We leave him," Dee agreed.

Ethan looked up as Dee and Scully walked out of the hut. He was glad they hadn't been very long. Lorna kept shuffling around behind him and Ethan worried she would soon pass out. She looked flushed and sweaty—not a good sign. Scully went to the Sapoquate he had been talking to before and said something that Ethan couldn't hear.

"Can you hear them?" Lorna asked. Her voice sounded strained.

"Yes," Dennis said. "He's telling the Sapoquate that they've concluded any business they had with Aquatis. The Sapoquate wants to know what the business was. Scully's telling him that Aquatis owed them money and that he won't hold the camp responsible. He just wants to leave peacefully. The Sapoquate says that's fine, and they will lead us out of the village. But first another villager wants to talk to us about a trade."

"Trade?" Ethan remarked. Scully and Dee were led back to the rest of them, and a villager came out with a human male, a rope was around his neck. He looked badly beaten and ill. Ethan guessed him to be sixteen or seventeen.

"He would like to know if you would be willing to trade one of your horses for this human," Said their interpreter.

"Which horse?" Scully asked quickly, knowing they couldn't afford to give up any of the horses. Losing one would mean some would have to walk. It would slow them down tremendously.

"He favors the black horse," the Sapoquate said.

"What if I offer something better?" Dennis said.

133

"What do you have to offer? The sword? The pouch of powder?" The Sapoquate chuckled at his jokes.

"This," Dennis fumbled in his front pocket and pulled out the white dragon gem. He didn't know how to use it, though, or give the Sapoquates a demonstration.

"A rock?"

"A Royal Dragon Gem, taken from one of their very own maidens. This is a healing gem. You can heal injuries with it. It is of greater value than a horse," Dennis said.

The Sapoquates seemed interested. The boy looked at them with dull eyes; he looked like he was dying. They had to save him; Ethan hoped they could.

The Sapoquate took the gem. He looked at it skeptically. Then he turned to the Sapoquate with the human and spoke in their native tongue. The other Sapoquate took the gem. The Sapoquate looked at Dennis.

"Show us how to use it, and we will accept your deal. He has a cut on his hand; use the stone to heal it, show him how to do it, and the child is yours," the Sapoquate said. Dennis hesitated, not sure how to proceed. Scully had a pained look on his face; he didn't know what to do either. The silence dragged on.

"I'll show you," Dominique said, realizing no one knew what to do. Ethan wondered what the simple potato farmer hoped to accomplish.

"Very well, untie him and come forward," the Sapoquate told him. Dominique looked at the ill child as he passed him, then took the white gem from the Sapoquate. He placed the gem gently on the Sapoquate's palm, where the injury was. Then he blew gently on the gem. The Sapoquate's eyes grew wide in amazement. He picked up the gem and started talking excitedly. A small crowd had formed, and they all started cheering. One took the gem and tried it. Sure enough, when the Sapoquates blew on it, it worked its magic and healed whatever injury the Sapoquate had. The Sapoquate with the boy took the gem back with a few sharp words. Then he handed the boy's leash to Dominique.

"He is satisfied with the trade. Allow us to blindfold you once more, and we will lead you a safe distance from the camp, where you will be freed," the Sapoquate said.

"Thanks," Scully said as he and Dee allowed themselves to be tied once more.

Dennis blinked in the bright sunlight as the blindfold was removed. He didn't pay attention to where the Sapoquates had left them; he just wanted to find Dominique. The Sapoquates quietly disappeared into the trees overhead. Dennis glanced around quickly, they were at the edge of the swamp. There were thick trees to one side, and a golden meadow stretched out ahead of them.

"Dominique!" Dennis cried. He hurried past the others and threw his arms around the farmer. "How did you know how to use the gem?"

"I learned it in school. I come from a very religious family; I know all about the dragons. Did none of you know how to use it?" Dominique asked, puzzled.

"Not a one of us," Scully said.

"I am in your debt, Dominique. Anything you need, just ask," Dennis said with a smile.

"It's the boy who needs us now. How is he Lorna?" Dominique asked.

They had put him on the Friesian to travel; he was too weak to walk on his own. Rick and Lorna pulled him down. His skin was clammy and green.

"There's a White Dragon Village not far from here. If we move quickly, we should be able to reach it by sunset," Scully said. The black and white dog, who had been very calm during the Sapoquate adventure, perked up as Dominique pulled some jerky from Lorna's pack. He intended to give it to the boy, but gave a slice to the dog, as well. Dennis was hungry, too; he couldn't wait until they reached the village. A home-cooked meal would be great.

"Dee, why don't you see if you can help the kid?" Scully said as he led the way through the knee-high grass. "We'll have to take turns riding the horses for a while; they're tired."

"Dennis and I are good to walk," Rick said.

"Is that what I am now? The medic?" Dee asked.

Lorna climbed onto her horse. Her ankles swollen, she would have to ride the rest of the trip. Ethan looked tired, as well. Dennis thought he had probably lived a pampered life. He could tell Ethan wanted to get on one of the horses, but was hesitating.

"Dee, the boy needs help. You can help him, so why don't you?" Scully said, as kindly as he could. Dennis was starting to like him.

"Get on the horse, Ethan; I'll lead him. You need to get some rest," Dennis said, boosting the young man onto the large work horse. Ethan nodded his thanks. Dennis took the reins and followed Lorna.

Dee still hadn't helped the kid, who Dominique and Rick were helping to stand. Scully walked over to them. He glared at Dee, but said nothing. He looked instead at Dominique.

"Climb on my horse, Dominique. We'll put the boy on your other draft," he said. Dominique nodded and allowed Scully to boost him up onto the young mare. Then Scully pulled on the reins and left Rick, Dee, and the boy alone—the other draft horse standing nearby.

"Fine. But if anyone starts calling me a cleric, I'm not going to be pleasant," Dee stammered. He put his hands on the boy's face and tilted his head so he could look him in the eye. Rick helped steady the boy.

"What's your name?" Dee asked.

"Shia," the boy said weakly.

"Well, Shia, this might hurt a bit, but you're going to feel a lot better. Do you know who I am?" Dee asked. The boy shook his head.

"Hold up," Scully called to Lorna. "We don't want to leave them behind."

Dennis stopped walking and brought the mighty horse to a halt. He watched Dee talking to the boy.

"I'm Dee, as in Decompose. Have you heard of me?" Dee asked. The boy got a terrified look in his eyes and nodded his head.

"Well, that's good. Those stories are true, every last one of them. But I'm not going to kill you; I'm going to make you better. Are you ready?" Dee asked.

The boy had no choice, so he nodded. Dee's eyes glowed red, as if crimson light bulbs had just been turned on inside his head. Shia's eyes glowed red for a moment, then the boy started to scream; it was a painful sound. Dennis covered his ears. The boy would have fallen to his knees if Rick hadn't been holding him. But the sound hurt his ears, too, and Rick finally let go, covering his ears. Dee caught the boy and let him bend down. The boy's scream became muffled and a green, chunky slime erupted from his mouth. Dennis watched in amazement: the kid had thrown up at least two gallons of the slime. Then Dee pulled him away from the puddle, his eyes no longer glowing.

Scully walked back over and looked at the slime. Curious, Dennis gave the reins to Ethan. He kept a safe distance from the puddle. Mouse-sized tadpoles were flopping around in the goo.

"Larva," Rick said solemnly.

"Larva?" Scully asked.

"More like tadpoles, but Sapoquates refer to them as larva. They raise their young in an inner bowel until they reach a human-like form," Dennis explained.

"How did they get inside him?" Scully asked, disgusted.

"Someone must have raped him," Rick said matter-of-factly.

"Sapoquates can breed with humans?" Scully asked.

"No, but a human can act as host to Sapoquate larva. He was probably raped by a female Sapoquate, and she laid the eggs inside him. Then a male Sapoquate did the same thing and fertilized the eggs," Rick explained.

Scully looked as if he were about to throw up. "Why would they give us a human boy with their children inside him?" Scully asked, trying not to be sick.

"My guess is that they didn't know they were inside him. I doubt the larva were planted on purpose," Rick said. Scully looked back at the boy.

"Well, I didn't think you wanted me to leave those in him. He wasn't built for that kind of thing. He would have died," Dee said.

Scully looked sternly at the boy. "Lorna, light the larva on fire. Dee, can you get inside the boy's mind, make him forget about what happened to him at the Sapoquate camp?" Scully asked.

"What are you talking about?" Dee asked, puzzled.

"If he was raped by a Sapoquate, I don't think it's something he wants to remember," Scully snapped.

"What?" Shia spoke up. "What kind of wak is that? I didn't have sex with any of them."

"What?" Scully asked, now it was his turn to be puzzled. "Rick, I thought you said he was raped."

"He was," Rick repeated.

"I think this is a language problem," Dennis decided. "Maybe our definition of rape isn't quite right. He was unintentionally impregnated."

"Wait, wait," Rick interrupted. "Do you know how a Sapoquate reproduces? It can be as simple as covering another's mouth. The spores on their hands go into their mouths and reach the stomach, where they lie until fertilized, then they grow."

"Or touching his food before he eats it," Dennis finished. "There was probably very little physical contact."

"Dude, that is wak," Shia said. Everyone looked at him. He was using words they didn't understand.

"Fine, but next time, be a little more clear on matters like this. You have no idea what I was picturing," Scully told them. "Now let's get moving. I still want to reach that village before dark."

"You hear that, Dennis?" Rick asked. Dennis listened, he could hear something, all right. It was the sound of wings, large wings, the kind only found on dragons. But these wings didn't sound like any he had heard before. There was something different about them.

"Dragons?" Dennis asked.

"Just one, I think. A big one," Rick agreed.

"Dragons?" Scully asked. They all looked to the sky, searching for the dragon. It didn't take long before Dennis spotted it. He pointed so the others would know where to search.

"What color is it?" Dee asked.

"Too soon to tell. Why?" Dennis asked.

"Well, depending on what color of dragon it is, I'll know how to fight it. Red ones are easy; they just blow fire. You can hit them just about anywhere, so long as you avoid the fire. White ones are a little tricky because they're covered in spikes. It's harder to reach their bodies, but they don't have any real powers. They can heal things, but they can't heal themselves. Fire works good to take care of them. Black dragons are pushovers; their only defense is invisibility—once you see them, it's easy to kill them. Silver dragons are covered in armored plates, impossible to penetrate. Fire won't even hurt them. They're only vulnerable on their soft underbellies. You just have to get under them— the tricky part is avoiding their claws and teeth," Dee explained as they watched the speck in the sky get larger.

"What about gold dragons?" Rick asked.

"There's only one," Scully corrected.

"I don't know. I've never fought him," Dee said calmly.

"The Gold Dragon is a very peaceful dragon; he doesn't fight. In school, we were taught that he just sits around and makes gold all day. The Queen wouldn't send him," Dominique said.

Twilight of One: The Plague of Decompose

"She can't send him," Dee said, staring at the sky. "When I was on that island, I could touch the minds of all the dragons, except his. All that gold on his body blocks telepathy. I'm guessing the Queen is the same way. Her powers work the way mine do. If I can't control him, neither can she."

"Explains why there's only one of him. Why would she want more dragons she can't control?" Rick deduced.

"Why would the Gold Dragon come after us?" Dennis asked.

"I don't know, why do you ask?" Dominique asked.

"Because that looks like a gold dragon—or a flying sheepdog," Dennis said.

"What should we do?" Rick asked.

"If the Queen's not controlling him, we should find out what he wants," Scully decided. He looked around; no one objected.

Dennis watched as the beast descended. He didn't look hostile. His body was covered in long strands of hair. He landed, his feet crushing the golden grass. He stood on all four legs and had long ears. His golden hairs moved oddly, though. The wind was blowing from the north, but his hair didn't move with the breeze. Dennis stared. Some moved in one direction, others a different way. And the hairs were longer than they appeared. They reminded Dennis of a swarm of snakes weaving around each other.

Scully motioned for everyone to get behind him as he stepped forward to face the beast. The dragon's golden eyes looked at him. Pure gold eyes with a little black dot. They looked intelligent. The hair parted perfectly around his eyes so he could see. The dragon towered above them, the size of a two-story house. But Dennis didn't worry; Dee was that size when he morphed into Decompose.

"Gold Dragon, to what do we owe the honor of your presence?" Scully asked. The dragon cocked an eyebrow, then lowered his head to look Scully in the eye.

"You are familiar to me," the great beast said in a grandfather's voice. Scully smiled at the dragon and said nothing. The dragon searched the group. Finally, his eyes fell upon Dee.

"The great Decompose. The Queen is looking for you," the Gold Dragon said.

"I know," Dee responded.

"Has she sent you to retrieve him?" Scully asked.

"I have come of my own accord. You threaten everything for which we dragons have strived. Peace—this world has experienced a level of peace humans never reached on their own. You threaten to take it all away. I can't let that happen, Decompose," the dragon said.

"Peace?" Lorna exclaimed. Her temper showed for the first time in days. "What part of this existence that you dragons have created do you consider peace? The cult you call religion? The kidnapping and forced slavery of young women? The use of cannibals to keep humans reliant on dragons?"

"I would not be so quick to complain. Judging by your size, I assume that life has been good to you," the dragon said sweetly. Lorna fumed at his mockery. She wanted to kill him right then and there, but Scully shook his head and she restrained herself, although it was difficult.

"What do you want?" Dee asked.

"I want to put an end to this before more blood is shed. Come peacefully with me, back to the island. Let us put you somewhere safe, where you can't hurt anyone ever again," the Gold Dragon said.

"He hasn't hurt anyone this time," Lorna snapped. "You're just upset because all your cannibals are gone. You don't have any leverage over the humans now."

"That leverage kept peace. What do you say, Decompose?"

"I say no. This way of life is over," Dee said with a hint of anger in his voice. "I will slay as many dragons as I must to end the slavery of humanity and put things back the way they were."

"The way they were before you came along? This is all your doing, Decompose. All you can do is make things worse."

"I can fix this. And you and your Queen can't stop me," Dee said coldly.

"You can't fight the Queen, Decompose. Her body is covered in those beautiful gems that make you all sleepy. And me—well, you can fight me if you like. But you can't win," the dragon boasted.

Dee's eyes started to glow red; Dennis couldn't tell if it was because he was mad or because he wanted to accept the challenge. Dee morphed into Decompose, giving off a revolting odor. He smelled like a rotting compost pile. Decompose was a fitting name.

Dee wasted no time. He lunged at the dragon. The Gold Dragon responded with a speed no sheepdog could have equaled. The long strands of hair perked up, shooting straight up in the air, exposing the dragon for what he truly was, a scaled reptile, just like the other dragons. The hairs ran along the top of his back, the length of his body, from the top of his head to the tip of his tail. When he was relaxed, they covered his body all the way to his feet. But now, preparing to fight, they swirled above his body, like thousands of trained snakes. His scales glimmered. He was covered in golden plates of metal, and they glared in the sun, hurting Dennis's eyes. His snout, once as cute as a puppy's, now resembled an alligator's, with rows of tiny needle-like teeth. He reared and on the tips of his fingers were long golden nails. The dragon dodged Dee's attack. It was like watching a bear try to catch a dragonfly.

Dee skidded to a stop, and the dragon landed next to him. The long hairs grew longer as they swarmed above the dragon. Dennis couldn't breathe, he just stood and watched, much like the others. Even Dominique seemed amazed.

The dragon opened his jaws, exposing shiny golden teeth. His chest heaved, but this dragon didn't blow fire—he blew gold. Before Dee could recover, the dragon shot yard-long golden sticks at Dee. The first bombardment hit him in the skull. Dee batted at them, as if he were being attacked by bees. The dragon puffed again, and this time shot the sticks at Dee's feet, pinning him to the ground. Dee squirmed, but it was no use. He was stuck.

Scully snapped into action. "Scatter!" he shouted. None of them stood a chance against the dragon. Dennis didn't hesitate. He smacked the rear end of Ethan's horse, and Scully did the same to Dominique's. The horses fled in opposite directions. Dennis turned back to the woods. It was a distance away, but it was the safest place he could think of. The dragon was too big to fit between the trees, and all those golden strands would get tangled in the branches, whether he could move them at will or not. Lorna shouted to her horse, and they dashed off in another direction. Dennis's lungs burned as he ran towards the woods. He had to make it.

"How about we take along a few of your friends, as collateral—just to make sure you don't try anything stupid," the Gold Dragon said. He heard Dee roar with fury, then he tripped, falling into the golden grass. Dennis rolled over and stayed very still. The grass would hide him unless the dragon was right on top of him. He parted the grass a little and peered through. Dee had morphed back into human form, which freed him from the golden stakes. The Gold Dragon noticed and tossed a red gem at him.

"I'll take care of this, Dee. You get some sleep," the dragon said with a grin. He went up to Dee's limp form and picked him up with his golden hairs, rolling him up so that he looked like a little hot dog in a bun. The Gold Dragon kicked into the air and flew over the field of grass. Dennis watched him dive and pluck someone up with his long hair. Dennis squinted, moving the grass gently so he could see who the dragon had caught. It was Rick, rolled up just like Dee. Dennis saw him squirming, but with his arms pinned to his sides, there was nothing Rick could do to free himself. Dennis considered attacking; he couldn't let the dragon kidnap his only friend. The dragon grabbed someone else, tossing him into the air with his forearm and catching him with his hairs on the man's descent. It was Ethan. He was screaming like a little girl; the sound hurt Dennis's ears. The dragon dove down one more time and plucked another person from atop a horse. It was Dominique. He cried in alarm, then fell silent.

Then the dragon rose high into the air, flying off in the same direction he had come from. Ethan's screams slowly lessened as the dragon turned into nothing more than a speck on the horizon. They were gone. Dennis stood up with his mouth dry and his breath coming in little gasps. The dragons had won. They had all thought Dee was invincible, impossible to beat, but now they had been proven wrong.

"Dennis! Dennis!" Scully shouted. Dennis turned and saw him running through the grass, chasing after his appaloosa mare. "Help me gather up the horses, we have to get moving!"

Dennis didn't move, he couldn't think, he was in shock. Then Lorna was next to him, still atop her black stallion. She looked down at him.

"Ethan is my cousin. I intend to get him back. I assume you feel the same way about your friend Rick," Lorna said. Lorna was used to getting her way. He had a feeling she would do whatever was necessary to accomplish just that. Dennis couldn't speak, but he nodded.

"Then help us gather the horses; we have a lot of work to do."

Part IV

Dragon Island

He heard the knocking on the door, distant, as if it was very far away. *Maybe it's not real, maybe it's all in my head.* He had started to fall back to sleep when he heard the knocking again. Jonathan Wescott opened his eyes and looked at the ceiling, in a room clouded with gray smoke from incense. He watched the swirls drift about and took a deep breath of scented air. Forgetting why he had awoken in the first place, he closed his eyes. Then he heard the knock on the door again. Jonathan opened his brown eyes, the irises nearly as dark as his pupils. He sat upright and the room seemed to swirl, much like the clouds dancing above him. He put his hands on his forehead and ran his fingers through his dark brown hair. It fell back onto his shoulders. He considered cutting some of it off; a man should not have hair that long, he recalled his mother saying. Again he heard the knock. Jonathan finally stood, the room swimming once again. Jonathan swayed for a moment before he managed to get his balance.

"Must have drunk a bit too much rum last night," he muttered. He glanced at his bare feet and made sure he was wearing pants and a shirt before making his way to the door. Pieces of literature and partially eaten food cluttered his path. He wiped the back of his hand across his greasy face and wondered if he should stop at the restroom and wash up a bit. He heard the knocking again. Whoever was at the door had been very patient thus far; he shouldn't keep them waiting any longer. Jonathan put his right hand on the door and twisted the knob, unlocking the bolt with his other hand. He pulled the door inwards and blinked his eyes at the light that streaked in from the streetlights. Or was that moonlight? Jonathan ignored the man standing on his porch and instead looked at the night sky, looking for the moon.

"Hello?" the man greeted him, but it sounded more a question than a greeting. Jonathan lowered his gaze and rested his eyes upon the tall man on his porch. He looked Asian, but his voice betrayed an Australian accent. Jonathan would have found such a combination odd, if it wasn't for the fact that his girlfriend had the same heritage. He found it amusing to meet another person of the same mixture.

"Well, a hello plus question mark to you, too, my dear stranger," Jonathan said with a slight bow, tipping an imaginary hat with his right hand. The Asian man didn't seem amused. He looked at Jonathan without breaking a smile.

"Is Melanie here?" the man asked seriously.

"Well that depends; I'm not keen on talking to strangers who show up asking me questionable hellos on my porch," Jonathan said, trying to imitate his seriousness.

The man looked as if he expected Jonathan to say more. The two looked at each other for what seemed, to Jonathan, like hours. His eyes drifted to the bottom of the porch steps, where three other people stood. One was a fat woman, another a man wearing sunglasses—even though it was dark outside—and the third was a skinny teenage boy. What an odd bunch to come visiting Melanie at this time of day.

"Let me repeat the question." Jonathan told the stranger. "How do you know my dear Melanie?"

"She's my sister," the man said flatly. Jonathan's eyes widened, and he took an exaggerated gasp. He clasped his hand over his heart as though he were having a heart attack.

"*The* Mak Scully? You are *the* Mak Scully? One and only sibling to my dear lover, Melanie? I never thought the day would come that I would meet such prestige—such—such—well, such a presence—that I'm at a loss for words," Jonathan rambled with exaggerated joy.

"Lover? What happened to Freddy?" Scully asked.

"Well my dear Scully, I'm afraid Freddy is a little deaddy, if you know what I mean. But he's still around if you want to say 'ello. Ha-ha—we had the poor chap cremated; Melanie couldn't bear to part with him."

"We?" Scully questioned.

"Yes, we—as in Melanie and I. We used to have the most wonderful threesomes I've ever experienced. But now Melanie's melons are all mine! Ha!" Jonathan exclaimed with a chuckle. No one seemed amused by his cheerful banter. "But we let Freddy watch sometimes, for old times' sake."

"Thank you," Scully interrupted. "But I don't think any of us care to hear about that."

"Still protective of your little sister after all these years? She's told me quite a bit about you as well. Quite the ladies' man, aren't you? Ha-ha," Jonathan joked. Again, the humor was lost on his crowd.

"Is Melanie here?" Scully asked again.

"Well now that depends," Jonathan told him, trying to keep a straight face.

"I am no stranger; I believe we have already completed our introductions," Scully said.

"I have not introduced myself to you, so technically, we are still strangers. Not to mention these ther tthr three—there we go—three—count 'em—one, two, three," Jonathan counted on his fingers and held them up for Scully to see. "The *three* strangers you have brought with you."

There was a brief flash of reflected light, then Jonathan felt cold hard steel against his neck. He looked down with his eyes and saw the handle of a blade in Scully's grip.

"I need not know your name. I'll just call you Freddy the second, since you are twice as annoying as he was. I don't think it really matters who my friends are now does it?" Scully said grimly.

"Well, that depends," Jonathan began, then he felt the blade cut easily into his flesh; he winced and closed his eyes, "on whether that friend of yours with the shades is hiding iridescent Zalite eyes."

"And if he is?" Scully asked. Jonathan opened his eyes and peered at the Zalite.

"I'd never refuse a guest from another galaxy," Jonathan finished with a smile.

Rick was awakened by a cold splash of water upon his face. He opened his mouth to keep from inhaling water through his nose and gasped. The last thing he remembered was the suffocating pressure of the golden strands of hair. He had been kidnapped. The memory rushed back and his eyes filled with hate as he opened them. Instinctively, he tried to move, but he was immobile. His hands and ankles were chained to a wall behind him. He looked at the chains on his wrists, then down to the ones on his feet. It wasn't that uncomfortable, he'd been in worse. His wrists were tied together then looped through a metal hoop in the wall. But the walls were red and powdery, so he gave the chain a slight tug. The stake holding the hoop in place began to slide forward. He paused when he heard Ethan scream. Looking to his right, he saw Ethan and Dominique bound in the same fashion as he.

A woman in baggy silver pants and matching halter top was tossing buckets of water on them. Dominique was already awake, and Ethan thrashed against his chains as water trickled down his back. The woman giggled playfully. She sat the gray bucket down and picked up her silver staff. She had matching silver hair and boots; Rick was starting to see a pattern with the maidens.

"Where's my daughter?" Dominique asked.

"Daughter?" the silver woman asked.

"Molina, you took her."

"Oh, she died. Couldn't cut it as a maiden," the woman said with a sly grin.

"Why are you doing this?" Ethan asked, his voice as high as a child's.

"The Queen wants to keep you around for leverage," the woman said.

"Is that all we are?" Rick asked. The woman looked at him and smiled.

"I would think you'd be happy to be so important," a familiar voice said. Rick turned and saw the cat-like Darlene stand. She had been kneeling next to an opening in the rock. Six thin red bars walled off the cavern. It was only six feet wide—maybe four feet tall. The floor was level with the ground, and on the other side, Rick saw Dee's unconscious form. He had one of the red gems tied around his neck.

"So you survived," Rick told her, not really surprised.

"So I did. Don't you wish you'd killed me when you'd had the chance?" she asked. "Vivian, leave us. I want to speak to the prisoners alone."

The Silver Dragon's maiden departed the room, taking her staff with her. Darlene placed her staff against the wall and walked up to him. She stood only inches away. He remembered how easily he had loosened the chains.

"You're happy to see me again. Missed me, didn't you?" Rick mocked.

She smiled, a menacing grin. He knew what she was going to do; he had seen other human females do the same thing. Concentrating, he flared the sharp, needle-covered flesh covering his testicles between his legs. As he had expected, she kicked, intending to knee him in the groin. Her tender flesh hit the spikes. Like Velcro, they held her knee in place. Her eyes widened in surprise, and she tried to pull away. The sensation was oddly arousing, which caused his spikes to fasten themselves more securely in her flesh.

"What the—" Darlene began, but before she could finish, Rick relaxed, the spikes let go, and she stumbled backwards, clutching her knee in pain. She was wearing another belt of gems, so the tiny punctures in her knee quickly healed. She looked at her knee, confused. After testing it, she picked up her staff.

"Did the kitty cat get hurt?" Rick asked. She swung her staff at him, aiming for his forehead. This time, the tiny quills clutched her staff, making it stick to his forehead. She tugged on it, then let go, not sure what to do. He retracted the spikes, and it fell to the floor. He put his foot on it, holding it in place. She twisted her fingers and an invisible force tugged on the staff, but she couldn't free it.

"Come on, kitty cat; come get your stick," Rick taunted. She had proven what he wanted to know. He had put her in danger, and no one had come to help her. The Queen couldn't see through her eyes. If something were to happen to Darlene, it would be a while before someone found out.

"Are you sure taunting her is something you should be doing?" Ethan asked. "We are her prisoners, at her mercy. Darlene, I want it noted that I disapprove of his actions. I don't think I should be held accountable for what he's doing. I was an ally to the dragons once, remember? Doesn't that earn me some sort of leniency?"

"Shut up, Ethan," Darlene snapped.

"Yes, Ethan, shut up," Rick mocked. That did it. She moved forward, fast, but not faster than him. He pulled forward, and the chains holding his hands to the wall broke free. He swooped down as she reached for the staff and wrapped his chains around her neck. Then he remembered the belt. He pressed her against the cave wall and pressed his knee against her waist, on the belt. His little spikes sprang up on his knee and caught it. He yanked the belt off, then relaxed and let it drop to the ground. He slammed her head against the wall. She went limp.

Rick waited a few moments, keeping the chains tight. Then he dropped her to the ground, making sure she was a fair distance from the belt.

"I can't believe you did that," Ethan gasped.

"That was great," Dominique said as Rick took the keys from Darlene and unlocked his chains. He shook his wrists as the chains fell away, then he freed Dominique.

"That was insane," Ethan snapped. "We should have waited for Scully and the others to rescue us."

"I'm not much for playing the damsel in distress," Rick said as he unlocked Ethan's chains.

"I'm not much for getting myself killed, and that's what's going to happen. What do you plan on doing next? Didn't think that far ahead, did you?"

Rick went to the bars separating them from Dee. He kicked at the bars, and they crumbled as easily as the chains had pulled from the walls. This was too easy. If Rick didn't know the dragons didn't realize how strong a Zalite was, he would have figured this was all a trap.

"What is your plan?" Dominique asked. Ethan's paranoia was spreading.

He pulled Dee from the crevice and yanked the red stone from around his neck. He slung him over one shoulder, hoping he would wake soon.

"We get out of this room. Ethan, you've been here before. Do you know where we are?" Rick asked.

"No, no, I do not. These caves are like a maze. I have no idea where we are. We'll be lost in here forever," Ethan complained.

"We could use her as a guide," Rick suggested.

"No we can't! We can't control her!" Ethan exclaimed.

"Then we go forward blindly. Maybe we'll get lucky," Rick decided.

"We can't leave this room," Ethan said. "You have to have a dragon gem to get from room to room. We don't have any."

"Will those on her belt work?" Rick asked. Ethan's jaw dropped. Dominique bent down and pulled the five gems off. He handed a gold one to Ethan, kept a black one for himself, tucked the white one and a red one in his pocket, and handed the silver to Rick.

"So now what? You're just going to blindly walk through the wall?" Ethan said dryly.

"Sure. Which way should we go?" Rick asked.

"This is insane. This place is one giant maze. We'll get lost."

"Seeing as how we don't know where we are, I'd say we're already lost, so there's no harm in getting more lost," Rick surmised. Ethan looked at him, speechless.

Rick went opposite the direction the silver maiden had gone. A passageway opened, exposing a black cave. He moved forward cautiously, carrying Dee with him. He stepped through and found the cave deserted. Dominique followed and so did Ethan, muttering under his breath.

"It's a hallway," Dominique pointed out. It dead ended to one side and continued in the other direction. Rick couldn't see how far the hallway went; it curved.

"I don't believe it," Ethan said, astonished.

"What?" Rick asked.

"I know where we are," Ethan said, surprised at himself. He turned to the dead end and a passageway opened, and Ethan looked back as sunlight shone into the black cave.

Things hadn't changed much from what Scully remembered. The house reeked of incense, so thick Scully couldn't see across the room. He heard Dennis cough as they entered and guessed the scents had to be torture to his sensitive nose.

"My name's Jonathan Wescott, by the by," the skinny man with overgrown hair told him. He smiled, showing various crooked teeth. Scully guessed the man to be about five-ten, if you didn't count the crazy hair.

"Shia Belmont," Shia said and reached to shake his hand. Jonathan seemed confused by the friendly gesture and paused awkwardly before he took the hand and gave it a brief shake.

"Dennis," Dennis managed to say between muffled coughs. He waved his hand at the young man. Jonathan returned the gesture with a nod of his head.

"And the lady?" Jonathan said with a forced smile.

Scully searched the room—it likely had once been a living room. Now it was just a garbage bin. "That would be Lorna McPowin," Scully said, without bothering to look at the man.

"Do you have a bathroom?" Lorna asked.

"Of course, my dear, although I fear it may not be large enough for you," Jonathan joked.

Everyone fell silent. Even Dennis stopped coughing. Scully couldn't read Lorna's expression through the smoke.

"I was referring to your prestigious stature as a McPowin."

"You're just loads of laughs, aren't you?" Lorna asked.

"Why, my dear, I have yet to begin," Jonathan countered. "You'll find the bathroom down the hall, third door on your right."

"And where would I find my dear sister?" Scully, asked mocking the man's way of speaking.

"She—she will most likely be found passed out under some pile of garbage," Jonathan said. Scully looked at him, expecting him to break into laughter. But he was serious. The two of them stared at each other.

"So should we start digging?" Shia asked, trying to keep a straight face.

"Ha, and have her slice off your head when you wake her? Melanie is not a woman to contend with, no, sir. We best wait her out. She'll wake up sooner or later and come staggering out looking for food or another drink. 'Til then, make yourselves at home. Take a bath; get some sleep. You all rather stink. I'd think you'd spent the whole day trouncing around in the swamp if I didn't know better."

"We don't have that kind of time," Scully said.

"I was afraid you'd say that. Well, hmmm," Jonathan murmured. His eyes glazed over as he stood there, staring at nothing. He was crazier than Freddy. At least Freddy had been somewhat with it when he was sober. Scully had a feeling this behavior was normal for Jonathan.

"I can't stay in here. I'm going back to the stables and staying with the horses and dog tonight," Dennis said with a cracked voice.

"We aren't staying here long."

"It'll take you hours to get an answer out of that man," Dennis said. He turned and dashed out onto the porch. The sound of the door slamming startled Jonathan awake. He blinked.

"Oh, dear, leaving already? But you haven't seen your sister," Jonathan mumbled.

"Do you care if I search your house for her?" Scully asked.

"House search? Well, that depends," Jonathan began.

"Shia, go outside and find Dennis; get him back here. Wait on the porch if he can't come inside," Scully ordered. Then he turned to the narrow hallway without waiting for permission from Jonathan.

"Now, hold up, I don't want you tripping on some heirloom," Jonathan called after him. Scully forced the first door open. It was a bathroom, with a toilet, shower, and sink.

"Why didn't you have Lorna use this bathroom? Why send her all the way to end of the hall?" Scully asked, irritated.

"This is the *men's* bathroom; I couldn't very well have a lady use it, now could I?" Jonathan said, equally annoyed at having to answer such a silly question. Scully ignored him and threw open the door on the other side of the hall. It was a storage closet, full of linens and bed sheets. Scully moved farther down the hall and forced open another door, this time finding what seemed to be a bedroom. He kicked some clothes out of his way as he entered. Jonathan followed close behind.

There she was, lying half-naked on the bed. It wasn't really a bed—just a few mattresses stacked on top of each other and some sheets tossed across. She didn't even have a pillow. Scully found a light switch and turned it on. The grimy room was cast into dim light, the bulb covered in dust. Scully crossed the room and kicked the mattresses, but the Asian woman didn't stir. She lay face down, her arms sprawled around her.

"Melanie!" Scully shouted. The woman groaned, and Jonathan grabbed his own head in animated pain. Scully kicked the bed again. "Wake up!"

"Stop shouting; that's really not a good idea," Jonathan started. Melanie moved swiftly. She pulled a samurai sword from under the sheets, then Scully felt it against his neck. He could have blocked or dodged it, but he didn't see the point. She wasn't out to kill him, just warn him.

She was on the mattresses, on her knees, her petite figure barely reaching his shoulders. Her brown eyes grew large as she recognized him. Scully tried to ignore the fact that the sheet had fallen away and her breasts were exposed.

"Mak?" she said, puzzled, and Scully fought to restrain himself. He didn't get along well with his sister. "I never thought I'd see you again. But then again, when you live as long as we do, I suppose it's unlikely. It's a small world, you know, or at least that's what Mother always said. Wasn't it? I doubt you're here by chance. You want something, don't you?"

She dropped the blade from his neck and plucked a shirt from the floor.

"Melanie, I need to use your mirror," Scully said softly. She looked at him, her five-foot-six figure tiny next to him. Scully found it hard to believe she was the same height as Lorna. Lorna seemed so much bigger.

"My mirror?" she frowned. "I don't have it anymore. The dragons took all the mirrors. If you want to use one, you'll just have to go to the temple like everyone else. No one has full length mirrors of their own anymore—you know that. I know you like looking in the mirror, but you'll just have to admire that handsome face of yours in a little five-by-five, like everyone else. It just drives you nuts, doesn't it?"

"Melanie, I know you still have the mirror. Don't play games with me. Just let me use it."

"Fine, no games. No. N-O, no. Do you understand that? I know you aren't used to hearing it. But I'm standing up to you, Mak. No, you may not use my mirror. And don't try to bully me. I don't care if you threaten my life. I don't care if I die. I welcome it. I've been alive so long it's fine with me if I die. You'd love to kill your baby sister, wouldn't you? Probably been dreaming of it for a long time. And don't get any ideas of threatening Jonathan, either, although I'm sure you already did. I don't care if you kill him, so don't waste your time. Freddy I loved, but he's gone now. Look, I kept his ashes."

She jumped down from the mattresses and plucked a copper urn from the floor, holding it up for him to see.

"All that's left of my darling Freddy," she sighed, staring into the copper.

"Where is everyone?" Lorna asked from the hallway.

"Dennis couldn't stand the smoke, so he went back to the stables with Shia," Scully said. Lorna was about to say something, but Melanie beat her to it.

"Is this your girlfriend? Jeez, Mak, your tastes have gone downhill. You'll sleep with just about anyone, won't you? You can do better, Mak, this old cow is going to break you. Not going to let her be on top, are you? Or is that your death wish?" Melanie rambled. She always talked too much, and without thinking.

"This is Lorna McPowin. I believe you slept with her father, Jafar, once," Scully said coldly. A flash of awareness crept across Melanie's face, but she held her ground.

"Don't look much like him, do you? Guess he got all the good looks in the family," Melanie continued.

"You ignorant child," Lorna snapped. She flicked her wrist and sent Melanie flying across the room. She crashed into the wall and fell to the floor, pieces of plaster tumbling down after her. The white dust coated her black hair.

"Stupid cow," Melanie growled back. She rose to her feet, sword at the ready.

Scully raised his own sword and blocked Lorna's path.

"No one calls me a cow and lives to talk about it," Lorna growled. Scully was debating if he wanted to let them hash it out when he heard a clatter from the living room.

"Scully!" Dennis cried. "The dragons know we're here. They were at the stables, they found our horses. We have to get out of here. I'm sure they followed us." Dennis appeared in the doorway, his expression flushed. Hank was at his side, barking loudly.

"Shia?" Scully asked.

"Here," Shia said timidly. Scully nodded. Lorna's temper dwindled as she realized the danger they were all in.

"Melanie, we need to use your mirror now," Scully said.

She looked at him harshly. "I already told you no. And get that dog out of here," she growled. The two stared at each other, neither giving an inch.

"I'll make her talk," Lorna growled, pushing at Scully's sword.

"No," Scully said simply. He looked at Jonathan. "Jonathan—can I call you Jonathan?"

The scraggly man seemed to have forgotten he was an active participant in the scene developing around him. He focused his eyes on Scully and blinked, as if surprised Scully was talking to him.

"Sure," Jonathan said. Scully silently thanked him for not rambling about what that question depended on.

"Good, Jonathan, I'm happy to hear that," said Scully, hearing a dragon at the front door. He couldn't tell what it was saying. Jonathan was their only hope. Scully's calm rubbed off on Jonathan. He relaxed a little.

"Can I call you Scully?"

"Sure, mate, that sounds fine. Now how about we go find that mirror?" Scully asked. Jonathan looked at everyone crammed into the little room. Dennis had taken off his sunglasses, and Jonathan's gaze lingered on the man's strange eyes. Scully knew they didn't have this kind of time; the dragons were knocking on the door, shouting. Melanie saw Jonathan looking at her.

"Don't you show him that mirror! You hear me? I'll cut you like a turkey if you show him that mirror, Jonathan!" Melanie screamed.

Jonathan's eyes got big. Scully could almost see the rusty gears in his brain trying to solve the dilemma. He looked at Scully.

"Don't you do it, Jonathan! He's evil!" Melanie screamed. Jonathan turned and left the room. He pushed past Dennis and Shia. Dennis looked at Scully questioningly, but Scully nodded, indicating that they should let him pass. Scully hurried after him, telling Dennis to not let Melanie leave the room. It was hard to keep up over the piles of miscellaneous items in the hall. Scully followed Jonathan into a room filled with large boxes and shelves covered with sheets and dust and watched him go to the corner and pull a sheet off a full length mirror. Jonathan took a few steps back then looked at Scully.

"You're going to Dragon Island, aren't you? To save someone?" Jonathan asked. Scully stepped up to the mirror and touched the reflective surface. "Someone taken as a dragon maiden?"

"No, just some old friends of ours," Scully looked at the young man, who was acting fidgety. "We need dragon gems to pass through this mirror."

"Melanie has some in the urn," Jonathan told him. "Are you taking us with you?"

"I don't seem to have much choice, do I?" Scully said softly.

"I know how to get to Jaff's lab from here," said Ethan as they walked next to the black-rock cliffs. Dee was waking up; Rick was helping him walk, his arm slung around his shoulders. Dominique was on lookout, keeping an eye out for dragons.

"I figure it's safer to travel outside than inside. We'll at least be able to see the dragons coming," Ethan said. Rick looked at the burnt, dead tree on the other side of the moat. Even the water looked black.

"This is where Jaff kept me," Dee mumbled softly. "Right inside these caves. There's an entrance around this corner."

"Seems like a fitting place for a monster to live," Rick agreed. They walked on, concentrating on their footing; the ground was slick.

"Some of the caverns are underground, others above ground. It's really confusing. There are white, gold, red, and silver caves in the

Black Dragon Territory, but they are all underground. The only ones above ground are the black ones. The same thing is true in the other territories. Only the red caves are visible in the Red Dragon Territory, and so on," Ethan explained.

"So we're in the Black Dragon Territory?" Rick asked.

"Yes, the island is split up into five territories. One for each of the Royal Dragons. We walk around this black cave formation up ahead and enter from the other side. We just have to go through that one cavern to reach the lab."

"So you can only enter the black caves from the outside when you're in the Black Dragon Territory. You can't enter through a silver or white cave?" Rick asked.

"That's right. There's actually a white cave between these two black caves, but it's underground. And on this side of the black cave, there should be a silver room, then a gold one," Ethan explained.

"I can see how you thought we'd get lost," Rick commented.

"Yes, well, this is the only part of the island I know. This area and some of the caves in the White Dragon Territory, which is just a little farther ahead."

"To the east," Rick said.

"I don't know. I don't know directions," Ethan said.

"Zalites are good at knowing directions. I'm guessing the shore line is that way, which means we are in the southernmost part of the island."

"If that's true, then the White Dragon Territory would be on the east coast. The Silver Dragon's along the northeast coast, the Red along the northwest, and the Gold to the southwest," Ethan decided.

"Good to know," Rick nodded. "Shall we go in?"

"I suppose. Who wants to go first?" Ethan asked.

"I will," Rick volunteered. "Here, hold Dee."

Jonathan went through the mirror second to last, with Scully quickly behind him. Jonathan had gone to temple only as a child, when his mother had insisted, saying the dragons had saved her life. She had lived through the plague and been a witness to the dragons' salvation. Jonathan had heard of the magical caves in which the dragons lived, but nothing could have prepared him for what he saw.

The cave was made of a red, powdery stone. No windows or doors—just a sealed cavern. It should have been dark, but scattered in the walls were glowing stones that matched the red of the walls, which curved around a perfectly round, red room. He looked at Scully as he entered through the passageway in the wall. He saw a musty storage closet on the other side. Then Scully stepped out and the passageway disappeared. He felt his heart putter faster; it was easy to get claustrophobic.

"Do you know where we are?" Lorna asked. Scully looked at the room.

"It's round. There are only five round rooms on the island. The passageways that lead off the island are only found in these rooms. So, yes, I know where we are, but I don't know where they took Dee," Scully said.

"We won't have much time before the dragons figure out we're here. They were almost ready to bust down that door," Dennis commented.

Jonathan didn't understand the problem. They were on the island, their friends were on the island. Why weren't they moving?

"I can get us to Jaff's lab. It used to be mine. But I don't know if there will be anything there that will help us find them," Scully said.

"You guys didn't plan any further than this?" Shia asked, perplexed. No one had an answer for him. Even the dog seemed ashamed and curled his tail between his legs.

"Are you all witches and warlocks?" Jonathan asked. Melanie had her arms crossed. She looked up sharply when he spoke. "Can't you cast a spell or something to find them?"

"Yeah, exactly. A spell," Shia agreed, looking at Jonathan, grateful for the support.

"I don't know any finder spells," Lorna snapped, annoyed.

"But such a spell does exist?" Shia insisted.

"I'm sure one does, but I don't know any," Scully admitted. Dennis took a deep breath, he didn't have any ideas either. Melanie ignored them.

"What about you, Melanie?" Jonathan asked. She glared at him sharply; Scully noticed.

"Melanie, do you know a finder spell?" Scully asked. She stared at the dusty floor. "You do, don't you?"

"You selfish little brat, people are dying!" Lorna shouted.

"Melanie, we don't have a lot of time. The dragons will kill all of us—you included. I don't care if you have a death wish or not. I don't think anyone here wants to die by the hand of a dragon," Scully said.

"Melanie, he's your brother," Jonathan whispered to her.

"Fine. I'll help," Melanie said sarcastically. She wrung her fingers together and checked to make sure her sword was fastened tightly to her belt. Then she closed her eyes, put her hands out to her sides, and shook them limply. "Have some of that pixy dust on you?"

"Always do," Scully told her. "Although I wish you'd stop calling it that."

"Throw some of it in front of me," Melanie said. Scully reached in his pouch and tossed a handful into the air in front of her. The pinkish dust floated in the air, then began to sink to the ground.

"Dust to dust, ash to ash, show me where these louts' friends are," Melanie said.

"That was uncalled for," Lorna snapped. But she silenced herself as the small particles of pink sand gathered and formed a solid orb. It shot forward, passing through the walls as if they weren't there at all. "Where did it go?"

"I can see the path. You can't because you didn't cast the spell," Melanie told her.

"Well, I'd rather not go that way," Scully said. "That will take us closer to the center of the island, and the Queen's nest is there. If we go a different way, will you still know how to find them?"

"Yeah, sure, Mak. We can go wherever you want," she said, still sarcastic.

"Good, hopefully it will turn out that they are on the other side of the Queen's nest," Scully said. "This way, everyone; there should be a long corridor out here that we can use to cover some ground."

Jonathan fell in behind Melanie and Scully, who took the lead. Scully, Dennis, and Lorna had the only three dragon stones, all of which were white. So Lorna went last, Scully went first, and Dennis was in the middle, falling in behind Jonathan.

Scully led them into a black cavern—a long, narrow hallway. It was just wide enough for a dragon to walk through, although he doubted two could pass each other. In one direction, the passageway opened up to a larger room, but boulders blocked his view so he couldn't tell if there were dragons inside. The tunnel curved, so a dragon could easily appear out of nowhere. According to Scully, there were passageways all over, so it was indeed a dangerous route.

"I think they're down farther this way," Melanie said.

"Let's go; everyone keep quiet and keep an eye out," Scully said as he took Melanie's arm and walked with her down the tunnel. The cave was dark and damp. There were little black stones in the walls giving off light, but it was still dark. Jonathan slipped on the damp floor and almost fell, but Dennis steadied him from behind. Jonathan glanced down; the rocks looked sharp. He was glad Dennis caught him.

❖❖❖

Ethan was amazed at how easy it had been. They were in Jaff's deserted lab. The one white dragon cave they had passed through had been empty. The lab looked just like he remembered, only everything was covered in a thick layer of dust.

"Is there a map somewhere?" Rick asked. "So we can figure out how to navigate?"

"Yeah, that would be nice wouldn't it?" Ethan remarked. He went to the center of the room and put his hands on the table. All the spellbooks were placed neatly on the bookshelves. The vials of potions were labeled and resting on other shelves. The table was empty. He ran his hand across it, taking a layer of dust with it.

"There's still running water," Dominique called from the other room as he washed his face.

"Well, that's good," Rick agreed. Dee sat on the cot, sending a cloud of dust into the air. He was awake, but very quiet.

"There used to be a map carved into this table. Jaff had a spell to show where all the dragons were at any time. He liked to sneak around. I never understood why. I guess it makes sense now that I know about you," Ethan said as he looked at Dee.

"Let's get that thing dusted off and turned on, shall we?" Dominique decided. He came back into the room holding a damp towel. He wiped vigorously at the table.

Ethan turned to the shelves. He blew the dust off and searched for the slip of paper with the activation spell Jaff had hidden amongst them.

"Is there a way to get back to the mainland, off this island?" Rick asked.

"Five passageways lead off the island. They are in the five round rooms. I don't know how to control where you come out, though. The maidens always did that part for us," Ethan explained as he searched the decaying books. Rick and Dominique looked at the freshly cleaned table, and Rick pointed out the five round rooms.

"Where are we?" Rick asked. Ethan stood, clutching a small piece of paper with a few lines of text scribbled on it. The paper was so old it almost crumbled away in his grip. He walked up to the map.

"That's the room we were in. This is the room we are in now," Ethan pointed to a red cavern. The rooms on the map were tinted five different colors, showing the five colors of the Royal Dragons. A rough outline of the dragon territories was shown on the edge of the map, but it was almost impossible to tell where one ended and another began in the crazy labyrinth of underground caverns. The only distinguishable pattern was the oval room in the center, which Ethan pointed out as the Queen's nest. There was a larger oval encircling it, divided into five rooms, each a color of the Royal Dragons. Another oval formed around it, misshapen on the outer edge; there, the colorization of the rooms seemed random. The five round rooms were next, but they seemed thrown into the mix. The rest of the rooms were arranged randomly. There were five larger rooms on the outer edge of the caves. Nests, according to Ethan.

"This big black cave was where they kept Dee," Ethan said.

"I was kept in a nest?" said Dee, speaking for the first time since they entered the lab.

"They didn't have a queen at the time, and they needed to put you in a big room," Ethan explained softly.

"Hurry up and activate this thing. Maybe we can find a maiden and force her to activate one of those passageways so we can get off this island," Rick said.

"All right—here goes," Ethan looked at the slip of paper.

"We'll be able to go outside from here. It might be easier to figure out where the others are from out there," Scully said. Jonathan had managed not to fall, although he noticed Lorna was having difficulty. Hank's claws made little clicks on the stone, and the sound seemed loud in the cavern.

A passageway opened before they reached it. Scully hadn't activated it. A red dragon peered in, sunlight behind him. Scully grabbed Melanie as he dashed to the left. A passageway opened, and Jonathan felt Dennis push him in after them, almost falling on the slippery ground. Dennis grabbed the back of his shirt, practically carrying him through the passageway. He was disoriented for a moment, then he looked around, glad to see everyone had made it.

He fixed his gaze on the scene before him. They were in a huge black cave, surrounded by eggs. Three-foot tall eggs. They spread all over the room, in no pattern he could see. They were different colors, not just the Royal Dragon colors. It seemed odd to have so many colors in the dark cave. Then he heard the sounds—squeaking, chirping, and low guttural sounds. He saw movement. Dragons. There were black dragons walking around, checking the eggs as they hatched. Scully motioned for everyone to get down. Lorna had some difficulty. No one said a word. Shia grabbed the dog to make sure he didn't run off.

Melanie waved her arms around, gathering everyone's attention. Then she pointed across the room, to the other side of the nest. Scully nodded, understanding. He let her lead the way as they began to crawl single file across the room, trying to keep the eggs between them and the nursery dragons.

❖ ❖ ❖

"It worked," Rick exclaimed as the carved wooden map came to life. It turned into a holographic version of itself, covering the table and extending a foot above it. Many different dots of color littered the map.

"What do the dots mean?" Dominique asked. Ethan paused and flipped the little piece of paper over.

"The red are red dragons, silver are silver dragons, gold are—" Ethan began.

"We get it," Rick interrupted. "What are the other colors?"

"The big, purplish-pink one is the Queen," Ethan said. "These orange dots are the dragon maidens, and the blue dots are unidentified. I think it's us."

"But why are there blue dots over here?" Rick asked. The three of them looked over at the six blue dots in the Black Dragon's nest. There were so many Royal Dragon colors in that room they overlapped each other. The blue dots were barely visible.

"That would probably be my rescue team," Ethan said breathlessly.

"You think it's Scully and the others?" Dominique asked.

"Why are they in one of the nests?" Rick asked. "That's like walking into a death trap."

Dee walked over to the map. He looked at it carefully.

Twilight of One: The Plague of Decompose

"Where were they holding us? You left Darlene there, right?" Dee asked.

"Here," Ethan pointed. There was a solitary orange dot in the room.

"Then the dragons don't know we escaped," Dee surmised. They were all silent.

"I don't think they know the others are here either," Dominique commented. The blue dots were arranged in a neat row. The dragon dots seemed unaffected.

Being back in the dragon caves was not pleasant, but Scully was dealing with it. Being with his sister again, back on the island that had almost destroyed him, it was a lot to handle. He tried to concentrate on the task at hand and not think about it. Melanie led him across the room, darting behind eggs as she went. Scully did his best to stay close and avoid the dragons.

He counted six adult black dragons tending the eggs. All kinds of dragons were being born. Melanie paused as a hatchling darted past her. Scully saw a flash of red, then the turkey-sized dragon's head peered around an unhatched egg, playing peek-a-boo with Melanie. She froze, uncertain. The dragon chirped at her, then dashed off. She took a deep breath and moved forward. Scully hurried across an opening between the eggs and put his back against one. He looked back at the others.

He couldn't see Lorna or Shia anymore; they were lost in the abundance of eggs. Jonathan was doing his best to keep up; he was only a few yards behind, Dennis right on his tail. A white dragon jumped on top of an egg, directly above Jonathan. It gave a shrill cry. Scully hugged his egg and peered around it, where the adult dragons were gathered. They looked at the infant. Then one moved in their direction. Scully motioned for his companions to hurry. Dennis moved to the side, putting an egg between him and the oncoming dragon. But it didn't matter where Jonathan moved—the dragon would see him.

Scully shouldn't have worried about Jonathan. Before the dragon reached them, he heard another frightened scream. This time, he didn't have to search the rows of eggs for the source. It was Shia. He was standing up, screaming. An infant red dragon was on top of his head. Shia thrashed about, trying to dislodge the dragon, but he wasn't looking where he was going. Shia was bumping into eggs and infants, and all eyes in the room fell upon him.

Jonathan heard Shia's screams. But he didn't dare move. The small white dragon was staring at him. If he moved, the dragon would pounce. Then to his surprise, Dennis stood and batted the dragon off the egg with one sweep of his arm and grabbed Jonathan with his free hand.

"You're with me," Dennis said as he pulled him to his feet. Jonathan had no option but to keep up as Dennis pulled him along. They dashed around the eggs, trying not to trip or step on the infants. One of the eggs they were passing was freshly cracked. A small pink dragon huddled on the ground next to the egg. It had marble-sized gems imbedded in its skin.

Suddenly a black dragon was in front of them. Dennis fell to the ground trying to stop his forward momentum. He let go of Jonathan as he fell. Jonathan froze, as if the dragon wouldn't be able to see him if he didn't move.

The black dragon's two whiskers looked like a moustache, although they moved as if alive. The black eyes settled upon him, and Jonathan tried not to shudder. He felt Dennis grab his leg, trying to pull him down.

Then the dragon looked away and focused on the infant. Jonathan thought for a moment that the infant was pretty; he'd never seen a dragon like it before. The black dragon lunged with the speed of a snake striking at a small field mouse. It bit the infant and shook its head violently before taking a few gulps, forcing the carcass down its long, snake-like throat.

It had just eaten a baby. The dragons were cannibals. How could that be? Why were they eating some of their offspring? Was it sick? Weak? Jonathan didn't have time to ponder the idea. Dennis was back on his feet and pulling him away from the bloody scene.

Shia shrieked and batted crazily at the infant dragon on his head. Hank watched him, uncertain what to do. Their cover was blown. Lorna got to her feet and to aid the boy. She saw Dennis stand up and grab Jonathan, the two of them running off in some random direction. She grabbed Shia's shoulder with one hand and the neck of the infant with the other. She pulled it off, flicked her wrist, and the red dragon went limp in her hand. She had broken its neck. Repulsed, she dropped it to the ground.

They were surrounded. One of the black dragons had encircled them with his long, narrow body. His little whiskers twitched as he lunged, ready to take a bite out of her. Then she saw Scully leap upon the dragon's back and slice the beast's head off. The dragon fell to the ground, his body twitching.

"Get out of here," Scully told her.

"Come on, kiddo," Lorna said as she grabbed Shia under the armpit and steered him away from the bloody mess. He wiped at his scalp with his free hand. Blood was trickling down into his eyes from deep cuts on his head. He kept wincing as he wiped it away.

"I think they were discovered. Look at the dots," Rick said. They watched as the dots representing the dragons began to move toward the nest the others were in.

"The Queen controls them. All it takes is one dragon to see them, and she'll know. She gives the order, and all the dragons on the island move in," Dee said soberly.

"We have to help them," Rick decided.

"How?" Ethan asked skeptically. "As soon as one of us leaves this room, he will be lost. I know my way around a few caves, but if I'm fighting for my life, I'll get lost."

"But I won't," Rick said. "A Zalite doesn't get lost."

"Is Darlene still in that room?" Dee asked.

"Yeah, she hasn't moved," Ethan said.

"Okay, we have a chance. Let's go rescue our rescuers," Dee said as he stood. "Rick and I will go get them. You two stay here and keep an eye on things. One of you will have to come get us if we do get lost."

Ethan was about to object, but before he could, the two slipped through the passageway. Ethan muttered that they were all going to get killed. He watched as the six blue dots scattered.

Jonathan was pulled through a passageway; they didn't even look at what was on the other side. He winced at the bright light. They were outside, surrounded by leafless trees and faced with a moat filled with murky black water. Then he heard the dragon cries; they sounded upset. He looked at the sky and saw countless dragons flying towards them.

"What do we do?" Jonathan gasped.

"Can you swim?"

"I'm not going in that water. It's filthy and there's no telling what is in there," Jonathan objected. He looked back into the cavern and remembered the dog. He put his fingers to his lips and whistled for the dog.

"What are you doing?" Dennis shouted, annoyed. Jonathan ignored him as he saw Hank racing towards the passageway, bounding over the eggs. He leaped through just as Dennis grabbed Jonathan and pulled him into the water. A red dragon swooped down, like an eagle going for prey. Jonathan barely had a chance to take a gulp of air before the icy water rushed up to meet him.

Down they went, the darkness of the water blocking the sunlight. Dennis let go so he could swim better. Jonathan struggled and finally managed to swim up. He broke the surface of the water and took another breath of air, his lungs burning. The dragons were overhead, ignoring him. He swam to shore, towards the opposite side he had been on. He dragged himself up the beach. The black sand clung to his damp clothes, and he shivered in the slight breeze. A white dragon landed next to him.

He froze, hoping the dragon wasn't after him. The dragon's hide was covered in spikes that seemed to spring out of his body at random. He looked like a scaly porcupine. The dragon lowered its alligator face and peered at him with all white eyes. For a moment, he thought the dragon was blind. Then he saw the tiniest speck of a black pupil. The dragon opened its mouth, showing him rows of needle-like teeth. Jonathan wanted to scream, but his breath was gone.

What Jonathan had at first thought was a giant tree trunk, suddenly came smashing down on top of the dragon, breaking his back. The dragon gave a pathetic cry and went limp. Jonathan looked up and saw that the trunk was actually an arm. A four-legged, deformed monster hovered above him. The beast didn't even have a head—just an empty skull with two glowing red eyes.

The beast opened its jaws, showing him how hollow the skull truly was. Then it came down upon him, swallowing him whole. Jonathan was inside the skull, unharmed, but trapped. He stood and grabbed at the beast's nose holes. He saw sky on the other side. Then a scaly hand grabbed the skull where the nostrils were. Jonathan screamed and let go, falling to the hard surface of the bottom jaw. The dragon tried to reach him through the holes, then the entire skull whirled around like a roller coaster. Jonathan's stomach lurched. He closed his eyes; when he opened them again, the dragon was gone.

Melanie and Scully hacked at the dragons with speed and skill. It reminded Melanie of the old days when her and her brother fought side by side. But this time, she didn't see an end in sight. More dragons came into the cave—it didn't matter how many they killed, more just kept coming. She jumped from egg to egg, sometimes cracking the shell with the impact of her body.

She jumped, landing perfectly as a white dragon came down upon her. She jumped back, slashing with her sword as she went. She cut the beast under its jaw, and it fell to the ground. Her back slammed into an egg, and she slid to the ground. She moved quickly, using the eggs as cover.

Then someone reached out and grabbed her. It was Scully. His blade was covered in blood. For the moment, the dragons didn't seem to know where they were. He mouthed the words, "Where are they?" She looked at him, puzzled, wondering who was he talking about. Then she remembered the finder spell she had performed. The pink light was still showing the path that led to Scully's friends. It had been dizzying darting around the cave with the pink streak moving with her, constantly realigning itself. She had gotten so used to it that she had forgotten what it was. She pointed in the direction the light was showing. Scully nodded, and with a quick tug on her arm, dashed in the direction she indicated.

With a huff of aggravation, she hurried after him, slicing down two white dragons and a silver as she went. She grabbed Scully, pulling him through the correct passageway.

Suddenly, they were outside. She blinked her eyes at the sudden onslaught of sun, then saw the most horrendous scene she had ever laid her eyes upon. She had lived through the plague and seen mankind at its worst. She had watched mother and child fight to eat each other. She herself had hidden in a closet for weeks, unable to bear watching another abandoned child allow himself to be eaten alive, but what she saw now, chilled her to her bones. A monster, its flesh decomposing, worked its way through the dragons. Heaps of corpses already littered the ground. But it was the way the beast fought that terrified her. It tore at the dragons like a mad dog.

The worst part was the way the pink light that led her to Scully's friends led her right to the beast. She watched for a moment as the beast moved. The beam of light moved with it. This was Scully's friend. She waved her hand in front of her face, and the beam of light disappeared from her sight.

"Melanie, this is Decompose," Scully said softly. Her heart skipped a beat as he said it. So it was true. The Plague of Decompose had been caused by an actual being—the beast the dragons claimed was the devil. Why wasn't he in the Valley of Death?

Dennis swam to the surface. He had lost track of Jonathan. He searched the beach frantically for him. He heard Hank barking and Dennis called for him. The wet dog dashed up to him and whined. Then he saw Rick. Soon the two were in a warm embrace. Then he heard the loud roar of Decompose.

"You guys are free?" Dennis asked, astonished.

"Of course. We escaped," Rick said with a grin. "Dominique and Ethan are in Jaff's old lab. We need to get back there. We'll make it our stronghold."

"Right," Dennis agreed.

"I saw Scully and some woman on the other side of the moat. Is she with you?"

"Yes, that's Scully's sister, Melanie."

"Who else came?" Rick asked.

"Lorna, Shia, and a friend of Melanie's."

"Where are they?"

"I—I don't know. We got split up," Dennis said, fearing the worst.

Melanie watched, horrified, as the dragons fought the beast. It was a blur of red, silver, white, and black, mixed with flashes of the beast's rotting flesh. They should have taken him down easily. Some were larger than him, and they had him outnumbered. Then they backed off. The dragons took to the air and vanished inside the black caves.

"Where are they going?" Melanie asked in a hushed voice. The Decompose monster stood silently on the black sand next to the moat.

Then she saw it. A giant dragon had come up out of the ground. It was unlike any dragon Melanie had ever seen. It had vibrant, dark pink scales with matching spikes along its back that turned dark red at the tips. A crest of longer spikes on the head made the beast look as if it was wearing a crown. But the size was what took Melanie's breath away. The dragon was the size of a four-story building. None of the other dragons came close to matching it. Even Decompose looked like a child next to the giant dragon.

"That," Scully began, "would be the Queen."

Melanie said nothing. The other dragons were gone. The giant dragon flapped her wings, making a thunderous noise. A powerful gust of wind hit them. Melanie ducked, but the impulse wave wasn't aimed at them. Decompose drove his mutated claws into the ground, but it was no use. The soft sand gave way, and he slid back, leaving claw marks as he went.

Decompose sent a telekinetic wave of his own, but the dragon clapped her wings again and easily overpowered it. She sent another wave and another, driving him slowly, but surely, away from her.

"She's pushing him into the ocean," Scully said. "Come on, we have to help him."

"What?" Melanie exclaimed.

"He's my friend, Melanie; we have to help him."

"How? We can't fight that dragon."

"She's no different from the other dragons we've already slain," Scully said. "She's just bigger and has telepathic powers."

He said it as if those things didn't matter. She followed him as he jumped into the moat, swimming to the other side.

Dee knew he was losing ground. He heard the roar of the ocean behind him. So that was what she was doing. Did she know he couldn't swim? Or was it just a lucky break for her? It didn't matter. What did matter was that she was winning. He passed a grove of trees, probably the last ones before he reached the beach. He clawed frantically at the dirt, but it was no use. She was pushing him away, but it wasn't the wind; it was…something else. Like they naturally repelled each other. Like magnets. He remembered playing with magnets as a child. If you put the same polarity together, they would repel. No matter how hard you tried to force them together, they pushed each other away. Maybe the same thing was true for them. Their telepathic powers were so alike that they repelled each other, and her flapping wings just kept her from moving away from him. He waited for a pause between her wing flaps, then opened his jaws, spitting out the terrified man he had picked up earlier. Then he morphed into his fully-clothed human form, grabbed the man, and pulled him behind a tree.

He felt the wind, but now in his human form, he wasn't pushed nearly as much. He could hold his ground, so long as he stayed next to the tree.

"Who are you?" the bewildered man asked. Dee felt like asking the same question. Then a shadow came over them. Dee looked up and saw the Queen above the ocean. He had hoped she would give up and go back to the caves.

Dee only had a few moments before she spotted them. So he did the only thing he could think of—he ran towards her. He waited until he felt the tug pulling him away, then he morphed into Decompose and jumped forward. He wasn't sure how, but he grabbed hold of her hind leg. The extra weight pulled her down and they crashed into the salty water. The nagging pull was gone, but now the Queen was fighting back with all her might, and she was a lot bigger than him. Dee was pulling her down with him, and she was fighting to regain the surface; she needed air. Dee looked down. He couldn't see the bottom—just inky darkness. He stopped struggling as he realized that if she managed to dislodge him, or she drowned, they both would plunge to the bottom.

❖ ❖ ❖

Scully raced towards the ocean, hearing Melanie breathe heavily as she struggled to keep up with him. They reached the last of the trees. From here on out, it was just pure black sand. He paused, waiting for Melanie to catch up. The waves lapped against the beach. There was no sign of Dee or the Queen.

"Hey! Hey!" Jonathan shouted. Scully hadn't even known he was here. He turned his eyes from the ocean and saw Jonathan a few trees away, waving his arms frantically. Scully waved back. Jonathan found some courage and made his way to Scully. Melanie came up next to him on the other side. She was breathing in ragged gasps, trying to catch her breath.

"Scully!" another man shouted. Scully turned to see Rick and Dennis jogging up, the dog trotting alongside. "Did you see that? Dee pulled her down with him!"

"Yes, Rick, I saw it. Where are Dominique and Ethan?" Scully asked.

"Safe. We found Jaff's lab. They're waiting for us. It's about a half-hour walk from here," Rick said. "It didn't take Dee long to cover the ground once he morphed into that monster."

The five of them silently stared at the ocean as the loss of Dee began to dawn on them.

"Why aren't the other dragons coming to help her?" Dennis asked. No one answered.

"Aren't we a few short?" Jonathan asked. Everyone turned to look at him. "The young boy and the fat woman—where are they?"

"I thought they were with you," Dennis said to Scully.

"I thought they went with you," Scully returned.

"They weren't with anyone," Melanie snapped. She was shaking; Scully didn't know why. Maybe she was cold from the water—but everyone was soaked except for Rick, and she was the only one shivering. "Lorna had her own gem; she didn't go with any of us."

Suddenly, they heard a painful roar and a thunderous splash. Scully looked at the ocean. Near the beach, they saw the Queen break the surface. She stretched her neck up and took a breath. Her wings flapped uselessly at her sides as she tried to raise them high enough to catch the air. Waves splashed roughly against the beach, rising higher, almost reaching them, but falling short. She gave another cry, and Scully began to ponder Dennis's question. Why weren't the other dragons coming to her aid?

Suddenly she broke free, lunging up and unfolding her wings, she caught a current of air and rose a few feet, but half of her body was still in the water. She thrashed violently and began rising, but something was weighing her down. Decompose clung to her hind leg, his jaw and front claws holding tight. Blood trickled down her side; he had hurt her bad. She flapped her wings frantically, but couldn't go any higher, not with her injury and Dee's added weight. She turned her long neck and snapped at him, ripping large chunks of flesh from his body. She faltered and almost fell back into the ocean, then managed to get her other hind foot on Dee's exposed ribcage. She dug her claws into him and pushed. He took a good chunk of her flesh with him, but he lost his grip, dangled for a moment from his teeth, then let go. He morphed back into his human form before he hit the water. Then he was gone. The Queen rose higher and soared off, injured and bleeding badly, but alive. The fight was out of her, though, and she retreated to the caves from whence she had come.

"He can't swim!" Rick cried. And he was off, sprinting to the shoreline. Dennis raced after him and both disappeared into the lapping water. If anyone could get Dee back, it would be them. Scully looked at the shuddering Melanie and the frightened Jonathan.

"Two of us should look for Lorna and Shia," Scully said slowly. "One of us will stay here to tell the others where we went."

"We should all wait," Jonathan answered. "Regroup and replan."

"We have to move now; the Queen is injured. They won't mount another attack until she's better, which won't be long—not with the white dragons helping them. We don't have much time to find Lorna. Now, which of you is going with me?"

"Well, not me," Jonathan said matter-of-factly. "I just got eaten by that monster. I'm in shock. I think it'd be best if I stayed here."

"In shock," Scully repeated, and Jonathan nodded. Scully looked at Melanie; she had a glazed look to her and was shaking badly. "Melanie?"

She didn't answer. He shook her shoulders gently, and she finally looked at him.

"How can you want to help him? He killed people. Didn't you live through it, too?" Melanie asked. She was sweating.

"You should take her," Jonathan suggested. "You two are good with swords—it'd be best. Maybe the dog could go with you—"

"No, I'm taking you," Scully decided as he pulled his sword out and looked back at the caves.

"What? No, I'm in shock, remember?" Jonathan said.

"She's coming down from a high—going into withdrawal. What use is she going to be to me?" Scully asked.

"We could give her another hit," Jonathan suggested.

"A hit of what?" Scully exclaimed.

"Hey! We need to get you guys out of here!" a man was shouting at them. Scully saw Ethan standing inland, next to a black rock formation, waving his hands wildly.

"We have to find Lorna!" Scully shouted.

"No time! Darlene is on the move! She's headed this way! We have to get out of here *now*!" Ethan shouted. Scully wondered how Ethan knew such things. He didn't see Darlene. He looked at the shore and saw Rick and Dennis pulling Dee up the beach. He was coughing, but otherwise seemed okay. They pulled him to his feet, supporting him.

"We have to move! Now!" Ethan shouted. Something about his tone told him to listen. Scully grabbed Melanie, pulling her along, while Jonathan followed.

"I will not help you," the Gold Dragon said calmly in his grandfatherly voice. Usually, his voice calmed people, but this time it only aggravated his audience.

The other Royal Dragons stood around him, the Queen in the center. Unhatched eggs filled the room, for this was the Queen's nest. He saw the fins on the Red Dragon ruffle in anger.

"Why not? You brought him here," the Red Dragon argued.

"That was when he was a threat to the world. Now he is on this island. I feel no need to fight him. He can do no harm trapped on this island," the Gold Dragon surmised.

"No harm?" the Queen asked, pushing away the white dragon that tended her wounds. "Did you see the mockery he made of me? The dragons he murdered?"

"He was provoked," the Gold Dragon said simply.

"He was in my nest!" the Black Dragon snapped.

"They killed no one until you attacked them. I will not fight Decompose unless he starts the fight," the Gold Dragon said. The other dragons fumed, but he saw amusement on the White Dragon's face. Silence filled the room. The Gold Dragon wished the other Royal Dragons could think for themselves; some might have agreed with him.

"If all he wants to do is hide in Jaff's old lab, I say let him," the Gold Dragon continued. "He won't cause anyone harm if he is trapped, whether it is of his own accord or not."

"You are the only one of us who has fought Decompose and defeated him," the Queen reminded him. She paused, as if expecting this to change his mind. When silence was all she got, she continued. "We will let Decompose be, but we will surround Jaff's lab. If any member of Decompose's party leaves that cavern, they are to—"

She paused, her thoughts elsewhere for a moment, then she curved her mouth into a smile. The gems covering her body glowed a little brighter.

"Two of his friends have been found," the Queen said. Again she paused, as if expecting someone to comment. "Silver Dragon, take them to one of your caves, far away from Jaff's lab. Have Darlene help you contain them. When Decompose comes to their rescue we will atta—wait for them to attack us. Only then will we strike them down."

"I will not condemn Decompose for coming to the aid of his friends. If you ask me, it's a blessing he has friends. If you had any humility, you would return them to Decompose and hope for his mercy. A good gesture on your part might go a long way."

"Do you really think they are his friends? He has mind powers, Gold Dragon; those fools were manipulated into being his allies."

"Two are Zalites. You know as well as I, he can't control them," the Gold Dragon reminded her.

"Think what you will, but I am showing humility; I'm not killing them. Silver Dragon, go, have Darlene help you. Don't attack Decompose's allies. Let them wander the caves, searching for their friends. Have Darlene hide them. Let them get lost. Then, when Decompose's true colors show, and he attacks us for no reason other than his own frustration at losing all his 'friends,' perhaps Gold Dragon will help us."

"And when Decompose doesn't attack us?" the Gold Dragon asked.

"If he doesn't attack, the peace will not be broken, will it?" the Queen said smartly, but the Gold Dragon knew she was up to something. He turned his back to her and departed.

Ethan led them to Jaff's lab without incident, relieved everyone was safe. Rick and Dennis sat Dee down on the cot against the side wall, and the others crowded around the table, amazed at the interactive map. Dominique embraced his dog.

"Can you use this to find Lorna and Shia?" Scully asked.

"Sure. These blue dots are us; we are all in this room—except for two," Dominique explained. Ethan backed away from the table, confident Dominique could show them what they wanted to see. He went to the shelf of vials. They were covered in dust; he had to pick them up and smear it off the labels to read them.

While the others were gone, he had gone through a similar process with the spell books until he had found Jaff's journal. It hadn't taken him long to find the spell they used to destroy the Meta-morphs. Now he just needed to find the ingredients they used. He hoped everything was on the shelf. He wasn't sure if Dee wanted him to balance out the disease, but he had nothing better to do with his time. And since they were already here…

"I couldn't fight her," Dee mumbled over and over. Dennis comforted him, saying he had given her a scare. They all seemed to doubt the dragons would give them trouble anytime soon.

"We have to get Lorna back. One person should come with me to get her and Shia, while everyone else stays here, where it's safe," Scully decided.

"It's doubtful the dragons will attack us while we are all together. We should be safe," Dominique agreed.

"And since we know where Lorna is, it should be easy to get them back," Scully continued.

Ethan found vials labeled as blood samples. He needed three samples of blood for the spell, didn't he? He started opening the vials, checking the contents. The blood was all dried up—practically dust. That was to be expected, he thought. It's been nearly sixty years. He moved on to the next level on the shelf and found those vials perfectly preserved. He located six ingredients he needed, and was ready to move on to the next shelf, when an argument broke out. He hadn't been listening to the conversation, but now it was impossible to ignore them.

"You can't just go and get them," Rick pointed out.

"Rick, you don't know these dragons; they won't expect us to—" Scully continued, indifferent to the man's objection.

"I don't know a thing about these dragons. That's Dominique's department. We all have special qualities that will help us. Dominique knows more about dragons than they know about themselves. Ethan is the only one who knows how to read these spells and make the potions. You've been here before—that gives you a background knowledge, plus you know how to do magic with nothing more than dust. The sword is an added bonus, I'll admit. Lorna is the most powerful witch I've ever seen, and from the way you talk about her, she's probably the best there's ever been. But Dennis and I are Zalites."

"Yes, you're stronger than us, and you have enhanced vision and hearing; I already know that," Scully said dismissively.

"We can do a lot more than that, but that's not my point. Zalites are conquerors. You have no idea how many planets we rule over. War is what we do. And this is war," Rick said. "This is what we were made to do. Our physical skills make us the perfect warriors. Enhanced vision, hearing, smell, reflexes, strength, skin. We know war. It's taught to us from birth. You've been around a long time, Scully, and you've seen your fair share of wars. But the wars Zalites have fought make your planet's wars look like a friendly game of football.

"All I'm asking is that you listen to me. I can win this, without the dragons ever knowing we started," Rick said, never taking his eyes off Scully. Silence fell over them; Ethan didn't think anyone had really thought of what they were doing as war, until now.

"Okay, it's war. But before we start drawing up battle plans, let's get our friends out from behind enemy lines. Okay?" Scully said slowly, trying not to aggravate Rick more than he already was.

Rick pointed to the map. "The dragons don't know we have this. But if we go directly to Lorna and Shia, they are going to know that we knew where they were. That's an advantage we can't lose. We can't let them think for a minute that we know our way around these caverns. It gives us an advantage."

"What do you suggest? Take a zigzag route to them?" Scully asked.

"No, that's too obvious. If only two people leave, the odds are great they would never find Lorna. We wouldn't send only two people unless we knew where they were."

"Hey," Melanie said, speaking for the first time since they arrived. Dee had earlier cured her of her shakes, although Ethan suspected she would have rather had another hit. "No one's mentioning that this might be a set up."

"No," Dennis added. "If they wanted to spring a trap on us, they would put the hostages somewhere we would easily find them. They've taken them up north. They don't want us to find them."

No one argued.

"I suggest we send out three groups of two. Two groups will act as decoys, roaming around, pretending to search for Lorna, but actually just acting as a distraction," Rick said.

"A wild goose chase," Jonathan added.

"Actually," Ethan stood up, placing the six vials on the table, making sure they weren't on the map. "It wouldn't have to be a wild goose chase."

"I don't even know what a wild goose chase is," Rick remarked.

"I need blood samples to make the Decompose plague with which we infected Dee. The samples here are no good. The other two groups could get those samples for me. The dragons wouldn't know the other groups have a different mission, and it would serve the same purpose."

"Hitting two birds with one stone," Jonathan added. Rick gave him another glare, not liking that he didn't understand Jonathan's idioms.

"Why do we need the plague? I already told you I don't want to be 'cured,'" Dee said.

"I can use the original plague not only to cure you, but to mutate the plague and make the dragons vulnerable to it," Ethan explained.

"Now that I like," Dee agreed.

"What are the samples?" Scully asked.

"Well, that's another problem," Ethan began. He opened Jaff's journal and looked again at what it said. He hoped he read it wrong the first time. "The easiest to get will be a Meta-morph blood sample."

"I thought you killed them all," Scully countered.

"We did, but we also brought them back to life. The ones the dragons didn't kill, that is."

"He's right," Dee agreed. "I controlled majority of the wildlife on this island once, and there are quite a few Meta-morphs. I didn't know what they were at the time, but I couldn't control them."

"A side effect of the plague keeps the Meta-morphs from morphing. We forced the Meta-morphs into the shape of white unicorns, so the dragons wouldn't recognize them."

"Why a unicorn?" Dee asked.

"Their true form is a black unicorn. It was easy to just change their color. They blend in with the normal unicorns this way," Ethan explained.

"Dennis and I should be able to get a sample from one," Rick agreed.

"Well, that settles that. You two will get the Meta-morph blood," Scully decided. "What else do you need?"

"Well, a McPowin's blood. Mine and Lorna's will suffice." He paused. "And Barbie's blood."

"Barbie?" Scully asked.

"Jaff's wife. She used to be a cat, but he turned her into a human. Since she morphed, although it was via magic, her blood was vital in creating the plague."

"Why don't we just get another cat and morph it?" Scully asked.

"Won't work. I need the same cat Jaff used, otherwise the spell won't be the same."

"But you don't need the same Meta-morph," Scully countered.

"Meta-morphs are different from humans and cats. I need Barbie."

"And how do you propose we find a cat that's been missing for sixty years?" asked Scully.

"Well, Jaff made her immortal, so she should still be alive," Ethan said calmly, though he knew the odds were against him. "And we do have the world's best telepath."

Everyone looked at Dee. Dee seemed puzzled at first, then shook his head.

"You want me to find a cat?" Dee asked.

Dee couldn't believe he was going after a cat. His brother's wife, actually. The idea gave him the chills. The caves muffled his powers. He'd been forced to step outside to telepathically search the villages. He'd almost hoped the cat was dead; it would have saved them a lot of trouble. But finding a cat full of human memories wasn't too hard, although he was pretty sure the memories were corroded enough that the cat probably wouldn't remember anyone she had met when she had been a human.

"I found her," Dee said softly. He closed his eyes and let the gentle breeze brush his face. He heard birds in the trees. The island had been unaffected by his plague; the birds here were still alive and flourishing.

"Great, I don't like standing around out here; makes me feel vulnerable," the scraggily man next to him said. He had been introduced as Jonathan Wescott, but Dee could tell he was still a little jumpy from when he had scooped him up in his skull.

Behind them, a passageway opened up in the white rock formation. There was a white cave next to Jaff's lab, making access to the outside convenient. There hadn't been any dragons in the cave, either, nor were there any outside. Dee thought it was strange; it was almost as if they were avoiding them. Dennis walked outside, holding something in his hands.

"Here, take this with you. I don't know if it will work once you get off the island, but at least you can let us know when you're back," Dennis said. He handed a small electronic device to Dee, and another one to Jonathan.

"What is it?" Dee asked.

"I found some electronic scraps in Jaff's lab. An old set of walkie-talkies, a radio, and some CD players—at least, that's what the labels said. Anyway, I'm good with electronic stuff, though these were primitive. I worked up some two-way radios. I'm passing them out to everyone. You put it in your ear like this," Dennis said, putting one in his ear for show. "Just press this little black button to talk. You'll be able to listen to everyone else's conversation, too, unless you turn it off."

"Well now, that would defeat the purpose, wouldn't it?" Jonathan said as he peered at the small item.

"Rick and I are going to travel in the caves, see how well the reception works. Scully and Melanie already left to get Lorna and Shia. Which route are you guys taking?"

"That depends," Jonathan began. He looked at them. "I believe that's where you should jump in and finish the sentence."

"Right," Dee looked at him oddly for a moment, then looked back at Dennis. "We need to find a mirror. We'll be heading to one of the round rooms. I figure we'll zigzag around aimlessly for a while and see how well-protected the rooms are."

"Push the button and tell Dominique, he's playing navigator with the map. Should be able to help us avoid the dragons."

"All right, come on, Jonathan," Dee said as he began walking. "There's a round room next to a white rock formation up ahead—just on the other side of a small pond and cluster of trees and down a slight hill."

Dennis nodded and turned back to the cave. Dee trudged on, not really paying attention to Jonathan.

Melanie and Scully took the most direct route they had seen on the map. Scully saw no reason to beat around the bush, and Rick certainly hadn't thought they needed to. They left Jaff's lab and crept into a silver dragon cave. Scully managed the ice-coated floor well. He kept his sword drawn, ready for action. Melanie mumbled to herself and Scully thought he heard her cuss. There weren't any dragons. Scully found that odd. He stepped to the wall on his left and opened another passage. This led to a red room. Again, he saw no dragons.

"This is odd," Scully murmured. He was starting to wonder if Dennis was wrong. Maybe it was an ambush. It was too easy to navigate the caves. He stepped into the room and the red rock sent up a puff of dust under his feet. Melanie stumbled and grabbed the wall next to the passageway for support.

"You always complain too much. Just be grateful this is so easy, okay? Count your blessings. Not everyone is out to stab you in the back," Melanie said as she found her footing. She stepped ahead of him into the room and stood in the center of the room with her hands on her hips. "Now where?"

Scully didn't even bother to answer. He walked around her and went to his right. The room narrowed, then opened up on the other side. It was an easy fit, although he wondered how the dragons managed to squeeze through. He looked at his sister; he wished he hadn't brought her.

"On the other side of this wall is a tunnel. We're going to follow it to the end. There are passageways on either side the whole length of the tunnel. So be careful."

"Careful is as careful does, my dear brother," Melanie mocked as she pushed past him and entered the next cavern. Again, they found it deserted.

"So you're the great and powerful Decompose," Jonathan said. Dee didn't even bother looking at him. He was starting to understand why Jonathan had been partnered with him. Maybe Scully was secretly hoping he would kill him.

"The dragons gave me that nickname; just call me Dee."

"Rather fitting, though, isn't it? I wasn't alive, of course. My parents were. They lived through the great Decompose plague. Told me horror stories of their experiences. The screams, the horrible screams. Some nights growing up, I could hear screams. Unlucky souls that wandered off. But most of the time, there were no screams. Pops told me that was the worst. To see someone getting eaten, smiling, not caring at all. At first, people thought the cannibals had some sort of drug in their saliva, like a narcotic. It was years before we found out they had telepathic abilities," Jonathan continued. Dee wished he could block out his voice. He wished they could walk faster.

"I remember the first time I saw one of those cannibals. I'll never forget the crunching of bones. The sickening sound of—"

"Can we talk about something else?" Dee asked, stopping and turning to face the scraggily man. He still had a shadow of a beard and his hair was long and unkempt.

"Sure, sure. Did you know Melanie, my girlfriend, once had sex with your father? Or so I'm told—I mean, Jafar is your dad, right?

There's been confusion about that one. Was he your father, grandfather, or great-great grandfather?" Jonathan chuckled at his own comment.

"Maybe he was yours," Dee snapped, quickening the pace.

"Oh, don't be silly. Humor isn't your thing. Stick to that serious, monotone nature you've got going. It works well for you."

"Maybe you should try it."

"Oh, no, me a boring—boring—well, a boring something. See there, just thinking about it makes me lose my train of thought and get bored myself," Jonathan mused. "Maybe we should try singing. Did you know they made a song about you?"

"I had no idea," Dee mumbled. He expected Jonathan to break out in tune, but he didn't. He didn't say anything. Dee reached the top of the hill. Looking down, he could see the white cave, which would be next to the white round room. And using that room, Dee would access the mirror in the temple nearest Barbie. It was a twenty-minute walk to the cavern. Jonathan was still quiet. Dee started to wonder if he had hurt his feelings. "Jonathan, if you want to sing the song, go ahead."

Silence. Dee turned and looked down the hill. Jonathan wasn't there. Dee's heart started to race. How had he lost him? How could he possibly lose a smelly, noisy person like Jonathan? He made sure his mike was turned off. There was no need to tell anyone about this problem. He didn't want Scully's sister to fret about her lost boyfriend. They'd probably paired him with Jonathan because they figured he would keep Jonathan safe. And now Dee had lost him. Stay calm, stay calm, Dee told himself. Just do a telepathic sweep and find him.

Then he saw it. Something on the ground was reflecting sunlight. Dee walked back down the hill, towards the reflective object. A mirror. There was a full-length mirror on the ground. It had been buried. Evidently Jonathan had walked across it, his dragon gem had activated it and he had fallen through. The dirt and grass that covered it had gone with him. Dee knelt next to the mirror and flashed his gem across the surface. A passageway opened up, and Dee saw himself looking into a storage room filled with mirrors. It was disorienting—the mirror was standing up in the room, but lying on the ground on Dee's side.

And there was Jonathan—down on his hands and knees, thrashing about with a white sheet. The sheet had probably been covering the mirror. Dee reached through the glass, grabbed Jonathan, and pulled him back through partway. Then he pulled the sheet off and threw it back in the room. Jonathan crawled out on his belly, making sounds like an injured bear cub.

"I do not want to do that again. Oh, my Quaker, I thought the dragons were going to get me. Those mirrors are kept in a back room in one of the temples. A few of them broke. And, oh, Quaker Queen almighty, you should have seen how crazy it is to fall in that thing. Quaker, Quaker," Jonathan rambled.

"Who's Quaker?" Dee asked.

"Quaker Crackers—they're my favorite. You should really try some," Jonathan said. Dee wasn't sure what to say.

"I'm glad you liked the trip, 'cause we're going to use this mirror to get to Barbie."

"No, no, Quaker is something I say when I'm frazzled. It's not a happy expression. If I was happy, I'd have said, 'Oh, Pilgrims, Pilgrims! My favorite pie—Pilgrim Pies.'"

"Well, you sounded happy to me," Dee said. He grabbed Jonathan and pulled him through the mirror with him. Jonathan had been right; it was disorienting. Dee fell to the ground, hitting his shoulder hard. They were in another storage room, filled to the brim with mirrors.

"Freaking Pilgrims," Jonathan muttered.

"I thought you said that when you were happy," Dee said as he stood. The room was chilly.

"I said I say, 'Oh, Pilgrims.' 'Freaking Pilgrims' is quite different," Jonathan said as he, too, stood. "Where did you take us? It's freezing in here."

"We're in a Silver Dragon Temple. Barbie is in this town."

"Silver dragon? You did *not* just say you brought us to a Silver Dragon Temple."

"And what's so *Quakering* wrong with that?" Dee asked.

"Well, the three feet of snow is a starter. Need I say more?"

"We'll steal some warmer clothes on our way, then."

"And you used Quaker totally out of context. Fluke Sickles would have been more appropriate. Fluking Sickles! See how that just flows off the tongue?"

Dennis barely felt the cold of the snow, though it came up to his chest as he crawled on his hands and knees. The needles on his skin, feather-like, kept his body warm in the cold. Zalites were built for all kinds of weather. Rick, at his side, shuffled through the snow like a grizzly bear.

They reached the top of the hill and looked down at a cluster of silver pine trees. Everything in the Silver Dragon Territory seemed to glimmer. Even the unicorns had a silver shine to their coats. There was a herd at the bottom of the hill. They lowered themselves to the level of the snow.

"I count fifteen," Rick said so softly that only someone with a Zalite's hearing could have heard him.

"I agree, but there were sixteen. I think one wandered off," Dennis answered in an equally quiet voice.

"One missing unicorn won't change things," Rick decided.

"How do we figure out which ones are Meta-morphs?"

"We take one that isn't afraid of us," Rick said. "Normal animals flee at the sight of an animal they don't know. But a Meta-morph has a more advanced mind; they won't flee unless they are given a reason."

"Sounds logical. What do we do if they all run?"

"They won't," Rick said. Just then, he heard the crackling of snow behind them. Something was approaching from behind. It sounded like a large animal with hooves. Rick heard it, too. He tensed, but kept his eyes on the unicorns below. The shuffling was close now. Rick gave a slight nod, and the two rolled to their backs in unison.

Their attacker stopped in its tracks, showing no fear; its black eyes stared at them, unflinching.

"We take this one," Rick said, a bit louder this time. The white unicorn shook its head, tossing its mane in the air. Dennis pulled a syringe from his black trench coat and got to his feet. Rick distracted the unicorn while Dennis jabbed the syringe into its neck. The sedative took effect quickly, and the unicorn fell to the ground. Dennis pulled out an empty syringe and filled it with blood. As he finished, he looked up to see the herd of unicorns approaching.

"Get moving; Scully said they can't go in the caves," Rick shouted.

The room was deserted, just as all the other caves had been. Scully didn't like how this was turning out. It felt more and more like a trap. He tapped the microphone, barely visible next to his ear.

"Dominique, we're in the room you said Lorna and Shia are in, but I don't see them," Scully said, trying to keep his voice calm. It was a trap—he knew it was. He started to sweat, despite the frigid cold of the Silver Dragon's cavern.

Melanie reached up and tapped her microphone as well. She walked around the icy chamber admiring the natural designs in the ice.

"You're right on top of them. I don't understand. Shia should be directly to your left, and Lorna behind you to your right," Dominique told him. Scully turned and found only a solid block of ice in the corner of the room where Dominique had claimed Lorna would be. He looked to his left and saw a silver boulder where Shia should be.

Melanie looked at the ice boulder and ran her fingers across it. She looked at him, her brown eyes deep in thought.

"Didn't you say once that Jaff hid a small boy inside a rock?" Melanie asked.

Scully's mind raced. She was right. Jaff had done such a thing. He had hid Emil inside a red boulder.

"Yes, he did. But I don't know how to undo the spell. I don't know that kind of magic," Scully said.

"Neither do I. But there's more than one way to crack an egg." She pulled her sword out and raised it high, then slammed the tip of the blade into the ice. Scully cried out in surprise.

"What are you doing? If he's in there you might have killed him!"

But Melanie didn't pay attention, she twisted her sword, forcing the ice to break away. Scully began to help her. He put his blade in the crack she had made and used it like a lever, forcing the crack to widen. Bits of ice splintered off and struck Scully in the arms and face. Then he saw fingers, human fingers, reaching out of the crack.

"Shia! Shia is that you?" Scully shouted, his voice echoing in the icy chamber. No answer came back, but Scully knew it was him. He put his foot against the rock and pushed. Melanie did the same. She pulled her sword out and struck the ice column again. The half she struck shattered.

A very cold Shia fell to his side, curled up in a fetal position, his skin almost blue. Melanie went to his aid, feeling for a pulse.

"Use the White Dragon gem; see if it can heal him," Scully said. He turned to the corner of the room where Lorna was supposed to be. If Shia had been hidden in the boulder, it was logical to assume Lorna was hidden in the wall.

The air was bitter and cold. The sun had long ago set, leaving Dee and Jonathan to walk the darkened streets. They had 'acquired' some silver dress gowns from the temple before departing, so the cold didn't bother them as much as it would have. Jonathan looked at the sky, which was overcast with gray clouds. He rubbed his arms, trying to keep warm. He wished he could see the moon or stars. The blue-tinted streetlights didn't provide enough light to make him feel safe. He looked at Dee, whose eyes were glowing red. With his hood pulled up over his head, he looked like a demon. All he needed was a scythe, and he could be the ghost that came at night and stole your soul, or the demon guarding the gates of hell, or the monster that ate little children when they snuck out late at night. All the bedtime stories Jonathan had been told as a child seemed to focus on evil creatures that resembled Dee.

Jonathan shivered as he realized he had been helping the very creature he had always been taught to fear. He tried to think about something else. The dark, gloomy alleys did nothing to comfort him. There didn't seem to be a single soul awake in the town. Just a demon and his henchman on an errand to steal a mother cat. He could already imagine the tales that would be created by this adventure. He thought it would make a good story.

He heard the feathery sound of wings and looked up to see a silver dragon overhead. It paid no attention to them, but Jonathan knew it had seen them. Dee suddenly stopped walking. Jonathan nearly bumped into him as he came to halt. He slid on the frozen ground, but managed to keep his footing. Dee's eyes stopped glowing, and for a moment, he looked like a normal person. Jonathan tried to conceal his anxiety.

"The cat is in here." Dee's breath made puffy white clouds as he spoke. He's actually warm, Jonathan thought. He's alive. Jonathan had always thought him a cold, undead creature. "I'm impressed you've managed to keep so quiet."

Jonathan managed to smile, but said nothing. He had been too busy being terrified to talk, but he figured that wasn't something he should mention. Dee walked up the three stairs to the wooden door and twisted the knob.

"What are you doing?" Jonathan gasped. Dee looked at him with eerie purple eyes.

"I'm going to get the cat," Dee said, not understanding the problem.

"People live here. You can't just walk into someone's house," Jonathan whispered, feeling even his whisper was a shout in the silent street.

"So you'd rather knock and wake them up? It's the middle of the night. They aren't going to be happy to see us."

"It's better than breaking and entering. I'm not here to commit any crimes," Jonathan said as he crossed his arms.

"We're here to kidnap a cat," Dee said slowly. Silence hung in the air.

"Well, if we wake them up we can ask them to loan us their cat."

"Oh, yes, I'm sure they will be perfectly willing to give their cat to a couple of strangers who woke them up in the middle of the night," Dee said sarcastically.

"It's better then getting shot by a panicky person who thinks they're being robbed in the middle of the night," Jonathan said, starting to get louder.

Dee dropped his hand from the doorknob and turned.

"Jonathan, I can kill someone with a thought. I could destroy this entire village in the blink of an eye. I could turn this house into rubble and pick the cat out of the remains. Now, if you really want me to wake these people up and risk having to do that, I'll do it. Why don't I enter their puny little minds and make them think we're their long-lost children? We can stay for cake and cookies. Is that what you want? Would you have me tell all the women in the house to have sex with you before we leave? I can do it. You name it—I can do it. I want to make it simple and just snatch the cat without anyone being the wiser. But if you'd rather do it some other way, tell me. Please, just spit it out, because it's incredibly cold out here, and I haven't been able to feel my toes for the past hour."

Jonathan realized he was breathing through his mouth. He clamped his jaw shut with a sharp clunk of his teeth. In the distance they heard a drunkard shouting profanity. A dog started barking.

"When you put it that way, a simple breaking and entering doesn't sound so bad," Jonathan agreed with a nervous twitch.

"Good," Dee said flatly. He twisted the doorknob and entered the house. Jonathan hurried up the stairs after him. The house was completely dark inside. He stood in the doorway and felt along the wall for the light switch, then paused, wondering if he should turn it on or not.

"Ah, what the—" Dee cried. Jonathan heard a muffled pounding as Dee protested. He felt along the wall and found the switch. Then something hit him across the face. He grabbed the wall to keep from falling back down the stairs. He flipped the switch, and his eyes burned at the sudden burst of light.

He ducked as the attacker took another swing at him. It was a broom. He was being beat in the face with a broom! He stood, just to feel the prickly straw strike him again.

"Think you can break into an old woman's home in the middle of the night and rob her blind, eh?" the attacker yelled. Jonathan tried to get away, but the woman was relentless. He moved around the table in the center of the room, but she followed him step for step. She traded the broomstick for a frying pan as they passed the stove. Jonathan finally got a good look at her. She had to be in her eighties; her hair was done up in rollers, and she was wearing a pale blue night dress. Her wrinkled face was contorted in anger.

"Dee!" Jonathan shrieked as he dodged her first attack with the pan. It slammed into the counter with a bang.

"Woulda been a hoot if you'd gone with the sex plan, huh?" Dee joked. Jonathan looked at him—he was just standing on the other side of the kitchen, not doing a thing.

"A little help here?" Jonathan asked. Then he felt the pan slam into his forehead as the woman found her mark. Jonathan cried out in pain and reached up to his forehead. He felt blood.

"She's just an old woman. What do you want me to do? Kill her?" Dee asked. Jonathan closed his eyes and tried to deal with the pain ringing in his skull. Through clinched teeth he managed a response.

"I would like you to keep her from killing *me*," he grumbled. The woman hadn't struck him for a few moments. He kept a hand on his forehead and lifted his head.

Dee stood in front of him, twirling the black frying pan in his hands. He was staring at it as if he'd never see one before. Jonathan looked past him and saw the woman clutching her broom, ready to strike Dee, but hesitating. Obviously she didn't like that he had taken her other weapon.

"I think I have a concussion," Jonathan told him, seeing little spots of light in the room. He sank slowly to his knees. Dee looked away from the mesmerizing pan and grabbed Jonathan's forehead. He used his hair to pull him back to his feet. Jonathan reached out and batted him away with his hand.

"Stop pulling my hair," Jonathan complained. He paused; the pain was gone. He touched his forehead to find it healed. "How?"

"It's a miracle," Dee said dryly. He turned away and his expression dimmed. Jonathan was still feeling his forehead, amazed the pain was gone.

"What is it?"

"We have a problem," Dee said softly, gesturing with the frying pan. Jonathan turned to look. From the other room a parade of black cats was walking into the kitchen. Jonathan counted at least a dozen.

"You're telepathic, right? Just figure out which one she is," Jonathan said. The woman behind Dee swung her broom. Dee raised his free hand and caught the stick in midair. The woman's eyes grew large.

"You're right. How silly of me." His eyes glowed. "She's the second on the left. Right next to the one with the white patch on his chest, and one pink pad on his paw."

Jonathan just looked at him dumbly, how was he supposed to understand those directions?

"Either get the cat, or hold off the old lady," Dee told him.

"All right, all right; just tell me if I pick up the right one," Jonathan said. He walked up to the cluster of cats and picked one up.

"No," Dee said flatly. He picked up another and got the same answer. He tried again and was again rejected. "Listen, she's right next to the big tom there, licking his paw. Second from the back. No, third— there's a little kitten back there. Do you see the kitten?"

"Oh, my Queen, you two will be here all night at this rate," the old woman complained. "She's right there."

The woman let go of the broom and waved her hands wildly at Jonathan. Dee turned and almost grabbed her, but stopped at the last minute.

"Come here, Ebony; here, kitty, kitty," the old woman crooned. She bent down as a single back cat slinked up to her. The woman picked her up and put her on the counter. She looked at Dee. "Is this what you were after?"

"Yes," Dee said softly.

"Why are a couple of fools like you trying to steal one of my cats in the middle of the night? What do you want with her? I wouldn't think anything of it, but you were mighty particular about which cat you wanted to take."

Jonathan pointed at his head and mouthed for Dee to mess with her head. Dee quirked an eyebrow and pretended not to understand.

"That cat, is my—my sister-in-law," Dee said gently as he tried to figure out the actual relation he was to the cat. "My brother was married to it."

The woman stroked the cat, which purred gently. The woman looked at them with smoky gray eyes.

"Well, that would explain why you turned into a cat-napper. But there's no way this cat is your sister-in-law. She's too young."

"You're right," Jonathan said. He moved closer. "I mean, this cat probably isn't his *real* sister-in-law. In fact this is the third cat he's made me kidnap, claiming it was his dear old sister."

Jonathan rolled his fingers in a circular motion next to his head, motioning that Dee was crazy. The woman nodded slowly as she started to understand.

"But it would mean a lot to my friend if you'd let him have the cat. I promise she will receive nothing but the finest of a brother's love. His other sisters-in-law all died with their bellies full of milk and, and—"

"Catnip mice. They were sis's favorite," Dee finished.

Jonathan looked at him and smiled. "Right—milk and catnip mice. So what do you say? Can my friend have his dear old brother's wife back?"

The woman's face relaxed, and she seemed to warm up to them.

"Of course you can have Ebony. But if you really are her family, I imagine you won't have a problem taking her latest litter of kittens with you. They're too young to be weaned." The woman bent down and picked up a wicker basket from the floor. She pulled back a worn red blanket and exposed five little black kittens. Barbie, or Ebony, as the woman called her, jumped into the basket with the kittens. They were so small, they couldn't even open their eyes yet.

"Of course. I would love to take my nieces and nephews with me. I wouldn't have it any other way," Dee said, trying to sound serious.

"I'll have you know that over half these cats are your relatives."

"Wow, sis has been busy," Jonathan remarked. "What would your brother say?"

"He'd understand; she actually left him because he was fooling around with a yellow tabby," Dee said, managing to remain serious. The woman looked at them for a moment, concern on her face.

"You two aren't into that kind of thing, are you?"

"What? No, no, no, no, we aren't, no, no," Jonathan repeated, shaking his head.

"All right, and your brother—is he?"

"Dead," Dee said flatly. "Died of worms."

"Oh, how—uh, sad," She turned back to the basket of kittens. "Well you go ahead and take them. This is Bonnie, Ben, Billy, Bret, and Ball."

"Why did you name him Ball?" Jonathan couldn't help but ask.

"I couldn't think of any more names that rhymed with Parsley," she said simply. They all fell silent, unsure what to say. Then Dee broke the silence.

"Thank you, ma'am. I promise to take wonderful care of them. Jonathan, pick up the basket and let's go," Dee said as he walked out the door, being careful to not step on any of the cats wandering around the room. Jonathan quickly followed suit, covered the cats with the blanket, picked the basket up, and hurried after Dee.

"You take good care of my precious pets!" the old woman called as Jonathan hurried out into the bitter cold air.

Scully slammed his blade into the stone. The ice cracked and chipped off, leaving him the hardened silver stone to contend with. It took a few strikes, but finally a chunk of boulder fell off. Inside a cavity in the stone was Lorna. She was frozen, her flesh blue and stiff. Scully's breath caught in his throat. He could only see her face through the opening, but she didn't look alive.

"Dominique, are you there?" Scully asked.

"Yeah, I'm here. Is everything okay?"

"We need Dee. I think Lorna is dead," Scully said softly. He heard coughing behind him. He turned to see Shia sitting on the floor. He was shivering, but seemed okay.

"Try the stone," Melanie suggested. She hurried over. "It worked for Shia."

"No time," Dominique said. "Dragon maidens are on their way. You need to get out of there, now."

Another voice crackled on the microphone.

"Where are they? Dennis and I can head them off," Rick said, slightly out of breath.

"I'll see what I can do. Scully, get out of there," Dominique said, then he clicked off the line to another frequency to talk privately with Rick.

"We're in a silver dragon cave. We had to get inside pretty quick. The morphs weren't happy when we took the sample. We'll have to have to stay inside from here on out," Rick explained.

"Sure thing. You need to go through a black cave on the east side of the cave you're in, then go straight, and it should take you to a long corridor. The maidens are coming up that way," Dominique explained.

"We're on it," Rick said. "Be sure to have Scully take a different route back."

Rick charged ahead, and Dennis followed, carrying the filled syringe.

"Rick, I have a better idea," Dennis said as he grabbed his arm. "Why don't we take another trip outside? And take a few friends with us?"

Rick grinned. He liked where this was going.

It wasn't long before Jonathan's fingers were cold and numb from carrying the basket of kittens. Barbie's added weight wasn't helping. Dee kept walking, heading back to the temple. They passed a sea dock. To Jonathan's amazement, the water wasn't frozen. Dee walked onto one of the docks and gestured for Jonathan to follow him.

"Why are we stopping?" Jonathan asked.

"It seems the most humane option," Dee said as he pulled the blanket off the basket. "I thought about just leaving them on the street. But the water will be less—well, less of a torment than slowly freezing to death."

"What?" Jonathan exclaimed, pulling the basket out of Dee's reach. "You want to kill the kittens?"

"Well, we aren't taking them with us," Dee snapped. "What good would five whiny kittens do us? And how is Barbie going to take care of them when we turn her into a human?"

"No, no—that is just sick. You want to drown them. You told that old lady you would take care of them," Jonathan argued.

"Oh, boo-hoo—so I lied. I didn't kill her, did I? We got out of there nice and peaceful. Isn't that what you wanted?"

"We are not killing these kittens," Jonathan snapped as he pulled the blanket back.

"Don't make me force you," Dee growled.

"What? Oh, that's right, you can do whatever you want, can't you? If I don't want to play along, you'll just mess with my head and make me forget these kittens ever existed, right?"

"That would be easier," Dee agreed.

"You wouldn't dare."

"I made my own father forget about me. Don't think for a second that I won't make you forget about a litter of kittens."

"Is that supposed to make up for it? You had a rotten childhood, so now you have the right to be heartless? You're not the only one with a sad childhood, you know."

"What are you talking about? You're too young to have lived through my plague. Let me guess—the dragons were mean to your family," Dee suggested.

"No. My mother was a drunk. And my father was—unfaithful. She lived through your plague; she was only fifteen when it happened. She drank to bury the memories. She never told me what happened, but every time I looked in her eyes, I knew it had destroyed her. She was empty inside. Her body survived, but her soul died. My father went to other women for comfort, to help fill the void my mother left. I think the plague scarred him, too, but he never talked about it. He brought home women and my mother would be in the next room, and we could hear him, but they never left each other.

"It went on like that for as long as I can remember. Then they got into an argument. My father was entertaining one of his lovers in the other room, and he went into the kitchen to get more wine. My mother was already there, drunk. I heard them shouting from my bedroom. I was only thirteen at the time, old enough to understand how dysfunctional we were. When I opened my bedroom door, I saw my mother holding a broken wine bottle. She had broken it over my father's head. She killed him," Jonathan paused as his mind traveled back to that horrid night. "Then she killed herself. Slashed her wrists with the broken bottle. Looked right at me as she did it. I watched as she bled to death."

"That's horrible," Dee agreed. "My father killed my mother for adultery, too. Then he tried to have me committed for animating her dead corpse. I was only five, so I guess I can use that as an excuse. I have to say, though, you turned out better than I did," Dee said as he reached for the basket again.

"My father's lover took me in. She and her husband raised me," Jonathan said, moving the basket out of his reach.

"I spent the rest of my childhood in a coma, courtesy of the dragons," Dee said.

"Melanie was my father's lover," Jonathan finished.

"But I thought you two were—" Dee began, but didn't finish the sentence.

"We are," Jonathan confirmed.

"Wow. My biological father and grandfather might be the same person, but that—that is just—well, the word *wrong* comes to mind," Dee said. "I think this conversation has gotten a little off track. Those kittens are going into this river."

"No. You'll have to throw me in, too," Jonathan decided. Dee quirked an eyebrow, then nodded.

"All right, but Barbie stays with me," Dee said.

"What?" Jonathan had barely spoken when he saw Dee wave his arm. The air lifted him, and the basket, too. The black mother cat was lifted out of the basket, and Dee rolled her up in the blanket like a little sausage. The basket of kittens and Jonathan floated in mid-air for a moment. Then Dee's eyes quit glowing, and Jonathan felt the icy water strike. The inky darkness engulfed him.

Rick stepped into the ice-covered hall. Somehow, they had gotten ahead of the maidens, between the maidens and the cavern. Rick saw their shadows reflected on the ice; they were just about to round a corner and come face to face with him. He counted three. Rick touched his mike and clicked it on.

"Is there a way for me to get outside using this cave?" Rick asked. The earpiece crackled, and he heard Dominique, his voice small and hollow in the headpiece.

"If you head north, away from the maidens, you'll come to what looks like a dead end. But if you keep going, it should take you outside."

"That's all I need to know. Tell Scully to count to ten, then head into this passageway; it should be clear by then," Rick said, then clicked off the mike before Dominique could object. Dennis stood in the passageway. "Count to ten, then come through," Rick said to him.

Dennis nodded and took a step back, letting the passageway close. Soon, Rick saw the first of the maidens. She was the same silver maiden he had seen earlier. She stopped when she saw him. Then Darlene came into view, along with another maiden Rick hadn't seen before. She was smaller than the other two—at least a head shorter. Her robes were of a white see-through material, her most private parts covered with a thicker white cloth. Rick leveled his eyes on Darlene and saw the hatred rising in hers.

"So we meet again. How about you and I have another go at things?" Rick asked. He didn't wait for an answer as he took off down the winding tunnel. He knew she couldn't catch him, or risk using magic in a tight tunnel such as this. He saw the dead end ahead and forced himself to ignore his instincts. He charged into the wall, closing his eyes.

Dee looked into the dark water. He couldn't see below the surface. The blue-tinted lights reflected off the surface, making it impossible to see below. He watched the gentle waves, hoping for a sign of Jonathan. The black cat squirmed in his arms. Dee was glad he'd wrapped her up; he felt her claws trying to get at him. He walked to the edge of the dock and peered down. He didn't realize how foolish he was being until he felt something grab his ankle and knock him off balance. The next thing he knew, he was falling face-first off the dock and into the icy water below. He threw the cat from his arms, not wanting to pull her down with him. But as he saw her come short of the shore and fall into the water, he realized she wouldn't be able to swim wrapped in the blanket. She would drown.

Then he was under the water. He held his breath, wanting to delay the inevitable drowning for as long as possible. He sank like a cement block, but he opened his eyes and saw a set of legs churning in the water under the dock. It was Jonathan. He'd pulled Dee off the dock. Dee was outraged. Without thinking, he grabbed Jonathan's leg and pulled him down with him.

Dee started to feel the pain in his chest from lack of oxygen. Jonathan was squirming. Dee climbed Jonathan, grabbing his knee, then his belt, until they were face to face. He looked him in the eye. Dee knew he only had a few more minutes before he drowned and Jonathan froze to death. Barbie was sinking in the water a few feet away. Jonathan was holding something in his fists. Kittens—he was holding a kitten in each hand. Dee thought they had died upon impact with the icy water,.

The burning was intolerable. Dee needed a breath of air. He just wanted to drown and get it over with. But if he drowned, so would Barbie. Dee pushed away from Jonathan and morphed into Decompose. He sank faster as his body weight increased. But Dee wasn't drowning anymore. He was always dead in this form. The pain screaming through his body blocked out any pain he otherwise felt. So maybe he wasn't really dead, just always at that last moment of life. But the pain never ceased, at least not for long. His body's rate of healing and dying seemed to increase in this form. He wouldn't completely drown as long as he stayed in the form of Decompose. It was more painful, and he would have rather just drowned, but he couldn't keep Jonathan and Barbie alive if he did. He opened his jaws, scooped Jonathan and Barbie up in his empty skull, and filled it with air from his lungs. Then he sank to the bottom of the river. It was a saltwater river, which meant it led to the ocean. And Dragon Island was in the ocean, wasn't it?

Dennis finished counting to ten and stepped forward. The passageway opened, and he stepped onto the icy floor. Daylight shone through the tunnel, from an open passageway leading outside. He turned just in time to see a blur of silver and white rush down the tunnel and out of the cave. He heard someone scream for Darlene to stop. Then the passageway closed.

Another passageway opened, and Dennis saw Scully and Melanie struggling to carry Lorna's unconscious form. They made it into the tunnel then settled her to the ground while Melanie caught her breath. Dennis hurried over, heading to the passageway that led outside, needing to help Rick. Shia stepped into the hall, pale and barely awake himself. Scully grabbed Dennis's arm as he passed.

"We need your help. Melanie and I can't carry her alone," Scully said. Dennis looked at Lorna. She was barely breathing.

"Rick needs my help," Dennis said curtly.

"Switch with Melanie. She can help Rick," Scully decided. The two men stared at each other for a moment. Then Dennis consented. He handed the syringe to Shia, then pointed at Melanie.

"There are three maidens and an island full of unicorns out there. Watch his back, okay?" Dennis instructed. Her face begged him to be joking. Scully looked at her sharply.

"Get going," Scully said as he put Lorna's arm over his shoulder. Dennis did the same as Melanie mumbled a curse word or two that Dennis didn't know the meaning of. Then she hurried down the hall.

"You can't kill him!" Vivian shouted. Rick had to admit he was surprised she was speaking on his behalf. He stood next to the silver boulder in the white snow. The white maiden was cold in the harsh temperature, but it didn't seem to bother the other two. The sun was shining, reflecting off the snow, but the air was still bitter.

Rick squinted against the bright sunlight. He guessed Darlene was doing the same. He walked carefully along the side of the boulder, keeping it to his left so he wouldn't be attacked from that angle. Already, white unicorns approached.

"No more games," Darlene said. One of the unicorns kicked at her; she flicked her fingers at the animal and sent it flying away in sparks of fire. She raised her hand, and Rick had a feeling she intended to do the same to him. The two maidens were behind her, the silver one still protesting. Rick tried to dodge the blow, but he knew he was going to come up short. He hit the snow with a thud, sending up a puff of white, snowy powder. Where was Dennis?

With Dennis helping, they made quick time down the silver passageway, into a white cave, then a black. Scully almost slipped on the damp floor, but managed to keep his footing. Shia went ahead of them, making sure the caves were clear before they entered. They passed into another silver cave.

"Dude, I am really getting sick of all this ice," Shia mumbled as he slid across the frozen ground.

"One more, and we'll be in the lab," Scully reassured him.

Melanie leaped through the passageway, seeing the problem as soon as she hit the ground. She was behind the maidens, and Rick was on the other side. She wasn't sure why she cared so much, why she was risking her neck for someone she barely knew. This was her brother's escapade, not hers. But she could do this, and the fact Dennis had doubted her made her want to prove her capability even more. She jumped on the silver boulder and raced along its top. She ignored the clustering unicorns, although she was surprised at how many there were. She heard the woman she assumed was Darlene say something. She didn't know anyone else who was covered in black fur. Scully had told her how powerful the woman was. She had been his match when she was just a witch. Now she had the power of not just one, but all Five Royal Dragons. She was the best there was, better than Scully, better than Lorna, and most definitely better than her. But everyone had weaknesses—at least, Melanie told herself so as she jumped down, landing between Rick and Darlene. She pulled her sword out as she landed. Sparks flew from Darlene's fingers. Scully said that was how Darlene did magic—the same way her father and her father's father had. Both Melanie and Scully had studied magic with the great Jafar McPowin; she knew how his magic worked. Her sword had been cast with a counter spell—any magic cast with McPowin chants was deflected by its blade. Same as Scully's, if he still had the same sword, and she guessed he did. The sparks hit the blade as she moved it to absorb every flame. She felt the snow behind her fly up from the ground and hit her back.

"Counter-flick, bitch," Melanie retorted. The flames jumped from the blade back to Darlene. She was confused by Melanie's sudden appearance, and the sparks hit her face, temporarily blinding her.

"Get up and move!" Melanie shouted at Rick, who had fallen into the snowdrift behind her. His eyes widened at the sight of her.

"We have to go now!" Melanie said again. He got to his feet and nodded at Darlene. She turned to look.

"Cute trick," Darlene commented. She flicked her wrist again and Melanie moved her sword to absorb the spell. Then Darlene raised her staff. The rainbow gem changed to bright silver, then she aimed it at them.

Melanie had no time to recover. Before she could block the dragon magic, a thick layer of ice covered her sword. She dropped it before the ice could encompass her hand. Another burst of sparks shot past her, hitting Rick. She felt scorching heat as the flames just missed her. She tried to jump out of the way, but she felt something tearing at her hair.

Darlene was pulling her hair! Melanie screamed as Darlene slammed the side of her face against the silver boulder. Darkness threatened to overtake her. She saw spots of bright light.

"I think it's time for a truce," Rick said. Melanie twisted until she could see him. Lying on the ground was the woman dressed in silver, his right foot planted firmly on her neck. In his hands he held the white-clad woman—one arm across her chest and the other across her face. "Let her go, or I snap both their necks."

"I could kill you long before you could kill them," Darlene spat.

"Maybe, but you'll have to let her go to do it. Won't you?" Rick taunted. He almost sounded like he was enjoying this.

Darlene paused. The white maiden whined.

"What kind of truce?" Darlene asked.

"I don't kill anyone. You don't kill anyone. We both walk away and go our separate ways. The next time our paths cross, all bets are off. Deal?" Rick asked. Darlene hesitated then loosened her grip on Melanie, shoving her away, knocking her into the snow.

Rick tossed the white maiden to the side. Her head hit the boulder, knocking her out. In the same motion, he was airborne, crashing into Darlene. In a blur of motion Melanie couldn't distinguish, Rick attacked. He knocked Darlene down and pulled her belt from her waist. In a few seconds, it was over. The three maidens were unconscious on the ground. Rick tossed the belt away as if it were a useless parcel.

He reached down and helped Melanie to her feet. His skin felt strange. Like pine needles on a tree. She felt dizzy for a moment, then remembered her sword. Ignoring the pain in her skull, she searched the snow for her lost blade.

"I don't believe it," Rick said softly. Melanie found her sword, the blade still coated in ice. She picked it up, then looked where Rick was staring. On the shoreline, not far away, something monstrous was breaking through the surface of the water. At first she thought it was a dragon, then she saw the deformed flesh clinging to its body.

It was Decompose. He crawled out of the ocean onto the silver sandy beach. His jaws opened and a human figure and a smaller object fell out, and Decompose shrunk into his human form.

"Come on; we have to get them before the Meta-morphs come back," Rick said. She hurried after him when she realized the human figure was Jonathan. He seemed okay, getting to his feet and shouting.

❖ ❖ ❖

Everyone had regrouped in Jaff's old lab. It didn't take Dee long to tend Lorna and Shia's injuries. Dee felt cramped and out of place in the tiny lab. It hadn't been made to be occupied by this many people. Lorna and Shia sat on one of the beds in the side room, while Dee made sure they were completely recovered. He heard the sink running behind him; Melanie was washing her hair. Everyone else was in the lab, crowded around the table map.

"Where did my bags end up? You guys brought them, didn't you?" Lorna asked.

"Yeah, I think so," Melanie answered as she dried her hair in a towel. The towel looked dusty to Dee; he didn't see what good all the washing had done. Melanie pulled over a few packs and started searching them.

"I have some beef jerky that should hit the spot, if you fools remembered to bring it," Lorna said. Shia gave her a disgusted look, but said nothing. Melanie pulled out a shiny container and cradled it gently in her arm. She dug a little deeper, found Lorna's jerky, and tossed the bag of dried meats at her. Lorna caught it in mid-air and broke the seal. The teriyaki smell filled the small cavern. Dee felt the pains in his stomach worsen. He looked at the container Melanie was holding.

"What's in there?" Dee asked. Melanie looked at him with a smile on her face.

"The ashes of my dead husband," she told him sweetly. "My dear Freddy—he goes everywhere with me."

"Well that's got to be a good omen," Shia muttered. Lorna offered Shia some jerky, but he politely declined.

"Meeting time, everyone. Come in here, if you will," Scully said, poking his head in the room.

The small cavern felt even more cramped as they all squeezed into the same room. Dee hung back and let the others crowd around the table. Lorna ended up next to him, and he felt nauseous listening to her as she chomped on the jerky. Dennis and Rick smelled the meat and joined in the feasting. Even Dominique took a strip. Jonathan started to ask for some as well, but Scully cut him off.

"People, please; we can eat later. Right now, we need to figure out a plan. We can't just stay in this cave. We have the Meta-morph blood and Barbie, so Ethan should be able to recreate the plague he and Jaff originally cast. He can create a cure for Dee and modify the plague to make the dragons vulnerable to it."

"Let's deal with the dragons first, shall we?" Rick asked.

197

"My thoughts exactly. Ethan thinks he can make a liquid form of the plague and infect Dee with it. Then Dee can infect the dragons," Scully continued.

"One problem with that," Dee pointed out. "I can't use my powers against the dragons as long as the Queen is around."

"I can fix that," Lorna said, still chewing jerky. She swallowed the food before continuing. "We can create a force field to go around the Queen's nest. It can block her mental powers, keeping her from contacting the other dragons. It would be just like the one the dragons used to trap Dee in the Valley of Death."

"You can make something like that?" Scully asked.

"Sure, especially if Dennis helps. If you can make these radios out of scraps, you can help me make force fields," Lorna said.

"Sounds good. How soon do you think you two can make something like that?" Scully asked. The two of them looked at each other for a moment. Then Lorna looked at the map, staring at the Queen's nest.

"I'd say we need to modify five stones. We'll put one in each room surrounding the Queen's lair. We should be able to program them to activate on command," Lorna began.

"Six hours," Dennis said.

"Sounds like a good estimate. Ethan, how long to make the potion?" Scully asked.

"I still need to turn Barbie into a human. Her sample needs to be human blood. But I'd say I could make their time line—six hours, maybe a few more," Ethan agreed.

"I think we should plan on twelve hours before we try to instigate the plan. We'll have to split into groups to get the stones planted. Until then, we can sleep in shifts so we'll all be rested. Dominique, you help Ethan with the potions, Lorna and Dennis, get started on the stones. Melanie, you take first watch to guard the passageway and keep our force field in place around the lab. Everyone else go to the side room and try to get some sleep. Lorna, you can pass out some food; we need to keep our strength up. And Dominique, try to keep Hank away from Barbie."

Scully slept for six hours, then took Melanie's position as guard. Dennis and Lorna finished programming the stones in five hours, then slept for the next seven hours. Shia, Jonathan, and Rick slept the full twelve hours, since their services were not needed. Dee tended Barbie once she was turned human again. She was quite frightened to be back in a human woman's body. She had forgotten all about being on the island. She didn't know anyone or remember Darlene or Jaff. Dee spoke to her telepathically, and she was thrilled someone could understand her. Hank got along with her better than they expected, but Dominique ensured they stayed separated. She took a liking to Rick, and he let her curl up with him on one of the cots. Dee never slept, but he wasn't much help to anyone.

No one noticed when Ethan told Dominique to go to bed; they had both been up for six hours. Ethan stayed up. He had to finish the potions. He didn't see that he had any choice. As the shift change concluded, Ethan thought Scully would tell him to go to bed. When Scully noticed his hands shaking, Ethan thought for sure he had been caught.

"Ethan, have you gotten any sleep?" Scully asked.

"Yes, of course I did. I took a nap during Melanie's shift," Ethan said casually. And with that, Scully dropped the topic. But Ethan didn't get any sleep; it had been nearly thirty hours since he had rested. His eyes felt heavy as the hours dragged on, but he was almost done, and he could sleep after he was finished. He poured the liquid contents into one large beaker, stirred it gently, then got out five little vials to divide it. The mixture was done. He reached across the table and got another large beaker into which he had melted dragon scales. All he needed was to pour the potion into the five vials. It all seemed simple to his sleepy mind. He lined up the vials and grabbed the beaker. His hands were shaking, and he realized he wouldn't be able to pour the liquid into the small vials. But he had to, they connected to a syringe they were going to use to infect Dee. He grabbed the vial at the top to help steady it, then carefully placed the tip of the beaker on the rim of the vial. He managed to fill three. As he filled the fourth, his hand gave an extra tremble—or maybe he nodded off—he wasn't sure which. But he felt the liquid trickle onto his hand and begin to burn, reacting to his skin much as a chemical would. Suddenly fully alert, he dropped the containers and pulled his hands away. He dropped his hands under the table to hide them as Scully looked at him, hearing the crash of broken glass. He had been studying the dragon map on the other table.

"What happened?" Scully asked, seeing the broken glass. Ethan wiped the potion off his hand with his shirt, keeping it under the table.

He glanced down and saw blood. The beaker had broken his skin, drawing blood. He was infected with the Decompose plague. His head spun as he realized what that meant. He wasn't tired anymore, the fear of becoming a cannibal erased all desire to sleep.

"Ethan? Are you alright?" Scully asked. He moved closer. Rick came out of the side room, having heard the noise.

"I'm fine," Ethan said. "Just dropped the beaker. Get me a towel to clean this up with, will you, Rick? Don't worry. I still have three full vials—plenty to use. I'm just going to wash my hands, I cut myself on some of the glass."

Ethan hurried past them and went into the other room; he turned on the water and washed the wound. But he could already see he was infected. The skin on his hand had the pasty gray look the cannibals always had. He splashed water on his face. Rick grabbed a towel to clean up the mess.

"Don't touch the liquid, it's like acid," Ethan said, hiding his wound from Rick's sight. Rick said nothing, he just quirked an eyebrow. Ethan tried to remember what he knew about the cannibals. Not everyone turned into a cannibal. There was a fifty/fifty chance. He had heard stories. People had described it as an insane feeling of hunger. Your stomach felt like it was on fire, and all you wanted to do was eat. But food lost its flavor—only salty things tasted good. Like blood. He trembled at the thought. The people who didn't turn were the ones that resisted, or weren't smart enough to figure out that they were craving blood. If you didn't eat anything for forty-eight hours, the plague would pass, and you would be no worse for the wear. But it wasn't as easy as starving yourself for two days. Not everyone could do it; some would die trying to resist the temptation. Their bodies couldn't cope. He wondered if Dee would be able to cure him, but the thought of asking him for help and admitting his mistake wasn't an option. He couldn't tell anyone he was infected. He washed off a cloth and wrapped it around his hand. He felt fine; maybe he was wrong. Maybe he had washed the potion off before it infected him.

He walked back to the lab to find that Rick had cleaned up the mess. Dee disposed of the fouled towels used to clean up the spill. Ethan was just short two vials; the others were okay. Ethan showed Scully how to inject the potion, and Scully injected the plague into Dee's arm.

"When this is all done, I can use one of the other vials to make a cure for you. It won't be hard," Ethan promised. Then he went into the other room to get a few hours of sleep before the others got up.

It seemed Ethan had barely closed his eyes when he felt someone shaking his shoulder. He sat up, nearly hitting his head on the bunk bed above him. Dennis stood next to him, looking at him with iridescent eyes. Ethan stared back at him, wondering if his eyes tasted like fish eyes—not that Ethan could recall having ever eaten fish eyes. The entire question puzzled him.

"Time to get up; we're having a final meeting before we take off. We need to pick partners and get our instructions," Dennis said. Then he left to wake Shia on the bunk above him.

Ethan swung his legs off the bed and tried to stand. He felt an awful cramp in his stomach. The pain was unbearable, and for a moment he thought he was going to be sick. He sat and took a deep breath. His hands were trembling; they looked very white. He was starting to get a headache, and he was thirsty, so thirsty. Was he allowed to drink water? His thoughts were fuzzy; he wasn't sure if that was from lack of sleep or infection. What was he saying? If he didn't drink water for two days, couldn't he die from dehydration? Not eating for two days was one thing, but water—he had to have water. His mouth was so dry. He got up, ignoring the cramps, and turned on the sink in the corner of the room. It was a large sink, big enough to climb in and take a bath. He turned on the water and drank it from the faucet.

"There are cups, hon," Melanie said. Ethan looked up to see her standing next to him, tying her hair back in a pony tail. Ethan didn't say anything as he wiped the water from his mouth with his sleeve.

"I have bananas and corn bread for breakfast, people. Here you go, Melanie, Ethan." Lorna was walking around, handing food to everyone. Lorna held out food for Ethan, but Ethan just stared at it. His stomach rumbled in hunger, but he shook his head, refusing. "You feeling okay, Ethan? You look pale."

"I'm fine. Just didn't get much sleep," Ethan said sharply. He moved around her, making an exaggerated amount of room for her as he passed into the other room.

"No telling how long we'll have to camp next to our assigned stone, so here's a jar of water," Rick said as he passed containers of water to everyone. He handed one to Ethan. Ethan opened the lid and hungrily drank the water. Rick paused. "Make sure you refill that before you leave."

"Everyone gather around," Scully called. Ethan stayed back and leaned against the wall, his jar already half-empty. "Everything is prepared. Lorna, why don't you explain how to operate the gems."

"Right. We have five gems." Lorna held up a pale blue stone, flat—only an inch thick, but nearly five inches in diameter. And true to tradition, it was a five-sided shape; Ethan couldn't remember what the shape was called. It was flat in the center, then curved towards the outer rim, so the rim was thinner than the center. "You have to touch all five sides on the top of the stone, pressing them in counter-clockwise order, then touch the center last. This will activate the force field. Be sure you aren't standing directly above it because it will injure you if you come into contact with it. This field is capable of blocking mental thought waves; it will prevent even the Queen from breaking through. I'll be creating a secondary force field on the inner side of the circle as an extra precaution."

"You should also partially bury the stone in the ground," Dennis added. Lorna nodded. Ethan had already stopped paying attention; he was debating whether to get more water from the sink.

"Sounds easy enough. Once the force field is up, Dee should be able to cast his plague, and the dragons should be taken care of. Once they are down, we can take on the Queen without the male dragons interfering," Scully said. "Dominique will stay here with Hank and keep track of everyone. We'll be using the radios, like last time. The rest of us will break into groups of two and stay in the rooms with our gems to be sure no one disturbs them. Our job is to get the stones in place and keep them activated. If just one of them goes down, the Queen will escape, and Dee won't be able to cast his plague."

"The stones don't need to be turned on at the same time," Dennis added. "The Queen won't notice until all five are activated. Activate your stone as soon as you arrive in the cave."

"All right, any questions?" Scully asked. Jonathan and Shia asked to be shown how to operate the stone again. Everyone else seemed satisfied. Ethan refilled his jar of water and came back as they were deciding who should pair up with whom.

"I'll take the cat," Rick announced. The black-haired woman was standing next to him, attached to him like a puppy to a child.

"I'll take the kid," Dennis said quickly as he realized he couldn't pair up with his fellow Zalite.

Jonathan seemed about to say something, but Melanie cut him off before he could say a word.

"I think Lorna and I should pair up. Us ladies should stick together. Plus, I'm curious why my Maky is so interested in a woman of your size. I mean, you must have a stunning personality. We are going to have so much fun. We can share stories about—" Scully interrupted her before she could continue.

"Then Dee and I will pair up. That leaves Jonathan and Ethan. Now we just need to pick rooms, and we'll be off," Scully said.

"Wait a minute," Ethan said. "Why do I get the crazy kid? I'm not playing baby sitter. It's not like he's going to be of any use."

"I'm not thrilled about it, either, pretty boy. I doubt your hair gel is going to be of much use," Jonathan shot back.

"You petty little infant," Ethan growled, pushing past the others to reach him.

"We will take the white room," Rick said, cutting Ethan off. "Anyone mind if we head off?"

"I could pair up with you, Jonathan. Maybe we can go swimming again," Dee commented. He glanced at the map.

"And drown some more kittens," Jonathan added.

"We'll take the red cave; it's the farthest from here," Dee decided.

"I don't remember you being so sarcastic before," Jonathan remarked.

"I'm a quick learner," Dee quipped. He passed one of the blue stones to Scully and headed through a passageway.

"Right, let's go, Barbie, come on," Rick said.

"We'll take the silver cave, next to yours. We can travel together," Lorna suggested, obviously not excited about being alone with Melanie. Dennis leaned over the map and pointed to a room.

"Shia and I will take the black cave; it's close," Dennis told Dominique and they departed as well.

"Well, I guess you two get gold. Good luck with that. Buzz me on the radio if you get lost," Dominique said. He handed a stone to Jonathan. Ethan sighed and waved his hand dismissively.

"Think you can hold on to that stone?" Ethan asked. He bent over the map and tried to figure out the route they would have to take, but looking at the glowing dots hurt his eyes and made his head hurt more. He closed his eyes and looked away. "Figure out a route for us. You know—be useful."

"I'm not your slave," Jonathan snapped.

"No, but you'll be dragon lunch without me, so pick a route already," Ethan growled. Jonathan took a deep breath and looked at the map.

Rick led the way out of the lab. The three women followed. They crossed the icy floor slowly in silence, but the silence didn't last long. Not with Melanie present.

"So how long have you and Scully known each other?" Melanie asked.

"I don't think right now is the time to discuss that," Lorna said. Rick opened the passageway to the next room—a red cave, empty like the one they were in. It was strange that the dragons were never around. It was almost as if they were avoiding contact.

Dee and Scully took the longer route to the center cave. They went into a different silver dragon cave. The cave was deserted. The two moved on silently, crossing the ice with ease. Scully was glad Dee didn't want to talk. He didn't feel much like talking. He was too busy worrying about whether this was going to work. Everything hung in the balance. If just one group failed, they would all fail. He took a deep breath and opened the next passageway, a white cave—again abandoned. He gestured for Dee to follow and then stepped through, sending a white cloud of dust into the air.

❖ ❖ ❖

Dennis and Shia chose the most direct route—through the scroll room next to Jaff's lab, then a black cave, a white cave, and then their final destination—another black cave. It seemed easy enough.

Dennis was amazed at the rows of scrolls. Golden walls reached the ceiling, covered in slots filled with scrolls. Dennis couldn't tell how many walls there were; it was like a maze. Shia was astounded at the dazzling array of gold.

"This place is amazing," Shia whispered.

"Yeah, it sure is something," Dennis said, unimpressed. He walked down another hallway of scrolls, hoping he wouldn't get lost. The room hadn't appeared this confusing on the map.

Twilight of One: The Plague of Decompose

Ethan walked into the silver dragon cave that a moment ago Rick and the women had walked through. He slipped on the icy ground and cursed. He fell to the ground, hitting his hip hard. He barely felt the pain, he could only feel the screaming hunger of his stomach and the throbbing migraine in his head.

"You okay?" Jonathan asked. Ethan looked at him; he seemed so agile on the icy surface.

"You had to pick this route, didn't you? I suppose we will be traveling through mostly silver dragon caves—just so you can watch me fall," Ethan said harshly. Jonathan didn't react.

"Of course not. This is the only silver room we have to go through," Jonathan told him sweetly, annoying Ethan even more. Everything was annoying. He struggled to his feet, refusing to accept help.

"You know, I'm amazed at how well everyone is working together," Dee said, breaking the silence. Scully looked back as he prepared to open the next passageway.

"You're right. I never thought my sister would be so—cooperative," Scully finished. He stood aside as Dee moved toward the passageway. He stepped from the chalky white room into the sandy red cave. He hadn't taken more than a step when he felt a hard blow on his head. Dee fell to the ground, more out of shock than anything. When he looked up, he saw Darlene holding her staff in the air, preparing to take another swing at him.

Scully caught her off guard. She looked up as Scully tossed a handful of pink dust into her face. The powder created a flash of light, temporarily blinding her as Scully kicked her in the stomach, sending her across the cave, into the wall behind her.

Dennis rounded another shelf full of scrolls, starting to get frustrated. Were they going in circles? Then, directly ahead of them, was the Gold Dragon—the same dragon Dennis had watched carry away his best friend. A furry of anger built up inside him as he remembered what the creature had done. The dragon was looking at some of the scrolls, writing on them. The beast looked up and saw them, its tentacle-like hairs wiggling around like antennae.

"Oh, no," Shia gasped. Dennis held his ground. He saw a wall not covered in cubby holes. That had to be their way out, Dennis decided.

Somehow he had to figure out a way to get past the dragon. Shia's breathing came in ragged gasps; he was panicking.

Ethan quickened his pace, deciding the faster they got through the caves and put the stone in place the sooner he would be rid of Jonathan. Jonathan nonchalantly followed, talking to him as if they were out for a friendly stroll.

"You know," Ethan interrupted—he hadn't even been listening to Jonathan. "I'm starting to think it's a good thing I was paired up with you."

"Really?" Jonathan said as they crossed a red cavern.

"Yeah, sure."

"What made you change your mind?"

"Well, if I turn into a cannibal you'll be the first person I eat. I'll be doing everyone else a favor," Ethan said nicely. Jonathan looked at him, puzzled, he couldn't decide if Ethan was joking or not.

"What do you mean?"

"I accidentally infected myself with the Decompose plague while making the potions," Ethan said casually. Jonathan's jaw dropped as he realized Ethan was serious.

"You're infected? Why didn't you tell anyone? Dee could have fixed you!" Jonathan exclaimed.

Ethan couldn't remember why he hadn't told anyone; he knew there had been a reason, but he couldn't think of it.

"I don't believe this; I mean, honestly, you warlocks and witches have so many issues. I thought—" Jonathan fell silent as he looked through the passageway he opened. Ethan walked up next to him, the conversation forgotten. He looked into the black cave ahead and saw a large pit in the center of the room. There was a narrow ledge that went around the edge of the cavern, but it was easy to slip and fall into the pit.

"Not a problem, we'll just go a different route," Ethan said.

"No, no we can't. It'll take too long. And we'll probably get lost," Jonathan said stubbornly.

"That's why we have these." Ethan tapped his headset for emphasis. "We just ask Dominique to give us an alternate route."

"But we aren't that far. We'll be really careful," Jonathan encouraged. Then they both heard deep breathing, unmistakably a dragon. They fell silent again, still in the doorway. It sounded like more than one dragon. Ethan pushed Jonathan aside and walked into the cavern.

The black rock was covered in condensation, making the surface slippery. He grabbed the wall for balance. "What are you doing? There's someone in there."

Ethan ignored him and moved closer to the edge of the pit. It was roughly an eight-foot drop, and at the bottom were six black dragons. At one time, the pit had been filled with water, something black dragons adored. Now there were only a few puddles of water here and there. He looked back at Jonathan.

"They're asleep," he whispered. "If we're quiet, we can reach the other side without waking them."

Jonathan turned white as he shook his head. He mouthed the word 'no' over and over, and he shook his head. For a moment, Ethan thought he had gone into some sort of fit.

"We'll be fine. Just follow my lead," Ethan encouraged.

"I thought you didn't want to go this way," Jonathan snapped, finding his voice again.

"I changed my mind."

"You just want to go this way because I don't want to."

"That's ridiculous," Ethan dismissed, although a part of him enjoyed watching Jonathan squirm. He moved along the wall and made his way to the other side of the room. He heard Jonathan mumble something under his breath then the soft sound of his footsteps as he followed. "I just realized something."

"What?" Jonathan whispered back.

"I don't know where we're going. You should be leading us, not me," Ethan said with a grin as he looked back.

"I'm not passing you on this ledge. Just keep walking; I'll tell you when we need to exit," Jonathan said, trying to keep his voice low. Their headsets made a crackling sound. They reached up and turned their headsets off, casting the room into silence. They waited to see if the sound had woken the dragons. Confident they were still sleeping, the men moved on, Ethan trying to ignore his throbbing head. His hands were shaking, making it hard to grip the wet rock on the cave wall. He was starting to feel dizzy when Jonathan grabbed his shoulder. "This is it. We go through here."

Ethan nodded and held up his gem, the passageway opened, and Ethan saw a gold room ahead. He walked in, Jonathan on his heels. They waited until the passageway was closed before they spoke.

"I didn't think you were going to make it back there," Jonathan said as he exhaled. "You didn't look too good."

"Thanks for that, Jonathan; you don't look good, either," Ethan snapped. Jonathan led him across the room, still jittery from the stress.

"Well, coming from you, that's probably a good thing. When I start looking good to you, that probably means you want to eat me," Jonathan remarked as he opened the next passageway. Ethan almost smiled, then he followed him into the next cavern. He looked down as he entered, and when he looked up, it was at the pointed edge of an arrowhead.

Scully had hoped to avoid this confrontation. He watched Darlene slam into the wall, sending up a cloud of red dust. She let out a scream, but it was anger, not pain. Dee was still on the ground, out of the way. She was after Dee, not him. Dee couldn't fight her; she was bound to have one of those Royal Dragon Gems. Scully pulled the pale blue stone out of his pouch and tossed it to Dee. He caught it and looked at Scully, confused.

"Have Dominique guide you the rest of the way," Scully said.

"No, no. I'm not leaving you here to fight her by yourself," Dee refused.

"You're more important than I am. Now go," Scully said. Dee opened his mouth to object, but Darlene was already back on her feet. He gave Scully one last look, then made a mad run for the passage that would lead him to the Queen's nest.

"Not so fast," Darlene said. She raised her hand and moved her fingers. She was going to create a block on the passageways, trapping them in the cavern. Scully charged, forcing her to block his attack. The spell incomplete, Dee passed through the passageway, unharmed. She kicked Scully away, and he recovered and prepared for her next attack, his sword ready.

"Mak Scully. I'd wondered what had become of you. Got your flesh back, I see," Darlene mocked, showing him cat-like fangs.

"No thanks to you," Scully snapped. He knew he couldn't fight her. Back when she was a sorceress, he would have stood a chance, but now with her dragon powers, he was no match for her. His best bet was to stall her. She turned away, as if he meant nothing to her. Scully blocked her path. She glared at him.

Twilight of One: The Plague of Decompose

"My feud is not with you," Darlene said calmly.

"Well *mine* is," Scully shot back. She looked at him with yellow eyes; the seconds ticked by. Scully started to sweat as he wondered what she was thinking.

"I loved you," Darlene said simply. Scully stared at her in shock. She had said it bluntly, as if it explained everything. "You hate me because I never gave you back your flesh. But if I had, you would have left me."

"You never told me that," Scully said. He felt like she had kicked him in the gut. He'd had no idea.

"Would it have made a difference?" Darlene asked. Scully felt like he was missing part of the conversation. It was as if she'd already had this talk planned out; she wasn't even responding to what he said. "If I had restored your flesh, would you have stayed with a freak like me, or would you have run off with your beauty queen models?"

Scully stared at her, he didn't understand what she was talking about. She kept looking at him as if he should say something.

"You loved me?" Scully asked.

Her face contorted in anger and frustration. "You wouldn't leave me as long as we were both freaks. No other woman would have a man that looked like a skeleton," Darlene said as if he were stupid for not figuring that out himself.

"I didn't *look like* a skeleton; I *was* a skeleton. That was the problem!" Scully shouted. "I couldn't have a woman because I literally couldn't have her!"

"That's all this is about to you, isn't it? You couldn't have *sex* while you were a skeleton?"

"What *else* is this supposed to be about?" Scully shouted in frustration.

"Fine, Scully; if you love the physical pleasures in life so much, you'll cherish this," Darlene snapped.

She swung at him with her staff. Scully dodged, then he realized her swing had been a distraction. He felt her kick his calf. He stumbled, but managed not to fall. That didn't matter to her; she grabbed his wrist and twisted it—the same arm that held his samurai sword. She had already dropped her own staff; she didn't need it anymore. She wanted his sword. He backed away, trying to regain some leverage, but soon felt the cool red stone behind him. He was against the wall. He twisted his body and tried to wiggle free, but he couldn't so long as he held the sword. He had to let go.

Knowing he would be powerless against her without his sword, he let go. He'd thought he would be able to free himself, but she was too fast. He didn't even see her flip the blade around, didn't see her drive the cool steel into his body. He only felt the blinding pain as she ran his sword into his chest.

"Tell me, Scully, do you love your flesh now?" Darlene asked. She took a few steps, pulling his sword out as she moved away. The pain was worse after she pulled it out. He clutched his stomach and looked down to see the blood beginning to soak his clothes. He pulled away one of his hands and saw it covered in blood. He felt faint. Slowly, ever so slowly, he sank to the floor, not wanting to fall.

He looked at Darlene to see her standing over him, watching him die. It sickened him. He wanted to take her with him, finish her before he died. That was all he wanted; his last wish was revenge.

Dominique stood over the glowing map, looking at the dots that represented his troops. That was what he had decided to call them—his troops. He held their fates in his hands. He saw when Dee and Scully split up.

"Dominique!" Dee's voice shouted in his ear.

"Don't shout; I'm here," Dominique responded.

"Scully needs backup; it's Darlene."

"I'm on it; you keep going to the Queen's nest. I'll send someone else."

"All right, but send it quick," Dee agreed. Dominique pressed the button on his headset so he could talk.

"Ethan, Ethan come in," Dominique called. Ethan and Jonathan were in the cavern next to Scully's, it would take no time at all for them to reach him. Silence. "Jonathan?"

Again, no answer. Had neither of them turned on their headsets?

"Idiots," Dominique cursed. He pressed the speaker button again. "Dennis? Dennis are you there? Shia?"

They were both in the scroll room, right next to the room Scully and Darlene were in, but he didn't get an answer. Something was wrong. Surely, not everyone had turned their mikes off. He looked under the table at Hank. "Can you believe this?" he asked the dog, but Hank had no response for him.

"Rick? Rick, do you read me?" Dominique asked. He prayed he did. There was a crackle of static, then he heard Rick's voice.

"Yeah, I'm here. What's wrong?"

"Scully needs assistance. No one else is answering their mikes," Dominique said, loving that he was giving orders.

"We are," Lorna snapped over the radio. Dominique winced at her sharp tone.

"You're farther away, and Rick's had experience with Darlene before."

"Darlene?" Rick asked.

"Darlene," Dominique told him simply.

"Enough said; where do we go?"

"There's a black cave south of you. Go through it, but be careful, there are dragons in it. They'll leave you alone, though; go south, and you should enter the room Scully is in."

The Gold Dragon had noticed them. Dennis was sure of it. The beast raised its head and spread its wings, completely blocking the passage they needed to reach.

"Shia, I'll deal with the dragon. You make a run for the passageway," Dennis ordered. Shia looked at him with fear in his eyes. "You can do it; just run. If you get lost, contact Dominique."

He reached up to the kid's ear and turned his headset back on. Dennis gave him a final nod, then charged around the shelf, towards the dragon.

Dennis flared his skin and the barbs on his body attached themselves to the Gold Dragon, who wrapped his golden hairs around Dennis. Dennis pulled, forcing the dragon to move, creating an opening for Shia. Shia took it, running like a crazed jackrabbit and disappearing through the passageway.

Dennis felt his tender flesh being literally torn away by the struggling dragon. Dennis fought back, refusing to give ground. The two became a mass of golden hair and flesh. Dennis crashed into one of the shelves, pulling the dragon with him. It caused a ripple effect, and rows upon rows of scroll-filled shelves tumbled down, eventually the toppling shelves circled the room and came back to where they were.

Dennis tried to free himself before the shelf fell on top of them, but his flesh was embedded too deeply. The shelf toppled, with the weight of the shelves behind it. Dennis felt the impact, and darkness engulfed him.

Ethan went cross-eyed staring at the arrow pointed at his forehead. Then he focused his eyes on the man before him. He had a hood covering his head, but the black fur on his hands and arms were unmistakable.

"McCaw?" Ethan asked. The man kept the crossbow bolt aimed at his head and reached up with one hand to remove his hood.

"Step over there," the man said, and Jonathan and Ethan sidestepped to the left, allowing the passageway to close.

"I thought Darlene had black fur," Jonathan pointed out. "I thought Darlene was a girl."

"I'm not Darlene," the man snapped, aiming the arrow at Jonathan.

"No, you're McCaw, Jaff's son. We thought you were dead," Ethan said in surprise.

"How do you know who I am?" McCaw asked.

"Well, like Jonathan pointed out, not many people have black fur," Ethan looked at Jonathan. "He's Darlene's brother."

"Really? Wow, you guys should have a family reunion," Jonathan quipped.

"That's not what I meant! How do you know me?" McCaw shouted. Ethan closed his eyes as his migraine grew worse.

"I'm Jaff's cousin," Ethan answered. "I can't believe you aligned yourself with the dragons. I thought you were better than that."

"I'm not anyone's ally. I'm here of my own accord. Tell me where Dee is."

"Dee? Why are you after him?"

"I spent forty years making sure he didn't escape; now I have to set things right and catch him," McCaw said.

"Catch him? With a bow and arrow?" Jonathan asked. "You do know Dee is Decompose, right?"

Ethan laughed; it did seem humorous when Jonathan said it like that. Maybe the plague was just rotting his mind. He didn't really care which, he laughed anyway.

"Are you mocking me?" McCaw asked, pressing the point of the arrow into Ethan's forehead.

"May as well; I'm as good as dead, anyway. You're McCaw. McCaw!" Ethan proclaimed. Jonathan looked at him like he was crazy. "Darlene's only full-blooded sibling, Jaff's only male descendant. You are McCaw—the best of the best; no one is better than you. Not Lorna, not me, not Scully. Not even Decompose! Did you know he single-handedly killed a Queen dragon? Ask Scully; he'll tell you all about it. That is how powerful this guy is. He's practically a—" Ethan paused as something Jaff once told him came back. "Tell me something, McCaw—are you still refusing to practice magic?"

"Huh—that would explain the bow and arrow," Jonathan agreed.

"I do not need magic to defeat Dee. I haven't needed it before, and I don't need it now."

"That's why you hate Dee so much, isn't it? He used his powers, and now people think of him as the devil, an evil god. That's what you've always feared—that you would become so powerful you would turn into a god," Ethan finished.

"Dee represents everything I oppose. Plus, he killed a lot of people. So why don't you tell me where he is?"

"Jonathan," Ethan looked at him, then at the stone Jonathan had tucked in his belt. "I think I'm going to have someone else for dinner."

Jonathan's eyes widened for a moment, then he understood. Ethan screamed and charged McCaw. Jonathan ran in the other direction, and Ethan pushed McCaw back through the passageway, into the room from which they had just come. He wasn't sure how he managed to reach the other side. A thirst for blood overtook him, and he attacked, much like an animal.

Ethan opened the passageway leading into the black cave with the dragons and backed into it, stepping onto the slippery stone. McCaw tossed his broken crossbow and bag of arrows to the ground. He charged Ethan, but Ethan didn't budge. He wrapped his arms around him as if they intended to hug, then they toppled backwards into the pit, landing hard and waking the dragons.

Rick paused before he entered the room with Scully and Darlene inside. He turned off his radio. He wanted to keep the element of surprise as long as he could. Barbie didn't have a radio, so he didn't worry about turning hers off. He stepped into the cavern, Barbie at his side, but he paid no attention to her. He saw Scully sitting on the floor, and he smelled the blood long before he saw it. Darlene held a sword at her side, admiring the blood on it. She had her back to Rick.

"Now to decide if I want to leave you to slowly die, or finish you off now," Darlene said. "Or you could repent, Scully, and I could turn you back into a skeleton. You won't die if you don't have any flesh from which to bleed."

Rick waited no longer. He didn't care if he made noise or not. He charged, but she heard him. She intended to stab him, much as she had Scully, but Rick knew hand to hand combat. She swung the blade, and he grabbed it. The blade sliced into his hand, but he didn't care. It confused her enough that he had time to punch her in the face. He twisted the blade, forcing her to let go. The sword fell to the ground with a clang. Rick head-butted her, sending her to the floor. He knew she would recover, and he ducked as her staff flew through the air and into her awaiting hand. He couldn't fight her magic, and she knew it.

"Why don't we finish this, now?" Darlene growled. Her growl was met by another—Barbie; Rick had forgotten about her. Barbie leaped between them, her face contorted into a snarl. She hissed and growled, protecting Rick. Darlene's expression changed. "Mother?"

Rick grinned. He had forgotten that Barbie was Darlene's mother.

"How is this possible?" Darlene gasped.

"And you know what's funny, Darlene? Spending over half a century in the form of a cat can rot your memory. I'm betting she doesn't remember you," Rick said.

"Mother, it's me—Darlene," she said, trying to make her remember. Rick put his hand on Barbie's shoulder and whispered in her ear.

"Kill her," Rick said, just loud enough for Darlene to hear. Barbie attacked, something Rick hadn't really expected. She jumped at Darlene, biting her and clawing away with her fingers. Darlene went on the defense, but was reluctant to strike her own mother. It reminded Rick of a literal cat fight; he started to chuckle as he realized it was considered a cat fight when two women fought. The irony of the human culture was not lost on Rick. He shook off his amusement and reached for Darlene, tearing her belt off; he wondered how many more times he would have to remove it.

Then Rick turned his attention to Scully. There was an awful lot of blood. Rick crouched down and touched Scully's forehead gingerly. He pulled one of his eyelids open and jumped as the pupil reacted to the light and Scully blinked. He was alive. Barbie cried out in pain. Rick decided to end things.

He walked behind Darlene, who had Barbie pinned to the wall. Rick grabbed the sorceress and slammed her head into the wall. He heard a crack, and wondered if he'd fractured her skull. She fell limp to the ground. Satisfied, Rick went back to Scully.

"How are you?" Rick asked. Scully licked his lips. There was no blood coming from his mouth—that was a good sign.

"Been better," Scully admitted. He sounded weak, but stronger than Rick expected. He ripped Scully's shirt open and looked at the wound. Blood was everywhere, but the bleeding seemed to be slowing. Rick took his belt off and put it around Scully, using it to hold a bundled piece of cloth in place. It would have to work as a temporary bandage.

"I don't think it hit any main arteries," Rick said, "but you won't last long if we don't stop the bleeding. And even if we do, you're going to get a nasty infection."

"Thanks for the pep talk," Scully murmured.

"Don't worry, we'll send Dee to fix you. I'll—" Rick dropped off as he heard a crunching sound behind him. Scully looked at him, puzzled as well.

"What was that?" Scully asked, putting his hands back on his chest. Rick had a feeling he already knew. Barbie was standing over Darlene, and in her hands was Darlene's staff. She was pushing down in a twisting motion, as if driving a stake into the ground. Rick felt sick. He'd just let Barbie kill her daughter. Barbie didn't know any better; she didn't remember, but Rick knew he should have stopped her. He hadn't thought she would continue to beat Darlene after she was unconscious.

"We should move you," Rick said quickly.

"What? I'm bleeding to death; I don't think moving me is a smart idea," Scully snapped.

"Don't be silly; you've lost a lot of blood. You don't know what you're talking about," Rick said, and he picked Scully up gently. He couldn't leave him lying in plain sight of Darlene's body. He guessed that wasn't something Scully would want to see. He moved him to a corner of the room where a rock formation blocked the view of the rest of the cavern. Scully winced in pain as Rick laid him on the ground again, making sure he was propped up on the wall behind him. Then he went back to Darlene.

He took the staff from Barbie's grasp and tossed it across the room. He grabbed her wrist and pulled her over to look at Scully again. He tried not to look at Darlene, but Barbie had done a good job of working her over with the blunt end of the staff. There was no point in checking to see if she was alive.

"Scully, do you want us to stay with you until Dee comes back? I can leave Barbie here," Rick said. Scully's eyes were closed. He looked at the pools of blood on the floor and decided there was no point in checking for a pulse. He left the cavern, pulling Barbie behind him.

Shia had run faster than he ever remembered running in his life. He reached a square room and paused to catch his breath. This was it, wasn't it? He looked at the black walls; this had to be it.

He knelt in the center of the room and placed the blue stone gently on the ground. He was supposed to partially bury it. He rubbed his fingers on the hard rock. He needed to something with which to dig. He looked around the empty room for a moment. Then remembered his jar of water. He shattered the glass and used a broken piece to dig a hole. Shia carefully placed the stone in the shallow hole, then pressed the sides and center of the stone in the sequence he had been shown. Instantly, a bluish tint was cast over the room as a force field divided the room in half. Shia remembered to stay on the side of the room not connected to the Queen's nest. He sat back and tried to catch his breath. Then he remembered his radio. He reached up, clicked it on, and heard the steady hiss of static.

"Dominique? Are you there?"

"Shia, is that you? What happened? Why isn't Dennis with you?" Dominique asked.

"We had a problem; Dennis had to stay behind and fight the Gold Dragon. I—I don't think he made it," Shia said, trying not to get too emotional.

"He's still in the scroll room; I haven't seen him move in a while," Dominique confirmed.

"I have my stone in place," Shia said, trying to brighten the mood.

"Okay, that's good. You're the first one. Just stay put and keep your radio on," Dominique said.

"Okay." Shia looked wearily around the dark cavern. It was creepy. Why did he have to be stuck in the black cave?

Jonathan was terrified. He ran and ran, not thinking about where he was going. Ethan was turning into a cannibal and there was a monster man running around with a bow and arrow—it was too much to handle. Now he was by himself. He ran and ran; some of the caves had dragons in them, but they didn't have time to react to him. He was moving too fast. Splash—he was in a black cave, then he slid on icy silver stone, then through a steamy golden room, then a white one, then a silver one, then a black one—and on and on he ran. It began to dawn on him that he should have reached the Queen's nest by now. But it didn't occur to him to turn his radio on and ask for directions. He'd forgotten all about it. He just wanted to get as far away from Ethan and McCaw as he could.

Melanie and Lorna reached their room without any problems. Melanie knelt on the floor and used her sword to break the ice. Then she dug a hole with her hands for the stone and activated it. A blue force field went up with a slight crackle. Melanie stepped back, looking at it proudly, then cupped her hands over her mouth, blowing on them for warmth; the silver cave was cold.

"Dominique, our stone is activated," Lorna announced. "Should I create the secondary force field?"

"No, not yet. Only you and Shia have your stones in place," Dominique said.

"Does anyone need help?" Lorna asked. There was a pause on the other side of the radio. Melanie tapped her headpiece to see if it was still working.

"My stone is in place," Dee's voice said. "Is that three?"

"So far, but Rick and Barbie just reached their cave. Hold on," Dominique said.

Rick put his stone in place and activated it. Barbie jumped in fright at the glowing force field. Rick warned her to not go near it, then he spoke into his mike, but only silence answered. He had forgotten to turn it back on after fighting Darlene. Rick corrected his mistake.

"Dominique, what's our status?" Rick asked.

"Good. We're still waiting on Jonathan and Ethan, though. I can't reach either of them."

"Where are they?" Dee asked.

"Jonathan is moving around a lot. I think he's lost, but he's turned off his mike. Ethan hasn't moved in a while; I think something happened to him," Dominique said.

"Is everyone else okay?" Melanie asked.

"Dennis hasn't moved in a while either," Dominique said.

"Where's Dennis?" Rick asked.

"He sacrificed himself so I could get away. I'm sorry, Rick," Shia said softly. Rick closed his eyes and said a silent prayer for his fallen friend. He promised he would go back for his body when this was over.

"We lost Scully, too," Rick said, trying to put it as kindly as Shia had. Everyone was silent for a moment.

"They would want us to finish this," Lorna said.

"I agree," Dee commented.

"Jonathan had the stone when they left here," Dominique offered.

"There are six of us and five rooms to protect," Rick said. "I say we fan out, one to a room, then someone can leave to look for Jonathan."

"What about Ethan?" Lorna asked.

"We can't divide up like that. That's defeating the whole point of us doing this in groups of two," Dee argued. "Besides, Barbie can't watch a room by herself—she is a cat!"

"Freddy can partner up with her," Melanie offered.

"Who?"

"My dead husband—in the urn," Melanie said, as if they were stupid for not knowing. "I have him here with me."

"No, no, no," Dee snapped. "No one is going to leave a cat or an urn in charge of guarding a room. And we aren't going to put Hank in a room, either. Everyone is going to stay where they are, and I am going to go find Jonathan. Melanie and Lorna, you are in the room next to mine—send Melanie over here so she can watch my room while I'm gone."

"Why do they get to split up? What about the buddy system?" Rick asked.

"You're the only one with a buddy right now, Rick. And your buddy is a cat!" Dee shouted. Rick started to grind his teeth together.

"Technically, I still have Freddy, so I kind of have a buddy," Melanie added.

"Everyone stay where you are. Okay? Just stay put. Dominique, tell me where Jonathan is," Dee ordered. Rick bit his lip; he didn't like being told what to do. It was different when Scully gave the orders—he trusted him. But he didn't trust Dee.

There was only silence on the radio as they waited for an answer. Then they heard a loud explosion. A hiss came over the radio, and Rick realized his ears were ringing. He put the earpiece on his other ear.

"What just happened?" Dee shouted. Rick took a deep breath; things weren't looking good.

"I think someone just took out Dominique," Melanie said glumly.

"No," Rick said calmly. "That was an explosion. Someone just took out Jaff's entire lab, with Dominique in it."

The reality of the situation sank in. They had no map, no navigator. Scully, Ethan, Dennis and Dominique were dead, and it was likely Jonathan would be next.

"I can do a finder spell," Melanie said, breaking the silence. "I can do it for Dee so he can find Jonathan."

No one objected—even Rick had no argument left in him.

Jonathan wasn't sure how long he had been running. His lungs were starting to burn. He dashed through another passageway and kicked something with his feet. Jonathan hit the ground hard, rattling his teeth in his skull. He coughed as he pushed himself up with his hands, a puff of red dust billowing around him. His feet were still tangled in something. He rolled over and sat up, feeling a dribble of blood on his forehead. He reached down and grabbed the object tangling his feet.

Bones. Ribs. His feet were tangled in a human rib cage. Jonathan gasped and recoiled, kicked viciously, and scooted away. He paused as his hand came to rest upon another object. This time, Jonathan screamed in horror at the human skull next to him. Jonathan sprang to his feet, winced, and favored his left foot as he felt a flash of pain in his ankle.

"Don't worry, Richard won't hurt you," a voice said gently. Jonathan turned and saw a woman at the other end of the room. He was still trying to catch his breath as he stared at her. She was dressed in white, and for a moment, Jonathan thought she was an angel. She smiled sweetly at him. "Sit down; rest a spell."

Jonathan didn't move. He wasn't sure what he should do, and he wasn't sure who she was. She was holding a white staff with a glowing white orb that floated a few inches from the tip. Only dragon maidens had those—Jonathan knew that much from his trips to the temple as a child.

"Who was Richard?" Jonathan asked as he backed towards one of the walls, which he hoped had a passageway.

"Richard was the stepfather of the triplets. They didn't take him when they left, and he died, trapped in this room," the woman said in an alluring voice. She started to walk towards him.

"How did that happen?"

"His friends forgot about him, and he lost his dragon gem. Much like what's going to happen to you."

"I don't know what you're talking about, I have—" Jonathan reached to where he had the red dragon gem tied around his neck. It was gone. It must have fallen off when he tripped over the bones. He looked at the floor just in time to see his gem fly through the air and land in the woman's welcoming hand. She held it up for him to see.

"That's mine!"

"I think you stole it," the woman accused. "I'll give it back if you make it worth my while."

"What do you want?"

"Your other stone," she said gently. "The blue one."

"No, I can't give you that. I—" Jonathan began, but she moved towards him and pinned him against the wall, her staff across his neck. For a moment, Jonathan couldn't breathe, then she pulled the staff away and hit him across the ear. Jonathan grabbed his head and cried out in pain. On the floor, he saw his two-way radio. He'd forgotten about it.

"Won't be contacting your friends now, will you?" the woman mocked. "Now give me the stone."

Jonathan looked at one of his hands and saw it covered in blood. He focused on the woman.

"Never," Jonathan said. He charged, hoping to catch her off-guard. For a moment, he did; she stumbled backwards and dropped the red gem. He snatched it from the air and ran towards the wall, but instead of passing through it, he slammed full force into it. Jonathan cried out in agony and turned to face her.

"Didn't really think it would be that easy, did you?" she asked.

Dee morphed into Decompose so he could cover ground quicker. He followed the trail of light that led him to Jonathan. He passed through two caverns then a long red tunnel. He jumped forward to pass into the next room, but the wall was solid. Dee morphed back into his human form and looked at the wall. He ran his fingers along it, but found no opening.

"Didn't really think it would be that easy, did you?"

Dee turned to see a red dragon approaching. He took a few steps away from the wall and looked the dragon in the eyes.

"Why has this been so easy? Why didn't you just kill us all, oh, great Queen?" Dee asked. "Or can't you kill me?"

"You may be immortal in every sense of the word. But your friends are not. If I kill them, it leaves you no reason to not destroy the world again. I am impressed with your expression of human emotion. It's different from the old Dee."

"You're not much like the other queens, either. I don't recall them ever wanting world domination." Dee looked back at the wall. She was stalling, and he knew it. He wondered what was happening to Jonathan.

"Leave my island in peace, and I will hunt you and your friends no more. I will let you live your life, Dee. You can pretend to be normal. Isn't that what you want?"

"You're afraid of me," Dee said with a grin. He looked at the young dragon. "You weren't willing to negotiate before. What changed?"

The dragon's fins frilled in anger and the beast's voice filled with hatred.

"I control all the dragons in this world, Decompose. I will command them to kill all of the humans if you do not agree to my terms. Killing me won't stop them. Once a dragon tastes human blood, it's all he wants. If you are truly trying to make amends, take my offer."

"No deal," Dee said flatly. He morphed into Decompose and slammed his fist upon the dragon's neck. Then he turned and began digging vigorously at the wall. He would reach Jonathan one way or another.

The Queen cried out in frustration. The walls in her cavern shook, cracking a few of the eggs. She turned to the Red Dragon and tried to calm herself. The gems imbedded in her body glowed as if fueled by her frustration.

"He refused to make a deal. I am ordering the execution of all humans," the Queen said. "I want the Royal Dragons to stay in their nests until this is finished."

"My Queen, I know our losses have been great, but I don't think we need to resort to this level of—"

"The Gold Dragon is dead, and so is Darlene. This is a desperate time, Red Dragon. If it's genocide Decompose wants, then it's genocide he shall have, and no one shall question it, or I will have them executed. Now, follow your orders, send your troops out, and remain in your nest."

The Red Dragon wanted to object; he had never wanted things to go this far, but he couldn't refuse her. She was his queen. He departed the cavern, leaving her alone with her horde of eggs.

Dee pounded the wall until he reached the other side and saw Jonathan facing a white dragon maiden. He morphed into his human form so he could fit through the hole he had dug and tumbled clumsily through to the other side. Jonathan was bleeding in various places and looked about to pass out. The woman opened her mouth to speak, but Dee wasn't in the mood to listen. His eyes glowed red, and Dee telekinetically tossed the woman across the room, into the wall behind her. She fell to the floor, unconscious—dead, judging by the sounds of bone fragmenting Dee heard.

Dee grabbed Jonathan and healed his injuries. Awareness crept back into the youth's eyes, and he grabbed Dee's arm firmly.

"I didn't let her have it," Jonathan said. He pulled the blue stone from his pouch to show him. Dee smiled, then it faded.

"What happened to Ethan?"

"I'm sorry, we were attacked, he—" Jonathan began.

"It's okay, come on. We have to move. The Queen is rather upset with us."

Ethan's head hurt. He wished he hadn't woken; he just wanted to sleep forever. Maybe when he woke up, it would all be over. But it wasn't; it was nowhere near over. He heard the gentle trickle of water; it sounded like a waterfall to his sensitive ears. He opened his eyes, and even the dark light emitted by the glowing black stones in the walls was too bright. Ethan managed to sit up, regardless of the pain. He looked around and found himself in the pit. There had been dragons in the pit, hadn't there? And someone else—McCaw. He remembered the terrible tumble they had taken—and the battle. He reached up and touched his lips. He had bitten McCaw, hadn't he? The bitter taste of blood was still in his mouth.

Ethan dropped to his knees and forced himself to retch. He wasn't sure that would help, but he figured it was worth a try. He felt worse afterwards, and the pain in his stomach was overwhelming. Ethan sat down and concentrated on his breathing. Where was McCaw? He reached up to rub his temples, hoping it would ease the pain, and his fingers bumped something on his ear. He pulled it off and looked at it, his mind working slowly through the billows of pain. It was his radio. Ethan clicked it on and put it back on his ear.

"...Jonathan. I talked to the Queen, too, she seemed upset. I think the others made some dents in her defense," Dee was saying.

"Then Dennis managed to kill the Gold Dragon before he—" Shia began, then dropped off.

"Well, I'm sure Darlene's death made quite a blow to her ego too," Rick added.

"It should have been me," Melanie added quietly. "I should have been killed—not Scully. We need him more."

"Don't forget about Ethan taking care of McCaw for us," Jonathan added. Everyone murmured at that comment. Ethan looked around the empty room, filled with guilt. He didn't know if McCaw was really dead. He wasn't here, and if Ethan had bitten him—he forced the thoughts from his mind and turned the radio off. Scully was dead? It was impossible. Ethan couldn't grasp the concept. He had to see it for himself. It took a few tries, but he finally managed to climb out of the pit. He paused at the top and wondered which way he should go. He debated going back to Jaff's lab so he could look at the map and see where everyone was. He stood there for countless minutes and tried to come up with a plan. He didn't even know which way to go to find the lab. He was too disoriented to remember how to get around the caves. He took a step towards one of the walls and a passageway opened to a red cave. In front of him was a dead body. The black fur was unmistakable. It was Darlene.

Ethan hurried into the room and dropped to his knees next to her, a dribble of drool slipped from his chin, and Ethan quickly wiped it away. It was like a free buffet. Ethan grabbed her shoulder and bent to take a bite out of it, then he heard a groan. Ethan looked over his shoulder instinctively. It was his food—no one else could have it. He crawled across the floor, searching for the source of the sound. He rounded a boulder and came face to face with Scully, sitting on the ground, slumped against the wall. A pool of blood had formed around him. The rank odor made Ethan even hungrier. He reached out, intending to sink his fingers into the chest wound, when the corpse suddenly came to life. Scully's eyes opened and his right arm reached up, putting a smooth blade against Ethan's neck.

"You're alive," Ethan said softly.

"Are you?" Scully asked, his voice stronger than Ethan expected. He felt the blade press against his skin, almost cutting his flesh.

"So far," Ethan said as he focused on Scully. Suddenly, Scully moved the blade from his neck and jabbed the tip into Ethan's left eye. Ethan recoiled and moved out of Scully's reach, grabbing at his eye. He couldn't see through it anymore, but the pain barely registered. "Why did you do that?"

"Cannibals can't work illusions with only one eye," Scully said matter-of-factly. Ethan looked at him.

"Why would you say something like that?" Ethan asked.

"You infected yourself, didn't you?" Scully asked, but Ethan knew he didn't need to answer.

"I'm not a cannibal," Ethan said. "I haven't tasted any blood. I won't turn into a cannibal if I starve myself for two days. I know how this works; I created it."

"Just the same—it makes me feel better knowing you can't mess around in my head," Scully said.

"Why don't you give me that sword?" Ethan asked.

"I think not."

"Look, you're covered in blood, you have a chest wound, and if you get any of the blood on that blade in your wound, you'll be infected, too. Just give me the sword, and I'll clean it," Ethan said.

Dee looked at the glowing blue force field. Jonathan said nothing. Dee's eyes glowed red as he reached out with his mind, intending to infect the dragons. But he couldn't reach beyond the walls of the caves. The Queen's mind was blocked, but she still had power in the caverns. He needed to be outside.

"I have to get outside," Dee said softly. "I can't do it from here."

"It'll take too long," Lorna said over the radio. "We're in the center of the caverns. The Queen already knows something is up; I can't hold her for long."

"The roof," Jonathan said. Dee pulled his earpiece off as others volunteered suggestions.

"There aren't passageways on the roof," Dee said flatly.

"Then dig through it like you did to get to me," Jonathan offered.

"This is gold; it was just red rock last time. That's a softer stone," Dee said.

"Gold is a very weak metal," Jonathan said. Dee put the ear piece back and told them what he was going to do. Then he morphed into Decompose and started digging at the ceiling. Slowly, the gold peeled away; the minutes dragged on, then he saw a crack of sunlight. He dug faster as boulders tumbled into the cave. Jonathan stood in the corner, a safe distance away. Dee finally had a hole big enough for him to climb through in human form. He held on with a giant paw and morphed into his human form, then climbed out. The sunlight shone down on him; he was in the Red Dragon Territory. His eyes glowed as he used his powers, reaching out to the dragons and infecting them with the deadly disease. A few dragons fell from the sky as they succumbed.

Then he saw a herd of white unicorns making their way to his position, and they seemed to be immune to him. Dee cast a force field around himself just before the first reached him.

"We have a problem up here!" Dee shouted into his radio. "I don't suppose anyone pissed off some Meta-morphs earlier today?"

"You're weak; you could drop it," Ethan said as he reached for the sword. Scully's fingers felt numb, and he wasn't sure he really *could* hold the sword much longer without dropping it. He was weak, and Ethan knew it. "If either of us are going to get out of this alive, we have to trust each other."

It hurt to breathe, but Scully refused to let Ethan know just how badly he was hurt.

"You swear you haven't turned," Scully asked. Ethan nodded, but Scully couldn't help but notice the hungry look in his eyes. "Then why do you keep looking at me like I'm a steak?"

Ethan suddenly grabbed the blade. With one swift jerk, he pulled the sword from Scully's hand. Scully winced as the movement jarred his body, but he managed to keep from crying out in pain. He kept his eyes on Ethan and watched him wipe the blade clean. Then Ethan knelt next to Scully and offered the hilt of the sword.

"I trust you won't stab my other eye out," Ethan said. Scully took the sword back and tried to keep his hands from shaking.

"Where are the others?" Scully asked.

"Mourning our heroic deaths," Ethan said sarcastically. Ethan sat next to him and pulled his legs up to his chest. "Don't mind if I stay here and die with you, do you?"

"I'm going," Rick said over the headsets. "Dee needs backup up there."

No one objected as Rick dashed through the caverns, passing Shia in his black cave then entering Jonathan's gold cave. Jonathan was sitting on one of the fallen boulders. He looked at Rick and said nothing. Rick leaped to the top of the biggest boulder and jumped. He caught the bottom of the hole in the ceiling with his hands and pulled himself up and out. Rick rolled across the ground and quickly got to his feet. He spotted Dee on some boulders; he had a force field around himself, but he couldn't cast the plague while that was up. The white unicorns surrounded him.

Rick screamed, hoping to attract their attention, and he did—a large white unicorn charged him. Rick prepared for the attack too late, and although he managed to avoid being trampled, the beast drove its horn into his hand. Rick screamed in pain.

The beast took off running, dragging Rick with him. Rick grabbed at the unicorn's mane and pulled himself up so he wasn't being dragged along the ground anymore, then he saw where the horse was taking him. They were in the White Dragon Territory, heading for a small pond. Rick climbed up the unicorn's neck and tried to gain enough leverage to slide his hand off the horn, but the animal kept jerking its head around, making it impossible. Rick flared his needles and dug into the flesh of the unicorn's forehead, but it ran on.

Then the hooves were splashing in the water, and it wasn't long before they were under water. Rick took a last gulp of air before he submerged. Under the water, Rick could move in new ways; he figured he could easily free himself. But the unicorn drove its horn into the muddy pond bottom, trapping Rick's hand. Rick kicked at the unicorn's head, pounded on its eyes, but the animal wouldn't budge.

Dee dropped his force field as he reached the top of the pile of boulders. He kicked at one of the unicorns and watched it tumble off the boulders, knocking other unicorns down.

"Rick just got pulled under a—" He searched for the right words. "He's in a lake. One of the Meta-morphs is trying to drown him. We need someone else up here to get him."

Dee's eyes glowed red as he shook the boulders, sending loose rocks crashing down on the unicorns. They backed off a few feet, but kept Dee surrounded. Dee reached out with his mind and started to infect the dragons.

"I'm coming," Melanie said.

Jonathan wished he had a working radio; he felt cut off from the others in his golden cavern. He looked at the sky through the hole in his ceiling and thought that the blue of the sky was similar to the color of the glowing force field. He heard a crunch in the gold rubble and turned to see who it was.

Standing in the cavern was McCaw, wounded. His features had hardened, and he looked more like a panther than a man. His clothes were torn, and a smear of blood trickled from his lip. Jonathan quietly moved behind one of the boulders, out of sight of the beast. He heard McCaw's ragged breathing. Jonathan wondered what a cannibalistic McCaw would be like. He hoped he wouldn't find out. He tried to keep his breathing quiet, not wanting the monster to hear him.

He heard another sound in the room and peered around the boulder to see Melanie entering the cavern. Without thinking he stood up and shouted a warning to her. She didn't even look at him as McCaw charged her. She jumped up in the air and kicked him on the forehead, used the gained momentum to jump up to the hole in the ceiling and was quickly out of sight.

Jonathan stood there dazed. She had left him. Then his eyes fell upon McCaw, who was eyeing him with a hungry look upon his face.

"I never thought I would die in the same room as Darlene," Ethan said in a dazed voice. Scully kept a firm grip on his sword, he didn't trust Ethan at all.

"What are you talking about?" Scully asked, trying to ignore the dizzy feeling in his head.

"Didn't you know? Darlene's body is right over there," Ethan pointed, but Scully was too tired to look. Then a thought occurred to him. Darlene always had all five gems around her belt; if her body was here, then so was her belt. And if Scully could get his hands on her white gem, he could heal himself.

"Ethan," Scully said, despairing as he heard how weak his voice sounded. "See if you can find her belt."

He heard Ethan moving around next to him, then he was directly in front of him looking at him with his one eye. It gave Scully the creeps to look at him.

"I don't really feel up to it," Ethan said flatly, then he sat back against the wall. Scully felt like he was keeping company with a vulture.

"Fine, I'll look for myself," Scully decided. He placed his sword across his stomach and set about dragging himself across the floor. The pain was worse when he moved and it made the bleeding increase. Yet, somehow, he managed to keep moving, dragging himself on his back, a little closer to passing out and never waking up with each inch he moved.

Melanie saw Dee on top of the boulders and he pointed her to the correct lake. Then she was running, pulling out her sword and cutting down Meta-morphs that got in her way. It no time, she had reached the body of water and jumped in the lake. She opened her eyes and searched for Rick.

She was almost ready to go back up for air when she saw him. He was thrashing, wildly fighting a unicorn. With one mighty thrust, she cut the beast's head off. Instantly, the water filled with blood, and Melanie couldn't see.

Jonathan didn't know what to do. He couldn't get over the fact that Melanie had just left him to face this monster on his own. How could she do that? After all they had been through. It would have taken her no more than a few seconds to chop McCaw's head off, and she hadn't even taken the time to do that. He had given away his location, risked his own safety for her, and she left him. That bitch, Jonathan thought.

McCaw gave an inhuman roar and ran towards him, his hands reaching out like claws. Jonathan gave a scream of his own and ran in the direction from which Melanie had come. He tripped over something as he entered the cavern and rolled over to find an urn. She had left Freddy's urn in the center of the room. He was really getting tired of tripping over dead people. Jonathan grabbed the urn in anger and almost tossed it across the room. Then an idea hit him; he twisted the lid off the urn and looked at the ashes inside.

McCaw charged through the passageway into the room, still roaring. Jonathan tossed the contents of the urn into McCaw's face, temporarily blinding him. McCaw screamed, and Jonathan turned to run away again.

Ethan watched his friend drag himself along the ground, inching ever so slowly towards Darlene's body. He got a strange satisfaction out of watching his friend suffer. The pain on Scully's face almost fed Ethan's empty stomach. It was like a cat playing with a mouse before he finally killed it. Amazingly enough, Scully managed to reach Darlene, but he was too weak to search her body. Instead, he had to lie next to her and feel her with his right hand. Ethan relished the moment, then Scully's eyes rolled back in his head, and he went limp.

Ethan jumped up and hurried to his side. Scully was still breathing; he had just passed out from the pain. Ethan backed a few feet away from him, afraid Scully would wake and stab him as he had done before. His foot kicked something. Ethan looked down and saw the belt. He picked it up. Then he went over to Scully and knelt next to him. He held the belt in one hand and paused. He reached with his other hand and touched Scully's open wound. The blood was warm against his fingers. He pulled his fingers out of the wound and raised them slowly to his lips, savoring the moment. Then he felt the cool blade of Scully's sword against his fingers. He looked at Scully, who had managed to raise his hand one last time, putting his blade against Ethan's hand.

"Lick those fingers, and I will cut them off," Scully said, but his voice was so weak the threat was barely a whisper.

"I wouldn't dream of it," Ethan responded, moving his fingers away from the blade. He paused, holding his fingers a few inches from his mouth, then he lowered his hand and wiped his fingers clean on his shirt, not that there was much clean left on it. His gaze never left Scully's, and finally Scully's hand shook and he lowered the sword, resting it on his chest.

Ethan remembered the object in his other hand. He tightened his grip on it and fought the numbing pain in his head. He raised his hand and held the belt up for Scully to see. But Scully's eyes were closed.

"Scully," Ethan said gently. He tapped the man's shoulder gently, but nothing happened. He picked up Scully's arm and slid his hand down to his wrist. He fumbled for a moment as he tried to find a pulse.

Melanie broke the surface of the water, gasping for breath. She started to swim towards the shore, but stopped when she saw the problem. Unicorns. Dozens of them had surrounded the lake while they were underwater. Rick surfaced next to her, but didn't seem out of breath, just upset.

"Can you believe what that qufritz tried to do?" Rick growled. Melanie paid no attention to him.

"We have a problem," she said flatly.

"My radio's fried—the water killed it," Rick said.

"Same here."

"Well, we can't stay here. I can already tell you they can swim and aren't afraid of drowning," Rick growled as he began swimming towards the shore. Melanie followed. Some of the unicorns were already slipping into the water and diving below the surface.

Jonathan ran through a passageway into Lorna's cavern. She was deep in concentration, keeping the secondary barrier up.

"Lorna, we have to run!" Jonathan screamed. She didn't even look at him.

"Why did you leave your cave? Jonathan, we are trying to accomplish something here," Lorna lectured.

Jonathan knew they didn't have much time. He dropped to the floor next to the stone and began punching the sides, deactivating it.

"What are you doing?"

"We're safer on the other side of this force field. Trust me," Jonathan said. She dropped her hands and her secondary field vanished. Jonathan tapped the top of the stone and the blue field went away.

"But this will interfere with Dee's spell. The Queen will be able to get out," Lorna argued. Jonathan grabbed her arm, pulling her to the other side of the stone. Then he bent down and began tapping the stone again.

"Do you realize we are now on the same side as the Queen?" Lorna asked.

Dee cried out in pain as the Queen's mind attacked his. His eyes stopped glowing, and he fell to his knees. He closed his eyes and listened to the drumming of the unicorns' hooves against the boulders. They couldn't climb the rocks to reach him. He heard Rick and Melanie screaming in the distance as the Meta-morphs attacked them relentlessly.

Dennis woke and felt pain. He tried to move, but he couldn't. There was something on top of him. He struggled a few minutes before he managed to free his arms and push the clutter off him. He twisted and dragged his legs out from under the fallen shelf, then he searched his body and was glad to find no broken bones. He searched the room for the Gold Dragon and saw strands of hair here and there. He crawled across the fallen shelves and scattered scrolls until he stepped on solid ground.

He looked back and saw the Gold Dragon's head stretching out from under one of the shelves. His eyes were wide open, but there was a glazed dead look to them. Dennis looked away. He stumbled over the ruins and made his way back to Jaff's lab. He needed to find out what had happened to the others. He hurt all over; Dennis didn't think he had ever experienced such pain.

He opened the passageway into Jaff's lab; the room was in worse condition than the scroll room. Hank was barking in the other room. He started to cross the room when he saw Dominique. The farmer had died instantly, Dennis was sure of that. There had been some sort of explosion, and Dominique had taken the brunt of the blow. Dennis could barely tell it was Dominique. The body reminded him of the charred corpses he found on the battlefields.

The table was destroyed, as well as the shelves and potions. The spell books had caught fire and were still burning into ash. He was about to call for Hank, when a woman walked into the lab from the other room.

The woman was dressed in gold, a turban on her head. Dennis didn't ask questions. He knew all he needed to know. He charged before she could react to his arrival. He snapped her neck and let her fall to the floor. Hank was still growling, but the dog seemed unhurt. He had probably been lying under the table when the explosion hit, and it had saved him from the flying debris.

"Come on, Hank. Let's go find the others," Dennis said grimly.

Scully opened his eyes to find Ethan holding his arm at the wrist, looking at it with a trickle of drool running down his face. Scully moaned and tried to pull away, but he was too weak. He tried to lift his sword, but couldn't. It wasn't painful anymore, just dark and cold. Ethan's good eye focused on him. For a moment, Scully saw excitement in Ethan's face. Scully winced, wondering if Ethan wanted him alive to watch him eat.

"I found it," Ethan said excitedly. Scully opened his eyes again, but it was hard to keep his eyelids open. Ethan was holding something in his hand—a belt, decorated with stones.

Ethan dropped his wrist, but Scully was too weak to stop its fall and barely felt the impact as his hand fell to the ground. Ethan ripped the white stone from the belt and laid the gem against Scully's wound. Scully opened his mouth to cry out, but he didn't have the breath. Ethan bent down and blew a breath onto the gem. Then he backed away, as if Scully were a piece of dynamite Ethan had just lit.

Jonathan tapped the top of the stone, and the force field went up again. He backed away, just in time to see McCaw walk into the room. The archer growled and lunged at the barrier, then howled in anger and pain as the force field sent a jolt of electricity through him. Lorna gasped.

"Is that McCaw? My dear child, what happened to you?" Lorna asked.

"He got bit by Ethan," Jonathan told her.

"What?"

"Ethan's a cannibal," Jonathan explained as if it were common knowledge. Lorna looked at him, surprised.

"What about the others?" Lorna asked. Jonathan stared at her for a moment not understanding. "Shia and Barbie—they're in the caverns next to us. If he gets bored pawing at the force field, he's going to find them."

"I could go get them, and you can stay here and keep him busy," Jonathan suggested.

"And when you lower the force field to let them on this side he can eat us," Lorna added.

"What about the radio?"

"Won't work through the force field; it blocks everything."

"Radio Lorna to help us!" Melanie shouted as she sent bolts of energy at the Meta-morphs; it was enough to frighten them into keeping their distance. Rick swung into the branches of a tree to escape the unicorns' stomping hooves. He tinkered with his radio. To his surprise, he heard a hiss of static.

"My radio is working," Rick shouted to Melanie. "Lorna, come in. We need help out here. Can anyone hear us?"

Rick tightened his grip on the branch as a unicorn slammed into the tree trunk.

"I'm here," Shia said over the radio.

"You're it?" Rick asked.

"How did we lose Lorna and Jonathan?" Melanie asked.

"Jonathan's radio wasn't working," Dee told them. "We need help. I can't hold these things off much longer. I've only covered ten percent of the globe. I'll never get finished at this rate."

Scully couldn't believe it. He reached down and touched his chest where the rip in his shirt was. The wound was gone. He pulled the white gem off and sat up. He looked at Ethan, who was leaning against the far wall, still eyeing him like he was looking at a spring chicken. Scully got up, not taking his eyes off him. He tucked the gem in his pocket and raised his sword, pointing it at Ethan.

"I saved you," Ethan said greedily. Scully wasn't sure what to say. Then he noticed a radio attached to Ethan's ear.

"You still have your radio," Scully said. Ethan looked puzzled for a moment then reached to touch the device. Scully covered the distance between them and angled his sword between Ethan's ear and his hand. "Mine broke; may I have yours?"

Ethan gave a trembling nod and didn't move. Scully plucked the earpiece from him and turned it on, placing it on his own ear.

"Hello? Hello, can anyone hear me?" Scully asked, keeping his blade on Ethan's neck.

"Scully? Is that you?" Rick asked.

"Yes, it's me," Scully said, then paused. "And Ethan."

"But we thought you were both dead," Rick said in surprise.

"So I've been told. What's our status?" Scully asked.

"The field is in place, but we're having trouble with the Metamorphs. We're outnumbered," Rick said glumly. "Don't suppose there's any way you two are in any condition to help us?"

"Dennis is dead too," Ethan murmured. Scully looked at him and had an idea..

"We're on our way, Rick. We're both fine," Scully told him. He looked at Ethan and turned his mike off. "Ethan, I have a question about the plague you infected yourself with."

"Accidentally," he said quickly. "I didn't infect myself on purpose."

"I know, Ethan. Now, listen to me. You once used this plague to kill all the Meta-morphs on the island. Is there any chance that what you are infected with could be used to kill them again?"

"They're immune to what's in Dee 'cause he had both infections. The cure and the plague," Ethan rambled.

"But you just have the one. You only made the plague, how do we infect them with it?" Scully insisted.

"Humans have a better immunity to it. They can only catch it if bitten, unless Dee works his magic and makes it an air virus or—"

"Ethan! We all know how humans catch it. I want to know how Meta-morphs catch it."

"It was made for them; they can catch it like a cold," Ethan said softly, with a twitch of his neck.

"So if I take you outside, just having you near them will infect them?"

"I'm a walking Meta-morph killer," Ethan said with a grin.

"Okay, good then. We need to go outside," Scully said. He lowered his sword and took a step back.

"No, no, I don't feel good. I'll just stay here," Ethan quickly sat down. Scully put the tip of his blade to Ethan's temple.

"If I have to carry you, I'm not carrying you alive," Scully growled.

"Okay, I'll run around and tell everyone what's going on. Maybe they can send someone to kill McCaw," Jonathan suggested.

"All right, but make it quick. This guy gives me the creeps," Lorna said. Jonathan hurried to the next cavern.

"Wait!" Lorna cried. Jonathan looked back to see Lorna waving her arms. "He's following you!"

"What? Why would he do that? It's not like I did anything that would—" Jonathan began, then he remembered that some scientists believed cannibals retained memories of their lives. But he was too late. McCaw entered the other room and saw Barbie napping on the floor. She didn't even see him coming. Jonathan turned away as he heard the cat-like howl Barbie cried.

"Keep going! Get Shia!" Lorna shouted. "While he's busy!"

"Right!" Jonathan shouted back. He started to move towards the other side of the room, but McCaw got up and threw himself against the force field. Jonathan cried out in surprise. "He's still following me!"

He accidentally saw Barbie's body. McCaw had attacked her in the throat, but there was a chance she was still alive. He'd gone back to trying to get Jonathan before he'dhad time to do much damage.

"Lorna?" Jonathan asked. He looked back at the silver cavern she was in to see her staring up at the ceiling in fear. "Lorna, what's wrong?"

Then he saw the problem. A large head—larger than any dragon head he had seen before—came down and grabbed Lorna, engulfing her entire body in its mouth. The dragon had pale pink skin with a hint of purple. He saw the crown on her head and remembered watching Dee try to drown this dragon. It was unmistakably the Queen. Her violet eyes rolled in her sockets and looked at Jonathan before she disappeared, Lorna's feet still kicking between her fangs.

"Lorna!" Jonathan screamed. Without thinking, he ran into the back wall of the cavern that led into the Queen's nest. He burst into the nest and stopped short. He couldn't take on the Queen. He watched the Queen toss Lorna's body across the cavern and against a wall. She was huge. The glowing gems embedded in her body made her seem like a walking building with little candles glowing in the windows. She gave a triumphant roar and then faced Jonathan.

Jonathan screamed and turned to run back into the cavern. As he jumped through the passageway, he came face to face with McCaw. He had returned to gnaw on Barbie but quickly returned to the force field to try getting at Jonathan again. He was doomed. Then Jonathan started thinking. Ethan had infected himself with the plague meant to infect the dragons. Without further thought, he dropped to the floor and began deactivating the stone.

He paused before he touched the top of the gem, waiting until he heard the snarl of the Queen. Then he tapped the stone and rolled onto his back, covering his face with his arms. He only had one shot at this, and his odds weren't good. But somehow it worked. McCaw jumped to land on top of him just as the Queen swept down to pick him up in her jaws. Instead of biting into Jonathan, she picked up McCaw. Jonathan lowered his arms and watched the Queen crunch into McCaw and shake his body viciously. Suddenly she paused and pulled her head back into her nest. Jonathan jumped to his feet and hurried in after her.

The Queen dropped McCaw, but it was too late to save McCaw and too late to save her. She coughed, and her entire body convulsed. In a few minutes, she was lying on the ground, unmoving. Jonathan wasted no time. He dashed across the room and searched until he found Lorna. She was alive. She had managed to sit up, her back against a few eggs. A trickle of blood ran down her chin, but Jonathan didn't see much blood.

"Lorna!" Jonathan shouted as he crouched next to her. She coughed, and her body trembled.

"I think I have broken bones, and I'm bleeding internally," Lorna said, gasping. "Probably punctured a lung too."

"Its okay; I'll get Shia, and he'll radio the others and get Dee in here to fix you."

"The Queen," she gasped.

"She's dead; I took care of her. It's going to be okay," Jonathan said. The realization of what he'd done dawned on him for the first time. He had killed the Queen. He wouldn't have believed it himself if he hadn't been able to turn around and see her unmoving body behind him.

Dee winced as the Queen again attacked his mind. Why did their force field keep malfunctioning? Then she was gone. Dee paused and stopped fighting the Meta-morphs. He reached inside the caverns and found no resistance. The Queen was dead. He refocused his power and wiped out the rest of the dragons in the caverns. That finished, he went back to the rest of the world. He had managed to keep the animals off the boulders, but it was slowing down his progress. He turned his radio on.

"Guys, the Queen is dead. What happened?" Dee asked.

Both Melanie and Rick told him they didn't know.

"Don't know about the Queen, but I'm about to take care of your Meta-morph problem," Scully said.

They stepped into White Dragon Territory. Ethan had slowed them down, saying he wasn't feeling good, but Scully finally got him outside. They were near the center of the island and Scully could see Dee up on a stack of red boulders and Rick in some trees near a lake. Scully could barely see Melanie through the unicorns surrounding her.

"Work your magic, Ethan," Scully said.

"I told you—it's an airborne disease. I shouldn't have to do anything."

A unicorn appeared from behind the white boulders, rose on its hind legs, and charged them. Then it dropped to the ground, convulsing. Ethan looked at him and nodded curtly.

"Come on, we need to get closer to the others," Scully said. He grabbed him by the scruff of his collar and pulled him along. But they didn't have far to go. The congregations of unicorns fell to the ground as if Ethan were emitting toxic radiation.

"Scully!" Melanie cried. She raced over and threw her arms around him.

"It's about time," Rick said as he jumped down from his tree.

Jonathan hadn't gone far before a passageway opened up and he saw the silhouette of a person walk through. Jonathan ducked behind some eggs and held his breath. He wondered if it was Barbie, returning from the dead.

"Hey? Is anyone in here?" A raspy voice called. It sounded familiar. Jonathan peered around the egg. The person was moving with a limp and there was an animal walking alongside him. Jonathan stood up and called out.

"Who's there?"

"It's me, Dennis," the man said as the dog barked in greeting.

"Dennis? Shia told us you were dead!" Jonathan exclaimed as another passageway opened. Jonathan held his breath again, but this time it was Shia.

"Dude, what happened? Why is the force field down?" Shia asked. Then he gasped, seeing Dennis.

"I'm okay. I'm pretty torn up, though. When I woke up, I went back to the lab. Someone worked that place over pretty well. I'm sorry to say Dominique didn't survive. Surprisingly, Hank here is okay. I found a woman dressed in gold that did not welcome me kindly. Let's just say we won't be seeing her anymore," Dennis said as he leaned against the eggs for support. He was indeed cut up; chunks of flesh were missing as if they had been ripped off.

"The Gold Dragon?" Shia asked.

"Buried under a pile of bookshelves," Dennis said proudly.

Jonathan suddenly remembered Lorna. "Shia, you have to radio Dee; Lorna's hurt and needs help."

Hank started barking as another passageway opened.

"Who killed the Queen?" Dee asked as he walked into the room. Rick, Melanie, Scully, and Ethan were with him. Rick ran across the room when he saw Dennis, but kept from hugging his friend when he saw his wounds.

"Lorna needs help," Jonathan said curtly. Dee hurried to her aid. Scully followed and knelt next to her. As the color started to come back into Lorna's cheeks, she smiled at Jonathan.

"Did someone ask who killed the Queen?" Lorna asked.

"Yes, who was it?" Dee asked as his eyes stopped glowing. He looked at Dennis, noticing his wounds.

"Jonathan did," Lorna said proudly as Scully helped her to her feet.

"Huh, guess it's a good thing I didn't eat you then," Ethan said softly. Jonathan thought he looked better than he had earlier. Everyone was looking at him, and Jonathan wasn't sure what to say. Melanie screamed with delight and ran towards him. He put up a restraining hand as she reached him and gave her a dirty look.

"You left me to die," Jonathan snapped.

"I had to help Rick. He was drowning," she tried to explain. Dee walked across the room to heal Dennis.

"Actually, I probably could have held my breath longer than the unicorn," Rick said softly. Jonathan glared at her, but she said nothing.

"It's okay, though," Jonathan said. "*Freddy* saved me."